Hamilton Hume

The Life of Edward John Eyre, Late Governor of Jamaica

Hamilton Hume

The Life of Edward John Eyre, Late Governor of Jamaica

ISBN/EAN: 9783743404403

Manufactured in Europe, USA, Canada, Australia, Japa

Cover: Foto ©Raphael Reischuk / pixelio.de

Manufactured and distributed by brebook publishing software (www.brebook.com)

Hamilton Hume

The Life of Edward John Eyre, Late Governor of Jamaica

THE LIFE

OF

EDWARD JOHN EYRE,

LATE

GOVERNOR OF JAMAICA.

BY

HAMILTON HUME.

LONDON:
RICHARD BENTLEY, 8, NEW BURLINGTON STREET,
Publisher in Ordinary to Her Majesty.
1867.

DEDICATION.

TO THE RIGHT HONOURABLE
THE EARL OF SHREWSBURY AND TALBOT.

My Lord,

WHEN it became known last summer that several gentlemen had formed themselves into a Committee with the object of collecting a sum of 10,000*l.* for the purpose of prosecuting the late Governor of Jamaica, the indignation of the country generally was very great. A Royal Commission having deliberately declared its opinion that, owing to the "promptitude and vigour manifested" by Mr. Eyre, the island of Jamaica had been saved, it was believed impossible that any body of men could be found who would deliberately seek to bring ruin and disgrace upon a public servant and upon his family, merely for the purpose, as we are told, of "settling a great constitutional question." You, my Lord, know well, and the members of the Jamaica Committee know well, that this "constitutional question" could have been settled without Mr. Eyre being arraigned on a charge of "wilful murder."

It is not for me to enter into the reasons that have actuated the prosecutors; it is not for me to point out how this blind and disgraceful act of public injustice might have been prevented: my object in the present volume is to let the world know something of a brave and good man who has done great service to the State. I am aware that in doing so I shall call down upon myself the censures of those who, in their desire to whitewash the black man, too often blacken the white man. I am also aware that, in a literary point of view, this volume will not stand the test of severe criticism; but you, my Lord, and the public generally, whatever its faults may be—and they are very many—will, I trust, deal leniently with them.

I have only to add the reason which induced me to ask your permission to dedicate this little work to you.

The moment it was known that Mr. Eyre was going to
be prosecuted by a number of private individuals, the
Eyre Defence and Aid Fund was organized, as a
solemn protest against such an unjustifiable proceeding,
and to prevent a public servant who had spent his
lifetime in the service of his country being utterly and
irretrievably ruined. Upon that Committee are men
holding various opinions in religion and in politics;
of men the most eminent in literature, science, and art;
of men distinguished for the services they have
rendered to this nation; of men whose names will
add lustre to the pages of future history. You, my
Lord, are its President.

I have the honour to be,

Your most obedient Servant,

HAMILTON HUME.

LONDON, *March* 15, 1867.

CONTENTS.

CHAPTER I.

CHAPTER II.

CHAPTER III.

CHAPTER IV.

CONTENTS.

CHAPTER VIII.

CHAPTER IX.

CHAPTER X.

CHAPTER XI.

APPENDIX.

EDWARD JOHN EYRE.

CHAPTER I.

BEFORE placing on record the services rendered to this country by the late Governor of Jamaica, it may be advisable to devote a few pages to a short history of his family and of his early life. It becomes absolutely necessary to speak of the former, since those persons who have so virulently assailed Mr. Eyre's character have also represented him as a man of no birth and without connections. That he is a "self-made" man no one can deny, and no doubt he himself is proud of having earned so honourable a distinction; but doubtless he is also proud of belonging to a time-honoured and ancient family.*

* Members of the different branches of the Eyre family have intermarried at various times with the families of De Padley, Fitz-William, Plumley, Wortley, De Willington, Reresby, Gorman Pole, Neville, Wastenys (Sir H., Bart.), Markham, Clifton (Sir G., Bart.), Babington, Neaton (Sir J., Bart.), Digby (Sir J., Bart.), Packington (Sir J., Bart.), Lyster, Cooke (Sir H., Bart.), Hickman (Sir W., Bart.), Skeffington (Earl Masserene), Turner, Bury, Thornhill, Dodsworth, Chambers, Bootle, Wainright, Armytage (Sir G., Bart.), Hay Drummond (Earl Kinnoul), Fountayne, Pierrepoint (Earl Manvers), Harcourt Vernon, Gally Knight, Foulis, Simpson, and many others.

B

Local tradition states that at the battle of Hastings, William the Conqueror was found lying on the ground breathless by the founder of the Eyre family in England—who dismounting, unloosed the bars of the King's helmet so that he could breathe, upon which the Conqueror cried out, " De l'Eyre ;" he then mounted the King upon his own horse, and fought the rest of the day himself on foot.   After the battle, William ordered his deliverer to be searched for, when he was found lying on the field with his leg cut off.   The King ordered him at once to be taken care of, and said, " Henceforth thou shalt be called De l'Eyre, because thou hast given me the air I breathe," and he gave him for his crest a leg in armour cut off above the knee as his was.   Also, he gave him lands in Derbyshire, which were called " Hope," because he had hope in his greatest extremity when he was lying on the battlefield dangerously wounded.   The arms of the family corroborate this legend, for they bear on a field, argent, a chevron, sable, charged with three quatrefoils, or; and the chevron, say the heralds, " is given for assisting a king,"—while the motto, *Si je puis*, attests their Norman or French origin.   At any rate, the De l'Eyres, as they signed themselves in old charters still extant, were for centuries a powerful family, spreading over that part of Derbyshire which is near the Peak, over Hallamshire, and towards Sheffield.   One of the race was lord of thirty manors, and the head of the family was usually knight of the shire. The estate of "Hope" continued in the family until the period of the Civil Wars, when the then head of the family, Sir Gervas Eyre, Governor of Newark Castle, sold it to raise the last loan ever contracted for King Charles the First. He was soon after killed by the waft of a cannon-ball whilst riding outside the gates of Newark, in company with his officers, surveying the neighbourhood. The local historians of the day speak of him as a man of irreproachable character, the best horseman in King Charles's army, and add, "that had the king had many such soldiers as Sir Gervas Eyre, he had neither lost his crown nor his life."

Sir Gervas Eyre married Elizabeth Babington, of Rampton, in the county of Nottingham, by whom he had several children.

His second son, Anthony Eyre (the eldest died an infant), married twice; first, Lucy, daughter of Sir John Digby, Baronet, of Mansfield Wood House, in the county of Nottingham, by whom he had one daughter; and, secondly, Elizabeth, daughter of Sir John Packington, Baronet, of Westwood, in the county of Worcester.

Gervas Eyre, son by this latter marriage, married Catherine, daughter of Sir Henry Cooke, Baronet, of Wheatley, in the county of York.*

* The following singular anecdote, from an ancient manuscript, has been preserved by Mr. Piercy, which is well worthy of perusal,

Their youngest son, Charles Eyre, became a physician, settled at Doncaster, and married Elizabeth, daughter of John Fountayne, Esq., of Melton-on-the-

and highly illustrative of the state of the times when it occurred. It is written in a clear and beautiful hand by Diana, wife of William Chambers, Esq., of Ruppon, one of the descendants of the same family, and is as follows:—

" Anthony Eyre, Esq., of Laughton-en-le-Morthen, and also of Kiveton Park, by his two wives had seven sons and gave to either three or four of them handsome fortunes, ye others he brought up to some profession and good business; his third son (from whom sprang our ancestors) had his estate in ye West-Riding of Yorkshire, at Kiveton and in that neighbourhood; Rotherham, ye nearest market town, after Laughton-en-le-Morthen, four miles from Kiveton, was reduced in the civil wars in Charles ye First's reign to a pretty large village town. Mr. Eyre's seat was at Kiveton, he had also lands in and about Laughton, and was Lord of ye Manor there. Some centuries before King Charles' reign, a descendant from ye eldest branch of ye Mr. Eyre's, married a young lady with a good estate, and very large house at Bampton, in Nottinghamshire, upon which Bampton was made ye family seat, Kiveton and his estate there (but not Laughton) was yn sold, and purchases made about Bampton. Their eldest son, and grandsons, always married into good families, and had genteel, sometimes large fortunes with their wives. Ye eldest branch of that family, who was married to a lady of distinction and had had some children, when ye rebellion broke out, went himself a volunteer in ye King's army, and a younger brother yt did the same, bravely lost his life in an engagement at, or near Nottingham.[1] The elder Mr. Eyre was a considerable sufferer by ye parliament partye, not only plundering his house, but also by damage done to his tenants, and £8,000 (intended for a purchase near Bampton) that he and a trusty servant hid underground in ye orchard, on a bright moonlight night, he was robbed on by a labourer yt saw them from ye top of the church steeple; he had

---

[1] This was at Newark.

Hill, near Doncaster, whose mother was the daughter, and ought legally to have inherited the estates of Sir Nicholas Carew, of Beddington Park, in Surrey, her

---

been suspected by living extraordinary well without work, but was soon reduced to poverty, and when near death confessed ye fact. My Grandfather,[1] Gervas Eyre, married Catherine, sister to Sir George Cooke, Bart., of Wheatley, Yorkshire, at ye age of 19, so early a marriage being desired by his mother, a widow, he being her only son; and her daughters she married early in their teens. As soon as he came of age, he was chose a member of parliament for ye county of Nottingham; and distinguished himself in ye house as a sensable, unprejudiced speaker, would accept no place from ye ministry, yt he might be free to speak and vote, as appeared to him best for his Queen (Ann) and country. My grandfather had a great impediment in his speech, but I was told by a gentleman yt sat in ye house with him, yt he would speak without any hesitation by tossing up an apple or an orange, and if by chance he dropped it, gave a full pause, till he got another out of his pocket. He died at ye age of 32 or 3 of ye smallpox when he was at London attending parliament, and was buried at Rampton. He was kind to ye industrious poor, was a cheerful and agreeable companion, ys death was much lamented both by ye rich and poor. He left 5 sons, viz.: Anthony, Henry, George, Charles, and Gervas, and 4 daughters, Elizabeth, Diana, Catherine, and Dorathe. My grandmother was with child when he died, but died of grief for his loss soon after him. The labour came upon her but could not be delivered. She spoke to my father yn but 13 or 14 years old, yt he would request his trustees to let ys overplus of his estate from what was spent and in his education and maintenance and repairs for tenants might go till of age, for ye use of his brothers and sisters, who otherwise would be very scantily provided for; my father's ready compliance with this, she told him gave her great pleasure and satisfaction;

---

[1] This person was Gervase Eyre, Esq., of Rampton, who was baptized there 20th August, 1669, High Sheriff for Nottinghamshire, and M.P. for the same county from 1698 to his death on the 16th Feb., 1703. His wife died 7th Nov., 1804.

father, since neither he, nor his brother who succeeded him, left any male heirs.

Dr. and Mrs. Eyre, of Doncaster, had one son, the Rev. Anthony Fountayne Eyre, Canon of York Cathedral, who married twice; first, Susannah, daughter of Kenrick Prescot, Esq., by whom he had four children, all of whom died unmarried; and, secondly, Honor, daughter of the Rev. Godfrey Wolley, and sister of Admirals Thomas and Isaac Wolley. By this second marriage, in the old residence house at York, the father of Edward John Eyre was born.

He was christened Anthony William, the first name having been borne, alternately with Gervas, by the head of the Eyre family, in memory of Anthony Babington, from whom the Eyres inherit it by the marriage of Sir Gervas Eyre with Miss Babington. Anthony William Eyre also became a clergyman, and

---

she prayed for ym all, but in a particular manner for blessings on my father, and dyed composed ye next day. My father did not only perform his promise to his mother, but was in many respects very kind to ym all after he was of age, but met with ungrateful returns from all but one brother, and his youngest sister. My grandfather kept a large stud of race horses, which was a great expense to him. Ye expense of his elections would not have hurt his family, but ye numbers of ye low class of freeholders yt frequented his house was a considerable charge to him. I have heard me father say, this made him decline ye solicitation to stand a candidate in ye neighbourhood where he lived, and though he was fond of a race horse, ye inconvenient expense he might by degrees be drawn into by keeping any, prevented his indulging himself in that pleasure."

held various cures and preferments, amongst others Stillingfleet, near York, and, at a later period, the vicarage of Hornsea and the rectory of Riston, in the East Riding of Yorkshire. These two latter preferments he held at the time of his death in 1848. He married Sarah Mapleton, the daughter of a physician in Bath, who is mentioned frequently by De Quincey in his Autobiography. Dr. Mapleton was a clever man, and one of his sons, Captain David Mapleton, R.N., was noted for his gallantry and daring. He was gazetted again and again for acts of bravery before he was one-and-twenty, and especially distinguished himself in cutting out boats under Sir Thomas Cochrane, afterwards Lord Dundonald. David, one of his sons, and a nephew, the son of his elder brother, Captain William Mapleton, R.A., were also well known as gallant and scientific naval officers. The last served in one or two Arctic expeditions with considerable credit. On all sides, therefore, Edward John Eyre came of a brave, energetic, determined race of men, and early in life he formed the resolution that he too would, if possible, distinguish himself.

He was the third son (the eldest died in infancy, the second at the age of fifteen), and showed no peculiar talent or bias towards any study or employment in his childhood. He was always fond of, and apt at arithmetic and algebra; devoted to carpentering, turning, and fishing, giving up all his half and whole holidays to these pursuits when able. He was a grave, quiet, self-centred, composed boy; remarkable only for the dogged resolution with which he pursued any amusement, study, or occupation he had once begun.* His memory was in childhood defective; but no youngster worked more thoroughly at school than he did, and all his masters predicted his future eminence in life. "He will one day be a blazing star in the literary horizon," was the grandiloquent speech in which one of his earliest tutors announced the improvement he had made during the half-year. Under this master it was that he learned to lay down maps and calculate heights and distances—knowledge that was to be so useful to him in after-life.

In his boyhood he occasionally, with his brother, spent his holidays at his uncle's, the Rev. Charles Wolff Eyre, rector of Hooten Roberts, near Doncaster. During these holidays, a gentleman of the neighbourhood took the two lads out fishing; it was a sunny day, and they had no sport; at last he unthinkingly said, "I wish we were on the other side of the river under those trees; I dare say there are fish there." He had scarcely uttered the words, when he heard a splash, and to his horror beheld the boy Edward, then about twelve years old, in the river. From infancy he never saw anything but the object he

* How forcibly, in after-life, his "dogged resolution" carried him successfully through unheard-of difficulties, dangers, and privations, will be shown when reference is made to his South Australian explorations.

had in view, and took no heed of any obstacles in the way of his attaining it. The gentleman had said there would be fish on the other side; of course he must get them; it never occurred to him that he might be drowned in the attempt, seeing that he could not swim a stroke. His elder companion had some difficulty in dragging him out safely, which he did eventually however, vowing mentally that "he would never again take Edward Eyre out fishing"—a vow he religiously kept.

At Thorparch, whilst spending another holiday with his grandmother and aunt, he caught a severe fever, contracted by sleeping in damp clothes. In order to lose no time in dressing in the morning to go out fishing, he used, unknown to any one, to take off the clothes he had worn at dinner in the evening, and put on the wet clothes he had worn in his fishing expeditions during the day, and which his family imagined were drying by the kitchen fire, and thus equipped, even to his boots, he was in the habit of creeping into bed.

Another of his holidays was spent with his brother and sisters at West Ella Park, near Hull, the property of Major Richard Sykes. Here he was missed one day for some hours, and being sought, was at last found perched on the very top of one of the highest trees in the park. He had got *up*, partly by swarming, but when he wanted to get *down*, he found the boughs were many of them too rotten to bear his weight; so with characteristic coolness he calculated that he would infallibly be missed and looked for, and that the wisest thing he could do was to remain quiet on his tree until assistance came. As he foresaw, search was made for him, but as he was at this period always alarming his family by getting into scrapes and risking his life, they resolved to punish him. Some time necessarily elapsed before three ladders could be procured and spliced together, so as to reach his perch at the top of the tree ; and whilst this was doing, Major Sykes, his family, and guests, the rest of the Eyre children, and all the servants, went to the tree where the young adventurer was pilloried and joined in laughing at him. The punishment was efficacious; he felt the ridicule of his position so keenly, that it cured him of his inveterate habit of climbing.

He was not in early life what is termed "a bookish boy." He did his work regularly to the best of his ability, and always held a foremost piace in his class. He was quite on a par with boys of his own age in classics, and in advance of them in mathematics ; but his work over, he preferred a long solitary ramble, a climb, fishing, shooting, skating, or any active exercise to reading; but *whatever he once began, he never left until he mastered it.*

He was successively at school at Thorparch, near Rotherham, at Grantham, at Louth, and at Sedbergh,*

* A well-known Yorkshire foundation school near the lakes.

where he had ample opportunities of indulging his passion for angling, and climbing difficult and dangerous rocks. From Grantham he went to the grammar school of Louth, in Lincolnshire, which Charles and Alfred Tennyson had left a year or two before. Their fame as poets was still traditionary in the school, and Edward Eyre seemed to feel a kind of noble envy, at once proud of the fact that two of "our boys" had actually published a volume of poems, for which a bookseller gave them ten pounds, and grieved he could not emulate them. Even then he craved distinction. He learnt much at Sedbergh. Many of his schoolfellows had a studious turn, and there he acquired some knowledge of chemistry, and occupied himself in making an electrical machine. He had also a turn for mechanical employments, and was handy at all kinds of carpentry; this was very useful to him in after-life.

He learned a little of astronomy, and used to try in the holidays to teach his sister to know the Greater and the Lesser Bear, and the names of many other stars. Neither then foresaw that in six or seven years from that time, or even earlier, he would be threading his way through an interminable untracked wilderness by calculating the altitudes of the stars.

When at sixteen he left Sedbergh, it was a difficult question to decide what he should be. His masters had, one and all, advised a college life, where, as they said, his talents insured him distinction and a fellowship. A constitutional delicacy of the chest, however, forbade his following any sedentary profession. His own wishes pointed to the army, but that was thought too expensive a profession; and, though the kindness of Lord Brougham had given his father a good living, that of Hornsea-cum-Long-Riston, in Holderness, Yorkshire, there was no spare cash in the family, who had always lived in the rank of gentlefolks, and had only that which enabled them to maintain their position. His name, however, was put down for the purchase of a commission, and the purchase money was lodged.

At this juncture, a friend advised his going out as a settler to Australia, where, at that time, there was an excellent opening for industrious, active young men. And so, at the early age of seventeen, with a good outfit, several introductions, and about 400*l.* in his pocket, he went forth from his father's house to seek his fortune in a new world.

He proceeded first to Sydney, and afterwards joined a settler in that colony, paying for his board, to enable him to acquire a practical experience as a colonist. Whilst living with this gentleman on the River Hunter, it happened that two men arrived one evening on the opposite side of the river from a very considerable distance. They were without food, and, as the river was highly flooded, sweeping along in a furious, boiling stream, carrying huge logs and trees with it, there was no possibility of the men crossing, or of any assistance being given to them that night. The following morning the river was higher and more furious than ever, and the question was, what should be done to aid the two men. At that time, Mr. Eyre, who was scarcely eighteen, could not swim; but, as none of those who could would face the raging stream, he volunteered to put on a mackintosh swimming belt, and try to carry a rope across.

One end of a very long rope was accordingly tied under his arms, and the other made fast to a tree on the bank, whilst several men stood by to pay out the rope as he progressed. He plunged in and struck out manfully for the other side, as the current swept him rapidly down-stream. At first he progressed very satisfactorily; but after passing the middle of the stream, the curve of the rope below him, pressed by the current, kept dragging him back, and his utmost exertions could not enable him to reach more than three-fourths of the way across. He was then completely exhausted. The party on shore, noticing this, hauled in the rope to drag him back; but when about half-way, the rope got entangled in the projecting part of a tree that had lodged in the river: here he stuck for some time, the rushing stream bubbling over him and all but drowning him. Eventually he managed to work himself free, and was dragged ashore almost dead. The men were obliged to remain starving until the river subsided. He learnt to swim almost immediately afterwards.*

Having gained some practical experience as a colonist, he then purchased a number of sheep, which he sold to advantage, and subsequently bought a

* It is singular the number of escapes Mr. Eyre has had from drowning during his eventful life. When a little boy, he went, on one occasion, with some schoolfellows to bathe in a canal. Not one of them could swim. On arriving and stripping, no one dared to venture in to try the depth (which turned out to be very great). Some one had two large bladders for learning to float, and young Eyre immediately volunteered, if the bladders were put on him, to go in and try the depth. He did so and got safely to the opposite side without finding bottom. After resting he set off on his return, and had got to the centre of the canal when the bladders slipped and tilted him head under. How he succeeded in struggling ashore no one knows to this day, but he did succeed, and was dragged out completely exhausted.

A still more extraordinary escape occurred when he was a very little child. He was left at home with a nurse one Sunday whilst his father, who was the clergyman of the place, went to perform duty in the church close by their house. It was winter time. The nurse soon occupied herself with her sweetheart and left the child to take care of himself. There was a pond in the orchard to which he soon found his way. It was well frozen over, but at one side had a large hole broken for the cattle to drink, and over this was only a thin coating of ice. After amusing himself for some time on the firm ice, he contrived to get on the portion covering the drinking hole, and of course fell through. He had no intentions, however, of being drowned, for he screamed most lustily before he went under. His father heard him in the pulpit, and he and half the congregation came rushing out just in time to prevent his career being cut short.

No doubt the Jamaica Committee will argue that Mr. Eyre cannot be drowned because he is reserved for the fate they have so kindly designed for him.

farm, which he disposed of to enable him to engage as an "overlander," in transporting stock from New South Wales to the newly-established colonies of Port Phillip and South Australia. In this he was eminently successful, and was the first to prove the practicability of driving sheep overland, by the route of the Murray River, from New South Wales to South Australia. Though accompanied by only a few convict servants, he succeeded in conducting his parties in safety, and without ever coming into collision with the numerous tribes of natives through whose country he had to pass, and by whom many subsequent parties were either partially or wholly destroyed. In the first of these journeys he brought 1000 sheep and 600 head of cattle from Monero, in New South Wales, to Adelaide, in South Australia, and was well rewarded for the labour and risk, as the price of cattle and sheep in Adelaide was, at that time, enormous, both sheep and cattle having previously been always taken from Sydney to Adelaide by water. The benefit he conferred on the then rising city of Adelaide was incalculable, and the settlers, with the Governor at their head, duly acknowledged it, by showing every possible honour to the daring adventurer. Eyre realized a handsome sum by the trip, which induced other bold men to follow in his steps, until the market at last became overstocked. From these journeys of his, and others, came the term " overlanders."

It was about this time that, writing home to a near relative, he said: "I have gone on in the spirit of the ancient motto of our house, *Si je puis.* ·If *I can* distinguish myself, *I will.*" The desire to earn honourable distinction marked his whole career at school and in manhood; and if the name of Edward Eyre was not familiar to English ears prior to the Jamaica insurrection, it arose from the fact that England was ungrateful to one of her noblest and bravest sons.

Having again purchased land on the Murray River, in South Australia, he once more set to farming his own estate. It was at this time, because of his great experience amongst the natives, and his tact and judgment in dealing with them, that he was appointed Resident Magistrate at the Murray, and "Protector of Aborigines," in which office he won their perfect love and confidence. In a letter to some friends in England, he says: " I have frequently slept unharmed and without fear, the only white man among 500 armed natives; I have travelled among them by day and by night; I have owed my life to them again and again, and I never received from them anything but the greatest possible kindness."

It is most important that, at the present juncture, the world should know the antecedents of the man who stands accused of being a reckless sacrificer of the black race; and no excuse, therefore, is necessary for making the following extract from the preface to the volumes published by himself upon his Australian explorations :—

"For the account given of the aboriginal tribes, the author deems it unnecessary to offer any apology; a long experience among them, and an intimate knowledge of their character, habits, and positions with regard to Europeans, have induced him to take a deep interest on behalf of a people who are fast fading away before the progress of a civilization which ought only to have added to their improvement and prosperity. Gladly would the author wish to see attention awakened on their behalf, and an effort at least made to stay the torrent which is overwhelming them. It is most lamentable to think that the progress and prosperity of one race should lead to the downfall and decay of another; it is still more so to observe the apathy and indifference with which this result is contemplated by mankind in general."

Mr. Kingsley, writing of Mr. Eyre's great march, prior to the insurrection in Jamaica, says :—

"Of this Mr. Eyre, who made this unparalleled journey, I know but little, save this: He knew more about the aboriginal tribes—their habits, language, and so on—than any man before or since. He was appointed Black Protector for the Lower Murray, and did his work well. He appears to have been (*teste* Charles Sturt, from whom there is no appeal) a man eminently kind, generous, and just. No man concealed less than Eyre the vices of the natives; but no man stood more steadfastly in the breach between them and the squatters (the great pastoral aristocracy) at a time when to do so was social ostracism. The almost un-exampled valour which led him safely through the hideous desert into which we have to follow him served him well in a fight more wearing and more dangerous to his rules of right and wrong. He pleaded for the black, and tried to stop the war of extermination, which was, is, and I suppose will be, carried on by the colonists against the natives in the unsettled districts beyond the reach of the public eye. His task was hopeless. It was easier for him to find water in the desert than to find mercy for the savages. Honour to him for attempting it, however."

CHAPTER II.

In the year 1840, public attention in Adelaide was considerably engrossed with the subject of an overland communication between Southern and Western Australia, for the purpose of opening up a traffic between the two places, with a view to the extension of their pastoral interests. So little did the gentlemen who assembled together to discuss the matter know of the dangers and difficulties that would beset the first exploring party, that they even proposed and agreed that cattle should accompany it. In the previous year Mr. Eyre, who was already well known as a determined and gallant explorer, had carefully examined the country to the westward of the located parts of South Australia, and fully satisfied himself of the utter impracticability of opening an overland route for stock in that direction ; and when, therefore, on visiting Adelaide, he heard of the wild schemes afloat, he at once came forward and used his influence to prevent them being carried out. His experience taught him that the vast extent of desert country, the scarcity of grass, the denseness of the scrub, and the all but total absence of water, even in the most favourable seasons, would utterly prevent any successful venture of the kind. While, however, discouraging the pet scheme of the Adelaide community, he endeavoured to turn their ardour into another channel, with what success will presently be shown. On the 23rd of May, 1840, he addressed the public in the columns of the 'South Australian Register,' and pointed out the possibility of the veil being lifted from the unknown and mysterious interior of that vast continent, and the probability of discoveries of importance being made, likely to prove beneficial to that and other colonies. He was listened to with marked respect, and directly he felt that he had been the means of diverting the public attention from a Western to a Northern exploration, he at once offered to encounter himself the risks and toils of the undertaking. Accordingly, he volunteered to take the command of any party that might be sent out, to find one-third of the number of horses required, and to pay one-third of the expenses. This generous and noble offer was at once accepted by His Excellency the Governor and by the Adelaide people, and seven days later he commenced the necessary arrangements for organizing his party, and getting ready the equipment required.

On the 2nd and 5th of June, meetings of the colonists were held, at which subscriptions were entered into for carrying out the object of the expedition. By the 13th inst., 541*l.* 17*s.* 5*d.* had been collected and paid into the Bank of Australia. On the 20th of June, the day upon which the expedition, which consisted of five Europeans, two aboriginal boys, and Mr. Eyre, was to start, a public breakfast was given by His Excellency the Governor. On leaving Government House, the party was accompanied by a large body of gentlemen on horseback, and ladies in carriages, desirous of paying the gallant adventurers the last kind tribute of friendship, by a farewell escort of a few miles. Mr. Eyre describes the parting in brief words :—" Carried away by the enthusiasm of the moment, our thoughts and feelings were wrought to the highest state of excitement. The time passed rapidly away; the first few miles were soon travelled over : then came the halt,—the parting,—the last friendly cheer ; and we were alone in the wilderness. Our hearts were too full for conversation, and we wended our way slowly and in silence."

It is not necessary to trace too minutely the course of Mr. Eyre in his journey towards the interior. His progress was very slow. How slow may be imagined from the fact that he was constantly obliged to halt his party, and proceed alone for days together, in order to find suitable camping ground ; and so, not expose his companions to the privations of want of water, and other dangers. Little indeed, as Mr. Eyre justly observes, are the public aware of the difficulties and responsibilities attached to the command of such an expedition. The incessant toil, the sleepless hours, the anxious thoughts that necessarily fall to the share of the leader of a party under circumstances of difficulty or danger, are but imperfectly understood, and less appreciated by the world at large.

Mr. Eyre, though struck down by illness, persevered. After three months, however, of continual marching and counter-marching, he was compelled to fall back upon Port Lincoln for supplies. During those three months he made three endeavours to force his way through a dreary region of arid waste, towards the north, but was thrice defeated. Each time, though taking a different northerly direction, he found himself hemmed in on every side by a barrier it was impossible to pass. The inhospitable shores of the desolate Lake Torrens frowned upon him on every occasion, and, at last, disappointed but by no means discouraged, he was obliged, from want of supplies, to retrace his steps towards civilization. The greater part of the vast area contained in the bed of this gigantic lake, though dry on the surface, consisted of a mixture of sand and mud, of so soft and yielding a character as to render perfectly ineffective all attempts either to cross it or reach the edge of the water, which appeared to exist at a distance of some miles from its outer margin. The lake, on its eastern and southern sides, was bounded by a high sandy ridge, with brush-wood growing upon it, but without any other vegetation. The other shores, which were distinctly visible, seemed to be one vast, low, and dreary waste. It therefore became evident that, to avoid Lake Torrens and the low desert by which it was surrounded, he must go very far either to the east or to the west, before again attempting to penetrate to the north. He accordingly fell back upon Port Lincoln, and remained there until he could obtain sufficient supplies from Adelaide to enable him to continue away five months longer.

While awaiting these supplies, a circumstance transpired in Port Lincoln which deserves special mention, not so much on account of the murder that then took place, as the reflections which that event caused in the mind of Mr. Eyre, and the record which he entered in his diary concerning the character of the aborigines in consequence. At a moment like the present, when he is lying under the stigma of excessive cruelty to the negroes, it is well that we should look carefully to his antecedents. The character of a man does not suddenly change in a day; and it is pleasing for those who repudiate with indignation the calumnies which have been unjustly heaped upon him, to read of his life, his actions, the very thoughts of his early years, and to find that they give the lie to the accusations now ruthlessly hurled against him.

While at Port Lincoln, a little boy, twelve years of age, of the name of Hawson, was left in a station hut whilst his brother came into town. Soon after his departure, about ten or eleven natives surrounded the hut, and wished for something to eat. The boy gave them bread and rice—all he had. As he fancied they would endeavour to force themselves into the hut, he stepped out and fastened the door, standing on the outside, with his gun by his side and a sword in his hand, which he held for the purpose of fighting them. He did not, however, make any signs of using them until he received from his cowardly assailants two long barbed spears in his chest. He then took up his gun and shot one of the natives, who fell, but got up again and scampered away, followed by the rest. The poor child remained with the two spears, seven feet long, sticking in his breast. He tried to cut and saw them without effect. He then sat upon the ground, and put the ends of the spears in the fire, to try and burn them off, and in this position he was found, at ten o'clock at night, upon the return of his brother, having been speared eleven hours. His brother immediately sawed the ends of the spears off, and placing him on horseback, brought him into Port Lincoln, where Mr. Eyre saw him. After the boy's death, it was stated that Mr. Edward Hawson had, some short time previously, shot at some natives to frighten them, after they had stolen something from the same hut where they speared his brother.

In referring to this melancholy occurrence, Mr. Eyre, in his journal, does not attempt to palliate the cruel barbarity of these savages; but it is the cause which induces him to jot down his views of the conduct of the aborigines of Australia generally towards the invaders and usurpers of their rights. It is to be regretted that limited space prevents the possibility of quoting fully all that he urges on their behalf; but sufficient may be given to show the utter falsehood of those who declare Mr. Eyre to be a man " destitute of the common feelings of humanity for the coloured people of God's earth."

" What are the relations," he writes, " usually subsisting between the aborigines and settlers, locating in the more distant and less populous parts of the country —those who have placed themselves upon the outskirts of civilization, and who, as they are in some measure beyond the protection of the laws, are also free from their restraints? A settler, going to occupy a new station, removes, perhaps, beyond all other Europeans, taking with him his flocks and his herds and his men, and locates himself wherever he finds water and a country adapted for his purposes. At the first, possibly, he may see none of the inhabitants of the country that he has thus unceremoniously taken possession of. Naturally alarmed at the inexplicable appearance and daring intrusion of strangers, they keep aloof, hoping, perhaps, but vainly, that the intruders may soon retire. Days, weeks, or months pass away, and they see them still remaining. Compelled at last, it may be by enemies without, by the want of water in the remoter district, by the desire to procure certain kinds of food, which are peculiar to certain localities, and at particular seasons of the year, or perhaps by a wish to revisit their country and their homes, they return once more, cautiously and fearfully approaching what is their own—the spot, perhaps, where they were born, the patrimony that has descended to them through many generations;—and what is the reception that is given them upon their own lands? Often they are met by repulsion, and sometimes by violence, and are compelled to retire again to strange and unsuitable localities. Passing over the fearful scenes of horror and bloodshed that have but too frequently been perpetrated, in all the Australian colonies, upon the natives in the remoter districts, by the most desperate and abandoned of our countrymen, and overlooking, also, the recklessness that too generally pervades the shepherds and stock-keepers of the interior, with regard to the coloured races—*a recklessness that leads them to think as little of firing at a black as at a bird, and which makes the number they have killed, or the atrocities that have attended the deeds, a matter for a tale, a jest, or boast at their pothouse revelries;*—overlooking these, let us suppose that the settler is actuated by no bad intentions,

---

* These lines have been printed in italics, because it has been loudly proclaimed that Mr. Eyre caused the blacks of Jamaica "*to be shot down like pheasants,*" without regard to sex or age.

and that he is sincerely anxious to avoid any collision with the natives, or not to do them any injury; yet, under these even comparatively favourable circumstances, what frequently is the result? The settler finds himself alone in the wilds, with but few men around him, and these, principally occupied in attending to stock, are dispersed over a considerable extent of country; he finds himself cut off from assistance or resources of any kind, whilst he has heard fearful accounts of the ferocity or the treachery of the savage; he therefore comes to the conclusion that it will be less trouble, and annoyance, and risk, to keep the natives away from his station altogether; and as soon as they make their appearance they are roughly waved away from their own possessions: should they hesitate, or appear unwilling to depart, threats are made use of, weapons, perhaps, produced, and a show, at least, is made of an offensive character, even if no stronger measures be resorted to. What must be the natural impression produced upon the mind of the natives by treatment like this? Can it engender feelings otherwise than of a hostile and vindictive kind? or can we wonder that he should take the first opportunity of venting those feelings upon the aggressor? . . . Nor ought we to wonder that a slight insult, or a trifling injury, should sometimes hurry them to an act apparently not warranted by the provocation. Who can tell how long their feelings have been rankling in

their bosoms—how long or how much they have borne?
A single drop will make the cup run over when filled up
to the brim; a single spark will ignite the mine that,
by its explosion, will scatter destruction around it : and
may not one foolish indiscretion, one thoughtless act of
contumely or wrong, arouse to vengeance the passions
that have long been burning, though concealed? With
the same dispositions and tempers as ourselves, they
are subject to the same impulses and infirmities. Little
accustomed to restrain their feelings, it is natural that,
when goaded beyond endurance, the effect should be
violent and fatal to those who roused them ;—the
smothered fire but bursts out the stronger from having
been pent up, and the rankling passions are but fanned
into wilder fury from having been repressed. .   . .
With reference to the particular case in question—the
murder of Master Hawson—it appears that, in addition
to any incentives, such as I have described as likely to
arise in the minds of the natives, there had been the still
greater provocation of their having been fired at, but a
short time previously, from the same station, and by
the murdered boy's brother. We may well pause,
therefore, ere we hastily condemn, or unjustly punish,
in cases where the circumstances connected with their
occurrence can only be brought before us in a partial
and imperfect manner."

This is singular language for a man to use, who is
now on his trial for ruthlessly slaughtering the negro!

To return, however, from this digression to the explorations of Mr. Eyre. Finding it impossible to force a passage to the north without proceeding first to the westward, Mr. Eyre moved for the head of the Great Australian Bight. After leaving Streaky Bay, he found gigantic obstacles to contend against; the heavy sandy nature of the country, its arid character, the scarcity of grass, and the very dense brushes through which the party had to clear a road with their axes, formed impediments which, but for the assistance of a cutter placed at the disposal of Mr. Eyre by the Governor, would have compelled them to give up altogether their plans. By putting on board the cutter the greater part of their dead weight, they relieved their jaded horses from loads they could no longer draw; and by obtaining from her occasional supplies of water at such points of the coast where they could procure none on shore, they were thus enabled to reach Fowler's Bay on the 22nd of November.

From this point Mr. Eyre could no longer avail himself of the valuable services of the boat—the wild unprotected character of the coast extending around the Great Australian Bight rendering it too dangerous for a vessel to attempt to approach so fearful a shore, where there was no harbour or shelter of any kind to make for in case of need.

Under these circumstances he left his party in camp behind Point Fowler, whilst he proceeded, accompanied only by a native boy, to examine the country ahead. For twenty-four days and nights he was engaged in attempting to round the head of the Bight; but so difficult was the country, that he was driven back from want of water, and obliged to abandon one of his horses. In no way dispirited, he made a secon_ attempt, accompanied by a native boy and one of his party, driving a dray loaded solely with water and provisions; but such was the dreadful nature of the country that, after penetrating to within twelve miles of the head of the Bight, he was again obliged to abandon three horses, the dray, and all the provisions. After reaching the nearest water, they made every effort to save the unfortunate animals. For seven days Mr. Eyre, his attendant, and the native boy were incessantly engaged, day and night, in carrying water backwards and forwards to them—feeding them with bread, gruel, &c.—but all their efforts were vain, and the expedition thus sustained a fatal and irreparable injury in the loss of three of its best draught horses.

In traversing the country along the coast from Streaky Bay to within twelve miles of the head of the Great Bight, the whole extent was totally destitute of surface water. Still his indomitable energy urged him on, and he confidently expected that, once able to round the Bight, the country might, perhaps, alter its character so far as to enable him to prosecute the main object of the expedition, that of examining the northern interior.

The very severe loss the expedition had sustained in the death of four of its best horses, added to the unfavourable season of the year, and the embarrassing nature of the country, rendered it at last impossible for them longer to carry provisions for so large a party, more especially since the wild and fearful nature of the breaker-beaten coast precluded the possibility of their making use of the assistance and co-operation of the Government cutter. Mr. Eyre was consequently under the necessity of reducing the strength of his already small party, and accordingly sent two men back to Adelaide, retaining only his overseer and one man, exclusive of Mr. Scott and two native boys.

From the reduced state of their remaining horses it became absolutely necessary for them to remain in depôt five or six weeks to rest them. The departure of the cutter and two men of their little band made the camp wear a gloomy and melancholy aspect, and cause a sad alteration in its hitherto cheerful character. The monotony of their life was very dispiriting, and Mr. Eyre frankly owns in his diary that he felt downhearted. He says :—" For a time, indeed, the writing up of my journals, the filling up of my charts, and superintending the arranging, packing, and burying of our surplus stores, amused and occupied me, but as these were soon over, I began to repine and fret at the life of indolence and inactivity I was doomed to suffer. Frequently required at the camp, to give directions, or to assist in the daily routine of duty, I did not like to absent myself long away at once; there were no objects of interest near me, within the limits of a day's excursion on foot, and the weak state of the horses prevented me from making any examinations of the country at a greater distance on horseback; I felt like a prisoner condemned to drag out a dull and useless existence through a given number of days or weeks, and like him, too, I sighed for freedom, and looked forward with impatience to the time when I might again enter upon more active and congenial pursuits. Fatigue, privation, disappointment, disasters, and all the various vicissitudes incidental to a life of active exploration had occasionally, it is true, been the source of great anxiety or annoyance, but all were preferable to that oppressive feeling of listless apathy, of discontent, and dissatisfaction, which resulted from the life I was now obliged to lead."

Christmas-day came, and made a slight though temporary break in the monotony of their daily life. The kindness of their friends had supplied them with many luxuries, and they were thus enabled, even in these desert wilds, to participate in the fare of the season. On the 26th they found that their remaining horses were falling off so much in condition, from the scarcity of grass and its dry and sapless quality, that it was absolutely necessary for them to remove elsewhere. Mr. Eyre accordingly marched the party five miles to a well in the plains, having first carefully buried all the surplus stores. The grass here was abundant, but very dry and without much nourishment, while the water was so brackish as to be hardly fit to drink. They were thankful, however, to get any.

The horses having enjoyed a rest of a few days, and being stronger, Mr. Eyre determined to make one more effort to get round the head of the Bight. On the 30th December he left the camp, the sheep, and four horses in charge of Mr. Scott and the youngest of the native boys, whilst he proceeded himself, accompanied by the overseer and eldest native boy on horseback, the other European driving a dray with three horses, to cross once more through the scrub to the westward. On the following day they found the little water they came to salter and more bitter.

On New Year's-day, 1841, they were joined by a large party of natives, who were very friendly disposed, and lamented, in pathetic terms, the death of the horses, the dead bodies of which they had come across in their wanderings. To all Mr. Eyre's inquiries about water, they persisted there was none inland, though they pointed out a hole where some might be obtained two miles distant. January 2nd the party started early; but after fourteen miles the horses could go no further, and they were obliged to come to a halt. There appeared to be a disastrous fatality attending all their movements in this wretched region. Every time that they had attempted to force a passage through it, they had been baffled and driven back. Twice before, Mr. Eyre had been obliged to abandon his horses; and now, after giving those that remained a long period of rest and respite from labour, and after taking every precaution which prudence or experience could suggest, he had the mortification of finding that they were in the same predicament as they had been before, with as little prospect of accomplishing their object. The horses were taken back by the overseer to the water to remain two days and rest, while Mr. Eyre stayed with the native boy and dray until their return. On the 5th they came back, but so little benefited that, upon being yoked up and put to the dray, they could not move it. The following day, therefore, the dray was sent back with the overseer, and Mr. Eyre determined upon pushing on to the north-west, accompanied by the native boy and the European leading a pack-horse with twelve gallons of water.

The weather grew intensely hot, while a strong wind blowing from the north-east, threw upon them an oppressive and scorching current of heated air, like the hot blast of a furnace. After a march of seventeen miles on the 6th, they sank down fairly exhausted. The European who accompanied Mr. Eyre was thoroughly beaten. His spirits failed him, and giving way to his feelings of fatigue and thirst, he lay rolling on the ground, and groaning in despair.   They had halted in the midst of a low sandy flat, not far from the sea, thinking that by a careful examination they might find where water could be procured by digging.   There being, however, no trees or bushes near them, and the heat of the sun and the glare of the sand being so intolerable, at all hazards Mr. Eyre was obliged to get up the jaded horses, and compel his thoroughly beaten companion to go on yet a little further to seek for shelter.   This they at last found under a rock upon the sea-shore.   The native boy and Mr. Eyre stripped themselves of every particle of clothing, and by constantly plunging into the sea and then returning to the shelter of the rock, they succeeded in keeping themselves cool.   But it was a long time before they could induce their companion to follow their example, either by persuasion or threats; his courage had failed him, and he lay down and moaned like a child.   When at last they succeeded in getting him to strip and bathe, he at once found the benefit of it.

It is not to be wondered at that Mr. Eyre should have resolved in his own mind as soon as possible to get rid of a companion who had now become not only useless but an actual clog to him.*   The following

---

* Writing subsequently of this individual, Mr. Eyre generously remarks :—" I had ever found him a useful and obedient man, and with the exception of his losing courage under the heat upon the

day, therefore, he was sent back to rejoin the overseer, with a note requesting the latter to send two fresh horses to meet Mr. Eyre on the 15th January, for, from the weak condition of the animals he had with him, and the almost total absence of grass where he purposed pushing to, he could not but dread lest he might be compelled to abandon them also, in which case, if he did not succeed in finding water, he would probably have great difficulty in getting back himself.

As soon as the man had gone, Mr. Eyre and the native boy moved on to the north-west, and at last arrived at the head of the Great Bight. Having successfully rounded this point, they proceeded some fifty miles, and met with a few friendly natives, who showed them where both grass and water was to be procured, at the same time assuring them that there was no more along the coast for ten of their days' journey (100 miles), or where the first break took place in the long continuous line of cliffs which extended to the westward of the Great Bight. Along these cliffs, lashed by the violent waves of the great Southern Ocean, Mr. Eyre trudged on for forty-five miles further, in the vain hope that some great and important change might take place in the features of the country inland, from which he trusted he might accomplish the object for which

---

occasion alluded to, he had been a hardy and industrious man, and capable of enduring much fatigue."

the expedition was fitted out.   Such, however, was not
the case; there was not any improvement in the appearance of the country, or the least indication that there
might be a change for the better within any practicable
distance. Having already examined the tract of country
from the longitude of Adelaide to the parallel of
almost 130° E. longitude, an extent comprising nearly
8½ degrees of longitude, without having found a single
point from which it was possible to penetrate far into
the interior, and finding himself in circumstances of an
embarrassing and hopeless character, he reluctantly felt
that he must give up all further idea of contending
with obstacles which there was no reasonable hope of
ever overcoming.

Having, therefore, retraced his steps, he found himself, on the 15th of January, at the appointed rendez-
vous, where he was to meet the two fresh horses. The
overseer himself had brought them, and the whole
party moved back to Fowler's Bay without further
delay. There they met Mr. Scott, who complained
bitterly of having been left alone so long.

The following brief abstract of the labours of the
party, and the work performed by the horses in the
three attempts to get round the head of the Bight,
will give the reader some notion of the gigantic difficulties this gallant band had to encounter. And when it
is borne in mind that, after all, the distance examined
did not exceed 135 miles, and might have been done

easily in ten days, and without any loss, had the situation of the watering-places or the nature of the country been previously known, one can only pause in admiration at the courage and perseverance of the explorer, who, baffled and defeated, still traversed, over and over again, the same dreary waste, gaining but a few miles of ground at each fresh attempt.

ABSTRACT OF LABOURS OF THE PARTY IN ROUNDING THE GREAT BIGHT.

Name.	Distance Ridden.	No. of Days Employed.
Mr. Eyre.	643 miles	40
Mr. Scott.	50 ,,	4
The Overseer	230 ,,	22
Costelow.	. .	22
Houston	. .	12
Corporal Coles	. .	8
Eldest Native Boy . . .	270 miles	19
Youngest Native Boy . .	395 ,,	23

Upon maturely considering all the circumstances of their position, Mr. Eyre resolved upon not returning to Adelaide without accomplishing something. His dauntless spirit could not brook defeat, and he decided, therefore, to force a passage round the Great Bight, with pack-horses only, and so make his way to Western Australia, a distance of over 1,000 miles of trackless desert. The Government cutter had been sent back to

Adelaide for forage for the horses, and Mr. Eyre now daily expected its return, and he accordingly resolved that, after a long rest at Fowler's Bay, he would make this terrible march, provided the instructions he might receive from Adelaide would justify him in sending the vessel so far beyond the boundaries of South Australia as Cape Arid, to convey the heavy stores and drays.

On the 26th their spirits were raised with the sight of a boat rounding to in the bay, and the consequent receipt of many English and colonial letters. On board the boat was a favourite servant of Mr. Eyre's, a native of King George's Sound, named Wylie, whom he had sent for, and who was wild with delight at meeting his master. Amidst all the kind letters received, came one of bitter disappointment from His Excellency the Governor. Although friendly in the extreme, it acquainted him that the ' Hero ' (the cutter) was entirely at his disposal *within* the limits of South Australia, but that, being under charter, he must not take her to Cape Arid or beyond the boundaries of the province. Thus all the plans he had formed were completely upset, and it became a matter of serious consideration what he should do under the circumstances. It was impossible for him to take his whole party and the drays overland through the dreadful country verging on the Great Bight; whilst if he took the party and left the drays, it was equally hopeless that he could carry upon pack-horses a sufficiency of provisions to last them 1,000 miles to King George's Sound. There remained, therefore, but two alternatives, either to break through the instructions received with regard to the 'Hero,' or to reduce his party still further, and to attempt this unparalleled journey almost alone. The first he did not, for many reasons, feel justified in doing—the second, therefore, he reluctantly decided upon adopting.

It was a painful step to part with his young friend, Mr. Scott, who had been with him from the commencement of the undertaking, and who had always been zealous and active in promoting its interests; but he felt that he ought not to allow him, however anxious, to be led into perils from which escape seemed all but hopeless. He accordingly seized the first opportunity when alone with Mr. Scott to explain the circumstances under which he was placed, and the decision to which he had been forced. Mr. Scott begged hard to be allowed to remain and share the dangers of his gallant leader, but Mr. Eyre was inexorable. The other men, with the exception of the overseer, were next spoken to, and, no doubt, tired and disappointed, they offered no objection whatsoever to get back to civilized life.

The only European of the party that now remains to be referred to was the overseer, John Baxter, whose subsequent melancholy fate during that fatal march deserves that his name should be handed down to posterity. Mr. Eyre sent for him and explained to him most fully the circumstances in which he was placed, the utter impossibility of taking on the whole party through so inhospitable a region as that before them, and his own firm determination never to return unsuccessful, but either to accomplish the object he had in view or perish in the attempt. He then left him to determine whether he would return to Adelaide in the cutter, or remain and accompany him. Baxter was not long in making up his mind. His reply was, that although he had become tired of remaining so long away in the wilds, and should be glad when the expedition had terminated, yet he would willingly remain to the last, and would accompany Mr. Eyre to the westward at every hazard.

Thus everything was arranged, and Mr. Eyre felt that the sooner the separation, the very thought of which had cast a gloom over all, was accomplished the better. The drays and such stores as were not required were shipped on board the ‘Hero,’ and on the 31st of January, his final report was addressed to the Chairman of the Committee, promoting the expedition, at Adelaide—that expedition being now brought to a close, and its members disbanded. The farewell was taken and the graceful cutter glided out of Fowler’s Bay, leaving these two gallant explorers to their fate.

They were now alone, with only three native boys, with a fearful task before them and with the bridge broken down behind them. They must either succeed in reaching King George's Sound, or perish in the attempt; no middle course remained. "It was impossible," writes Mr. Eyre, "for us to be insensible to the isolated and hazardous position we were in; but this very feeling only nerved and stimulated us the more in our exertions to accomplish the duty we had engaged in; the result we humbly left to that Almighty Being who had guided and guarded us hitherto, amidst all our difficulties, and in all our wanderings, and who, whatever he might ordain, would undoubtedly order everything for the best."

Having a large supply of the corn and bran sent from Adelaide by the 'Hero' still remaining, they determined upon staying in depôt until the horses were thoroughly set up again. They had many necessary and important preparations besides to make which kept them fully occupied. While Baxter made pack-saddles, extra bridles, and new hobbles, Mr. Eyre undertook the duty of stuffing and repairing the various saddles, making what extra clothes were required for himself and the native boys on the journey, weighing out and packing in small linen bags all the rations of tea, sugar, &c., which would be required weekly; preparing strong canvas saddle-bags, and making light oilskins to protect their things from the wet.

By the 23rd of February their preparations for entering upon their journey were nearly all completed; the horses had eaten up all their bran and corn, and were in good condition, all their provisions were packed, and everything in order for commencing the undertaking. The following afternoon the start was to be made. When the hour arrived, and the horses were just moving off, they were surprised by a shot in the direction of the Bay, followed by a second one, and presently two persons were descried in the distance. These turned out to be Mr. Scott and Mr. Germain, the master of the 'Hero,' who had been sent back by His Excellency the Governor, to entreat the return of Messrs. Eyre and Baxter. From the Governor Mr. Eyre received a kind letter offering to assist him in any further attempts he might wish to make round Lake Torrens, or to explore the Northern Interior, but begging him to desist from the dangerous undertaking he now contemplated. As a further inducement, and with a view to lessen the disappointment he might experience at the unsuccessful termination of an expedition from which such great results had been expected, the Assistant Commissioner wrote to him officially, communicating the approbation of His Excellency and the colonists of the way in which he had discharged the trust confided to him, and directing him to relinquish all further attempts to the westward and to return in the 'Hero' to Adelaide.

But Mr. Eyre had formed a resolution which nothing could make him depart from. He felt that the origin and commencement of the Northern expedition was due to him, he having been instrumental in changing the direction of public attention from the westward to the interior. He remembered also what publicity had been given to his departure, and how great was the interest felt in the progress of his labours; and how sanguine were the expectations formed as to the results; how signally all those hopes had been dashed to the ground, after the toils, anxieties, and privations of eight months, without any useful or valuable discoveries having been made; how, hemmed in by an impracticable desert, or the bed of an impassable lake, he had been baffled and defeated in every direction. To have returned, he considered, would have been to have rendered of no avail the great expenses that had been incurred in the outfit of the expedition; to have thrown away the only opportunity that remained to him of making some amends for past failure, and of endeavouring to justify the confidence that had been reposed in him, by carrying through the exploration which had been originally contemplated to the westward, when it was no longer possible to accomplish that to the north for which it had given place. He deemed himself in duty and in honour bound not to turn back from this attempt, so long as there was the remotest possibility of success. Returning, therefore, his best thanks to the Governor, to the colonists, and all his many friends who had expressed such kind interest in his behalf, he declined firmly to accede to their solicitations. Mr.

Scott accordingly sailed for Adelaide, once more leaving these two daring men to themselves.

And on the 25th they started—started on a journey that one of them was never to see the end of; a journey so full of horrors that the mere recital of their sufferings seems but the hideous revelations of a nightmare. It has justly been said that Mr. Eyre " did then what no man had ever done before, and no man will ever do again."

To this unparalleled journey, in the whole range of British adventure, a separate chapter must be accorded.

CHAPTER III.

In the whole civilized, or, indeed, uncivilized portion of the globe, not even excepting the eternal ice-bound regions of the Arctic Ocean, where lie bleaching the bones of many of England's noblest children, is there a tract of country to be equalled for desolation to that southern portion of the Great Australian Continent discovered by Nuyts in the ship 'Gulde Zeepaard' in the year 1627. If the reader will refer to the map of Australia, he will find that between 30 and 34 degrees of south latitude, and 118 and 134 degrees of east longitude, lies this fearful coast, lashed by the angry waves of the great Southern Ocean. The very map will speak of the hideous desolation: " Barren granite hills," " Barren sandy shore," " No water," " No vegetation ;" such is the information recorded upon it; while the only names set down by explorers to denote the more prominent points, bear the following signifi-cant titles : " Cape Arid," " Mount Barren," " Mount Ragged," and " Doubtful Bay." It has not inappro-priately been termed, " a blot on the earth's surface," and " the handiwork of Nature in her dotage."

Across this dreary waste we propose now to follow

the footsteps of Mr. Eyre and his companion Baxter, and to record their frightful dangers and privations, the violent death of the one, and the ultimate triumph of the other.

On the 25th of February, 1841, having bid Mr. Scott a final adieu, they set out upon their long and dismal journey. The party consisted of Mr. Eyre, Baxter, three native boys, nine horses, one Timor pony, one foal, and six sheep. Their starting point will be found marked on the map as " Cape Adieu." To the 7th of March their route was comparatively easy, for having been over the same ground previously, and buried water and provisions at favourable points, they knew where to halt. What they suffered most from during these few days was the sand which enveloped them, and never left them free from irritation and inconvenience. It floated on the surface of their water, every drop of which was far more precious to them than gold; it penetrated into their clothes, hair, eyes, and ears; their provisions were rendered almost un-eatable by it; and when they lay down at night they could get no rest, for their blankets were buried in it. It was a perpetual and never-ceasing torment; and to increase their miseries, they were afflicted with swarms of large horse-flies that gave them no peace.

But these were comparatively trivial annoyances for men who had set their minds upon a journey of over a thousand miles through trackless wastes, untrodden by

the foot of civilization, and incapable of affording even its savage children the merest necessaries of existence. Besides, Mr. Eyre had much to occupy his thoughts. There was the dim uncertainty of failure and death lying straight before him, and the knowledge that on his shoulders alone rested the responsibility of all that might happen. He knew that to get his party to the next water would be a task of no ordinary difficulty; and who can wonder that he lay down on his couch of sand restless and uneasy, and at last came to the determination that he would proceed in advance of his party in order that, by finding out where water was, he might be on the look out for them and guide them to it.

There is something inexpressibly grand and noble in this apparently trivial act. It demonstrates the generous bravery of Mr. Eyre's disposition. Leaving then the party, he pushed onwards, across those vast arid plains, taking with him only one of the native boys, the sheep, and two horses; one to carry provisions and water, the other for the native youngster to ride on. Day after day they trudged along, the little parched-up grass being all the food for their dumb companions. At length the horses began to feel the want of water; and though, as if to tantalize them, morning and evening the threatening clouds overhead seemed to promise relief, still no rain fell. Seventy-seven miles after leaving their companions, both sheep and horses refused to feed, being too much in want of water to attempt to eat the dry and withered grass around them. They lay down for an hour to rest, and then ten miles further were accomplished by moonlight, in the hope that some cliffs in the distance might bring them to it. Their hopes, however, had been excited but to render their disappointment the greater; on reaching the cliffs and examining spots where rain-water would have settled after heavy showers, not one single drop was to be found. Gloomily turning away, they struggled on yet another eight miles, and just as the day began to dawn they sank from downright exhaustion and fatigue. So thoroughly was Mr. Eyre done up, that he says in his diary: "I found myself actually dozing as I walked: mechanically my legs kept moving forwards, but my eyes were every now and then closed in forgetfulness of all around me, until I was suddenly thrown down by getting entangled amongst the scrub, or aroused by a severe blow across the face from the recoil of a bough after the passage of the boy's horse."

Two hours only could be spared for rest in this desperate march for life or death, and in that short period they were accordingly at work again. They continued along the line of cliffs, every moment expecting to find a break where it was to be hoped water might be found. Hour after hour passed away, mile after mile was traversed, but still no change took place.

At noon they had marched 110 miles from the last water, and Mr. Eyre found it necessary then to abandon the sheep, and by moving more rapidly with the horses, endeavour at least to save their lives. Foreseeing that such a contingency as this might occur, he had given Baxter strict orders to keep the tracks of the horses, that if he should be compelled to abandon the sheep, the overséer might find them and bring them on with his party.

Having decided on this plan, he made a yard of such high, withered shrubs as he could find, shut the sheep in, and left a slip of paper hoisted on a long stick for Baxter, directing him to bury the loads of his horses, and to hasten on with the animals alone, to save their lives. At dark they were fifteen miles from this spot, the two horses having been without a drop of water for four days, and Mr. Eyre and his native boy having no longer any for themselves. To add to the darkness that surrounded them, they had now got into a dense scrub. Still they kept perseveringly onwards, leading their horses, and forcing their way through it in the best manner they could. It was, however, all in vain. The poor boy, utterly worn out, and the horses in the same pitiable condition, at last refused to move, and for a few hours, therefore, Mr. Eyre was compelled to halt. The agony of their own sufferings was heightened by the knowledge that Baxter, the two boys, and the other horses, carrying heavy packs, must surely perish also,

unless the morning brought relief. As Mr. Eyre lay on
the ground, vainly courting sleep, the horrible thought
occurred to him, that the water he had expected to
find, from information given him by the natives on
starting, at a distance of one hundred and twenty miles,
might have been passed in the dark. The bare idea of
such a possibility was almost maddening, and as the
dreadful thought flashed across his mind, he almost
made up his mind to retrace his steps. If he went
back, however, and found it not, his horses were too
jaded to make up the lost ground, and if he had passed
it, every step forward they took would but carry them
further from it, and lead to their certain destruction.

It must have required a man of powerful nerve and
indomitable bravery to decide in this awful dilemma;
but Mr. Eyre was equal to the task. He determined
to press on, and Providence at last befriended him.
After a few miles they came to some sand drifts, and
turning into these, they struck the very place spoken of
by the natives. Thus, on the fifth day of their sufferings, they got relief, and were blessed with an abundant
supply of water. Mr. Eyre's first thoughts were now
turned to the party behind, and after some hours' rest,
absolutely needful, they set out to meet them, carrying
three gallons of water upon one of the horses for their use.
On meeting, they found both horses and people greatly
worn. The sheep and the loads of the pack-horses had
been abandoned many miles back. Mr. Eyre, there-

fore, directing Baxter and his party to the water, went in search of them, and luckily finding them, the whole party were soon afterwards, by God's blessing, once more together and in safety, after having passed over one hundred and thirty-five miles of desert country, without a drop of water in its whole extent, and at a season of the year the most unfavourable for such a journey. This may be set down as the first stage in this tremendous undertaking.

From the 12th to the 18th of March, they remained at the sand-drifts, attending to the horses, and sending back to recover the stores that had been left by Baxter.

The sand, as usual, was a dreadful annoyance, and large blood-sucking flies added to their discomfort. After a week's rest they again started, making a short stage of fourteen miles. At first they tried the beach, but were driven back behind the sea-shore ridge, and compelled to travel through a succession of low, scrubby undulations, and the beds of dried-up lakes. By the 19th they had travelled forty miles from the last water; and as it now became apparent to Mr. Eyre, from the villainous aspect of the country, that they would have probably another long push before they came upon any, and as the horses were already suffering much from thirst, he determined, on consultation with Baxter, to leave their baggage where it was, and to send back the horses to their last halting-place to rest for a few days, and then load them with as much water as they could carry. At midnight he accordingly sent the whole party back, remaining alone by himself to take care of the baggage and sheep, with an allowance of a pint of water per diem for six days, this being the contemplated period of Baxter's absence.

If we reflect upon the desolate feeling that creeps over a person when left solitary and alone for a lengthened period in even one of our fair English forests, some very faint and indistinct notion may be conceived of the sensations of Mr. Eyre under these unenviable circumstances. He must indeed have spent a miserable time. He had moments, long and weary ones, to reflect upon his position and prospects, which involved the safety of others as well as his own. He found, on consulting his chart, they had still 600 miles to traverse, measured as the bird flies ; but, taking into account the inequalities of the ground, and the circuit they would frequently be obliged to make, he could not hope to accomplish this in less than 800 miles of distance. With all the impediments and embarrassments they were likely to meet with, they could not possibly expect to accomplish it under twelve weeks. Their sheep were reduced to three in number, and their sole stock of flour amounted to 142 pounds, to be shared out amongst five persons. The task before them was indeed a fearful one ; but Mr. Eyre's motto was " Perseverance," and he firmly hoped that by patience and endurance he would safely and successfully accomplish his undertaking at last.

Before the six days had elapsed, when he might expect the return of Baxter, his little stock of water was exhausted. Evaporation had robbed him of some, and " *once or twice he spilt a little.*" What an ocean of suffering is conveyed in these few words!

At last his party came in sight. They had successfully accomplished their mission and brought a good supply of water, but only sufficient for themselves. On the 26th they moved on, and seventy-two miles further the scrub and sandy ridges became so heavy and harassing to the horses, that Mr. Eyre began to doubt whether he could get them on at all. Light as the loads were that they were required to carry, it became evident that they must be made even less burdensome. Allowing the native boys, therefore, to enjoy a good sound sleep, he set to work, with his overseer, to throw away every single article they could possibly dispense with. All except a single spare shirt and pair of boots and socks, a blanket, and the things they stood in, which consisted only of trousers, shirt, and shoes, were discarded. Most of their pack-saddles, kegs for holding water, all their buckets but one, their medicines, some of their fire-arms, a quantity of ammunition, and even a copy of Captain Sturt's Expedition, sent to Mr. Eyre while at Fowler's Bay, to amuse and cheer him, were here abandoned.

After all their arrangements were made, and everything rejected that they could do without, the loads of the horses were reduced in the aggregate about two hundred pounds. Having looked after the future welfare of the animals upon whose exertions their own lives now depended, Mr. Eyre ordered a sheep to be killed, as they had themselves been upon short allowance for some time, and were getting weak and hardly able to go through the toils that devolved upon them. The whole party ate a hearty meal, and at midnight, when the moon rose, moved on. To get clear of the dreadful scrub, for the next forty-eight hours they kept along the beach, but were frequently forced by the masses of seaweed to travel above high-water mark in the heavy, loose sand, the tide compelling them to halt at intervals. They had now, according to calculation, marched 102 miles from the last water, and expected to have to travel fifty miles further before they came upon any. By the 28th of March the horses became so jaded that one of them lay down, and Mr. Eyre was compelled to distribute its load amongst the others, and let him follow loose.

Their route continued along the beach, as the dense scrub inland prevented them from following any other course. They had, therefore, to go far out of their way, tracing round every point, and following along every bay, whilst the seaweed frequently obstructed their path, and drove them again and again to the loose sands above high-water mark, causing extra fatigue to their unfortunate horses. Sometimes they

were forced to go between these banks of seaweed
and the ocean, and even into the sea itself, on which
occasions it required their utmost vigilance to prevent
the wretched horses from drinking the salt water, which
would inevitably have destroyed them.

The Timor pony, which Mr. Eyre purchased at Port
Lincoln, at length broke down completely, and he was
compelled to abandon it to a miserable and certain
death, that by pushing on he might use every exertion in
his power to relieve the others, though scarcely daring
to hope that even one of them might be saved. "It
was, indeed," writes Mr. Eyre, "a fearful and heartrending scene to behold the noble animals which had
served us so long and so faithfully suffering the extremity of thirst and hunger, without having it in our
power to relieve them.   Five days of misery had passed
over their heads since the last water had been left, and
112 miles of country had been traversed without the
possibility of procuring food for them other than the
dry and sapless remains of last year's grass, and this
but rarely to be met with.   No rains had fallen to
refresh them, and they were reduced to a most pitiable
condition; still they travelled onwards, with a spirit
and endurance truly surprising.   Whenever we halted
they followed us about, like dogs, wherever we went,
appearing to look to us only for aid, and exhibiting
that confidence in us which I trust we all reposed in
the Almighty, for most truly did we feel that in his

mercy and protection alone our safety could now ever be hoped for."

The position they were in was a desperate one. The horses were nearly all exhausted, and if they failed them, they would be entirely dependent upon their own strength and exertions, nearly midway between Adelaide and King George's Sound, with a fearful country on either side, a very small supply of provisions, and no water. Yet in this fearful crisis Mr. Eyre never for a moment wavered as to the plan it would be necessary to adopt, in such a desperate extremity—at all hazards, he was determined to proceed onwards.

Unfortunately Baxter, though he still went through the duty devolving upon him with assiduity and cheerfulness, was evidently ill at ease, and had many gloomy anticipations of the future. He fancied that the party would never reach water by going on, and that there was little hope of saving any of the horses. In this latter idea Mr. Eyre rather encouraged him than otherwise, deeming it advisable to contemplate the darker side of the picture, and by accustoming themselves to look forward to being left entirely dependent upon their own strength and efforts, in some measure to prepare themselves for such an event should it unhappily befall them. But Baxter's mind was continually occupied with thoughts of returning, and he believed that the only chance of saving their lives was to return if possible to the water they had left behind themselves, and endeavour again to reach Fowler's Bay, where they had buried a large quantity of provisions. In discussing these subjects with him, Mr. Eyre carefully avoided irritating or alarming him by a declaration of his own opinions and resolutions; at the same time, he pointed out the imminent risk that would attend any attempt to get back to Fowler's Bay, and the probability there was of much less danger attending the effort to advance to King George's Sound. With respect to the native boys, they appeared to think or care but little about the future; they were not sensible of their danger, and having something still to eat and drink, they played, and laughed, and joked with each other as much as ever.

Digging a hole in the sand, they now abandoned everything they had with them, except two guns, a very little flour, and some tea and sugar, and then trudged onwards. Mr. Eyre's favourite mare soon dropped behind, and shortly afterwards another horse's strength failed. Day followed day, and night succeeded night, and their last drop of water was gone, while their feet became inflamed and painful to a degree, from constant walking in the salt water, whilst endeavouring to keep the horses from it. The pangs of thirst were slightly alleviated by some dew collected in a sponge, and they still contrived to crawl along in short stages, passing on their route masses of wreck upon the beach, oars, thwarts of boats, fragments of masts, spars, &c., strewed about in every direction; and which told in eloquent language their dismal tale of human suffering and human woe.

At length, as the mist gradually cleared away one morning, they found a slight change in the aspect of the country, and their hearts leaped with joy and hope. They staggered on and came to some ridges of white sand similar in formation to those where they had before found water. Selecting a hollow between two of these ridges, they all set to work digging with their hands in the desperation of despair, their suspense increasing every moment as the hole deepened. At about five feet the sand was observed to be quite moist, and upon its being tasted, was found to be free from any saline qualities. Another hour or more of desperate labour, and they came upon fresh water in abundance. In the last extremity they had been relieved.

Mr. Eyre thus records in his diary his feelings; he writes:—"That gracious God, without whose assistance all hope of safety had been in vain, had heard our earnest prayers for his aid, and I trust that in our deliverance we recognized and acknowledged with sincerity and thankfulness his guiding and protecting hand. It is in circumstances only such as we had lately been placed in that the utter hopelessness of all human efforts is truly felt, and it is when relieved from such a situation that the hand of a directing and beneficent Being appears most plainly discernible, fulfilling those gracious promises which he has made, to hear them that call upon him in the day of trouble."

As soon as each had satisfied his thirst, the suffering animals were attended to. The utmost caution became necessary in their management. They had been seven days without a drop of water, and almost without food also, and yet Mr. Eyre dared not give it to them freely. Of the two remaining sheep, one was now killed for food, and the meat lasted them for three or four days. It became apparent that some of the party must go back for some of the stores and other things that they had abandoned, forty-seven miles away. Baxter and one of the native boys accordingly started, and as it was probable that they would be away four days at least and have heavy work, Mr. Eyre gave him most of the food they had left. For this generosity he and the two boys who remained with him suffered acutely, and were obliged to resort at last to the roots of the gum-scrub for sustenance. When Baxter returned, it was to tell a pitiable tale. He had reached the spot where they had buried their stores and started on his return, when first one horse became blind and helpless, and had to be abandoned, with the things he had been carrying; then a second fell, and he too with his load had to be left; whilst the third managed to get within five miles of Mr. Eyre's halting place, and then succumbed also.

This latter intelligence was so far satisfactory that it enabled them, by sending that short distance, to get flour and tea, and so support life; but their situation was perilous in the extreme. They were still 650 miles from King George's Sound, with an entirely unknown country before them. Their provisions, when again recovered, would be barely sufficient to last them for three weeks and a half, at a very reduced rate of allowance. Their remaining horses were jaded and miserable beyond all conception; they could literally scarcely crawl. A single false step would be fatal. Everything depended upon Mr. Eyre's sole judgment and the determination he arrived at. Who can wonder that he felt deeply and anxiously the overwhelming responsibility that devolved upon him?

To attempt to move either backwards or forwards without the horses was at once dismissed; for, however revolting, it became apparent that before long their desperate circumstances would compel them to use the poor animals for food. Mr. Eyre never for one moment entertained the notion of retracing their steps to Fowler's Bay, though, unhappily, Baxter differed from him on this point. The last desperate march had unnerved him, and he gave way to the feeling that, if they advanced, they must inevitably perish. All Mr. Eyre's arguments were fruitless. With the characteristic obedience and fidelity with which he had always served his leader, he readily acquiesced in any plan that he might decide upon adopting; but Mr. Eyre perceived, with great pain, that he could not convince him that the view he took was a proper one, and that the plan he intended to follow was the only one which held out to them even the remotest hopes of eventual safety and success.

It now became necessary to turn their immediate attention to the recovery of their remaining stores. Baxter offered to attempt this object again; but, as he had just returned from a severe, though unsuccessful, journey on the same errand, Mr. Eyre decided upon going himself. He accordingly started on foot with one of the native boys, and, after an absence of four days, the two succeeded in bringing on their shoulders the stores necessary for their existence, everything else being left behind them. They luckily contrived during their journey to spear a sting-ray fish, which, though very unpalatable and unwholesome, nevertheless helped considerably to save their other provisions. During his absence, Baxter had reconnoitred the country a-head, and came back with gloomy misgivings, which he now unhesitatingly expressed. This only added to the dangers of their situation, for Mr. Eyre was afraid—with much good cause, as the sequence will show—that in addition to the other difficulties and anxieties he had to cope with, would be the still more fruitful one of disaffection and discontent.

Another cause of uneasiness was their diet. The sting-ray fish was beginning to make them all ill, and Baxter and the native boys declared they could no longer eat any more of it. In this dilemma Mr. Eyre determined upon having one of the sick horses killed for food, believing that this supply would last them over a few days, by which time they might again be able to venture on, and attempt another push to the westward.

They fed on this most unsavoury food until it became putrid, and both Mr. Eyre and Baxter were each seized with a violent attack of dysentery, which rendered them incapable of the least exertion of any kind, and left them very languid and weak. For several hours they were in the greatest agony, and could neither lie down, sit up, nor stand, except with extreme pain. Portions of the sick horse's flesh which they had dipped in the sea, and by this means salted and preserved, were, during the helplessness of Mr. Eyre's sickness, stolen and devoured by their native companions. The two eldest boys, both of whom had attained nearly the age of manhood, now became sulky and discontented. They had imbibed Baxter's idea that the party would never succeed in getting to the westward, and they got daily more and more dissatisfied, and, at length, decided upon leaving. Mr. Eyre in vain tried to dissuade them, but they left—not for very long, however. Four-and-twenty hours of starvation soon brought them to their senses, and they returned ; one of them apparently sorry for his insubordination, the other sulky and revengeful.

After a halt of twenty-eight days from the time they had come upon the water, they entered upon the next fearful push that was to decide their fate. They had lingered day by day, until it would have been madness to have waited longer. The remaining horses, notwithstanding their rest, were in a very poor condition, and carried the few little stores that remained with difficulty. The Rubicon was, however, now passed, and they had nothing to rely upon but their own exertions and perseverance.

We now come to that terrible night—the last that poor Baxter was to spend on earth. They had halted after a weary trudge of eighteen miles, and Mr. Eyre had intended to push on again during the darkness, on account of avoiding the day heat. Baxter, however, unconscious of the awful fate awaiting him, begged and entreated his leader not to move, as the clouds gathering overhead seemed to promise rain. Greatly against his own wishes, and in opposition to his better judgment, Mr. Eyre gave way and yielded.

The horses having been all hobbled and turned out to feed, the whole party proceeded to make breakwinds of boughs, to form a shelter from the gale, preparatory to lying down for the night. They had taken a meal in the middle of the day, which ought to have been deferred until night; and their circumstances did not admit of their having another, so that there remained only to arrange the watching of the horses before going to sleep. The native boys having attended them the previous night, the duty fell upon Mr. Eyre and Baxter this evening. The first watch was from 6 P.M. to 11 P.M., the second from 11 P.M. until 4 A.M., at which hour the whole party usually arose, and made preparations for moving on with the first streak of daylight.

Baxter asked Mr. Eyre which of the two watches he would keep, and as he was not sleepy, though tired, he chose the first. Trifling as this arrangement of the watches then seemed, yet was his choice the means, under God's providence, of his life being saved, and that of Baxter's being destroyed.

The night was cold, and the wind howled dismally over their desolate encampment, whilst scud and nimbus passed rapidly over the watery moon. Baxter laid down to sleep, that sleep which was to know no wakening, while Mr. Eyre kept his solitary watch. The horses fed tolerably well, but rambled a good deal, threading in and out among the many belts of scrub which intersected the grassy openings, until, at last, he hardly knew exactly where the camp was, the fires having expired. It was now half-past ten, and Mr. Eyre headed the horses back, in the direction in which he thought the camp lay, that he might be ready to call Baxter to relieve him at eleven.

Whilst thus engaged, and looking steadfastly around among the scrub to see if he could anywhere detect the embers of their fires, a sudden flash of light, followed by a loud report, which reverberated over the desert solitude, sent the blood tingling through his veins. The alarm was but momentary, however. He fancied that the overseer had mistaken the hour of the night, and, not being able to find him or the horses, had taken this method to attract his attention. He immediately called out, but no answer was returned. Again he shouted, and the wild wind only blew a mocking blast. His heart beat quicker, and an indefinite fear of some awful calamity came rushing upon him, as, reeling and stumbling in the darkness, he hurried on in the direction of the report he had heard. A few minutes, which seemed to him like hours, sufficed to bring him to the spot. And there, lying on the ground, weltering in his blood, and in the last agonies of death, was his faithful companion and friend!

Upon raising the body of his ill-fated follower, he found that he was beyond all human aid. He had been shot through the left breast, and expired a few moments after Mr. Eyre took him in his arms.

The frightful, the appalling truth now burst upon him, that he was alone in the desert with only Wylie, the King George's Sound native, the other two, who had committed the foul deed, having decamped. The man who had faithfully served him for many years, who had followed his fortunes in adversity and in prosperity, who had accompanied him in all his wanderings, and whose attachment to Mr. Eyre had been his sole inducement to remain with him in this last journey, was now no more. The horrors of his situation glared upon him in such startling reality, as for an instant almost to paralyze the mind. At the dead hour of night, in the wildest and most inhospitable wastes of Australia, with the fierce wind raging in unison with the scene of violence and blood before him, he was left, with a single native, whose fidelity he could not rely upon, and who, for aught he knew, might be in league with the other two, who even then were probably lurking about with the view of taking his life, as they had done that of poor Baxter. Can the most horrible imagination conceive a more ghastly picture?

Gently placing his murdered friend on the cold earth, Mr. Eyre turned to search for his double-barrelled gun. It was gone, as was also the weapon of the overseer. A brace of pistols, without cartridges, and a rifle, with a ball sticking fast in the breech, which Baxter had ruined by attempting to wash it, not knowing it to be loaded, a few days previously, were all the arms left to him. Luckily he found some ammunition shortly afterwards, which had been sewn up in a canvas bag, and had escaped the observation of the murderers.

Seizing this treasure, now more precious to him than gold, he hurried away from the fearful scene, accompanied by the King George's Sound native, to search for the horses, knowing that if they got away now, no chance whatever would remain of saving their own lives. They secured the wretched animals without much trouble, and Mr. Eyre sat down where he had found them, with an aching heart, to pass the remainder of this dreadful night. Every moment appeared to be protracted to an hour, and it seemed as if the daylight would never come. About midnight the wind ceased, and the weather became bitterly cold and frosty. He had nothing on but a shirt and pair of trousers, and suffered, therefore, most acutely from the cold; to mental anguish was now added intense bodily pain.

In his diary Mr. Eyre writes :—"Suffering and distress had well-nigh overwhelmed me, and life seemed hardly worth the effort necessary to prolong it. Ages can never efface the horrors of this single night, nor would the wealth of the world ever tempt me to go through similar ones again."

When daylight dawned once more, he visited the camp to witness a sad and heartrending scene. The corpse of his poor companion lay extended on the ground, with the eyes wide open, but cold and glazed in death; while all around the body lay scattered the harness of the horses, and the remnants of the stores that had been the temptation to the fatal deed.

It now became necessary to endeavour to extract the ball from the breech of the rifle before they proceeded: to effect this he took the barrel off the stock, and thrust the breech in the fire. He succeeded in his object, but narrowly escaped with his life, the bullet just grazing his head. The gun, however, was again serviceable; and, after carefully reloading it, he felt a degree of confidence and security he had before been a stranger to.

At eight o'clock they were ready to proceed. There remained but to perform the last sad offices of humanity towards him whose career had been cut short in so untimely a manner. Even this duty was rendered more than ordinarily painful by the nature of the country where they happened to have halted. One vast unbroken surface of sheet-rock extended for miles in every direction, and rendered it impossible to make a grave. Mr. Eyre could only, therefore, wrap a blanket around the body of his dead companion, and, leaving it enshrouded where it fell, escape from the melancholy scene, under the influence of feelings which neither time nor circumstances are ever likely to obliterate.

For some time they travelled slowly and silently onwards, and as the afternoon gradually ebbed away, and the shades of evening crept upon them, Mr. Eyre descried two white objects moving stealthily in the scrub at no great distance from him, and he at once recognized the murderers, covered with their blankets. They were following like wolves or bloodhounds on his track. Whatever their intention might be, he knew that, if they continued travelling in the same direction, his own life could only be safe by their deaths. He therefore came to the determination to shoot them, if they approached within what he considered a dangerous distance. The night, however, closed in, and they were lost to view.

Mr. Eyre now determined to make the most of the opportunity afforded him, and, by marching steadily during the night, to endeavour to gain so much in advance of them as to preclude the possibility of their overtaking him. After pushing on for eighteen miles, he felt satisfied that he had left the natives far behind, and, finding a patch of grass for the horses, halted for the remainder of the night. Moving on again on the 1st of May, as the sun was above the horizon, they passed through the same dismal dreary country, and, after completing a stage of twenty-eight miles, were compelled to halt. It was impossible they could endure this much longer, the horses having already been five days without water, and there being no chance of meeting any for two days more. One circumstance, however, tended to lighten the awful depression that was weighing so heavily upon Mr. Eyre, and led him shortly to expect some important and decisive change in the character and formation of the country. It was the

banksia, a shrub which he had never before found to
the westward of Spencer's Gulf, but which he knew to
abound in the vicinity of King George's Sound. "Those
only," writes Mr. Eyre, "who have looked with the
eagerness and anxiety of a person in my situation to
note any change in the vegetation or physical appearance of a country, can appreciate the degree of satisfaction with which I recognized and welcomed the first
appearance of the banksia. Isolated as it was amidst
the scrub, and insignificant as the stunted specimens
were that I first met with, they led to an inference
that I could not be mistaken in, and added, in a ten-
fold degree, to the interest and expectation with which
every mile of our route had now become invested."

Moving onward again with renewed hope, the unfortunate horses managed to crawl along; and though
the country was as desolate and inhospitable as ever,
still the banksias began to grow more common, and, as
if gathering courage from their master, the poor animals
plucked up spirit. But their gleam of hope was of
short duration. The seventh day's dawn since they
had left their last water found the road so rocky and
scrubby, or so sandy and hilly, and without a blade
even of withered grass, that they sank exhausted. A
merciful Providence, again, in their last extremity,
came to their relief, and two miles further, or 150
miles from their last watering-place, they came upon
some sand-drifts, where, by digging, they found relief.

Relieved from the pressure of immediate toil, and from the anxiety and suspense on the subject of water, —Mr. Eyre, having learnt from some natives whom he now met that there was every hope of their progress for the future being less difficult and dangerous—his mind wandered to the gap created in his little party. Out of five, two only remained; and he began to blame himself for yielding to Baxter's solicitation to halt on that fatal evening, instead of travelling on all night, as he had originally intended. Vain and bootless, however, were all regrets for the irrecoverable past, and it only remained for him to keep a sharp look out, lest the two murderers should travel up with them, now that they had come to a lengthened halt.

A striking example of the truly Christian spirit of Mr. Eyre is shown in the subjoined extract from his diary regarding these two bloodthirsty wretches. When he penned the following remarks, a quarter of a century since, he little dreamt that he would ever be arraigned on charges far more horrible than those of which these two Australian savages were guilty.

" The youngest of the two had been with me for four years, the eldest for two years and a half, and both had accompanied me in all my travels during these respective periods. Now that the first and strong impressions naturally resulting from a shock so sudden and violent as that produced by the occurrences of the 29th of April had yielded, in some measure, to calmer reflections, I was able maturely to weigh the whole of what had taken place, and to indulge in some considerations in extenuation of their offence. The two boys knew themselves to be as far from King George's Sound, as they had already travelled from Fowler's Bay. They were hungry, thirsty, and tired, and without the prospect of satisfying fully their appetites, or obtaining rest for a long period of time; they probably thought that, bad and inhospitable as had been the country we had already traversed, we were daily advancing into one still more so, and that we never could succeed in forcing a passage through it; and they might have been strengthened in this belief by the unlucky and incautiously-expressed opinions of the overseer. It was natural enough under such circumstances that they should wish to leave the party. Having come to that determination, and knowing from previous experience that they could not subsist upon what they could procure for themselves in the bush, they had resolved to take with them a portion of the provisions we had remaining, and which they might look upon, perhaps, as their share by right. Nor would Europeans, perhaps, have acted better. In desperate circumstances, men are ever apt to become discontented and impatient of restraint, each throwing off the discipline and control he had been subject to before, and each conceiving himself to have a right to act independently when the question becomes one of life and death.

" Having decided upon leaving the party, and stealing a portion of the provisions, their object would be to
accomplish this as effectually and as safely as they could ;
and in doing this they might, without having had the
slightest intention originally of injuring either myself
or the overseer, have taken such precautions, and made
such previous arrangements, as led to the fatal tragedy
which occurred. All three of the natives were well
aware that, as long as they were willing to accompany
us, they would share with us whatever we had left ; or
that, if resolutely bent upon leaving us, no restriction,
save that of friendly advice, would be imposed to prevent their doing so ; but at the same time, they were
aware that we would not have consented to divide our
little stock of food for the purpose of enabling any one
portion of the party to separate from the other, but
rather that we would forcibly resist any attempts to
effect such a division, either openly or by stealth.
They knew that they never could succeed in their
plans openly, and that to do so by stealth effectually
and safely, it would first be necessary to secure all the
fire-arms, that they might incur no risk from our being
alarmed before their purpose was completed. No
opportunity had occurred to bring their intentions into
operation until the evening in question, when the
scrubby nature of the country, the wildness of the
night, the overseer's sound sleeping, and my own protracted absence (at a distance with the horses) had all

conspired to favour them. I have no doubt that they first extinguished the fires, and then possessing themselves of the fire-arms, proceeded to plunder the baggage and select such things as they required. In doing this they must have come across the ammunition, and loaded the guns preparatory to their departure; but this might have been without any premeditated intention of making use of them the way they did. At this unhappy juncture it would seem that the overseer must have awoke, and advanced towards them to see what was the matter, or to put a stop to their proceedings, when they fired on him, to save themselves from being caught in their act of plunder. That either of the two should have contemplated the committal of a wilful, barbarous, cold-blooded murder, I cannot bring myself to believe—no object was to be attained by it; and the fact of the overseer having been pierced through the breast, and many yards in advance of where he had been sleeping, in a direction towards the sleeping-place of the natives, clearly indicated that it was not until he had arisen from his sleep, and had been closely pressing upon them, that they had fired the fatal shot. Such appeared to me to be the most plausible and rational explanation of this melancholy affair. I would willingly believe it to be the true one."

On the 7th of May they proceeded on their journey, and on the following day had to kill another horse for provision. The poor beast being very ill previous to execution, the meat was of a most unwholesome nature, and both Mr. Eyre and his native companion were seized with a violent illness, suffering for many hours at a time the most excruciating torture. Day by day they felt themselves getting weaker and weaker, whilst the intense cold that was now setting in, and their being reduced almost to a state of nakedness, rendered their condition almost unbearable. When they again attempted to march they found themselves desperately weak and languid. It became at last an effort to put one foot before the other. If they rested for a few moments—and they were compelled constantly to do so—it was with the greatest unwillingness they ever moved on again. There was a dreamy kind of pleasure —that most fatal of symptoms—which made them forgetful or careless of dangers and difficulties. They felt as if they could sit down quietly and contentedly, and let the glass of life glide away to its last sand.

In this lamentable state they were gazing one morning at the ocean, oblivious of the world and of everything else, when Mr. Eyre was suddenly aroused from his stupor by what he fancied to be a boat, every now and then appearing on the crest of the waves. With the eagerness of a desperate man he watched this tiny speck, until his startled senses became alive to the fact that it was no day dream or phantom of the imagination, but a reality. Hastily lighting a fire on a sandhill, they fired shots, shouted, waved handkerchiefs, and made every signal they could to attract attention, but all in vain. The boat was too far off to see them, and they stood silently and sullenly gazing at it until it was lost to view.

A few minutes of calm reflection, and Mr. Eyre came to the conclusion that the boat must belong to some whaling-ship. Anxiously scanning the horizon in every direction, he at last perceived to the westward the masts of a large ship, peeping above a rocky island which had hitherto concealed her from their view. The poor native skipped with joy, and Mr. Eyre fervently offered up a prayer of thanksgiving. He could not help fearing, however, that she might disappear before they could get to her, or attract the notice of those on board. He therefore pushed along by himself, as rapidly as the heavy nature of the sands would allow, leaving the native to follow with the remaining horses. In a short time he arrived upon the summit of a rocky cliff, opposite to a fine large barque lying at anchor in a well-sheltered bay (which he subsequently named Rossiter Bay, after the captain of the whaler), and at less than a quarter of a mile distant from the shore. Lighting a fire on the rock, he hailed the vessel with desperate eagerness, and soon saw a boat put off, and in a few moments had the inexpressible pleasure of being again among civilized beings, and of shaking hands with a fellow-countryman, in the person of Captain Rossiter, commanding the French whaler 'Mississippi.'

His story was soon told, and the native shortly afterwards coming up, they were both treated with the greatest kindness and hospitality.

For fourteen days Mr. Eyre remained on board; and, as if to make their escape from a terrible death more miraculous, during those fourteen days the weather was so boisterous, cold, and wet, that it would have been impossible for them to have survived it, had they not thus in their direst extremity been provided for by a merciful Providence.

Most men, after the awful ordeal Mr. Eyre had passed through, would have refused to quit the friendly shelter of the 'Mississippi,' and would have sailed in her whithersoever she was bound ; but his sense of duty was so strong, and his English pluck so indomitable, that he determined to persevere to the end. Accepting, therefore, the generous supply of stores, and a suit of warm clothes for each, on the 15th of June they left their kind friend, Captain Rossiter, determined to finish their unparalleled journey to King George's Sound.

CHAPTER IV.

On the 14th Mr. Eyre landed the stores, to arrange and pack them ready for the journey. They consisted of forty pounds of flour, six pounds of biscuit, twelve pounds of rice, twenty pounds of beef, twenty pounds of pork, twelve pounds of sugar, one pound of tea, a Dutch cheese, five pounds of salt butter, a little salt, two bottles of brandy, and two tin saucepans for cooking, besides some tobacco and pipes for Wylie, who was a great smoker, and the canteens filled with treacle for him to eat with rice. The great difficulty was how to arrange to pay for the various supplies so mercifully furnished to them at a moment when all hope seemed to have vanished. Mr. Eyre had no money with him, and it was a matter of uncertainty whether the ship would touch at any of the Australian colonies. Captain Rossiter intimating that possibly he might call at King George's Sound when the Bay whaling was over, and as that was the place whither Mr. Eyre himself was bound, he gave an order upon a gentleman who had previously acted there as his agent.

In arranging the payment Mr. Eyre could not induce the captain to receive anything for the twelve days that they had been resident in the ship, nor would he allow them to pay for some very comfortable warm clothing. To the honour of Captain Rossiter it must also be added that to this day the order first alluded to has never been presented.

After loading their horses, and bidding their kind and hospitable host farewell, they once again commenced their long and arduous journey, and were wending their lonely way through unknown and untrodden wilds. Mr. Eyre was, however, in very different circumstances now to what he had been in previous to meeting so opportunely with the French whaler. The respite he had had from his labours, and the generous living he had enjoyed, had rendered both Wylie and himself comparatively fresh and strong. They had now with them an abundance, not only of the necessaries, but of the luxuries of life; were better clothed and provided against the inclemency of the weather than they had been; and entered upon the continuation of their undertaking with a spirit, an energy, and a confidence that they had long been strangers to.

The first evening of their march set in with heavy rain, which continued without intermission the entire night. The drenching rain soon made them very wretched, and in the morning Mr. Eyre could scarcely move, having contracted a severe cold, and feeling dreadfully ill. Notwithstanding, they were compelled to proceed onwards, passing through a country consisting of the same sandy plains and undulations covered with scrub, until, after a few miles, Mr. Eyre was so exhausted from illness as to be compelled to halt.

Again the pitiless rain came down upon the shelter-less travellers, and continued without ceasing throughout the entire of the night and following day; and but for the warm clothing given by Captain Rossiter, the probabilities are, they would have died solely from the extreme inclemency of the weather.

When they started next morning the character of the country had, to a great extent, changed, their route being over a rich, swampy, grassy land. Indeed, they literally walked for miles in water, besides having to ford two rivers. It was some little satisfaction when they had to ascend an undulating and more elevated tract of country, of an oolitic limestone formation, most luxuriantly clothed with the richest grass, and having several lakes interspersed among the hollows between the ridges. Near one of these they halted for the night, under some of the coast sand-hills, after a day's stage of twelve miles.

The elements seemed to be at deadly enmity with them, for once more the rain came down all through the night in torrents. On June the 18th they proceeded onwards, and at a little more than three miles came to the borders of a large salt lake. Following the borders of the lake for a mile, they found abundance of fresh water under the banks by which it was enclosed, and which, judging from the rushes and grasses about it, and the many traces of native encampments, appeared to be permanent. The day being fine, Mr. Eyre halted at this place to rearrange the loads of the horses, and to take bearings. A year had now elapsed since he first started upon his expedition. That day twelve months he had left Adelaide to commence his journey, cheered by the presence and good wishes of many friends, and proudly commanding a small but gallant party. Alas! where were they now? Painful and bitter were the thoughts that occupied his mind as he contrasted the circumstances of his departure with his position at that moment, and when he reflected that of all whose spirit and enterprise had led them to engage in the undertaking, two lone wanderers only remained to attempt its conclusion.

They did not start till late the following day. When they did move they had to travel through a very grassy country, abounding in fresh swamps of a soft, peaty soil, and often with broad flag-reed growing in them. All these places were boggy and impassable for horses. In attempting to cross one a horse sunk up to his haunches, and they had much difficulty in extricating him. Suddenly they came upon a succession of barren, sandy, and stony ridges, and as there appeared little chance of finding permanent water in such a miserable region, Mr. Eyre took the opportunity of halting at a little rain-water deposited in a hole in the rocks; here they procured water for themselves, but could not obtain any for the horses.

The two next days they had to trudge along under great difficulties, owing to the desolate and trying nature of the country. The traces of natives were numerous, and they actually saw some in the distance, but considered it wiser and safer to pass them by without noticing them. The horses were now beginning again to knock up, whilst the wet overhead and the damp grass under their feet made it equally harassing to themselves. The constant travelling through the drenching rain began to affect their limbs considerably; and upon halting at nights they found their feet always much swollen, and their legs generally stiff and cramped.

It was impossible, however, to delay; and when they started on the morning of the 22nd, they were condemned to wade for three hours up to their waists in the wet brush. Fortunately, the weather cleared towards the afternoon, and they got on pretty fairly till they were suddenly brought to a dead stop by a deep salt-water river, fully a hundred yards wide, and increasing to three or four times that size as it trended to its junction with a large lake, and which was visible from the hills above the river. Mr. Eyre was compelled to trace its course upwards for the purpose of crossing. He would have liked much to have examined its mouth to ascertain its junction with the sea, but he dared not leave Wylie in charge of the camp for the time that it would have occupied him. Moreover, he did not feel justified in running so great a risk as it would have been, to take the horses such a distance, and through a rough and heavy country, with the certainty almost of not being able to procure for them grass or water.

After tracing the river northerly for two miles and a half, Mr. Eyre found it divided into two branches; and though these were still of considerable size, yet a ledge of rocks extending across the channels enabled him to effect a passage to the other side. At the place where he crossed, the stream running over the rocks was only slightly brackish, and he watered the horses there; had he traced it a little further, it might possibly have been quite fresh; but they had no time for this, for Wylie having taken charge of the horses but for a few moments, whilst Mr. Eyre was examining the river for a crossing place, contrived to frighten them in some way or other, and set them off at a gallop; the result being that their baggage was knocked off and much damaged, and great delay was caused in securing the animals again and rearranging the loads.

The country changed in aspect on the 23rd, and became once more barren and desolate, with nothing but scrub, and dried-up withered grass. On the night of the 24th they nearly lost the whole of their baggage and provisions from a spark having been carried by the wind from their camp fire to a piece of tarpaulin, which immediately ignited, and, but for Mr. Eyre observing the accident in time, they would have been left without a particle of food or clothing.

June the 25th they commenced their journey early, but had not gone far before the rain began to fall heavily. Occasionally the showers came down in perfect torrents, rendering them cold and miserable, and giving the whole country the appearance of a large puddle. They literally marched in water. It was dreadful work to travel thus for so many hours, but there was no help for it, as they could not find a blade of grass for the horses to enable them to halt sooner. After a dreary trudge of fifteen miles they came to a valley with some wiry grass in it. At this Mr. Eyre determined to halt, there being no prospect of getting better grass, and the water left by the rains being abundant. The latter, though it had only fallen an hour or two, was in many places quite salt, and the best of it brackish, so thoroughly saline was the nature of the soil upon which it had been deposited.

The following day Mr. Eyre determined to remain in camp to rest the horses and themselves. They had walked for eleven days, during which they had made good a distance of one hundred and thirty-four miles from Rossiter Bay; and as Mr. Eyre calculated that they ought under ordinary circumstances to reach their long-wished for goal — King George's Sound — in ten days more ; and as their provisions with economy were calculated to last that period, he resolved upon taking the much-required rest.

It was well they did so, for on the 27th they were severely taxed. Upon moving they passed towards the Mount Barren ranges* for ten miles through the same sterile country, and then observing a watercourse coming from the hills, Mr. Eyre became apprehensive he should experience some difficulty in crossing it near the ranges, from their rocky and precipitous character, and at once turned more southerly to keep between the sea and a salt lake, into which the stream emptied itself. After getting nearly half round the lake, their progress was impeded by a dense and most difficult scrub of the Eucalyptus dumosa. Upon entering it they found the scrub large and strong, and growing very close together; whilst the fallen trees, dead wood, and sticks lying about in every direction to the height of a man's breast, rendered their passage difficult and dangerous to the horses in the extreme. Indeed, when they were in the midst of it, the poor animals suffered so much, and progressed so little, that Mr. Eyre feared they would hardly get them either through it or back again. By dint of great labour and perseverance they passed through a mile of it, and

* They will be found marked on any map of South Australia.

then emerging upon the beach, followed it for a short distance, until steep rocky hills, coming nearly bluff into the sea, obliged them to turn up under them, and encamp for the night.

Three days more of fearful fatigue, suffering, and disappointment, and then the sun, as it were, broke through the dismal cloud that had been facing them for so long, and before the evening of the 30th of June closed in they obtained a view of some high, rugged, and distant ranges, which Mr. Eyre at once recognized as being the mountains immediately behind King George's Sound. At last they could almost say they were in sight of the termination of their long, harassing, and disastrous journey. Early in the morning Mr. Eyre had told Wylie that he thought they should see King George's Sound hills before night, but the boy at that time appeared rather sceptical; when, however, they did break upon their view, in picturesque though distant outline, his joy knew no bounds. For the first time in their journey he *believed* they would really reach the Sound at last. The cheering and not-to-be mistaken view before him had dissipated all his doubts.

But, although they appeared so near the end of their journey, they had yet some days of hard work and disappointment to undergo; but the almost certain knowledge that they would in the end succeed buoyed them up. On the 4th July they crossed the tracks of horses, apparently of no very old date, this being the first symptom they had yet observed of their near approach to the haunts of civilized man; and on the following day, with an exclamation of frantic joy, Wylie recognized, as a place he had once seen before, a fresh-water lake, in a valley between some hills, and he declared that he now knew the road well, and could act as guide. Thereupon Mr. Eyre resigned the post of honour to him, on his promising always to take them to grass and water at night.

The morning of the 6th July was very wet and miserably cold. The rain having fallen in torrents the previous night, they were completely drenched, and could only keep life in them by standing or walking before the fire the whole night. Mr. Eyre was glad to crawl onwards at daylight. With Wylie acting as guide they reached the Candiup River, a large chain of ponds, connected by a running stream, and emptying into a wide and deep arm of the sea, with much rich and fertile land upon its banks. The whole country was now heavily timbered, and had good grass growing amongst the trees. From the very heavy rains that had fallen, they had great trouble in crossing many of the streams, which were swollen by the floods into perfect torrents. In the Candiup River Mr. Eyre had to wade, cold and chill as he was, seven times through, with the water breast-high, and a current that he could only with the utmost difficulty stand up against, in order to get the horses over in safety. He now began to suffer intense pain, owing to the incessant wettings he had been subject to for so many days past.

Four miles beyond Candiup River, they came to King's River, a large salt arm of Oyster Harbour; here Wylie, who insisted that he knew the proper crossing-place, took Mr. Eyre into a large swampy morass, and in endeavouring to take the horses through they got bogged, and were nearly lost, and Mr. Eyre was detained in the water and mud for a couple of hours endeavouring to extricate them. At last he succeeded; but the poor animals were sadly weakened and strained, and Mr. Eyre was compelled to return back to the same side of the river, and encamp for the night, instead of going on to King George's Sound, as he had intended.

Of this bitter disappointment Mr. Eyre says in his Diary: "Fortunately there was tolerable grass, and fresh water lay everywhere about in great abundance, so that the horses would fare well, but for ourselves there was a cheerless prospect. For three days and nights we had never had our clothes dry, and for the greater part of this time we had been enduring in full violence the pitiless storm—whilst wading so constantly through the cold torrents in the depth of the winter season, and latterly being detained in the water so long a time at the King's River, had rendered us rheumatic, and painfully sensitive to either cold or wet. I hoped to have reached Albany this evening, and should have done so, as it was only six miles distant, if it had not been for the unlucky attempt to cross King's River. Now we had another night's misery before us, for we had hardly lain down before the rain began to fall in torrents. Wearied and worn-out as we were, with the sufferings and fatigues of the last few days, we could neither sit nor lie down to rest; our only consolation under the circumstances being that, however bad or inclement the weather might be, it was the last night we should be exposed to its fury."

On the 7th July they made several attempts again to ford King's River, but failed, and Mr. Eyre at last determined upon leaving the horses and proceeding on to the end of their journey at once. Having accordingly turned the horses loose, and piled up the remnants of their baggage, Mr. Eyre took his journals and charts, and, after much labour and difficulty, succeeded in fording the river. The rain continued falling heavily; but they cared little for it now, and pushed on. Before reaching the Sound, they met a native, who at once recognized Wylie, and greeted him most cordially. From him they learnt that they had been expected at the Sound many months before, and that nothing having been heard of the party, they had long been given up for lost, whilst Wylie had been mourned for and lamented as dead by his friends and his tribe.

They soon found themselves on the brow of a hill immediately overlooking the town of Albany, in Western Australia.   Mr. Eyre makes the following entry in his journal :—" For a moment I stood gazing at the town below me—that goal I had so long looked forward to, had so laboriously toiled to attain, was at last before me. A thousand confused images and reflections crowded through my mind, and the events of the past year were recalled in rapid succession. The contrast between the circumstances under which I had commenced and terminated my labours, stood in strong relief before me. The gay and gallant cavalcade that accompanied me on my way at starting—the small but enterprising band that I then commanded, the goodly array of horses and drays, with all their well-ordered appointments and equipments, were conjured up in all their circumstances of pride and pleasure; and I could not restrain a tear, as I called to mind the embarrassing difficulties and sad disasters that had broken up my party, and left myself and my native companion the two sole wanderers remaining at the close of an undertaking entered upon under such hopeful auspices."

Two hours afterwards Mr. Eyre was visited by Lady Spencer, and all the principal residents and visitors, who vied with each other in their kind attentions and congratulations, and in every offer of assistance or accommodation that it was in their power to render. He learnt from them also, that he had long been given up for lost both in Southern and Western Australia.

On the 13th of July he embarked for Adelaide, and

on the afternoon of the 26th arrived, after an absence of one year and twenty-six days.

Wylie remained at King George's Sound with his family and relatives, and as a reward for the fidelity and good conduct he had displayed whilst accompanying Mr. Eyre in the desert, he was ordered to receive from Government for the rest of his life a weekly allowance of provisions.*

In taking a cursory view of this great journey, the beneficial results may perhaps appear very small. Mr. Eyre had no important rivers to enumerate, no fertile regions to point out for the future spread of colonization and civilization, or no noble ranges to describe from which were washed the *débris* that might form a rich and fertile district beneath them; on the contrary, all was arid and barren in the extreme. Such, indeed, was the sterile and desolate character of the wilderness he traversed, and so great were the difficulties thereby entailed upon him, that throughout by far the greater portion of it he was

---

* Mr. Eyre writes :—" It was an interesting and touching sight to witness the meeting between Wylie and his friends. Affection's strongest ties could not have produced a more affecting and melting scene—the wordless weeping pleasure, too deep for utterance, with which he was embraced by his relatives; the cordial and hearty reception given him by his friends, and the joyous greeting bestowed upon him by all, might well have put to the blush those heartless calumniators who, branding the savage as the creature only of unbridled passions, deny to him any of those better feelings and affections which are implanted in the breast of all mankind, and which nature has not denied to any colour or to any race."

never able to delay a moment in his route, or to deviate in any way from the line he was pursuing, to reconnoitre or examine. But in a geographical point of view the result of his labours was neither uninteresting, or incommensurate with the nature of the expedition placed under his command, and the character of the country he had to explore. Mr. Eyre, by his indomitable fortitude and perseverance, passed through regions never before or since traversed by civilized man ; and, at the risk of his own life, opened the eyes of his fellow-colonists to the hopelessness of ever being able to establish an overland communication between Southern and Western Australia.

CHAPTER V.

In the year 1845 Mr. Eyre returned to England on leave, after an absence of twelve years from his native country. To beguile the tediousness of a long voyage, he prepared, from his journals, two large volumes giving an account of some of his explorations in Australia. These volumes were published almost immediately after his arrival in England.*

On the voyage home the vessel touched at the Cape of Good Hope, and, although they remained there only two days, he determined to see as much of the country as possible. Having landed in the afternoon and had dinner on shore, he persuaded one or two other fellow-passengers to attempt with him the ascent of the Table Mountain by night. They accomplished the undertaking successfully, arriving at the summit before daybreak, and being well rewarded by a most magnificent view as the day dawned. They saw sun, moon, and stars all at the same time. The rest of his time was spent in seeing Constantia and other points of interest within reach of Table Bay.

Mr. Eyre brought home with him two young aboriginal Australian boys, and kept them in England at his

* "Discoveries in Central Australia." By E. J. Eyre. London. T. and W. Boone.

own expense. They went with him to Buckingham Palace, and were introduced to the Queen and the late Prince Consort, who seemed much interested in them. One of the boys proving of a vicious temper, Mr. Eyre sent him back, the other the home Government took charge of and put to school, under the care of the Quaker philanthropist, Dr. Hodgkin. Eventually he caught cold and died from a pulmonary attack when about seventeen years of age. He was well-conducted and intelligent, and though not clever, read and wrote very well, and was learning the business of a saddler very creditably when he died.*

* Sir James Clark, in a letter to Sir Roderick Murchison expressing his regret that ill-health prevented his attending a meeting of the Committee of the " Eyre Defence Fund " at Willis's Rooms, thus speaks of Mr. Eyre and these two aboriginal Australian boys :—

" My first acquaintance with Mr. Eyre was his bringing to me two little native Australian boys, whom he had brought with him to this country with the object of giving them some education, and then returning them to their own country. This thoughtful attention and kindness to these little black fellows produced on me a very favourable impression of Mr. Eyre's benevolent disposition, and all our intercourse since that time—some twenty years ago—has been to satisfy me that the impression then made was a correct one—that Mr. Eyre was a kind-hearted man, who had the good of his fellow-creatures at heart. I can now add that nothing which has transpired of Mr. Eyre's conduct during the suppression of the unfortunate Jamaica insurrection has diminished the high opinion I had formed of his character. Mr. Eyre's position was one of the most anxious and responsible in which a man could be placed : the preservation of an important colony and the lives of many thousands of his countrymen and their families hung upon his conduct. He preserved both by his judgment and decision. Had he failed by lack of either,

When Mr. Eyre reached England he was in delicate health, the consequence of much over-exertion, fatigue, and privations of all sorts. He remained two years among his relations in this country, when, having recruited his strength, he again left it; under more favourable circumstances, however, than on a previous occasion.

Early in the autumn of 1846, Mr. Eyre received a flattering letter from Earl Grey, then Secretary of State for the Colonies, offering him the appointment of Lieutenant-Governor of New Zealand, and in December of the same year the appointment was gazetted.

On his arrival in the colony he was stationed at Wellington, and administered the government of New Munster, the southernmost of the provinces into which New Zealand was at that time divided—Sir George Grey, the Governor, residing at Auckland and administering the government of New Ulster, the northernmost of these provinces.

The now flourishing settlements of Canterbury and Otago were established in his division of New Zealand whilst he was Lieutenant-Governor. The first Whanganini war had not terminated when he arrived in the

those who are now accusing him of cruelty, and even murder, would have been equally ready to stigmatise him as unfit for his position. I can only add that my own conviction, founded on my knowledge of Mr. Eyre's character, is that in his whole conduct during the Jamaica insurrection he was guided by the purest motives, his sole object being to save the colony."

colony, and it was brought to a close and peace re-established with the natives under his auspices.

In New Zealand Mr. Eyre married Miss Ormond, daughter of Captain Ormond, R.N. It was an attachment he had formed in England; and as his duties as Lieutenant-Governor precluded him from going home for the lady, she went out to the colony to marry him.

When he had been in the country some few years, and on the termination of his appointment as Lieutenant-Governor, a change was made in the constitution, under which several provinces were created instead of the two formerly existing; and in place of a Lieutenant-Governor for each appointed by the Queen, the chief authority in each province was styled " Superintendent," and was elected to the office by the colonists themselves. Prior to his quitting New Zealand, the leading and influential colonists at Wellington invited Mr. Eyre to become their first Superintendent; but he declined, on the grounds that he was unwilling to retire from the more direct service of the Crown. It, at all events, showed that he had gained the good-will and confidence of those over whom he had been ruling for six years.

Some notion may be formed of the difficulties Mr. Eyre had to meet when he first went to New Zealand from the fact that New Munster was a newly-created colony, and that he had to organize and bring into working order all the departmental and other arrangements required in a government then established for the first time.*

Mr. Eyre was in New Zealand at the time the first severe earthquakes occurred—when every brick building and all the chimneys of the wooden ones were shattered to pieces. Lives were lost and a great deal of damage done. Mr. Eyre, without a moment's hesitation, turned Government House (which was a wooden building) into a barrack, and took in forty inmates, including some patients from the public hospital, which was destroyed. Crowds of colonists went on board the only merchant vessel in port, and wished at once to leave the colony; but Mr. Eyre, seeing the necessity for prompt and stern measures, immediately laid an embargo on her, and ordered a man-of-war to watch her, and prevent her leaving port. But for this wise though perhaps severe precaution the entire settlement would have been broken up, so great was the alarm and consternation; nor is it to be wondered at, for the shocks were terrific, sometimes occurring in the dead of the night, sometimes in the middle of the day, and in all weathers, calm as well as stormy. They continued for upwards of a fortnight.

* After Mr. Eyre had held the appointment of Lieut.-Governor of New Zealand for three years, Earl Grey, writing to Sir George Grey, Governor-in-Chief (*vide* Blue Book presented to Parliament on 14th August, 1850, page 151), says:—" I have the same favourable opinion of the zeal and intelligence of Mr. Eyre's administration, which I am happy to see that you entertain."

Whilst in New Zealand he ascended, accompanied only by a few Maoris, the highest peak of the Kaikoras in the middle island, called " Tappuanuco." It is supposed to be the most elevated point of that mountainous country, and is always covered with snow. He found the ascent exceedingly difficult and dangerous, but succeeded in reaching the summit on the second day, just as night was closing in. The wind was blowing a fierce gale, the snow was drifting, and there was every appearance of a storm. They had therefore barely time to take a hurried glance at the landscape around and make the best of their way downwards to seek for some sheltered place to pass the night. They had not proceeded far in a zigzag descent across a steep inclined plane of frozen snow before one of the Maoris slipped, and was hurried along downwards with fearful rapidity for upwards of fifteen hundred feet, striking against and bounding over ledges of rock which intersected and projected across the frozen snow at intervals of two or three hundred feet. Mr. Eyre himself had a terribly narrow escape at one moment. His foot slipped, and but for his presence of mind in striking an iron-shod pole he had with him into the snow, and lowering his hands, without a moment's hesitation, to the base, he would have been dashed to pieces likewise. As it was he managed to cling on for a few moments, and eventually regained his feet. It was impossible to proceed further as the night had closed in, and they were, therefore, obliged to lay down where they were upon a little ledge of rock which just kept them from following their unfortunate companion. It was so narrow that with outstretched arms Mr. Eyre could touch the brink. Here they passed the night in a state of bodily and mental torture that no words can adequately describe. At earliest dawn they again commenced their descent cautiously, and at last reached a point from which they could see the body of their unfortunate fellow-traveller, though they could not possibly reach it. The body had been projected under a huge ledge of frozen snow overhanging a small stream at the bottom of a fearful ravine. The poor fellow was evidently quite dead ; indeed, he must have been stunned and killed, long ere he reached his last resting-place, by the continual striking against the ledges of rock on his descent, from each of which a track of blood stained the frozen snow marking his course. Finding they could not even have the melancholy satisfaction of recovering the body of their unfortunate fellow-traveller, they made the best of their way down the mountain ; and as the Maoris were utterly disheartened, Mr. Eyre was reluctantly compelled to give up a projected trip across country to the Canterbury settlement.

Mr. Eyre remained in New Zealand the full period of six years for which a Governor is appointed, and then returned to England with his family, visiting

Sydney and Melbourne on his way. He arrived in this country in September, 1853, and after spending a year at home, was appointed by Sir George Grey, then Secretary of State for the Colonies, Lieutenant-Governor of St. Vincent, in the West Indies. This government he also held for the full period of six years, up to the end of March, 1861. Whilst still holding it he was specially appointed in 1859, by Sir E. Bulwer Lytton, then Secretary of State for the Colonies, to administer the government-in-chief of the Leeward Isles during the absence on leave of the Governor. This was a great and unusual compliment, it not being at all customary to call a Lieut.-Governor from one group of colonies to administer temporarily the general government of another and distinct group with which his own was in no way associated.

At St. Vincent Mr. Eyre laboured earnestly to effect a radical change in the constitution of the island, which, like the other West Indian ones, was utterly unsuited to the circumstances and requirements of the colony; and though unable to effect the change he desired and thought necessary, he succeeded in modifying it to an extent which made it somewhat similar to that effected by Sir H. Berkly in Jamaica.

Whilst Lieut.-Governor of St. Vincent he was, on one occasion, sitting at a Privy Council in the tówn of Kingston, when a gun was heard, and upon looking out of the window towards the Fort, some three miles off, they noticed the Union Jack half-mast high, and soon after saw dense masses of smoke curling up from the buildings. Hastily adjourning the council, Mr. Eyre ordered out the fire-engines, directed the police to attend, and a large supply of blankets to be sent up. Mounting his horse, he galloped towards the spot. When about half-way up, he met a gentleman on horseback coming down from the Fort as rapidly as he could. Having stopped him to make inquiries, the man immediately exclaimed, " For God's sake, Mr. Eyre, return, or you will be killed! The magazine is on fire, and the whole place will immediately blow up." Mr. Eyre replied with quiet firmness, that " though perfectly conscious of the danger, yet, as Governor, it was his duty to go and judge for himself." Leaving the gentleman to return to Kingston, he again struck spurs into his horse, and galloping onwards soon reached the scene of conflagration. He found that the magazine was not actually on fire, but that several wooden buildings adjacent to it were, and as there was a tunnel under the magazine, the smoke, drawn in by the in-draft at one end, went out at the other, and gave rise to the impression that the magazine itself was on fire. The matter, however, was quite serious enough, for the roof, walls, door, and windows of the magazine (the latter made of wood completely rotten) were so hot that it was impossible to bear the hand upon them ; and when blankets were subsequently applied, and kept constantly wetted by the engines, they were as rapidly dried, the water hissing off from the heated surfaces. Having hastily despatched on his own horse the only person he could find to hurry down the hill, and tell the people who were coming up (who otherwise would have turned back at the intelligence furnished by the gentleman who had first met Mr. Eyre) that he was at the scene, and that they were to make all possible speed to join him, he resolved in his mind the best plan of proceeding, and when the police, engines, and populace arrived, he so directed them that eventually the magazine was saved, and the greater portion of the barracks and other buildings. The magazine at the time was full of powder, and had it ignited, not only would the Fort have been entirely destroyed, but the town of Kingston itself would have been seriously injured.

It is worthy of remark that not a single member of the council which had been sitting with Mr. Eyre when the fire was first discovered attended or followed him to the Fort, with the exception of the senior member, a very old gentleman, who arrived some time after the populace had reached the spot. The latter, more especially the women, worked remarkably well. Had Mr. Eyre listened to the advice of the gentleman he met on the road; had he thought of the value of his own life, in preference to the stern dictates of duty; had he, in simple words, turned back, nothing would have induced any one else to have gone up, and the

catastrophe anticipated most certainly would have occurred.

The following despatch from Governor-in-Chief Sir
W. Colebrooke to Lieut.-Governor Eyre, will show the
estimation in which Mr. Eyre was held by his immediate superiors :—

" Windward Islands, Barbadoes,
Oct. 15th, 1855.

" Sir,

" Having been informed by the Secretary of
State that I am in a short time to be relieved in this
command, I take the earliest occasion of expressing to
you my sincere acknowledgments for the zealous and
able manner in which you have conducted the administration of the Government of St. Vincent. From
the period of your first arrival you have devoted yourself with untiring energy to the object of retrieving the
affairs of the island, and in a spirit to gain for you the
confidence of the colonists as well as that of the
government.

" I appreciate very highly the advantage to the public
service from the unreserved intercourse which has sub-
sisted between us; and I can assure you that it will
afford me the utmost satisfaction at all times to give my
testimony in favour of your public claims.

" I have, &c.,
(Signed)   " W. Colebrooke."

When Mr. Eyre was about leaving St. Vincent,

where he had secured the good wishes of all, he was presented with the following address from the President and Members of the Legislative Council :—

"*The President and Members of the Honourable Board of Legislative Council,*
"*To His Excellency Edward John Eyre, Esquire, Lieut.-Governor.*

"We, the President and Members of the Board of Legislative Council, have the honour to acknowledge the receipt of your Excellency's message, No. 13, announcing that the Right Hon. the Secretary of State had been pleased to instruct your Excellency to proceed to Antigua, to assume temporarily the administration of the government of the Leeward Islands.

"As your Excellency, in making this communication, refers to the possibility of your return to this colony, we are unwilling to take final leave of your Excellency; but, whilst congratulating you on this proof of confidence on the part of her Majesty's Government, we would respectfully convey to your Excellency the regrets of the Board at your temporary absence, assuring your Excellency that you carry with you the best wishes of its members for your Excellency's health, happiness, and success in the administration of the government which you are called on thus suddenly to assume.

"It must be as gratifying to your Excellency as it is satisfactory to the colony to be enabled to feel that, in leaving St. Vincent, your Excellency is enabled, with the greatest truthfulness, to say that the colony is in a greatly improved condition to that in which your Excellency found it on your arrival.

" The members of this board are pleased at the reflection that in all their intercourse with your Excellency, and their endeavours to promote the welfare of St. Vincent and its inhabitants, they have ever met with the most willing, active, and courteous co-operation of your Excellency.

(Signed)   " H. E. SHARPE,

" *President of Council.*"

As Lieut.-Governor of Antigua, Mr. Eyre was equally respected and beloved. It would be impossible, within the narrow limits of a single volume, to enter into details of all that he did for the colony; but the following extract from the ' Antigua Times,' on the occasion of his last opening of the legislature, will give a very fair notion of the light in which his services were held by those best able to judge.

" Governor Eyre's address, which will be found in our columns, delivered at the opening of the first session of our new legislature, is a document which, we feel assured, will be read with considerable gratification by all classes. Apart from its intrinsic merits as a production, the circumstances under which it was delivered, just on the eve of the termination of his official relationship with us—imparting to it more the character of a valediction than otherwise—the continued unabated zeal and solicitude for the future well-being of the colony, and the comprehensive and enlightened views given utterance to as to our most pressing wants and the measures best calculated, for the future, to conduce to our prosperity, all conspire to invest it with a peculiar and touching interest at the present juncture; and while they afford evidence of what might have been expected under a ruler already signalized by successes during his short sojourn amongst us, indicating the possession of considerable administrative abilities, intelligent discernment, prudence and judgment, the regret is rendered the more poignant that a connection which gave promise of so many advantages, at a period in the history of the colony when most required, should be thus abruptly severed. Assuming the government of the colony at a time of unexampled difficulties—depressed in its finances—but recently recovered from the whirlwind of internal distraction, it required no ordinary tact and discretion, no unskilful hand to guide the bark of state through the shoals and quicksands which beset her. Mr. Eyre may then, with pardonable complacency, look back upon the proud memorials which his short, but active and energetic career in this island will have left behind him, and which, while entitling him to the just commendation bestowed upon him by the two branches of the

Legislature, we trust will, in the proper quarter, secure for him that favourable consideration and appreciation which his services so richly merit."

Upon the termination of his governorship of Antigua in 1860, Mr. Eyre returned to England to recruit his health, which had greatly suffered from overwork, and from long residence in tropical climates. He was not, however, permitted to have long repose; for, in the early part of 1862, he was selected by the Duke of Newcastle, then Secretary of State for the Colonies, and specially commissioned to administer the Government-in-chief of Jamaica and its dependencies during the absence of Governor Darling, who had been compelled to return to England in consequence of ill-health.

CHAPTER VI.

BEFORE entering into the troubles that surrounded Mr. Eyre from the very moment he set foot upon the island, it may be as well to put on record the fact that the Governorship of the island of Jamaica, since the Emancipation Act, has been one of the most, if not *the* most difficult and trying appointments under the crown ; and the fact of Mr. Eyre having been chosen as the *locum tenens* of Governor Darling, conclusively shows the light in which his former services were held at the Colonial Office. Not one Governor has ever yet given satisfaction to the violent and turbulent people placed under his charge, with the solitary exception of Lord Metcalfe (then Sir Charles Metcalfe), who arrived in the colony with an authority in his pocket, if he found it necessary to use it, to ignore altogether the House of Assembly, and carry on the Government and requisite legislation with the Legislative Council only. This power, known to exist, though not exercised, at once brought the House of Assembly to reason.

Sir Charles Metcalfe was also an exceedingly rich man, without any family, and he could afford not only to spend his full official income, but a great deal more besides in hospitalities, subscriptions, and charities— always a source of popularity in any community. Moreover, Sir Charles Metcalfe's tenure of office in Jamaica only extended over three years instead of six, the usual period of service; and it rarely happens that a Governor comes much into collision with his subjects during the earlier part of his administration.

It is very necessary that these facts should be known; it is still more necessary to refer to the extraordinary mixture of races in the island, and to point out the dangerous materials of which its society was, has been, and ever will be composed. History has placed on record the atrocities committed on white men, women, and children in a neighbouring island; history has also shown that insurrections must be looked for and guarded against, for that they have been provoked in Jamaica four times within a century. Indeed, this statement is not sufficiently accurate. While there have been four serious insurrections within one hundred years, there have been no less than ten minor ones. Of the four serious ones, the first occurred in 1760, another in 1795, the third in 1832, and the last in October, 1865. Smollett thus describes the insurrection of 1760, which bears a singular resemblance in its commencement to the insurrection of 1865, if the massacre at Morant Bay be substituted for the butchery on Captain Forest's estate :—

"Assemblies were held, and plans resolved for this purpose. At length they (the negroes) concerted a scheme for rising in arms all at once in different parts of the island, in order to massacre all the white men, and take possession of the Government. They agreed that this design should be put into execution immediately after the departure of the fleet for Europe, but their plan was defeated by their ignorance and impatience. Those of the conspirators that belonged to Captain Forest's estate, being impelled by the fumes of intoxication, fell suddenly upon the overseer while he sat at supper with some friends, and butchered the whole company. Being immediately joined by some of their confederates, they attacked the neighbouring plantations, where they repeated the same barbarities, and seizing all the arms and ammunition that fell in their way, began to grow formidable to the colony. The Governor no sooner received intimation of this disturbance, than he, by proclamation, subjected the colonists to martial law. All other business was interrupted, and every man took to his arms. The regular troops, joined by the troop of militia, and a considerable number of volunteers, marched from Spanish Town to St. Mary's, where the insurrection began, and skirmished with the insurgents; but, as they declined standing any regular engagement, and trusted chiefly to bush fighting, the Governor employed against them the free blacks, commonly known by the name of the wild negroes, now peaceably settled under the protection of the Government. These auxiliaries, in consideration of a price set upon the heads of the rebels, attacked them in their own way, slew them by surprise until their strength was broken, and numbers made away with themselves in despair, so that the insurrection was supposed to be quelled about the beginning of May; but in June it broke out again with redoubled fury, and the rebels were reinforced to a very considerable number. The regular troops and the militia formed a camp, and sent out detachments against the negroes, a great number of whom were killed, and some taken; but the rest, instead of submitting, took shelter in the woods and mountains.

"The expense of putting down this rebellion was 100,000*l*."

The revolt of the Maroons in 1795 was not finally extinguished until 1796. That of 1832 (exclusive of the value of the property destroyed, viz., 1,154,583*l*.) cost 161,596*l*., and Parliament was compelled to grant a loan of 500,000*l*. to assist the almost ruined planters. Two hundred rebels were killed in the field, and about five hundred were executed.

Of the insurrection at St. Domingo, Alison, in his 'History of Europe,' has written :—

"This vast conspiracy (that of the negroes in St. Domingo), productive in the end of calamities in the island, unparalleled even in the long catalogue of European atrocity, had for its object the total extirpation of the whites, and the establishment of an independent black government over the whole colony. So inviolable was the secresy, so general the dissimulation of the slaves, that the awful catastrophe was in no way apprehended by the European proprietors, and a conspiracy which embraced nearly the whole negro population of the island, was revealed only by the obscure hints of a few faithful domestics, who, without betraying their comrades, warned their masters of the approach of an unknown and terrible danger. The explosion was sudden and dreadful, beyond anything ever before seen among mankind. At once the beautiful plains in the north of the island were covered with fires, the labours of a century were devoured in a night, while the negroes, like unchained tigers, precipitated themselves on their masters, seized their arms, massacred them without pity, and threw them into the flames. . . . The cruelties exercised on the unhappy captives on both sides in this disastrous contest exceeded anything recorded in history. The negroes marched with spiked infants on their spears instead of colours, they sawed asunder the male prisoners, and violated the females on the dead bodies of their husbands."

The object in referring to these subjects, painful though they may be, is to show the state of society in the island of Jamaica. What the negro was in 1795 so he is now. Emancipation has only made him more lazy, more cunning, more sensual, more profligate, more prone to ˙mischief, and more dangerous.   The mulatto is not less, perhaps more, to be feared even than the negro.   It is the mulatto who, after laying the train carefully for ignition, fires it, and takes care to have a place of safety for himself.   The negro left alone, with just sufficient to eat and drink without having to work, like any other animal, is quiet and happy enough ; but once rouse him, once let him taste blood, and you may as well try and stem the rise and fall of the ocean, or argue with a Soonderbund tiger upon the impropriety of seizing a *dak-wallah*, as to try and bring him to reason without physical force.

When Mr. Eyre reached Jamaica he had a difficult task.   He found the island in a state of retrogression. Cuba had usurped its trade, several of the richest estates in the island were uncultivated, and many demagogues were using inflammatory and seditious language, and inciting the negroes to rebellion, bloodshed, and crime.   When the markets rose, designing persons persuaded the ignorant people that they were unjustly taxed and oppressed ; while the real causes of the advanced prices were : 1st, the war with America, from which country the necessaries of life were chiefly drawn ; and, 2ndly, the scarcity of cotton.

It was not, as the negroes were taught to believe, that an extra tax was put on cotton, but that cotton goods in Jamaica, as in England, France, and all over the world, doubled and trebled in value, owing to the American war, and other manufactures of course rose in proportion, while wages necessarily decreased, not so much because of the importation of coolies as because the Jamaica planters depending on free labour could not compete with the Cuban planters. "How could they?" asks Mr. Ashley, formerly of Ashley Hall, in Jamaica. "*The Cubans would have no slaves but young men, and they worked them from eighteen to twenty hours a day.* Slavery was put an end to in Jamaica to give rise to a slavery a thousand times more cruel. Of course, the Jamaica planters could not compete with Cuba, and the richest estates fell out of cultivation. I once stated at a public meeting, that if a slaver could run one cargo of slaves out of three safely against the English blockade, it paid her. A man present rose and said I was mistaken. 'If a slaver could run *one* cargo of slaves *out of six it paid well*, and I know it,' he added, '*for all the slaves passed through my hands.*'"

The causes, therefore, which brought about the insurrection of 1865 were at work long before Governor Eyre reached the island; they were, that Cuban produce was cheaper than Jamaica produce; they were, the extreme indolence of the negro, which led him to do without, first one comfort, then another, until he almost lapsed into barbarism rather than work; they were, the mischievous and seditious harangues of low, despicable, mercenary agitators and unprincipled men, who saw in a rebellion aggrandizement for themselves; they were, the echoes, so to speak, of the American war, and the consequent emancipation of the negroes; they were, the close proximity of Hayti, where the black race had conquered the white *by murder*. The negroes of Jamaica wanted to rise simultaneously as the negroes of St. Domingo rose, massacre the whites, and make the island another negro kingdom.

All these elements of discord had been seething and fermenting in the mind of the coloured population of Jamaica long before Governor Eyre went there. His experienced eye at once detected the plague spot, and it was solely owing to his energy, courage, and determination that, in an island where there are twenty-seven black men to one white, there was not a second edition of all the horrors and atrocities of the Indian mutiny.

But the object of the present volume is to lean rather to a simple narration of facts than to offer any elaborate expression of opinion as to the steps taken by Mr. Eyre to suppress the rebellion.

When Mr. Eyre first went to Jamaica, he went, as before said, as the *locum tenens* of Governor Darling. He had not been there very long before he became unpopular with the House of Assembly. Having thought it beneficial for the interests of the service, he dismissed an official for misconduct. Mr. Eyre was requested by the House of Assembly to give up the correspondence that had passed between the dismissed official and himself; this he declined to do. The legislature then demanded copies of all the correspondence from the man himself, who also refused to surrender them, clearly showing that Mr. Eyre was justified in adopting the course he had. Whatever the faults of the man may have been, Mr. Eyre evidently considered that he had been sufficiently punished; and the delinquent preferred accepting the decision of the Governor to subjecting himself to other and probably harsher judges. Enraged at the refusal to surrender the documents, the two Houses of Assembly sent the man to prison, and addressed a complaint to the Home Government, petitioning for the removal of Mr. Eyre. No doubt the merits of the case were carefully weighed and both sides fairly heard. With that, however, we have nothing to do. The answer the Colonial Secretary and the Government gave was to appoint Mr. Eyre at once Captain-General and Governor, General-in-Chief and Vice-Admiral of the Island of Jamaica!

This proceeding on the part of the Home Government gave bitter offence to a few members of the legislative body, and henceforth Mr. Eyre was to encounter nothing but the most violent opposition and the most unscrupulous abuse. The most malignant misstatements and the grossest calumnies were published against the Governor; but, instead of serving the cause of his adversaries, they will conclusively prove to any intelligent reader that Mr. Eyre, because he was a high-minded, brave, and honourable man, above stooping to the dictates of a set of noisy demagogues, hunting after place and power, had to battle against enemies, and to overcome obstacles that would have appalled a less determined man.

It must not be understood, however, that Governor Eyre was without supporters amongst the influential and respectable colonists. By the clergy, the professional men, the army and navy, the planters, the Maroons, and even amongst the negroes, he was respected and beloved. As a proof of the violence and disgraceful proceedings adopted by a few of his enemies, it may here be mentioned that, finding they could not carry their own views with the Home Government, contrary to all etiquette and even to the simplest courtesy, they forthwith declined transacting any business with the Governor, and communicated direct with the Colonial Secretary, and even with her Majesty. The reply sent to them was forwarded through Mr. Eyre. It was very short, but to the point, simply stating that the Queen could give no directions respecting documents not transmitted through the officer administering the government of the colony.

Nine resolutions were thereupon published in the island, in which the Colonial Office and the Secretary of State for the Colonies were violently assailed in company with the Governor. These resolutions were ordered to be sent home, and published in the 'Times,' the 'Daily Telegraph,' and the 'Morning Star' newspapers. Mr. Eyre's conduct throughout these disputes was critically inquired into at the Colonial Office, with the following results :—

" Downing Street, April 1, 1864.

" SIR,

"I have to acknowledge the receipt of your despatches of the numbers and dates mentioned in the margin.

"I have received with satisfaction several addresses * and communications enclosed in your despatches, which addresses and communications express strong disapproval of the course of proceeding by which a minority of the Assembly has succeeded in obstructing legislative business.

"I entirely approve of the manner in which you have met this course of proceeding on the part of the portion of the Assembly by which it was adopted, and I have to express my sense of the firmness and moderation which you have evinced throughout the controversies in which, by no fault of your own, you have unfortunately . been involved.

"The conduct which you have pursued whilst admi-

---

* These addresses were from all parts of the island, and from colonists in every sphere of life, expressive of the greatest confidence in and affection for Mr. Eyre.

nistering the government of Jamaica, under a temporary commission as Lieutenant-Governor, will be duly
submitted to the Queen; and I hope to have it in my
power to give you an effective support in the further
prosecution of your endeavours to administer the affairs
of the island with advantage to the public welfare.

" I have, &c.

(Signed)   " NEWCASTLE.

" To Lieutenant-Governor Eyre."

The peculiar position occupied by Mr. Eyre on reaching Jamaica must not be lost sight of. His tenure of
office was very uncertain,—so uncertain, that he felt
unwilling to take any steps which, however right, might,
if a change in the administration of Government took
place, suddenly create difficulties and embarrassments
for any new Governor, who could not have that knowledge of the country and the people necessary to enable
him to understand and grapple with them.

There is scarcely any position so difficult and delicate
as that of the temporary administration of a government like Jamaica, where promptness, vigour, and independence of action are essential to inspiring confidence
and commanding respect. Unfortunately, during the
first portion of Governor Eyre's administration, he held
an anomalous and doubtful position. His first nomina-
tion was only for twelve months; a considerable amount
of feeling existed in reference to the gentleman whose

place he had taken; and as it was expected that Governor Darling would return, Mr. Eyre was bound carefully to consider how any act of his might affect his predecessor's position upon his resuming the administration. After it was decided Sir Charles Darling was not to resume his appointment, Mr. Eyre was never informed that he was to remain for any definite period, so that he actually continued on in his government from month to month, never knowing that any packet which arrived might not bring him an order to retire.

This extreme uncertainty had a prejudicial effect on his position. It enabled those who were hostile to him to keep the public mind in a constant state of excitement by circulating fresh reports of his recall, or of the appointment of a new Governor on the arrival of almost every packet. It prevented the colonists from having confidence in the stability of anything he might inaugurate, seeing he might not remain to carry it to a conclusion. It also deprived him of much of the active support which a more settled position would have insured, and it certainly made him feel unwilling to take many steps which, though right in themselves, might have led to temporary embarrassments, which some other person, newly appointed, might perhaps have been called on to meet.

Shortly after Mr. Eyre had been appointed Lieut.-Governor of Jamaica, Mr. G. W. Gordon was removed from the commission of the peace for having, according to the Duke of Newcastle's own words, made " a wilful and unpardonable misrepresentation" regarding the Rev. Mr. Cooke, the rector of Morant Bay. On the plea of exposing abuses, Mr. Gordon neglected his own duty, and leaving unremedied the evils which he said existed, made those alleged evils the groundwork upon which to build up a deliberate, unjust, and most malevolent imputation against a worthy clergyman, the rector of the parish. It became Governor Eyre's duty, upon ascertaining not only that this imputation was unfounded, but that Mr. Gordon knew it to be so at the time he made the charge, to remove from the magistracy one who so disgraced the Queen's commission, and whose retention on the bench after such an occurrence would have been an insult to all the other magistrates in the colony.

On the same date that the letter containing the " wilful and unpardonable misrepresentations" regarding the Rev. Mr. Cooke was sent to Mr. Eyre by Mr. Gordon, he also forwarded to the Secretary of State for the Colonies a communication making sweeping, scandalous, and libellous charges against the clergy of the Church of England in Jamaica, as a body, designating them as " the most immoral men" in the whole island, whose example was " exceedingly injurious and lowering to the inhabitants generally."

Prior, however, to Governor Eyre arriving in the

island, Mr. Gordon had been, by order of Governor Darling, superseded as a magistrate for improper conduct, but for some cause or other the writs of supersedeas were not issued. The following letter on the subject is interesting as showing the light in which Mr. Gordon was viewed by Mr. Eyre's predecessor :—

" Governor's Secretary's Office,
" 14th February, 1862.

" Sir,

" I am desired by the Governor to acquaint you that he has had before him copies of the several orders entered by you in the justices' visiting book of the Morant Bay District Prison on the 5th Feb. inst.

" I am desired to observe to you that in giving those orders you have usurped the prerogative of the Crown, the powers of the Governor in Privy Council, and those of the visiting justices of the prison ; and you have induced the superintendent of the prison to commit a dereliction of duty for which his just punishment would be immediate removal from office.

" Your conduct appears to his Excellency to exhibit such an unwarrantable assumption of authority, and such extreme ignorance of your proper functions as a magistrate, as to render it inexpedient that you should be any longer intrusted with these functions, and his Excellency therefore feels it his duty to supersede you in the commission of the peace for the several parishes in which your name is at present included.

"I have, &c.,

(Signed)   "HUGH W. AUSTIN,

" *Governor's Secretary.*

"G. W. Gordon, Esq., Kingston."

Mr. Eyre very soon understood the character of Gordon, and foresaw what a firebrand he would be amongst an uneducated and excitable negro population. In August, 1862, he wrote in these terms to the Duke of Newcastle: "I believe Mr. Gordon to be a most mischievous person, and one likely to do a great deal of harm amongst uneducated and excitable persons, such as are the lower classes of this country. His object appears, not to be to rectify evils where they exist, but rather to impress the peasantry with the idea that they labour under many grievances, and that their welfare and interests are not cared for by those in authority."

While referring briefly to Mr. Gordon, perhaps it would be as well to give here a specimen of his behaviour in the House of Assembly. The following disgraceful scene took place not very long before the insurrection broke out.

" Mr. GORDON.—It does not seem that his Excellency's natural endowments qualify him for the government of this country. (Cries of 'Order!') I desire to give honour to whom honour is due, and I respect every man in authority; but if a ruler does not sway the sword with justice, he becomes distasteful, and instead of having the love and respect of the people, he becomes despised and hated. All the privileges, all the rights, and all the purposes of the constitution should be maintained in their highest integrity and purity, by the gentleman who may from time to time be entrusted with the government of the country. So soon as he digresses from this, so soon does he descend from his high position, and become grovelling, portentious (*sic*), and prevaricating.

"Mr. SPEAKER.—Order! The language of the honourable member cannot be allowed. The honourable gentleman must know that he is out of order.

"Mr. GORDON.—I regret, Mr. Speaker, that I am out of order, but when every day we witness the maladministration of the laws by the Lieutenant-Governor, we must speak out. You are endeavouring to suppress public opinion, to pen up the expression of public indignation; but I tell you that it will soon burst forth like a flood, and sweep everything before it. There must be a limit to everything: a limit to oppression—a limit to transgression—and a limit to illegality! These proceedings remind me of the time of Herod—they remind me of a tyrannical period in history! I do not think that any Governor has ever acted so before. While he justifies himself in one case, he uses the police force to accomplish another illegality. What an example to the prisoners who were confined in prison ! what an example to the people ! If the Lieutenant-Governor is to go on in this way, what can you expect from the populace ?

"Mr. LEWIS.—Insurrection. (Laughter.)

"Mr. GORDON.—Ay ! that will be the result. When all our laws are put at defiance, the populace will break out from discontent, and the Lieutenant-Governor will be unable to allay their feelings. Mr. Eyre says that he is the representative of her Majesty the Queen, but it is clear that he lacks administrative capacity ; and, unless he is speedily removed, the country will be thrown into a state of confusion, by reason of his illegal conduct. When a Governor becomes a dictator, when he becomes despotic, it is time for the people to dethrone him, and to say—' We will not allow you any longer to rule us.' I consider the proceedings of Mr. Eyre especially dangerous to the peace of the country, and a stop should at once be put to his most dogmatic, partial, and illegal doings. The House will concede and concede—they will concede everything to the Governor ! If they did this in favour of a noble-minded man there might be some excuse ; but when they leave the well-being of the country, and the safety of society, to the keeping of an incapable, it is time for the people to exclaim—' Oh, the evil !' It is a reflection on this country—it is an evil to this country, that such impotent parties should be selected as Governors. Oh! I only wish that the honourable member for St. David, who is now defending his Excellency, would come under his lash, then he would see whether all that has been said of him is the truth! I do not propose to take any adverse opinion against his Excellency, because that would be a work of supererogation, as an adverse opinion has, and does, prevail against him. Had I succeeded against him the other night, I should not have considered it a great victory, for I do not believe he is a man of such great ability and honour as to have made a victory over him a great victory. (Cries of 'Order!') The honourable member for St. David must know that his Excellency has been guilty of a public wrong, and he knows what Blackstone and other commentators of a high degree of learning say of public wrongs.

"Mr. BARROW.—The House is a public wrong.

"Mr. GORDON.—I hope the honourable member of St. Thomas-in-the-Vale will make himself acquainted with these matters. The honourable member for Port Royal says we should be obliged to the Lieutenant-Governor and the Executive Committee for making the appointment; therefore, *per se,* as the honourable member for St. Catharine said, the people would be quite right to break out into open rebellion. If an illegality is permitted in the Governor, *an illegality may be permitted on the part of the people.* I have never seen an animal more voracious for cruelty and power than the present Governor of Jamaica.

"Mr. SPEAKER.—Order! Order! Such language cannot be allowed.

"Mr. HENDERSON.—I ask if these are words that should be used here of the Governor?

"Mr. SPEAKER.—I called the honourable gentleman to order as soon as he used the words.

"Mr. GORDON.—I say that if the law is to be disregarded it will lead to anarchy and bloodshed. (Cries of 'Order!' from the chair and in the House.) I speak the words of soberness and truth. I say there will be disorder, *and that we will have no Government at all,* and that the Lieutenant-Governor is setting the worst example to the people, because he is breaking through the law. You may say that the people are not discriminating; but I tell you that the poorest, the most miserable subject, is the best judge of practical oppression. The people feel that no justice is being done them, and that the axe is at the root of the tree, and this is what the honourable member for Port Royal says is quite right.

"Mr. HENDERSON.—I never did. When the honourable member says, in the face of the House, that I advised anarchy, I say he is incorrect. I use this mild phrase, but if the honourable member was out of the House, I would use a stronger term. What I really said was that, under the peculiar circumstances of the country, the Governor and his Executive Committee were quite justified in making the *pro tempore* appointment, and that it was as good as any that could have been made at the time. Circumstances alter cases.

"Mr. GORDON.—We see to-night who are for maintaining the principle of illegal appointments. Let justice be done, though the heavens may fall!—let this be done, notwithstanding all the honourable member for Port Royal has said. I tell him I will meet him on fair terms outside the House, if he desires it. *If we are to be governed by such a Governor much longer, the people will have to fly to arms and become self-governing.* (Loud cries of 'Order!') The honourable member for Kingston (Dr. Bowerbank) gave expression to an inuendo against me; he called me a reckless member. I think the honourable Doctor said we should not seize on the Lieutenant-Governor, or belch out our wrath against him. I know that when a stomach is out of order, rhubarb and other alteratives do a great deal of good. I think, therefore, that the learned Doctor would be acting exceedingly well if he could discharge from the mind of the Lieutenant-Governor some of the deposits that are there, and which are bringing him into collision with this House and the people.

"Dr. BOWERBANK.—He (G. W. Gordon) is a disgrace to the House."

In quoting the above, we merely give a very mild

K

specimen of this Mulatto's conduct in the House of Assembly. He was the same everywhere. A reckless, worthless, unprincipled demagogue; at enmity with every respectable man in the island of Jamaica.

CHAPTER VII.

A BRIEF sketch having been given of Mr. G. W. Gordon, it now becomes necessary to refer at some length to Dr. Underhill's most unwise and most improper letter to the Secretary of State for the Colonies, which materially helped to, if it did not indeed actually, fan into a flame the smouldering fires of rebellion.

The causes which brought about the insurrection, it has already been said, were at work long before Mr. Eyre reached Jamaica, and it is unnecessary, therefore, to recapitulate them. All the elements of discord referred to had been seething and fermenting in the mind of the coloured population of Jamaica when Dr. Underhill wrote the following letter :—

Copy of a Letter from E. B. Underhill, Esq., LL.D., to the Right Hon. Edward Cardwell, M.P.

"33, Moorgate Street, E.C.,
"January 5, 1865.

" DEAR SIR,

"I venture to ask your kind consideration to a few observations on the present condition of the Island of Jamaica.

" For several months past every mail has brought letters informing me of the continually increasing distress of the coloured population. As a sufficient illustration, I quote the following brief passage from one of them :—

" ' Crime has fearfully increased. The number of prisoners in the penitentiary and gaols is considerably more than double the average, and nearly all for one crime—larceny. Summonses for petty debts disclose an amount of pecuniary difficulty which has never before been experienced ; and applications for parochial and private relief prove that multitudes are suffering from want, little removed from starvation.'

" The immediate cause of this distress would seem to be the drought of the last two years ; but, in fact, this has only given intensity to suffering previously existing. All accounts, both public and private, concur in affirming the alarming increase of crime, chiefly of larceny and petty theft. This arises from the extreme poverty of the people. That this is its true origin is made evident by the ragged and even naked condition of vast numbers of them, so contrary to the taste for dress they usually exhibit. They cannot purchase clothing, partly from its greatly-increased cost, which is unduly enhanced by the duty (said to be 38 per cent. by the Hon. Mr. Whitlock) which it now pays, and partly from the want of employment, and the consequent absence of wages.

"The people then are starving, and the causes of this are not far to seek. No doubt the taxation of the island is too heavy for its present resources, and must necessarily render the cost of producing the staples higher than they can bear, to meet competition in the markets of the world. No doubt much of the sugar land of the island is worn out, or can only be made productive by an outlay which would destroy all hope of profitable return. No doubt, too, a large part .of the island is uncultivated, and might be made to support a vastly greater population than is now existing upon it.

"But the simple fact is that there is not sufficient employment for the people; there is neither work for them, nor the capital to employ them. The labouring class is too numerous for the work to be done. Sugar cultivation on the estates does not absorb more than 30,000 of the people ; and every other species of cultivation (apart from provision growing) cannot give employment to more than another 30,000. But the agricultural population of the island is over 400,000, so that there are at least 340,000 whose livelihood depends on employment other than that devoted to the staple cultivation of the island. Of these 340,000 certainly not less than 130,000 are adults, and capable of labour. For subsistence they must be entirely dependent on the provisions grown on their own little freeholds, a portion of which is sold to those who find employment on the estates ; or perhaps in a very slight degree on such produce as they are able to raise for exportation.   But those who grow produce for exportation are very few, and they meet with every kind of discouragement to prosecute a means of support which is as advantageous to the island as to themselves.   If their provisions fail, as has been the case from drought, they must steal or starve.   And this is their present condition.

"The same result follows in this country when employment ceases or wages fail.   The great decrease of coin in circulation in Jamaica is a further proof that less money is spent in wages, through the decline of employment.   Were Jamaica prosperous, silver would flow into it or its equivalent in English manufactures, instead of the exportation of silver, which now regularly takes place.   And if, as stated in the Governor's speech, the Customs Revenue in the year gone by has been equal to former years, this has arisen, not from an increase in the quantities imported, but from the increased value of the imports, the duty being levied at an ad valorem charge of $12\frac{1}{2}$ per cent. on articles, such as cotton goods, which have within the last year or two greatly risen in price.

"I shall say nothing of the course taken by the Jamaica Legislature; of their abortive immigration bills; of their unjust taxation of the coloured population; of their refusal of just tribunals; of their denial

of political rights to the emancipated negroes.   Could
the people find remunerative employment, these evils
would in time be remedied from their growing strength
and intelligence.   The worst evil consequent on the
proceedings of the Legislature is the distrust awakened
in the minds of capitalists, and the avoidance of
Jamaica, with its manifold advantages, by all who
possess the means to benefit it by their expenditure.
Unless means can be found to encourage the outlay
of capital in Jamaica, in the growth of those numerous
products which can be profitably exported, so that
employment can be given to its starving people, I see
no other result than the entire failure of the island,
and the destruction of the hopes that the Legislature
and people of Great Britain have cherished with regard
to the well-being of its emancipated population.

"With your kind permission I will venture to make
two or three suggestions, which, if carried out, may
assist to avert so painful a result.

"1. A searching inquiry into the legislation of the
island since emancipation, its taxation, its economical
and material condition, would go far to bring to light
the causes of the existing evils, and by convincing the
ruling class of the mistakes of the past, lead to their
removal.   Such an inquiry seems also due to this
country, that it may be seen whether the emancipated
peasantry have gained those advantages which were
sought to be secured to them by their enfranchisement.

"2. The Governor might be instructed to encourage by his personal approval and urgent recommendation the growth of exportable produce by the people, on the very numerous freeholds they possess. This might be done by the formation of associations for shipping their produce in considerable quantities; by equalizing duties on the produce of the people and that of the planting interests; by instructing the native growers of produce in the best methods of cultivation, and pointing out the articles which would find a ready sale in the markets of the world; by opening channels for direct transmission of produce, without the intervention of agents, by whose extortions and frauds the people now frequently suffer, and are greatly discouraged. The cultivation of sugar by the peasantry should, in my judgment, be discouraged. At the best, with all the scientific appliances the planters can bring to it, both of capital and machinery, sugar manufacturing is a hazardous thing. Much more must it become so in the hands of the people, with their rude mills and imperfect methods. But the minor products of the island, such as spices, tobacco, farinaceous foods, coffee, and cotton, are quite within their reach, and always fetch a fair and remunerative price, where not burdened by extravagant charges and local taxation.

"3. With just laws and light taxation, capitalists would be encouraged to settle in Jamaica, and employ themselves in the production of the more important staples, such as sugar, coffee, and cotton. Thus the people would be employed, and the present starvation rate of wages be improved.

"In conclusion, I have to apologize for troubling you with this communication ; but since my visit to the island in 1859-60 I have felt the greatest interest in its prosperity, and deeply grieve over the sufferings of its coloured population. It is more than time that the unwisdom (to use the gentlest term) that has governed Jamaica since emancipation should be brought to an end,—a course of action which, while it incalculably aggravates the misery arising from natural, and, therefore, unavoidable causes, renders certain the ultimate ruin of every class, planter and peasant, European and Creole.

"Should you, dear sir, desire such information as it may be in my power to furnish, or to see me on the matter, I shall be most happy, either to forward whatever facts I may possess, or wait upon you at any time that you may appoint.

"I have, &c.,

(Signed)   " EDW. B. UNDERHILL.

"The Right Hon. Edward Cardwell, M.P.

"P.S.—I append an extract from the speech of the Honourable A. Whitlock, in the House of Assembly, with respect to the condition of the people.

"'He (Mr. Whitlock) would make an assertion

which could not be gainsaid by his successor, that taxation could not be extended; not one farthing more could
be imposed on the people, who were suffering peculiar
hardship from the increased value of wearing apparel,
which was now taxed beyond all bounds; actually
they were paying 38 per cent. now, when $12\frac{1}{2}$ per cent.
was before considered an outrageous ad valorem duty.
Cotton goods, including osnaburgh and all the wearing
apparel of the labouring classes, had increased to 200
per cent. in value; what was bought at $4d.$ a yard
before was selling for a shilling per yard, therefore the people are now paying $1\frac{1}{2}d.$ of duty in every
yard of cloth instead of $\frac{1}{2}d.$, which has been justly
described as a heavy impost. The consequence is
that a disgusting state of nudity exhibited itself in
some parts of the country. Hardly a boy under ten
years of age wore a frock, and adults, from the ragged
state of their garments, exhibited those parts of the
body where covering was especially wanted. The
lower classes hitherto exhibited a proneness for dress.
And he could not believe such a change would have
come over them, but for his belief in their destitution
arising out of a reduction in their wages at a time
every article of apparel was tripled in value. . . .
This year's decrease in imports foreshadowed what was
coming. Sugar was down again to $11l.$ per hogshead;
coffee was falling, pimento was valueless, logwood
scarcely worth cutting, and, moreover, a sad diminu-

tion effected in our chief staple exports from a deficiency of rain.' "

On the receipt of this letter, Mr. Cardwell at once forwarded it to Governor Eyre, with a request that he would report on its contents. Mr. Eyre being anxious to obtain the fullest and most authentic information, called upon the custodes of the different parishes, and upon the heads of the different religious denominations, to favour him with their views on the various allegations contained in Dr. Underhill's communication.

In collecting and collating opinions from so many different persons, representing various interests and classes, and having reference to numerous localities widely apart from each other, and differing essentially in physical features, climate, and industrial occupations, it was only to be expected that there would be some diversity of opinion and many conflicting statements. But, on the whole, the evidence was of a decidedly uniform character, and went to establish several very important inferences :—

1st. That in consequence of the long-continued low prices of the staple products of the West Indies, and a diminished production occasioned by repeated droughts, all classes and interests had suffered severely, but that the pressure had fallen more heavily upon the *planter* than the *labourer*.

2nd. That distress did not exist amongst the labour-

ing population to the extent depicted by Dr. Underhill.

3rd. That owing to the immense extent of fertile
land open to the labourer at a mere nominal cost, his
position in Jamaica was very *far superior* to the peasantry of most other countries.

4th. That although the labourer could readily earn
1*s*. 6*d*. in from four to six hours, he invariably refused
to earn, as he easily might, double that amount by
extending his hours of employment.

5th. That one great reason of the non-existence of
cultivation, and the consequent increased means of
employing the people on estates, was to be found in the
fact that, whatever amount of labour might exist in the
neighbourhood of a plantation, that it was not pro-
curable with certainty or continuously; that the very
times when the planter most required the services of
his workpeople was the period best suited for the cultivation of provision-grounds, and that, therefore, the
labourer naturally deserted his employer to work on his
own land. In fact, that he only worked upon estates
when it suited his own purpose to do so, without any
reference to the convenience or requirements of his
employer. That on such occasions, and at August and
Christmas, when holidays of weeks together were taken
by the Creole peasantry, the estates would, in many
instances, be ruined but for the immigrant labour,
which supplied the place of the native, and which, how-

ever expensive or unsatisfactory in some respects, had at least the advantage of being always available.

6th. That as regarded clothing, the climate was of so genial a nature as to make little necessary, whilst the habit of the people was to go to their work in scanty, ragged, or dirty garments, reserving their finery for Sundays, holidays, markets, or courts, when for the most part they were neatly and respectably, often very expensively clad.

7th. That there was, consequently, no such general starvation and nakedness as so graphically pictured by Dr. Underhill.

8th. That crime, especially larceny, was fearfully on the increase ; but that it *was not due to want* compelling to steal. The young and strong of both sexes were those who filled the gaols. That the old, the decrepit, or the emaciated were rarely to be met with in a Jamaica prison.

9th. That the utter want of principle, or moral sense, which pervaded the mass of the people, the total absence of all parental control or proper training of the children, the incorrigible indolence, apathy, and improvidence of all ages, and the degraded and immoral social existence which they all but universally led, was quite sufficient to account for any poverty or crime which existed amongst the peasantry of Jamaica.

To substantiate the above very important facts, some extracts will now be given from the voluminous documents transmitted to the Colonial Office by Mr. Eyre.

Mr. Hosack, who was Finance Minister from June, 1855 to December, 1860, writes:—

"The first and most important statement made is, that every mail for several months past had conveyed letters from Jamaica to Mr. Underhill, informing him of the continually increasing distress of the coloured population. By 'coloured' he means, I presume, the black population. My answer to this is, that the Government have had no proofs of any such distress among that class, nor have the clergy or the public journals of the island indicated its presence.

*　　*　　*　　*　　*　　*

"The illustrations given by Mr. Underhill as to the true origin of crime in Jamaica entirely fail in their object, in my opinion. Since the extreme poverty referred to (where it exists) is, in nine cases out of ten, the result of sheer idleness, and a growing dislike to steady industry, and a consequent preference to a dishonest mode of living, with the risks of occasional imprisonment, to one of honest labour, with the remote certainty of independence. These, added to the ease with which provision-grounds can be plundered with little risk of detection, and the indifference with which imprisonment is now regarded, operate as a serious drawback and discouragement to industrious settlers.

It is notorious that a labourer, by working one day in a week, can, owing to the high productiveness of the land, keep himself in ground provisions all through the year; he, therefore, cannot starve, unless he returns to primeval barbarism.

*　　*　　*　　*　　*　　*

" There is always a want of capital when the staple produce is low in price, and losses have to be met; every other interest in the island is more or less dependent on sugar cultivation, and therefore suffers in the same proportion as the primary interest. But to say that ' the labouring class of Jamaica is too numerous for the work to be done' is another fallacy, when the fact is, that, compared with other populations, the work done (as evidenced by the exports) is miserable indeed. This has arisen, I believe, in some measure from the principles of self-reliance being adopted too soon by the people of Jamaica, after emancipation, under the advice of well-meaning but mistaken persons. The labouring population is not now numerous enough at the centres of industry (generally speaking), and time is wasted in going and returning to those centres."

The Rev. Samuel Oughton, a well-known and zealous Baptist minister, indignant at a circular issued by the Baptist Missionary Society in London, entitled ' Distress in Jamaica,' wrote as follows to the editor of the ' Jamaica Guardian :'—

" To the Editor of the 'Jamaica Guardian.'

" SIR,

"I have just read your leading article of this morning on a circular recently issued by the Baptist Missionary Society in London, entitled 'Distress in Jamaica,' and as it is desirable that all the Baptist ministers in Jamaica should not suffer in public estimation for the injudicious and exaggerated statements of one or two, I beg leave through your columns to declare that I have never made any such communications to the Society in England, and further, that I do not believe that they are fair and truthful representations of the state of things at present existing amongst the labouring population of this island.

"There can be no doubt that a large amount of poverty exists amongst us, and it is true that the attendance at places of public worship has very much declined, and that dishonesty and crime have increased to such an extent that our prisons are crowded to a degree corresponding to the emptiness of our chapels, whilst new and more stringent laws have become necessary to afford protection to property; but I do not believe that these accumulated evils are to be wholly or principally attributed to excessive droughts, inability to obtain employment, or dear salt fish and calico. These may indeed tend to intensify and aggravate the evils; but the real cause in the great majority of cases is, in my opinion, only to be found *in the inveterate habits of idleness and the low state of moral and religious principles which prevail to so fearful a degree in our community.*

" As you have invited protests from such Baptist ministers as dissent from the opinions set forth in the Baptist Mission Circular, I have felt it only just to myself and the public to send in mine, and am,

" Yours faithfully,

" SAMUEL OUGHTON,

" *Baptist Minister.*

" East Queen Street, Kingston, 25th Feb., 1865."

The Bishop of Kingston, in a letter to Governor Eyre, dated March 2nd, 1865, says :—

" I am glad to have this opportunity of expressing my conviction that the representations which have been made to the Secretary of State, and similar representations which have, as appears from the newspapers, obtained considerable publicity in England, of the increasing distress of the coloured population of this island are, to say the least, very highly coloured, very inaccurate. There is distress in this country, as in every other; but not, I am convinced, great distress, nor, so far as I have any reason to believe, increasing distress. And I know not of one person in this island of any class or colour who deeply grieves over the ' sufferings of the coloured population,' as Dr. Underhill says he did in 1860. Before I had received your Excellency's Despatch, my attention had been drawn by one of the clergy to certain statements in the newspapers on this subject which he considered false and disgraceful, and repeatedly said demanded emphatic contradiction. Such statements, if credited, would do more to deter capitalists and persons of enterprise from venturing hither than any legislation could possibly do to encourage them.

*　　*　　*　　*　　*　　*

"Local and temporary distress, and a state of comparative poverty (though not by any means of discomfort or actual want as the ordinary condition), must prevail amongst a people satisfied, as many are, to remain in a semi-barbarous state, taking no thought for the morrow, and satisfied with such food as their own grounds (or their neighbours') can supply, or with 'such things as grow of themselves.'

"If Devonshire were in Jamaica, the apple orchards would hardly continue to exist. The people—not all, but not a few,—would steal the fruit before it was ready for the cider press, cook it in some simple way, live on it so long as it lasted, and refuse to work for wages till they wanted money to buy food. And with all the wisdom of Parliament, all the energy of our Executive, the remedy would be hard to find.

*　　*　　*　　*　　*　　*

"But I believe the people in many districts are improving in steadiness and forethought, in morality, and in wealth. I do not forget the increase of petty larceny, or the increasing difficulty in the Plantain Garden River District and others of obtaining labour on the sugar estates. As the crust of the earth is geologically both rising and falling, so I believe are the people of this island both ascending and descending in the scale of civilization. It is not want, but idleness and profligacy, which lead to theft. Your Excellency has already proved this to demonstration. The thieves are young. The provision-grounds are not plundered by fathers of families starving, but by young men, worthless and reckless, who, if they have children, care not to maintain them."

In reply to a series of questions put by his bishop, Archdeacon Stewart writes:—

" I have no reason to consider the labouring class poorer than they were three or four years ago. As a body I think them better off than the peasantry of most other countries.

"I reside close over the public road leading into Kingston; the labouring classes daily pass along this road to and from the city, but I have not seen any of them indecently clad. While working for pay, or in the cultivation of their provision-grounds, they invariably put on their worst clothing. They are then loosely but not indecently clad, which is explained when the excessive heat of a tropical sun is taken into consideration. The East Indian labourer, coolie, is a vast deal more indecently clad, and that at all times.* I have seen them in my travels totally naked, except a twisted loin-cloth under and about their hips.

" On Sunday and other holidays the labouring class invariably appear well dressed, and I should say expensively. On a recent occasion I appealed to them on behalf of the ' Jamaica Home and Foreign Missionary Society.' There were between 600 and 700 labourers and artificers in and about the church, and they contributed liberally. Their very respectable appearance—and in very many instances expensive-attire, viz., the women and girls of eighteen or nineteen with crinoline, chip-straw hats trimmed with ribbons and artificial flowers, and the men with neat jackets, and many in the ordinary dress of a gentleman of the upper class —attracted the notice of Europeans who happened to be present. Raggedness is seen in the towns only ; it is attributable there, not to poverty, but to laziness, and to a determination not to seek work in the rural districts.

*   *   *   *   *   *

" I do not attribute the recent increase of petty larceny to increasing distress. I attribute it, among some, to their unwillingness to labour honestly for their daily bread, and for supplying means to satisfy their profligacy, and,

---

* What would Dr. Underhill think, if he visited Calcutta, or any station throughout the length and breadth of India?

among others, to the absence of all principle. It is not uncommon of late for decently-clothed labouring women from the country to purloin articles in the shops of Kingston while pretending to purchase, and to conceal such articles under their dress. Some have been detected with the articles so concealed. The lazy and unprincipled constantly stealing the provisions of the industrious, and to such an excess that many have given up the cultivation of their grounds."

The Rev. Jas. Williams, rector of Spanish Town, says :—

"If we could eradicate the fondness for 'making an appearance' in the matter of dress in certain classes and persons, the whole island would be one sink of abomination. The shame attendant on not being able to 'make an appearance' keeps very many from providing that creditable or decent clothing that in other countries the industrious amongst the lower classes are contented with, seeking nothing beyond it. For dress many will work, and their every-day raggedness is attributable to the gratification of their vanity on this head. It is far, very far, from being an uncommon thing to find individuals and members of a family which is supported by alms coming to church in a style which would apparently betray anything rather than poverty. The raggedness of clothing which is often witnessed is owing then, not to commiserable poverty, but to pride, yet to a pride which, if it existed not, idleness and beggary would increase. A stranger coming to the country, and forming his judgment of the people by their appearance, for instance, in our churches, would be greatly misled on the subject of their moral and social condition."

The Rev. T. Orgill writes :—

" Labourers in this district never work more than three or four days in the week, and not unfrequently refuse work when offered. They are nearly all freeholders, and keep their horses or other stock. I may mention that in the last twelve months properties have been bought by some of them to the extent of nearly 600 acres, at a cost of about 400*l.*"

The letter of Archdeacon Rowe to the bishop is so important that it must be given in full :—

" Archdeacon Rowe to the Bishop.

" 1. There is no distress among the labouring classes in the neighbourhood in which I reside, for many estates are in cultivation, and the people receiving their wages regularly, and not depending on the cultivation of their own lands.

" 2. I do not consider the people to be poorer than they were three or four years ago.

" 3. The people generally clothe themselves decently; I mean the natives of Jamaica. The coolies are indecently clothed, after the fashion of their own country. I am informed that in the French colonies they are compelled to appear in decent clothing from the day of their landing.

"4. The great increase of petty larceny does not arise from distress, for those who commit this crime are generally strong young men who can earn full wages or in other ways maintain themselves comfortably. But the punishment awarded to this crime is so light, and prison discipline so lenient, that it becomes to them a matter of indifference whether they are convicted or not.

"The peasantry of Jamaica are, generally speaking, a well-conducted, industrious people, kind to each other, and willing to attend to the instructions of the ministers of religion; *but in consequence of a misplaced leniency, which forbears to inflict proper punishment in cases of larceny, sorcery, bestiality, and other crimes, there is a race now growing up which are likely to prove the destruction of the community.* Honest and industrious persons are afraid to plant their provision-grounds, knowing that as soon as the products of the land arrive at maturity they will not only be stolen but wantonly rooted up and destroyed, and I am persuaded that whatever want now exists proceeds from that cause more than any other.

"5. A shilling a day for an able field labourer is quite sufficient to maintain him in comfort; but the people generally labour by the task or job, and make more than this. At the present price, however, of Jamaica produce, *i. e.*, the great produce of sugar, it is likely that many will be unable to carry on the cultivation of their estates at this rate, and that their properties will be abandoned in consequence.

"6. The people can of course only get wages for labour when they live in the neighbourhood of estates that are in cultivation.   But they can always turn their labour to account by growing corn, provisions, coffee, ginger, tobacco, sugar-cane, &c., for land can be bought in most districts at 40s. an acre, or rented at from 12s. to 20s.

"7. The people seek employment on the estates, or confine themselves to the cultivation of their own land, according to inclination or the profits derived from either course.   And, with the exception of the idle and wicked ones already spoken of, they are an industrious and contented people, and might, under proper and wholesome regulations, be made as good a peasantry as any in the world.   I have had long experience among them, and my duties call upon me to make frequent journeys, and I consider myself competent to form a correct judgment on the subject.

"8. If the crime of larceny is stopped by proper laws I do not anticipate an increasing want of the necessaries of life, but, on the contrary, an increasing abundance.   And if 'obeah' and 'sorcery,' which are only other names for secret poisoning, and are much on the increase, are, together with other heinous offences, severely punished, as they ought to be, I look for a corresponding increase of happiness and prosperity among our people.

"9. I consider the laws of Jamaica to be excellent in all other respects except the points in which I have stated them to be deficient. The taxes are light, and the people would be happy and prosperous if a stronger check were placed on the wickedness of the few.

"Slavery was a system under which there could exist no room for the exercise of proper parental discipline or the formation of social habits; and although a vast improvement has taken place in the condition of the people since the emancipation, parents have not yet learnt how to bring up their families respectably, and there has been, therefore, nothing to supply the place of that former discipline, which, hateful as it was in many respects, was still of use in restraining from the commission of crimes destructive to society.

(Signed)   "William Rowe, A.M.,

"*Archdeacon of Cornwall.*

"6th March, 1865."

Very many writers, clergymen, magistrates, and others, attribute what distress showed itself, as also the increase of crime, to the "revivals." The Rev. Mr. Sheam says that the great majority of cases of distress "must be attributed to idleness, the love of dress, and that entire destitution of religious principle which is so fearfully increased by the numerous rum-shops which have been opened in all directions, *and those midnight meetings which are held for immoral purposes, under the pretence of serving God:* and I know of none more calculated to bring His curse upon the land than those which are wickedly and falsely called 'revival meetings.'"

The Rev. C. A. Angell says :—

"If there is any distress in my district (comprising 4,000 persons), it is only among the strong young people, who are too lazy to work, and the aged people, who are invariably handed over by their relatives to the parish for support when too infirm to labour.

* * * * *

"The people who work obtain the necessaries of life from the soil, which is taxed at 1*d.* per acre only; besides they cultivate various products for exportation, *e.g.,* in my district coffee, which is purchased at their doors at the present time at 42*s.* per cwt., and the laws of the country in no way discourage their industry.

"How can any race of people be improved unless their intellectual culture is attended to? The negroes on the whole are in this country grossly ignorant, and believe as firmly in their African superstitions as they do in the teachings of the Christian religion. They are utterly indifferent about the instruction of their children; and, unless 'better legislation' introduce some scheme of compulsory education, I fear that the prospects of the country will every day become more gloomy."

Having given sufficient extracts to show the light in which Mr. Underhill's letter was regarded by the clergy

of all denominations throughout the island, the opinions
of others will now briefly be referred to.

The Hon. Mr. Westmoreland states:—

"Mr. Underhill's picture of the cond tion of the black
population of Jamaica is not a correct one. Taking
them as a whole, there are no people in the world occupying the station they do so well off, as evidenced by
so many of them possessing land and stock to no in-
considerable extent. No doubt the competition with
slavery has caused a diminution in the cultivation of
sugar, in the requirements of labour, and in the rate of
wages, and in many instances an inability on the part
of the planter to pay punctually those decreased wages;
but Mr. Underhill has far underrated the amount of
labour still used in sugar cultivation, and the other
sources of occupation.

*   *   *   *   *

"I think, as I have already said, that very many of
the people born since freedom have been brought up in
habits of idleness, and have taken much to thieving in
preference to showing any desire to earn an honest
livelihood, but that a large number of older people have
established themselves as small and even large freeholders, and that their circumstances are improving,
and by their industry the export of coffee is considerably on the increase.

*   *   *   *   *

"Mr. Underhill is incorrect in saying that 'the

sugar land of the colony is worn out,' &c. A vast quantity of it has relapsed into a state of nature, and has thereby been renovated, and requires but capital and labour to make it productive. Were it, as Mr. Underhill states, worn out, how could he fairly hope that ' by just laws and light taxation capitalists would be encouraged to settle in Jamaica, and employ themselves in the cultivation of sugar ?'

" Capitalists will not come to Jamaica and engage in sugar cultivation, when they can go to Cuba and invest their money in a similar way, and obtain an interest of 17 per cent., as shown by a statement now before me of the result of the operations of a sugar estate near St. Jago last year.

" Here, at the prices that have ruled the last four years, it is hardly possible to make both ends meet. When slavery is abolished, and our own and the Spanish colonies placed on the same footing as regards labour, then we may expect capitalists will embark here in sugar cultivation; and I would wish Mr. Underhill would direct his endeavours towards such a consummation, believing that by so doing he would conduce to the material interests of those whose cause he is ever advocating much more than by *making representations based on incorrect statements, calculated to lead persons to believe that the black people in Jamaica were better off as slaves than they are as freemen.*"

" March 10, 1865."

The Hon. Sir Bryan Edwards, Chief Justice of Jamaica, while believing that crime and indigence are on the increase in Jamaica, and that poverty to a certain extent exists, says :—

"But very few persons here, I suspect, will be disposed to assent to Dr. Underhill's conclusion, that with these people the alternative is to steal or starve; or that the present poverty of the emancipated peasantry—at all events the able-bodied part of them—is occasioned by circumstances over which they had no control. Indeed, by far the most serious charges of larceny are against persons who, from their appearance as well as from what is ascertained upon inquiry, are by no means destitute; and I think it may be received as certain that those who, being able to earn their living, are yet found in a state of indigence, as in too many instances is the case, are so simply because, though able, they are disinclined to labour, even when employment offers itself, or could readily be obtained if sought for.

* * * * *

"But Dr. Underhill besides complains of the unfairness of the Legislature, not only in respect of unequal, and therefore unjust, taxation of the emancipated negroes, but also of the refusal to them of just tribunals, and the denial to them of political rights.

"In candour, Dr. Underhill ought to have illustrated his meaning by explanation or example, and not have clothed his reproof in such vague and unintelligible terms.   For myself, I must confess I am not able to understand of what it is exactly he complains.

"Taxation, such as it is, applies equally to every one ; no distinction is or can be made ; and it should be borne in mind that it is not the emancipated population only who dress in calico, or who consume American pork or flour.   I know of no tribunals, just or unjust, which affect exclusively that class; and with respect to political rights, there is no pretence for saying that in this island all are not politically equal."

Mr. Salmon, a gentleman who has resided forty years in the island of Jamaica, remarks :—

"It seems to me, then, that if a coloured person chose to provide for himself, moderate labour will procure him all the necessaries of life.   How is it that now,—that at this time,—which is represented to Mr. Underhill as of increasing distress,—as large an amount of cash is taken over the counter at the stores for requirements for dress, and hoops, and bonnets, and calicoes, and ribbons, and boots and shoes, and ladies' and gentlemen's saddles, &c. &c., as for many years past, and this in spite of the increasing price?   With increased price of imported articles our prices for ground provisions have gone up.   Yams from 5s. per 100 lbs. to 6s., 8s., and 10s.; cocoes from 3s. and 4s. to 5s., 6s., and 8s.   These would pay well at 4s.   Tobacco yields a crop of 50l. per acre, sold in the markets by the yard ; corn sells readily ; pork and fowls in demand ; and on a market day, in the country, you will meet the carcasses of five or six hogs, of 100 to 200 lbs. each, taken to market, and which are sold. It would be a difficulty to find out how a man can complain, if it were not known he prefers 'sitting down' to the doing anything, and that generally the money he gets for the labour he does is spent in dancing and dress, and segars and pomatums. Noticing these particulars may be said to be trifling; it may be, but they are truths, and ought to be known. If so distressed,—' the continually increasing distress of the coloured population,'—how can be accounted for the large and increasing proprietorship of these persons in cattle, and especially in horse kind?—how are they purchased, and how is the pasturage paid where the owner has no land? I myself had 80 head, the property of black and coloured people, at pasturage on one property. I say then the people as they are are not starving, nor is the negro overtaxed, for he pays comparatively nothing; one penny per acre per annum tax on land, which cultivated will yield 10*l.* 6*s.* If he have a horse for his pleasure or profit he pays 16*s.* per annum, and taking provisions to market weekly carries not less than 10*s.* value."

The following extracts are from a letter written by the Hon. L. Q. Bowerbank :—

"The gross immorality and lewdness, especially of the lower orders of the women, is perhaps the greatest curse with which the city, if not the island, is affected;

and the fearful prevalence of concubinage and unchastity in both sexes, and the state of riot, disorder, and idleness, in which children grow up, are among the most prolific causes of distress and poverty.

"On several occasions attempts have been made to introduce a Bastardy Bill to compel fathers to provide for their illegitimate children. The attempt, however, has hitherto failed in consequence of the determined opposition offered to it by a very large majority of the members of the House of Assembly.

* * * * * *

"That the licentiousness and gross perversions of the truth so common in the newspapers of the island, under the plea of upholding the independence of the press, and which are, in too many instances, conducted by men whose station in society, their antecedents, their social and moral relations, unfit them to act as censors for the public, influence the conduct of the lower orders.

* * * * * *

"I believe that the increase of crime is to be accounted for, not by the necessity of starvation, or the failure of provision-grounds, or want of labour, or deficiency of wages, but from a spirit of dishonesty, love of plunder, idle and improvident habits, want of a just appreciation of the rights of property, laxity of law and impunity in doing wrong ; love of ignorance, vice, and vicious indulgences ; and the entire absence of all moral and religious feeling ; to which I would add, bad example set by the better class, in an open and unblushing manner, unknown in other British colonies or dependencies.

*   *   *   *   *   *

"To speak of the people of Jamaica generally as naked and starving is simply untrue and absurd. That in some localities there may be scarcity and distress is not confined to Jamaica, but exists to as great an extent at home, and is by no means so increased here as to warrant the conclusion drawn from it.

"It is not true that the labouring class is too numerous for the work to be done. In Kingston, as I have already stated, carpenters cannot at times be found ; weeks elapse before the smallest piece of work can be done ; and then, for a bungling, incapable, and lazy artisan, you must pay three shillings per day. Labour is wanted all over the island ; but the high wages, and little work given for it, causes people to let alone all improvements.

*   *   *   *   *   *

"In perusing Dr. Underhill's letter I am at a loss to understand what he means when alluding to the Jamaica Legislature. He alludes ' to their unjust taxation of the coloured population ; of their refusal of just tribunals ; of their denial of political rights to the emancipated negroes.' After many years' residence

M

here, and after sitting as a member of the House of Assembly for some three years, I feel bound in honour and duty to express my opinion that the House of Assembly is the curse of Jamaica. Still I am not prepared to agree in the charges he brings against it, unless he can more fully explain his meaning."

Four or five years ago Dr. Underhill visited the Island of Jamaica at the request of the Treasurer and Committee of the Baptist Missionary Society, to investigate "the religious condition of the numerous Baptist Churches formed in the Islands of the West, especially as that condition had been affected by the Act of Emancipation," and he took advantage of the opportunity to write a book. The subjoined extracts are worthy of note :—

" *Generally the people of Jamaica are great deceivers and liars.* It might be a remnant of slavery influences, but it seemed in most cases inherent in their character, almost a natural peculiarity. Among estates' people especially there are few individuals who, unless under intimidation, adhere to the truth ; and the ministers confess with sorrow and mortification their want of success in eradicating this evil.

*   *   *   *   *   *

" Offences against the law consist chiefly of petty larcenies ; graver crimes are few. The actual number of criminals is not large. The same individuals appear before the magistrates again and again. There is a great disregard for the sanctity of an oath in the courts of law, and perjury is frequent and manifest. *The poor, the widows, and the aged are often worse off than in the times of slavery.* Then they were secure of some sort of support on the estates. Now, if they have no relations to care for them, they become wretchedly poor and miserable. The negro is generally far from being kind and charitable to his own race."

At a gathering in St. Thomas-in-the-Vale, Dr. Underhill met a large number of the residents of the mountains. But few of them, he says, worked on sugar estates. He selected two men from the party, "who were particularly intelligent in their remarks; they had not worked on an estate for many years. They grew coffee for sale, and made sugar enough for their own use; they ate bread every day, also salt fish and herrings; and sometimes more than once a week they had fresh beef. Provisions, they said, were dear, but clothing was cheap. The soil of Jamaica, they said, was so rich that it did not require manure; the deeper it was dug the richer it became. When the soil was exhausted, they preferred to occupy new ground; after it had been fallow a few years they often resumed its cultivation, but virgin land was so cheap and abundant in the mountains that it was more profitable to take it than to manure or clear old lands. They had no idea of keeping a cow; they had no pasturage for one. Pigs and goats, the latter supplying them with milk, with their domestic animals. One had eleven children, the other nine; both had had thirteen. They lived most comfortably, and could afford something for their minister." Dr. Underhill had already remarked, that the major part of the population of the parish resided in the mountains, and cultivated lands there.

On the authority of a gentleman whose "position and character," Dr. Underhill thought, rendered his observations "worthy of the gravest consideration," he mentions that "very many estates in the district had been thrown up, not on account of the want of capital, for in many instances they belonged to men of great wealth;" and that "two more would shortly swell the expanse of bush. They were no longer profitable, because the people who cultivated them, when released from bondage, could better themselves, and naturally did so. If any amount of money were brought to bear, there are not hands to work, much less to reclaim them, unless hired at some enormous sacrifice. Of fifteen estates in the immediate neighbourhood, four only remained under cultivation, and two of these four but partially. During slavery they were amply supplied with labour, and carried on to their utmost limit. The few remaining proprietors, still struggling to survive, have the utmost difficulty in obtaining labour when desired."

In reference to every part of the island which Dr.

Underhill visited, he made the same remarks as to the dearth of labour for estate purposes, and the independence and thrift of the persons who became small settlers.

What becomes now of his statements that the labour market for estates in Jamaica is overstocked, and that the settlers and others are starving? Can it be credited that the industry of the settler has ceased to render him independent, and that numbers in consequence resorting to the labour market have made the supply too great for the demand? Upon no other hypothesis is it possible to reconcile the statements we have quoted with those recently made by Dr. Underhill.*

In reference to the decay of cultivation in St. Thomas-in-the-Vale, Dr. Underhill wrote :—

"Careful and respectable men are not usually willing to work on sugar estates, or to suffer their families to do so." In another place—"Few will labour on the estates for more than four days in the week, except in crop time, when they usually give a fifth day; scarcely any will work on a Saturday. There are, in fact, more than sufficient labourers, at least in St. Thomas-in-the-Vale, for the extent of sugar cultivation now carried on, and the abundance reduces the rate of wages; on the other hand, their labour is uncertain, is not always

* *Vide* Parliamentary Blue Book, in corroboration of all that is stated concerning his book.

available at the time when it is most required, and is limited by their habits, special occupations, and partial wants." Again he writes—" The best organization of labour for the planter is, undoubtedly, that by which it can be secured with regularity as well as cheapness; but this will only take place where the labourer depends on the wages he can earn. The universal possession of provision-grounds prevents this, and so great is the desire to obtain land that a regular supply of labour can only now be secured either through an artificial scarcity of land, or by a very large increase of population. To the question whether, if sufficient wages were given to cover both the present wages and the value of the produce of the provision-grounds, they would give up their small holdings, I received but one reply from the people:—No!"

It is in the face of the knowledge of facts such as these that Dr. Underhill denies the necessity for immigration, and wishes small settlements to be encouraged. What does he ask for but the annihilation of the planter?

Dr. Underhill's book is full of statements like those quoted above; and the tenor of all his remarks is to show that when on the spot, Dr. Underhill imbibed very similar impressions with regard to the position, character, and conduct of the peasantry of Jamaica to those expressed in the extracts quoted from the documents criticising his letter to the Colonial Secretary.

In every community there is always a certain amount
of pauperism ; there are always aged, infirm, or diseased
persons who require aid from their friends or from the
community ; but these classes were not more numerous
in Jamaica than in other countries, except in so far as
it is common in that island for relatives to desert and
throw upon the parish those members of their family
who are unable to support themselves; children thus
constantly deserting their own parents when well able
to support them ; and fathers almost invariably deserting their illegitimate children, leaving them entirely to
the mother for support. This latter circumstance of
itself adds considerably to pauperism, as the large
majority of children born in Jamaica are illegitimate.

That Jamaica, prior to the insurrection, was generally
in a most unsatisfactory state as regards its moral,
social, material, and political interests, nobody denied.
That deterioration, decadence, and decay were everywhere noticeable, and the elements which ought to
sustain and improve the national character, and promote
the welfare and progress of the country, were gradually
disappearing, every one connected with the island, and
more especially Mr. Eyre, frankly allowed ; but it was
due not to the causes assigned by Dr. Underhill. The
peasantry did not " meet with every kind of discouragement to prosecute a means of support." There was no
" unjust taxation of the coloured population." There
was no " refusal of just tribunals," and there was no

" denial of political rights to the emancipated negroes." White, black, and brown were all equally taxed ; while as to "political rights" of the forty-seven Members of Assembly, more than one-half were black or coloured men. The Hon. Mr. Georges, writing on the subject, asks, " Who are our barristers, our officers in the Legislative Department, in the Customs? Who are our magistrates, inspectors of police, coroners, clerks of peace, and clerks of vestry, &c.? More than three-fourths are coloured men!"

The extract from the speech of Mr. Whitelocke, upon which Dr. Underhill laid so much stress, was an opposition speech, for the purpose of inducing the House of Assembly to withhold additional revenue for his successors in office. So far, however, from the consumption of imports having decreased, on an average, for the five years prior to the rebellion, such consumption had steadily increased. At the same time the labouring classes, by the cultivation of coffee, honey, bees-wax, ginger, and other products, had themselves largely added to the value of the general exports of the colony within the same period. Dr. Underhill asserted that there was "a general decrease of coin in circulation in Jamaica," and " an exportation of silver now regularly takes place." The manager of the only bank in the island, in reply to this, states: " I cannot say whether any or what amount of British silver has been exported from the island, but, if any, the extent cannot be very great, and the present amount of British silver in this island is far in excess of its requirements as a circulating medium."

Very large sums were paid annually by the Colony for services of a charitable nature, for providing schools, for religious instruction, for the protection of life and property, and for the punishment of crime; from all which outlay the peasantry, who constituted the mass of the population, necessarily received their full share of advantage; whilst they had no direct taxes to pay, except on substantial property, such as the possession of houses above the annual value of 12*l.*, animals, vehicles, or land, or upon certain produce if exported; but all these charges were comparatively light. The Reports called for by Mr. Eyre abundantly proved that the peasantry largely possessed horses and other animals, carts and lands; and they further showed that they generally managed to depasture their animals, free of cost, upon the lands of the larger proprietors; and that where they bought or rented one acre of land they occupied and cultivated three or four more, and, in many cases, actually sub-let lands which in no way belonged to themselves. They were equally ready to evade the taxes, and very often succeeded.

It will thus be seen that Dr. Underhill's letter, from first to last, was written without a knowledge of facts. No one will impute to that gentleman a deliberate intention to mislead the Colonial Office, but it is impossible to deny that he allowed himself to be made the tool of such designing men as Gordon and others. All the misery that sowed itself broadcast over the land was due solely to the ignorance, idleness, vice, superstition and crime which so universally prevailed. The chief cause of all this evil was undoubtedly the total want of parental control and proper discipline over children, the absence of any suitable early training, and the constant presence of evil example and influence.

Since emancipation, vast sums had been expended in schools, and in affording religious instruction by different religious denominations. Great exertions had been made by able, zealous, and good men; but it must be confessed that all—if not a lamentable failure so far as general results were concerned—had, up to the period of the insurrection of 1865, miserably fallen short of what might reasonably have been hoped for. The people were more idle, more immoral, more wanting in anything like principle, and more vicious than at the time of emancipation; and thus the labours, the sacrifices, and the expenditure of seven-and-twenty years had been comparatively thrown away. The records of the Courts of Justice, and the state of the gaols throughout the Colony, amply testified to this unsatisfactory result.

To sum up the results of the inquiry in consequence of Dr. Underhill's letter in a few words, it may be noted that idleness and vice, combined with the infamous falsehoods propagated by designing agitators, were the ruling causes of the penury, nakedness, and distress.

Since emancipation, the negro, so far as he himself is concerned, has permitted his offspring to grow up neglected in mind, neglected in body, neglected as to education, neglected as to religion, neglected as to all moral principles and treatment, neglected in everything, in fact, and wilfully given up to moral and spiritual ruin and destruction. The transition from slavery to unlimited freedom was too sudden. Experience was wanting in so momentous a matter; and hence the great experiment, on which the whole world looked with expectant gaze, has proved a failure, involving alike in its ruin planter and peasant, European and Creole. The statesman who can point out the method by which the peasantry of Jamaica may be brought into habits of honest industry will deserve well of his country; for with all the advantages the island affords, there is no excuse for petty theft, or cause for destitution of any kind or degree, save such as are inherent in the dispensation of Providence.

The seditious teachings and preachings of Mr. G. W. Gordon, and of others acting under his immediate directions, had produced a lamentable amount of discontent of the most dangerous kind, when Dr. Underhill's pernicious and most unwarranted letter (as has been conclusively proved) arrived in the island, and was immediately seized hold upon by Gordon and others to further their own infamous designs.

Of the effect of this letter, no better illustration could be given than an extract from a speech made by the Rev. S. Holt (a black man) at Montego Bay, when addressing a large assemblage of people there. He said :—

"We all feel the hardship of the times, but did not know the cause of it. Sometimes we go to bed, and in the night we hear a rumbling, but we turn ourselves and do not know what the rumbling is. In the morning one man meets another, and he asks, did you feel the earthquake last night? then we know what was the rumbling. Just so we all felt the hardship of the times, but did not know what was the cause. We did not know what the rumbling was until every one asked, have you read Dr. Underhill's letter? then we know what all the disturbance was, and the rumbling, that bring us here to-day."

Some of the papers reporting this meeting, say: "We confess we are unable to do justice to this speaker in our report. His was the speech of the day; and such was the effect upon those whom he addressed, that he was cheered for some time after he had left off speaking."

It was at this meeting also that Mr. Henderson, a Baptist preacher, said: "If estates cannot give more, the people will have to *get possession of the ' back lands,' and endeavour to improve their circumstances."* The Report of the Royal Commission will show the views entertained by the black population with regard to these *" back lands,"* and that it also was a topic relative to which the greatest excitement existed.

CHAPTER VIII.

THE first fruits of Dr. Underhill's letter were shown by a petition addressed to her Majesty, purporting to be a statement of the distress and grievances under which the writers, "certain poor people" (as they called themselves) of St. Ann's, considered they laboured. These deluded people, worked upon by designing demagogues, no doubt fully believed that her Majesty's Government would directly contribute to their pecuniary relief. The reply of her Majesty was to the effect that the prosperity of the labouring classes depended in Jamaica, and in other countries, upon their working for wages, "not uncertainly or capriciously, but steadily and continuously," and warned the petitioners against placing any reliance in schemes suggested to them by designing persons.

This reply was declared to be "a lie." The petitioners were taught to believe that it had never emanated from the Queen, but was the work of Governor Eyre himself, who had never forwarded their petition to its proper destination.

Almost immediately after this petition a meeting was held at Kingston, at which G. W. Gordon presided; and amongst the resolutions then passed the following will be found:—"This meeting calls upon all the descendants of Africa, in every parish throughout the island, to form themselves into societies, and hold public meetings, and co-operate for the purpose of setting forth their grievances."

The consequences of these meetings were that others were convened all over the island, for the purpose of convincing the negroes that they were being trampled upon and defrauded. Mr. Eyre considered that it would be a great public advantage to make generally known the very just sentiments expressed, and the excellent advice given, in the reply of the Queen to the "starving people of St. Ann's," and he therefore directed it to be published in the 'Government Gazette' and in the local newspapers, in the hope of allaying the irritation and correcting the misrepresentations which had originated in consequence of Dr. Underhill's letter.

This proceeding was entirely approved of by Mr. Cardwell, in a despatch dated August 4th, 1865. It was subsequently considered, both by Mr. Eyre and his Executive Committee, that, as there were so many districts in which the newspapers were not seen, it would be better to print the reply in the form of handbills, and have it distributed and posted in all parts of the Colony. This was accordingly done, and 50,000 copies were thus circulated by means of the custodes,

the justices, the ministers of religion of all denominations, the inspectors of police, and other persons.
There were only a few refusals to circulate the reply,
and they all emanated from the parish of St. James, one
of the three districts where disaffection was currently
reported to exist, and in which it was thought prudent
to take precautionary measures to guard against any
possible aggressions.

It is quite clear that if men of any education, residing
amongst an ignorant, debased, and excitable population, took upon themselves to endorse and reiterate
assertions such as those in Dr. Underhill's letter, to
the effect that the people were starving, ragged, or
naked ; that their addiction to thieving was the result
of extreme poverty ; that all their troubles arose from
taxation being too heavy ; that such taxation was
unjust upon the coloured population ; that they were
refused just tribunals, and denied all political rights—
that such persons did their best not only to make the
labourer discontented, but stimulated sedition and
resistance to the laws and constituted authorities.
Moreover, it must be borne in mind the state of agitation that prevailed.

In the month of July, 1865, an insurrection was
anticipated. To use the words of Professor Tyndall,
in his admirable letter to the Jamaica Committee,*
"the colony then resembled the dried grass of a

* See Appendix marked B.

prairie, ready to be set on fire from beginning to end by a spark of successful insurrection." Governor Eyre received from all parts of the island reports of the most startling description ; reports, in fact, precisely similar to those received by the English Government immediately prior to the suspension of the Habeas Corpus Act in Ireland. Illegal drillings were reported all over the country ; seditious meetings, under the immediate control of some of the worst and most unprincipled agitators, were being held ; negroes were being enlisted ; and arms and ammunition were being collected and concealed in many of the disaffected districts.

But lest any doubt be thrown upon these statements, it may here be mentioned that in July and August of 1865 Mr. Eyre wrote to the Colonial Office, expressing his belief that an insurrection would, before long, take place in the island, and added, moreover, in one despatch, that it was his " firm conviction that the day will come when Jamaica will become little better than a second Hayti."

That he had justifiable grounds for arriving at these conclusions the following evidence will testify. Mr. Salmon, the Custos of St. Elizabeth, and President of the Legislative Council, wrote, on July the 22nd : " I think it my duty to inform your Excellency that the minds of many persons in this parish are distressed by rumours of intended disturbances by the negroes.

Among these, the resisting the payment of taxes, and the appropriation of lands to their own use, are said to be their every-day consideration. . . . It appears to me quite necessary that a strong hand should at once arrest a spirit now abroad, and which requires to be compelled to fear the law, and respect the rights and security of the community. The despatch from Mr. Cardwell, in reply to the St. Ann's Memorial to the Queen, is represented here as a false make-up."

Mr. Hudson, magistrate of Spring Vale, on the 20th July, says:—"I think it incumbent on me to inform you of reports of a serious nature which are in circulation in my neighbourhood. For the past few weeks there have been rumours of a rebellion among the peasantry, but I did not attach any importance to them, but conceived they originated from want of understanding the causes of the recent meetings held in this and other adjacent parishes, until lately I have been led, by sufficient information, to believe they are more than passing reports, and which require some notice. It appears that there is an organized plot among the people in this vicinity for a rebellion about the early part of August ensuing. I do not think it would be wise to treat these rumours merely as idle tales."

Mr. Greaves, a magistrate living in the Strype Savannah, almost entirely the property of small settlers, gave information that several of the small proprietors in his neighbourhood had let him know that they were fully aware that on the first day of August a large body of negroes from the neighbourhood, assisted by others from all parts of the country, had determined on proceeding to Black River, accompanied by their wives and the women of the neighbourhood, and that the purpose was, that the women should take anything they required from the stores. The people alleged that they had been informed that the Queen had sent a large sum of money to be laid out in the purchase of lands to be divided among them. They also said that they had been told they were to be made slaves again.

On the 24th July, Mr. Raines Smith, senior member of the Executive Committee, from November, 1860, up to March, 1863, writes :—" I wished, the other day, to put you in possession of information which Dr. M'Catty had, the day previous, communicated to me, which was that his dispenser had received a letter from St. James, in which allusion was made to 'a great thing which was to be done in St. James in August.' There is undoubtedly a spirit of disaffection abroad, and the remarks dropped here and there lead to the conviction that the people are ripe for mischief." Writing subsequently to Governor Eyre, Mr. Smith says:— " Considerable excitement has, for some time, existed in this parish, in consequence of rumours of a rising of the peasantry in this and some other parishes of the country, to such an extent that many families have fled from their homes seeking safety."

Mr. Vickers, Custos of Westmoreland, writes :—
"Considerable alarm prevails amongst the gentlemen residing near the confines of this parish, from the serious reports which daily reach them from the adjacent parish. This has been shown by the application made to the merchants of Savannah-la-Mar for gunpowder for the purpose of self-defence."

Mr. Manley, justice of the peace, writes on the 27th July :—

"I deem it my duty, as the only resident justice of the peace in the New Savanna neighbourhood, to bring to your honour's notice certain rumours that have come to my knowledge, to confirm what passed on Friday last at Black River as to the intended rebellious rising among certain indisposed parties in this parish. From what I can learn, the focus will be the parish of St. James, extending to this quarter, met and supported by those from the Holland and Y. S. districts. If there are any disposable public arms in Black River, I would (if your honour should so consider it requisite) request an order for such a supply as could be spared, so that I might, as a somewhat protection for property here, place them in the hands of such parties as might be trusted. I send this by our head constable, Adam Smith, who will better and more fully explain than I can write."

The statement of Adam Smith was as follows :—

Adam Smith's Statement.

"July 28, 1865.

" Adam Smith, head rural constable, New Savanna district, says, the constant conversation in the New Savanna neighbourhood is, that the St. James' and Westmoreland people are to meet some company from St. Elizabeth, and that they are coming to burn down the gentlemen's estates and houses, as they can't get anything to do ; that they sent word to Dr. M'Catty's dispenser (who is a Lucea black man) to come away from St. Elizabeth and join them, and that as they liked Dr. M'Catty, and did not wish to injure him, he must go away. A negro on Y. S. Estate Bridge, told William Stewart, a rural constable, that as soon ' as August come, they would know what to do with him, and his badge and his staff; that the buckras had gun, and the negro mascheat and fire-stick.' Stewart also says the people have constant night meetings in the Y. S. and Holland district. He, Stewart, has constantly heard in the market, and people have told him, that they will have a war ; they have determined on it. He inquired of Smith what the constables were to do. Private Mackenzie, of the police at Black River, told me this morning that a man told him that when the war commenced he was the first man he would kill in August."

Space prevents the possibility of quoting further evidence to show the state the island was in four months before the insurrection actually broke out. H. M. Ships 'Bulldog' and 'Cadmus,' and the gunboats at the disposal of the Commodore commanding the station, were sent to cruise round the island, and with orders to land men at any moment they might be required; the European inhabitants, conscious of impending danger, commenced arming themselves and discussing the best course to adopt for their mutual preservation; and Mr. Eyre, with the consciousness of what previous negro insurrections had been like, with Hayti in close proximity, and with a mere handful of troops scattered in isolated bodies over an immense tract of mountainous country, difficult to be communicated with, had to ponder in his own mind the best course to pursue for the general safety of the entire colony.

It was at this critical period that Mr. Gordon's evil influence and system of agitation now began to manifest themselves. There is abundant evidence that, during the months of July and August, he travelled round the island holding meetings and stirring up sedition wherever he could. It is sworn that in the parish of Vere he told the excited audience that surrounded him " to do as the Haytians had done." The Custos of Trelawney reports that, in August, Mr. Gordon obtained an opportunity of addressing the congregation of the Baptist Chapel in Falmouth; but " in consequence of the seditious advice and inflammatory language indulged in by him, he was stopped in his harangue, and was prevented by the Rev. Mr. Lea (the minister attached to the chapel) from continuing his improper course," and that he pursued the same system "in the Presbyterian Kirk at Green Island, where he was also, for the like reason, checked and compelled to discontinue his address."

Mr. Trench, Inspector of Revenues, met Gordon during the months of July and August, travelling in different parishes, and learnt from himself that he had been addressing the people. Mr. Trench remarks:— "From the character of the resolutions passed at these meetings, I have little doubt that sedition was abundantly inculcated in the minds of the people by the inflammatory harangues of Mr. Gordon and others who addressed them, for indeed there was no occasion or subject upon which Mr. Gordon addressed an audience that he did not level the most scurrilous invective against all authority, whether ecclesiastical or official."

Just about the time the Government were expecting an outbreak near Black River, Mr. Gordon was attempting to purchase a Confederate schooner, with arms and ammunition, for the purpose, as stated by Lieutenant Edenborough, the Commander of the schooner, of landing Haytians, arms, and ammunition at Black River, and Mr. Gordon spoke of "a new West Indian Republic."

Lieutenant Edenborough was prepared to swear as to his identity, and, even whilst the Royal Commission was sitting, volunteered to leave England and go to Jamaica, at great personal inconvenience, for the purpose of giving evidence.*

The following important documents are reprinted from the Blue Book, but no reference whatever is made to them in the Report of the Royal Commissioners :—

" The Right Honourable Edward Cardwell to Governor Eyre.

"Downing Street, Dec. 16, 1865.

"SIR,

"I transmit to you, for your information, the copy of a letter from Mr. H. B. Edenborough, late Lieutenant in the Confederate States Navy, communicating the substance of a conversation which he had with the late G. W. Gordon, in June last.

"I have, &c.,

"(Signed)   EDWARD CARDWELL.

" Governor Eyre, &c."

---

* Assuming for a moment that Lieutenant Edenborough was mistaken as to the identity of Gordon, the ugly fact still remains, that some one endeavoured to enter into negotiations with the Confederate officer to land arms, stores, &c., at Black River, thereby showing that there were other ringleaders of some weight and influence engaged in the conspiracy to turn the island into a second Hayti.

" *Lieutenant Edenborough to Mr. Secretary Cardwell.*[*]

" 6, Sheffield Gardens, Kensington, W.,
" Tuesday, Dec. 12, 1865.

" SIR,

" The evidence to which I referred in my letter to you of the 29th ult., connecting certain Haytian negroes with the rebel Gordon, and which you desire I should furnish you with, is that in June last, at Kingston, Jamaica, for a few days having landed from a vessel, the property of the Confederate States of America, which remained in the offing ; whilst in Kingston I was called upon by Gordon, who said he

* The above communication was sent direct to the Secretary of State for the Colonies, and forwarded by him officially to the Governor of Jamaica (Sir H. Storkes), but no effort was made by the home authorities to obtain further details from Lieut. Edenborough. He was not sent out to Jamaica to give evidence, as he ought to have been, nor did the Government direct the Royal Commissioners before leaving England to take his evidence, *then easily attainable.* When the official communication of Lieut. Edenborough was received in the colony, through the Secretary of State for the Colonies, and it was known that a Commission of Inquiry was about to sit in Jamaica, the Executive Committee gave directions for Lieutenant Edenborough to be sent for, as *he had volunteered to come.* Unfortunately, the instructions were sent to a gentleman in England who was himself about to return to Jamaica, and who had actually sailed from England before the instructions reached it; consequently Lieutenant Edenborough was not obtained, and when the miscarriage of the instructions was known in the colony, it was then *too late* to send again so as to have obtained him before the Commission broke up. It was most certainly the duty of the Home Government who had him in England, and were in communication with him, to have exhausted the subject, or to have sent him out to Jamaica to be examined by the Royal Commission.

was connected with the Government of the island. He stated he understood it was my desire to dispose of the vessel and armament, the war being concluded, and said he wished to purchase the arms on board and the vessel, a beautiful clipper schooner, if possible. The arms he wished to purchase consisted of breech-loading rifles, nine shooting pistols, hand grenades, small torpedoes, and whatever accoutrements, fixed ammunition, and gunpowder there might be on board. He wished them to be landed on the south side of the island, in the neighbourhood of ' Black River.' He expressed himself as a strong sympathiser with the Confederate States in their struggle for independence.

" On learning that I intended sending the crew of the schooner to England, on board a vessel then lying in Anotto Bay, on the north side, he proposed to charter the vessel for a voyage to the island of Great Inagua, and back, there to receive on board a certain refugee Haytian general, and one or two others, and to touch at St. Nicholas Mole, Hayti, for another, on the return voyage ; a quantity of arms and powder, which he stated had arrived at Inagua, from the United States, were also to be brought down to Jamaica, and landed in the neighbourhood of Black River.

" He was accompanied at the time by a bright mulatto, whom he introduced to me as a ' General,' and whom I frequently saw afterwards in Kingston, where he resides. He referred me to a mercantile house of credit in Kingston, who would become the purchaser of the vessel and armament, or the voyage to Inagua should be made, both of which I declined.

"I was then under the impression he was connected with the Dominicans against Spain, as, in his conversation, he and his Haytian friend inquired the practicability of converting ordinary small boats into torpedo rams against war-vessels blockading ports, &c. I imagined then he referred to the Spanish squadron blockading the coast of San Domingo, and that he was in conjunction with certain Haytians, organising an expedition in the cause of San Domingo at Black River.   He spoke of a 'New West India Republic.'

"When the late news from Jamaica arrived, connecting him with the insurrection, I deemed it my duty to make you acquainted with these facts before leaving England, and regretting that absence prevented my placing myself and crew at the disposal of Governor Eyre.

"I have, &c.,

"(Signed)   HENRY B. EDENBOROUGH,

"*Lieutenant late Confederate States Navy.*

"The Right Hon. Edward Cardwell,
    "Colonial Secretary."

"*Extract from Log of Confederate States' Schooner 'Happy-go-Lucky.'*

"*May* 31.— *   *   *   *   At Port Paix, Haiti. The cruise being at an end, disarmed the schooner

by stowing the Blakeley gun in her hold, and sailed
for Jamaica to arrange a passage to England for the
crew.

*   *   *   *   *   *

"*June 7.*—Off Port Royal. Boarded by pilot, who
took me ashore and advised anchoring schooner under
lee of Lime Key. I took lodgings in the town of
Kingston, and made inquiries as to vessels bound to
any English port. Heard of one loading at Anotto
Bay. A negro boy brought a note to say that a
gentleman desired to see me at Groome's Dining
Rooms ; went there and found ' the gentleman ' to be a
swell mulatto, who introduced himself as the Honourable Mr. Gordon, and stated that he was connected
with Government, was a strong Confederate, and had
been interested in blockade-running operations with
Galveston. With Gordon was a dark mulatto, introduced as ' my friend, General Profet, of Haiti, a gallant
soldier, brave as a lion.' Gordon said that, hearing I
had an armed schooner for sale, he had sent for me to
propose an arrangement which he thought would be
satisfactory to me, both as to the arms and the schooner,
which he would either buy or charter, but that he must
not appear in the transaction, owing to his connection
with Government. He inquired what arms were on
board, and said he supposed there was a lot of ·rifles.
I told him that there were not many firearms, but that
there was powder, fixed ammunition, and cutlasses.

Gordon expressed a great desire to arrange for the purchase of the arms and ammunition, for which a high price would be given; that he would guarantee the payment, and referred to a mercantile firm in Kingston as to his responsibility. He proposed that the arms and ammunition should be delivered at Black River; said he would provide a pilot to take the schooner from her anchorage at Lime Key by the inside passage, as her draft of water was light; that a person should meet her, and that she need not anchor, as the arms would be put into a boat which should be sent off, so there could be no difficulty. Gordon and Profet asked many questions as to the use of torpedoes, and particularly if they could be used in ordinary ships' boats, not propelled by steam, but row-boats. Gordon hearing that the crew were about to be shipped for England, inquired if there were any Americans among them who would take service where they would be well paid. He said that if the sale of arms was carried out, he would charter the schooner to proceed to Magna to take on board a cargo of arms and ammunition from the United States, to be delivered at Black River. I said I would think it over. The next day I saw Gordon again, and declined both proposals, as I was very desirous to get back to England at once. I thought at the time that the proposal was connected with the Haitian movement, but on asking General Profet if Soulouque was at the back of it, he replied, ' Oh no ; he is a damned old fool.'

"*June* 10.—Went off to the schooner, brought her in, and anchored here in Port Royal Harbour, alongside H. M. S. 'Aboukir.' Went on board and reported myself to the Commodore. Crossed the island to Anotto Bay, and secured passage in the 'Jane Doul,' loading for London.

"*June* 15.—Took the schooner round to Anotto Bay.

"*June* 26.—Shipped the men on board the 'Jane Doul.'

"*June* 29.—Schooner sailed for Cuba.

"*July* 5.—Chased by brigantine showing Yankee colours off the 'Grand Cayman.' Set fire to schooner, abandoned her, and landed in the boat on 'Grand Cayman.' Obtained passage to Aspinwall in small coasting schooner. Sailed for Jamaica.

"*July* 31.—Sailed from Anotto Bay for London."

The Parliamentary Blue Books contain numerous papers, showing the connexion existing between Mr. Gordon and other conspirators, evidencing that all were engaged in combination to madden the people and bring about a rebellion.

One of them is sworn to have stated in August that he " could swear that in less than five years there would not be a white man in Jamaica; that the black men would not hurt the white ladies, but have them as their wives, and just do with them as they did in Hayti;" and subsequently to the rebellion the same man is sworn to have stated that the blacks "took the wrong way to do it; they should have set the fire-stick;" that they were " damned fools for attempting to destroy the white and coloured people in the way they were doing; the better way would be for them to agree throughout the island, and in one night massacre them ; that the blacks should go to each estate in parties, when they might easily murder them all ;" and another individual states that he was writing editorial articles in his paper, " to second the noble exertions of the Vere people. What I desire is to shield you and them from the charge of anarchy and tumult that in a short time must follow these powerful demonstrations." Amongst papers found were lists of names of about 120 persons in Vere, and the lists were headed—" Names of persons enlisted for the volunteers." These had no connexion with any volunteers enrolled by or known to the Government. Similar lists of persons in St. Thomas-in-the-East were found amongst Mr. Gordon's papers.

There is evidence to show that before the outbreak in St. Thomas-in-the-East many captains were appointed, and 50 men told off to each, who administered oaths to them, and drilled them.

Such was the dangerous state of affairs, when the following proclamation was placarded about the parishes of St. Ann's and St. Thomas-in-the-East. This proclamation was traced to have emanated from G. W. Gordon.

" State of the Island.

" People of St. Ann's.

" Poor people of St. Ann's.

" Starving people of St. Ann's.

" Naked people of St. Ann's.

" You who have no sugar estates to work on, nor can find other employment, we call on you to come forth; even if you be naked, come forth, and protest against the unjust representations made against you by Mr. Governor Eyre and his band of custodes. You don't require custodes to tell your woes; but you want men free of Government influence; you want honest men; you want men with a sense of right and wrong, and who can appreciate you. Call on your ministers to reveal your true condition, and then call on heaven to witness, and have mercy.

" People of St. Thomas-in-the-East, you have been ground down too long already. Shake off your sloth, and speak like honourable and free men at your meeting. Let not a crafty jesuitical priesthood deceive you. Prepare for your duty. Remember the destitution in the midst of your families, and your forlorn condition. The Government have taxed you to defend your own rights against the enormities of an unscrupulous and oppressive foreigner—Mr. Custos Ketelhodt.* You

* Baron Ketelhodt was one of the first singled out for massacre at the Court House.

feel this. It is no wonder you do. You have been dared in this provoking act, and it is sufficient to extinguish your long patience. This is not the time when such deeds should be perpetrated; but as they have been, it is your duty to speak out, and to act too! We advise you to be up and doing; and to maintain your cause, you must be united in your efforts. The causes of your distress are many, and now is your time to review them. Your custos, we learn, read at the last vestry the despatch from Mr. Cardwell, which he seemed to think should quiet you. But how can men with a sense of wrong in their bosoms be content to be quiet under such a reproachful despatch?

"Remember that 'he only is free whom the truth makes free.' You are no longer slaves, but free men. Then, as free men, act your part at the meeting. If the conduct of the custos in wishing the despatch to silence you be not an act of imprudence, it certainly is an attempt to stifle your free expression of opinions. Will you suffer this? Are you so short-sighted that you cannot discern the occult designs of Mr. Custos Ketelhodt? Do you see how, at every Vestry, he puts off the cause of the poor until the board breaks up, and nothing is done for them? Do you remember how he has kept the small-pox money, and otherwise mis-distributed it, so that many of the people died in want and misery, while he withheld the relief? How that he gave the money to his own friends, and kept it himself, instead of distributing it to the doctors and ministers of religion for the poor ? Do you perceive how he shields Messrs. Herschel and Cooke* in all their improper acts? You do know how deaf he is on some occasions and how quick of hearing on others. Do you remember his attempting tyrannical proceedings at the elections? But can you and the inhabitants of St. Thomas-in-the-East longer bear to be afflicted by this enemy to your peace ; a Custos whose feelings are foreign to yours? Do your duty at the meeting to be held. Try to help yourselves, and heaven will help you.

" More anon !"

The publication of this incendiary document, coupled with warnings, official and anonymous, from all parts of the colony, put Governor Eyre somewhat on his guard, though he was scarcely prepared for the terrible blow dealt by the rebels on the 11th October.

---

* Messrs. Herschel and Cooke were also amongst the first murdered by the infuriated negroes. Of the former Gordon was heard to say, just prior to the outbreak, " That fellow Herschel talks a great deal too much, and *ought to have his tongue cut out*," which atrocity was actually perpetrated upon the unfortunate gentleman.

CHAPTER IX.

ON the morning of Wednesday, the 11th October, Mr. Eyre received a letter at Spanish Town from the Baron von Ketelhodt, Custos of St. Thomas-in-the-East, written the previous evening from Morant Bay, to inform him that serious disturbances were apprehended, and to request that troops might be sent. The circumstances stated in the Baron's letter were to the effect that, on Saturday the 7th October, whilst a black man was being brought up for trial before the justices, a large number of the peasantry, armed with bludgeons, and preceded by a band of music, came into the town, and, leaving the music at a little distance, surrounded the Court-house, openly expressing their determination to rescue the man about to be tried, if convicted. One of the party having created a considerable disturbance in the Court-house, was ordered into custody, whereupon the mob rushed in, rescued the prisoner, and maltreated the policeman in attendance. No further injury appears to have been done at this time, and the magistrates seem to have thought so little of the occurrence that no steps were taken to communicate with the Executive.

On Monday, the 9th October, the justices issued a warrant for the apprehension of twenty-eight of the principal persons concerned in the disturbance of Saturday, and confided it to six policemen for execution. Upon the arrival of the police at the settlement where the parties lived (called "Stoney Gut," and about three or four miles from Morant Bay), a shell was blown, and the negroes collected in large numbers, armed with guns, cutlasses, pikes, and bayonets. They caught and ill-treated three of the policemen, putting them in handcuffs and administering to them an oath upon a Bible, which they had ready, binding them to desert the whites and join their (that is, the black) party.

Governor Eyre lost no time, on receiving the Baron von Ketelhodt's letter. He immediately sent for the Executive Committee, and, after a hurried consultation with them and with the Attorney-General, an express was sent over to Kingston, requesting the General commanding her Majesty's troops to get ready 100 men for immediate embarkation, and an express was also sent off to Captain De Horsey, senior naval officer at Port Royal, to request that if possible a man-of-war might at once be sent up to Kingston, to receive troops and take them to their destination. Captain De Horsey at once got ready his own ship, the 'Wolverine,' and in the course of eight hours from the time the news was first received by Mr. Eyre, the troops were on their road.   Unfortunately, in the meanwhile, an insurrection had broken out, and a bloody massacre had taken place.

In consequence of the riotous behaviour of the black people from Stoney Gut and neighbourhood on the preceding Saturday an outbreak of some kind was anticipated at the vestry meeting at Morant Bay on the Wednesday, and every gentleman accordingly went down to the place well armed ; but instead of taking their weapons of defence with them into the Court-house, they foolishly left them at different houses in the Bay.   The Volunteers had also been ordered out by the Custos, and were marched down to the Court, house, having had ten rounds of ammunition served out to each man.

At the vestry everything went on quietly till about three o'clock, the only peculiarity noticeable being the absence of Mr. G. W. Gordon, whose duty it was to be present, and who invariably made it a rule never to absent himself from any of the meetings.

The ominous warnings and threats of the negroes to many of those in the Court-house, and also to the Volunteers when marching into Morant Bay, created great uneasiness in the mind of Captain Hitchins, and he objected to the Volunteers under his command leaving their posts even for a minute to get refreshment.   His uneasiness was not without cause, for suddenly Mr. Arthur Cooke (one of the rector's sons) came galloping at full speed across the parade to the Court-house, shouting out, "They are coming! they are coming! the rebels are coming in hundreds!—they are upon you!" Serjeant McGowan at once ordered the bugler to sound the alarm, and the Volunteers stood firm at their posts, fully prepared for any emergency. Prior to this the rebels had attacked and sacked the police-station, and seized upon all the arms and ammunition. Seeing the Volunteers drawn up in front of the Court-house, the negroes, to the number of 700, armed with muskets and fixed bayonets, cutlasses, fish-spears, long poles with bill-hooks securely attached to them, stones, bottles, &c., led by a negro carrying a pistol in his hand, advanced across the court-yard, with horns and shells blowing, and with drums beating.

The members of the vestry, in the meanwhile, had rushed to the door of the building, and Baron von Ketelhodt, the Custos, addressed the rebels, beseeching them to keep the peace. The reply was, " We want no peace," accompanied with a shower of stones and bottles. Captain Hitchins, Serjeant McGowan, and several others were severely hurt, and their hands and faces covered with blood. One of the Volunteers (James Ross) was struck down senseless, one of his eyes being cut out and hanging down his cheek. He was carried to one of the lower rooms of the Court-house, where he died. Still the Custos withheld the reading of the Riot Act, and waved a white handkerchief to show that he wanted peace. This was met with shouts of derision, and the negroes at once commenced striking at the weapons of the Volunteers, yelling out the most diabolical threats, and hurling stones and brickbats at the windows of the Court-house. At last the Riot Act was read, and, many of the volunteers being seriously injured, the order was given to fire. Several of the rebels fell at the first volley; but instead of being in any way deterred by the deaths of their comrades, they immediately, having been reinforced by some 500 more negroes, armed with guns and all kinds of dangerous weapons, set upon the small body of Volunteers and completely overpowered them. After a short but gallant resistance, the poor fellows were compelled to retreat into the Court-house, where they were fired into by the rebels, who now completely surrounded the building. A short consultation was held by the negroes, when they appeared to have quickly determined as to their next mode of tactics. A strong westerly wind blowing at the time, the building, constructed of the most inflammable matter, was set on fire at the western side. In the meanwhile, bodies of rebels were stationed so as to form a regular cordon around the town, and especially in the vicinity of the burning building, to murder every one who attempted to escape.

There were then in the Court-house the Baron von Ketelhodt and his son, several magistrates, Captain Hitchins, and other officers and men of the Volunteers who had not been killed, the rector with his three sons, the coroner and clerk of the vestry, Dr. Major, Dr. Gerrard, and other gentlemen.

Shots were now fired into the windows, and Captain Hitchins was dangerously wounded; notwithstanding he continued to give his orders with extraordinary coolness, and would not permit the doctors to attend to him whilst others were in want of assistance. The Court-house by this time was one mass of flame, and the molten lead was running from the burning roof into the interior upon the unfortunate victims. A few minutes more and it was clear that the roof would fall in and destroy them all. In these dreadful moments a consultation was held, the voices of the poor creatures being scarcely audible amidst the shrieks of the delighted fiends outside and the roar of the flames. By some it was proposed they should jump out of a back window, one by one; but this was objected to, on the ground that they would each be shot down as they appeared. It was finally determined that the front door should be suddenly thrown open, and a rush made down the steps for the school-house, where Mr. Georges, Mr. Price, and others had already taken refuge. All immediately consented, and, after removing the forms, tables, chairs, &c., with which they had barricaded the door to prevent the rebels entering, they made the movement so suddenly that the negroes were taken completely by surprise, and the poor creatures succeeded in reaching the school-house in safety. They had been in their new asylum but a minute or two, when the roof of the Court-house fell in with a terrific crash.

They had not been long in their fresh place of refuge before it was also set on fire. In these awful moments their courage never forsook them for a moment. The Rev. Mr. Herschel, who had been praying alone for some time, proposed that they should all unite in prayer. They at once agreed, and every one knelt down; before, however, Mr. Herschel had time to commence, several shots were fired through the jalousies by the rebels, and the Baron Von Ketelhodt, the Hon. W. P. Georges, and the coroner, Mr. McPherson, were severely wounded. A minute or two more and part of the burning roof fell in upon them, and the heat became so intense that they were compelled to leave the house, and take refuge behind the parapet wall at the back, where the shots were flying in all directions. Two or three of them were killed by bullets, and thus saved a more horrible death.

Now commenced those fearful and bloody acts which were scarcely paralleled by the massacre at Cawnpore. The cries for mercy, the savage yells of the women hounding on the men as each new victim was discovered, and the heavy thuds of the cutlasses on the bodies of the butchered, were heard even above the rattle of the musketry and the hissing of the devouring flames. The Baron Von Ketelhodt, the Rev. Mr. Herschel, and

Lieut. Hall were beaten to death with sticks. Capt. Hitchins, faint from loss of blood, owing to his numerous wounds, and utterly unable to resist, was slowly hacked to death by a negro with a cutlass, who sat down to his diabolical work as coolly and as slowly as if he had been chopping wood. The Rev. Mr. Herschel's tongue was cut out, and the fingers of the Baron Von Ketelhodt severed from his hands.

Night closing in alone put an end to this horrible massacre, and then, the negroes drunk with blood and mad with excitement, marched off in small parties in various directions to urge on other negroes to attack the plantations, and to carry the flame of insurrection throughout the colony. All the principal inhabitants of the district were killed,* and the entire Volunteer force (with the exception of two or three who escaped with frightful wounds, being left for dead by the rebels), consisting of twenty-two officers and men, nobly died at their posts gallantly doing their duty.*

The instant Governor Eyre received the news of this terrible calamity, he determined at once to proceed to the scene of action himself. In concert with General O'Connor he arranged that more men should without a moment's loss of time be sent off to Morant Bay, while a company of white troops from Newcastle were ordered to proceed along the line of the Blue

* Not one word of pity for these poor victims and their wives and families is ever heard from the lips of those who denounce Mr. Eyre.

Mountain Valley, to try and intercept the rebels, who were now known to be trying to force their way into the interior of the island, and were being joined by negroes from all quarters.

Great stress has been laid by a portion of the English press upon the fact, as they allege, that no lives were taken by the rebels after the first outbreak at Morant Bay on the 11th October. This, however, is not correct; Mr. Cockrayne, a bookkeeper at Sir W. Fitzherbert's, was killed at Blue Mountain estate, seven miles north-west of Morant Bay, on the morning of the 12th October ; Mr. Hire was killed, and several others left for dead, at Amity Hall, twenty miles from Morant Bay, in quite another direction (to the eastward) late at night on the 12th October. That other persons were not subsequently killed is due, not to the mercy of the rebels, but to the fact that for the most part their intended victims had escaped into the woods or cane-fields, or out to sea in canoes. Let the words of the rebels heard by Mr. Harrison of Hordley estate, the warnings given to Mr. Hinchelwood of the Mulatto River, and many other facts and statements given in the correspondence published in the Blue Books, declare what would have been the fate of the white men and ladies and children had they been got hold of.

Governor Eyre remained calm but very firm and determined. He called together his Executive Committee, and by midnight assembled his Privy Council. The result of the deliberation was, that it was considered expedient at once to declare martial law, and notices were forthwith sent out to the members of the Privy Council and members of Assembly to meet at eight A.M. next morning to hold a council of war, this being the legal formality required by the 9th Vict., cap. 35, sec. 95-98. They did meet. All the leading men in the island being assembled, came to the unanimous resolution that martial law ought to be declared forthwith all over the island. Governor Eyre positively refused to accede to these proposals, not considering such a step necessary, and not desiring to paralyse trade. Martial law was accordingly proclaimed in the county of Surrey only; and to prevent the suspension of business and other incidental inconveniences, Mr. Eyre even declared the town of Kingston exempt from its operations. On Friday, the 13th, martial law was accordingly proclaimed; and Governor Eyre, considering the magnitude of interests at stake, proceeded at once, in company with Colonel Nelson, Adjutant-General (appointed Brigadier-General by Mr. Eyre), to the scene of the disturbances.

Whilst proceeding down the harbour of Kingston they met H.M.S. 'Wolverine' from the scene of action, bringing up the ladies, gentlemen, and children who had escaped, and some few prisoners who had been captured.

It would be impossible to convey within any reasonable limits the prompt and decisive action of Governor Eyre at this critical juncture. So great was the danger of the whole of the black population rising, if the rebels were allowed to get beyond the Blue Mountain range into the interior of the island; so dreadful were the accounts of apprehended outbreaks in every district; so small was the force of military at his disposal for the protection of the entire colony, that the only surprise is that throughout that terrible period he remained so cool and collected, and was enabled to act with such consummate judgment. One single false step, one moment's hesitation, and Jamaica would have been taken from our grasp, to be reconquered only with a still more terrible loss of life, and at a price frightful to contemplate.

On the 15th October Governor Eyre reached Antonio, having completed arrangements with General Nelson just in time to save that settlement from the rebels, who were burning buildings and destroying property about twelve miles to the eastward, and were known to be intending a descent on Port Antonio. A large number of the principal inhabitants of the place had taken refuge on board the American barque the ' Reunion,' Captain Tracey, who had taken them out to sea for fear of having his vessel attacked. The joy and relief of the inhabitants at the arrival of Governor Eyre may be easily conceived. No time was lost in disembarking the troops, and by noon a strong detachment was on its way to meet the rebels, reported to be at Long Bay (twelve or fourteen miles to the eastward), and to protect the women and children and other refugees in that district, and in that of Manchioneal, to which they were to move in accordance with an arrangement concerted between Mr. Eyre and General Nelson.

By the intervention of Providence the Maroons, whose loyalty was doubtful, in consequence of their former rebellion which took upwards of twelve months to suppress, and with whom it was well known many of the rebel leaders had been tampering, happily decided to throw in their fortunes with the white people. Under the Hon. A. G. Fyfe, they did incalculable service.   They protected Bath, captured the leader of the Morant Bay rebels, Paul Bogle, hunted out other notorious ringleaders, and by their general behaviour showed how valuable their services were, and how dangerous they would have been had their sympathies been directed the other way.

The following description of this extraordinary people by the Hon. A. G. Fyfe is peculiarly interesting. Writing to Governor Eyre subsequently as to the future occupation of the Maroons, he says :—

" To employ Maroons in the occupation of military posts in the plains would at once divest them of that distinctive nationality to which they owe their somewhat mysterious power over the negro. The Maroons are 'the children of the mist' of Jamaica romance.

They have their haunted 'Namy Town' in the interior fastnesses, which they never approach; and even the white man, who, impelled by curiosity, has tried to penetrate its mysteries, has been scared by occurrences for which he has been unable to account. The sound of their wild war horns as they rush without warning and without apparent discipline to the plains, strikes terror into the heart of every one that hears it. Their charm consists in their very seclusion: bring them into every-day contact with the people, and that charm, which in effect quadruples their numbers, would be dispelled. Besides which, the Maroons have a strong aversion to be employed with troops. After the perfidy of the island to those who capitulated at the last Maroon war, they have an inherent dread of remaining long in positions in which they know they are powerless to frustrate treachery;—for the same reasons, a traditional warning is, 'Never trust yourself on the sea.'"

Having effectively disposed of the troops, by landing men on each side of the island and marching them down upon the insurgents, the wave of rebellion, which had spread with such appalling rapidity, was suddenly checked. By the celerity of their movements Governor Eyre and General Nelson got ahead of the rebellion, which, breaking out at Morant Bay, had proceeded with such speed along the south-east, east, and north-east corner of the island. By occupying Port Antonio in time, they not only saved that district from total destruction, but they met and stopped the further progress of the rebellion twelve miles east of it. They had indeed accomplished some most important results in a singularly brief space of time.

A military post was now established at Morant Bay and another at Port Antonio, whilst the centre of a line connecting the two was occupied by friendly Maroons. The greater portion of the actual rebels in arms were therefore hemmed in within the country east of this line, but the alarming reports from all other parts of the island, and the evident determination of risings in other districts, if opportunity offered, necessitated the most constant watchfulness, and caused the gravest anxiety.

On the night of Sunday, the 15th October, Governor Eyre, for the first time, got a little rest, but before daybreak he was disturbed by an express despatch from his Executive Committee at Kingston, and from the Custos and Justices, earnestly requesting him to return without a moment's delay and declare martial law in Kingston, considerable apprehension being entertained that a rising would take place in the capital, and reports being . brought that disturbances were momentarily expected at Linstead in St. Thomas-in-the-Vale, about fourteen miles from Spanish Town. Considering that his personal presence and the information and explanations he could give would do more to allay anxiety and calm apprehension than anything he could write, Mr. Eyre, leaving General Nelson to complete his military arrangements, started at once for Kingston.

During his absence General O'Connor had, in concert with the civil authorities, taken all measures and precautions in their power by increasing the number of the Volunteers, both infantry and mounted, calling out the pensioners, and making such other arrangements as were practicable.

Governor Eyre met the Custos, Mayor, and Magistrates of Kingston, and explained the exact position of affairs, and, after some trouble, succeeded in satisfying them that under existing circumstances it would not be expedient to extend martial law to Kingston. There was one very important point to be decided upon. Throughout his tour he found unmistakeable evidence that Mr. G. W. Gordon had not only been mixed up in the matter, but was himself, through his own misrepresentation and seditious language addressed to the ignorant black people, the chief cause and origin of the whole rebellion. Gordon was now in Kingston, and it became necessary to decide what action should be taken with regard to him. Having obtained a deposition on oath that certain seditious printed notices had been sent through the post-office, directed in his handwriting to Paul Bogle and others who were leaders in the rebellion, Mr. Eyre at once called upon the Custos to issue a warrant to capture him. For some little time he managed to evade arrest; but finding that, sooner or later, it was inevitable, he proceeded to the house of General O'Connor and there gave himself up.

All coincided in believing him to be the occasion of the rebellion, and that he ought to be taken, but many of the inhabitants were under considerable apprehension that his capture might lead to an immediate outbreak in Kingston itself. Mr. Eyre did not share this feeling, and knowing Gordon to be the chief instigator of the rebellion, he at once took upon himself the responsibility of his capture. In a moment of unparalleled danger, when even the name of Gordon would have been sufficient to cause a rising in any portion of the island, it was imperatively necessary that the disaffected should see that the man who was, to use Professor Tyndall's words, " the taproot from which the insurrection drew its main sustenance," could not and would not escape,

Possibly, had Mr. Eyre been a less brave and conscientious man, he might have carefully weighed and considered what the results might be to himself; but, feeling that he was doing his duty, he gave no thought to any pains or penalties that might arise in the future. Gordon was accordingly placed on board the ' Wolverine,' and taken to Morant Bay, where General Nelson had established his head-quarters.

It is a very extraordinary fact that the actual rebels

at Morant Bay did not proceed in any considerable numbers to the adjacent districts, but the people of each district rose, and committed the deeds of violence and destruction that were done within it. This fact shows how wide-spread the feeling of disaffection was, and how prepared the people of each parish were to catch the spirit and follow the example of their neighbours. It showed, too, the extreme insecurity which existed in nearly all the other parishes of Jamaica, where the same bad spirit prevailed.

Mr. Gordon having been taken to Morant Bay, he was put on shore as a prisoner on Friday evening, the 20th October.

The next day a Court-martial was sitting for trial of prisoners there, consisting partly of members of the Legislature. Brigadier-General Nelson, however, having deemed it right that Mr. Gordon should not be tried by a Court composed of persons who might be supposed to be influenced by local prejudices, adjourned that Court, and another was convened, before which, about two o'clock the same afternoon, Mr. Gordon was brought for trial.

This Court consisted of Lieutenant Brand, of Her Majesty's ship 'Onyx' (president), Lieutenant Errington, R.N., and Ensign Kelly, 4th West India Regiment (members). The charges against the prisoner were for furthering the massacre at Morant Bay, and at divers periods previously inciting and advising with certain insurgents, and thereby by his influence tending to cause the riot.

Two heads of offence were drawn up, one for high treason, the other for complicity with certain parties engaged in the rebellion, riot, and insurrection at Morant Bay.

The evidence taken consisted of documents and oral testimony.

Some of these documents were selected from the papers of Mr. Gordon by Brigadier-General Nelson, and others were statements of persons taken and sworn before magistrates, and then forwarded to Mr. Ramsay, the Provost Marshal. All these were laid before the Court by the Provost Marshal.

They consisted of—

> 1st. Statements of 21st October, separately made and sworn to by John Anderson and James Gordon, before a Justice of the Peace of St. Thomas-in-the-East. These two persons were prisoners, and were sworn and examined orally by the Court.
>
> 2nd. A statement of the 17th of October, purporting to be a dying declaration of Thomas Johnson.
>
> 3rd. A joint statement of 19th October, on oath, by W. R. Peart and J. F. Humber, made before a Justice of the Peace.
>
> 4th. A statement of 19th October, on oath, of

Charles Chevannes, at Kingston, before a Justice of the Peace.

5th. A statement of 18th October, of George Thomas, on oath.

6th. Printed placard, headed " State of the Island," above referred to.

7th. Statement of 17th October, of Elizabeth Jane Gough, sworn at Kingston. She was also orally examined by the Court.

8th. Three letters of Mr. Gordon—to Chisholm, September 11th, 1865; to E. C. Smith, October 14th, 1865; to Chisholm, June 19th, 1865.

The printed placard, headed " State of the Island," is a duplicate of that above mentioned as posted up on a tree, in August, at Morant Bay, the original draft of which was proved to have been in the handwriting of Mr. G. W. Gordon.

Five witnesses were sworn and examined for the prosecution, and one on behalf of the prisoner, and Gordon himself admitted that the circumstantial evidence was suspicious against him.

All those present at the trial, and there were several independent witnesses, deposed before the Royal Commission that the prisoner had a very fair and patient trial. He was found guilty, and sentenced to death.

After having approved and confirmed the finding of the sentence, Brigadier Nelson forwarded the proceedings of the trial to Major-General O'Connor, under cover of a despatch, dated 21st October, 1865, 8 P.M.

In this despatch he states, for the information of the Major-General, that he considered it his duty fully to approve the finding and confirm the sentence, and adds, " To-morrow being Sunday, and there existing no military reason why the sentence should not be deferred, I have preferred to delay its execution till Monday morning next, at eight o'clock." The whole proceedings of the Court were enclosed for the General's information.

These proceedings reached the General at Kingston on the morning of the 22nd October, who, after *reading them to two members of the Executive Committee,* forwarded them the same day to Governor Eyre, with a request that he would return them with as little delay as possible. These proceedings were returned to the General the same day by Governor Eyre, who wrote at the same time that he fully concurred in the justice of the sentence, and in the policy of carrying it into effect.

On the same day Governor Eyre wrote the following letter to Brigadier-General Nelson from Spanish Town, dated 6 P.M. : —

" MY DEAR BRIGADIER,

" Your report of the trial of George William Gordon has just reached me through the General, and I quite concur in the justice of the sentence, and the necessity of carrying it into effect."

This letter reached Brigadier Nelson before the execution of Mr. Gordon.

On the 23rd October, Brigadier-General Nelson sent a despatch to Major-General O'Connor, announcing the execution of Gordon at 7.10 A.M. that morning.

On the 24th October, General O'Connor transmitted, in letters to the Secretary of State for War, and to the Military Secretary at the Horse Guards, a copy of Brigadier-General Nelson's despatch reporting the trial, sentence, and execution of Gordon, and in both letters he adds, " A copy of his Excellency the Governor's letter approving the same is enclosed, *in which I fully coincide*."

A properly constituted Court having tried, passed verdict, and sentenced the prisoner, there was no necessity to have sent the proceedings to Mr. Eyre, and certainly it was not necessary for him to confirm them. The sending the proceedings, therefore, to the Governor was purely a matter of courtesy on the part of the military authorities. It is true that Mr. Eyre had the power of exercising the prerogative of mercy had he deemed it advisable, as in the case of any ordinary murderer under sentence of death ; but, for reasons which have before been given, he considered it right that the real head of the rebellion should suffer as well as his unfortunate dupes. Mr. Gordon was accordingly hanged on the ruined arch of the Court-house at Morant Bay, where the atrocious massacre of his victims took place,* and where the lives of all his personal enemies had been so horribly sacrificed.

* The evidence against Gordon will be found in detail in the Appendix, marked A.

CHAPTER X.

NOTHING can be more absurd than to compare a negro insurrection with a rebellion in England. The negroes, from being in the very lowest state of civilization, and under the influence of superstitious feelings, can never be dealt with in the same manner as might the peasantry of an English county.

To produce any adequate effect upon such a population as Jamaica, numbering as it did some 450,000 negroes and coloured people, as against about 13,000 whites, the latter being scattered amongst the former in isolated and unprotected positions, and widely separated from each other, it was of paramount importance that punishment for such serious offences as rebellion, arson, and murder should be prompt, certain, and severe. It could only be made so by the continuance of the military tribunals until all the parties captured as principals had their cases inquired into and dealt with summarily.

No doubt that within a short period from the first outbreak the rebellion was got under control; but a large number of the instigators of, and actors in it, were still at large, scattered throughout an area of between 400 and 500 square miles of mountainous and woody country.

To have withdrawn martial law, and have substituted the delay and uncertainty of civil tribunals, before the majority of the chief rebels were punished, would have done away with the impression which it was so necessary at the time to make upon the minds of the negroes throughout the island.

There is a point of some importance in connection with Gordon which has been left entirely unnoticed by writers on the subject. Long after martial law, and whilst Sir H. Storks was acting as Governor, a large number of prisoners were indicted before a grand jury (under civil jurisdiction), charged in at least seven out of eleven counts *for conspiring with G. W. Gordon and others* to commit treason, and the grand jury brought in a *true bill.* The proceedings were not carried further under this charge and finding, because the Attorney-General, of his own accord, and without consulting the Crown, chose to proceed for the lesser offence of felonious riot; and his alleged reason for doing so was, not that he doubted that the parties would be convicted of treason, but that he felt a personal unwillingness to prosecute such a large number of persons (between eighty and one hundred) for an offence (treason) which, if found guilty of, necessarily entailed a sentence of death upon all. There can be no doubt they would have been found guilty. All the proceedings connected with this matter, the indictment and finding of the grand jury, the summary of evidence and depositions, the points brought forward in the speech of the counsel for the prosecution, and the reasons given by the Attorney-General himself for not proceeding with the prosecution for treason after a true bill had been found by the grand jury, were all sent to the Secretary of State for the Colonies.

There is also a very important point in connection with the accusation made against Governor Eyre of having continued martial law, and trials, and executions by court martial longer than was necessary. Notwithstanding all the trials and executions which took place under martial law, the prisoners charged with the graver offences were not nearly exhausted. Martial law expired on the 13th November. Long after it was over, in fact in January, 1866, when Sir H. Storks was Governor, and whilst the Commission of Inquiry was actually sitting, a *large number* of prisoners were tried under civil law, and were found guilty of the graver offences committed during the rebellion. *Two were sentenced to death and were hung, and a large number* were committed and sentenced to very long terms of imprisonment. This ought to be a sufficient answer that martial law did not do more than was necessary, or was kept in force longer than it ought to have been, even if Mr. Eyre had not received daily and hourly communications from all parts of the island,

and from the most trustworthy sources, that risings were anticipated notwithstanding the terrible examples offered to the rebels.   But, moreover, the statute itself fixed the period of thirty days as the duration of martial law, and it is very questionable that even had Mr. Eyre desired it (as he did not) whether he could have curtailed that period by any act of his own ; and it is ridiculous to suppose that the Council of War, by whose authority and advice martial law had been imposed, would have concurred in terminating it before the statutory period of thirty days had expired.

A few examples need only be selected from the mass of evidence showing the grave probability of fresh outbreaks.   The following proclamation of Paul Bogle's was found, dated the day after Governor Eyre considered the insurrection got under :—

" Morant Bay, Oct. 17.

" Mr. Graham and other Gentlemen,

" It is time for us to help ourselves skin for skin. The iron bar is now broken in this parish.   The white people send a proclamation to the Governor to make war against us, which we all must put our shoulder to the wheels and pull together.   The Maroons sent the proclamation to meet them at Hayfield at once without delay—that they will put us in the way how to act. Every one of you must leave your house—take your guns ; who don't have guns take cutlasses.   Down at once !   Come over to Stony Gut, that we might march over to meet the Maroons at once without delay. Blow your shells! roule your drums! house to house; take out every man; march them down to Stony Gut; any that you find, take them in the way; take them down with their arms; war is at my black skin; war is at hand from to-day till to-morrow. Every black man must turn out at once, for the oppression is too great. The white people are now cleaning up their guns for us, which we must prepare to meet them too. Cheer, men! Cheer in heart; we looking for you a part of the night or before daybreak.

"We are, yours truly,

"(Signed)   PAUL BOGLE,   J. G. M'LAREN,
                 B. CLARKE,   P. CAMERON.

"Get a bearer to send us an answer to this, for they determine to make us slaves again. When you do come to Stony Gut or Hayfield, blow your shells, and tell what place you in from before entered.

"E. K. BAILEY."

"WALTER RAMSAY, you sure better take care of yourself how you paying money, you damn thief. I were having   at you a long time, for in a short time there will be fire, and fire enough in Spring Garden Plantation, for when I come down I not going too burn task-house alone, for I going to burn from still-house, boiling-house, and your house and self too, for I means to cool all of you St. George's fellows, for all of the solders in the camp can't cool me, for my troops are solders too. As for Spring Garden low lighten and wood stalks places are in hell fire, but we will put our life against them. I will rite George Solomon to let him know that in a short time Spring Garden will be burn down, for Ramsay is a dam thief, and yes we will do it. If you don't believe we will just show signs for it, for we are kill and can't cure."

Communication addressed to Mr. Lynch.

" I SENT to inform all gentleman in town that if we do not get justices in this October Court that we will burn down the town; and we have 1,500 man consent to raise a riot at the Court-house October the 23rd of this month, and Monday we looking out to see what trial will be, then we will commence. Lif for lif will be taken that day at the Court-house, for we do not fare, and that days of October, for we is well armidid with cutlass and gun appear and that day.

" Beside oman to helpe us 400 I sent to tell Francis Linch he better mind himself.

" October him best to setchonon whare him is, for he is a mudder to the people; but if he no what I no, that sum of the bad will be about thare to see what gone to be down in at that Courts-house, for the good will suffer for the bad that day.

" Powder we have plenty as much as to kill hold town."

Communication addressed to the Custos of Kingston.

"Beware of what you are about, beware, beware, if the hair of the head of one of those that are taken up be singed. I'll be the demagogue, and your life won't be worth a biscuit. Kelly Smith, Joseph Goldson, and Vaz, what are they to do with the riot?

"Kingston is quiet, tranquil ; do you want a whole-sale slaughter, conflagration, rapine, plunder, and wholesale destruction? If a stripe be put on Kelly Smith and Vaz you can tell the Governor that from him downwards shall be shot like a fowl, except he is going to walk or ride with a strong body guard. He ought to be shot long ago, the damn old scamp. Hell and scissors, if those men are flogged Kingston will be fired from east to west. Beware Custos; beware Custos, mind they don't make a custard of you ! Fire, fire, fire, fire, fire, fire, fire. It is true that these men are to hold their Underhill Conventional Meetings, but men like Kelly Smith, Vaz, Roach, Goldson, Harry, are not negroes of a rebellious character, nor would they excite or advise ignorant men like the lower orders of St. Thomas-ye-east barbarians to commit such barbarous and cruel deeds. They have no part or lot in the matter. You as a Custos, and a very un-popular one, you better beware or else you will be shot like a dog. Take care if these black men, who are keeping themselves respectably, be disgraced. Your blood will not be sufficient to atonement for them, they have done nothing worthy of chastisement. Revenge. Take care what you are about, take care."

On the 21st October the Custos of Clarendon reported an attempt to burn down the Court-house. The clerk of the vestry being absent, kerosine oil, together with matches and other combustibles were thrown into the building, which took fire, but was happily extinguished. At Brown's Town the most threatening language was openly indulged in, and documents seized, showing an intention of the negroes to rise in insurrection about the 2nd November, being the date when the next magisterial courts were to be held.

Writing to General O'Connor on the 28th October, Governor Eyre says :—

" In the existing state of Jamaica, with disloyalty and sedition latent everywhere, and threatening language openly used in many places, it is essential that the most prompt and decisive measures should be taken, and that the Executive should show itself not only ready to put down an outbreak should it occur, but able at once to capture and punish those who dare to make use of threatening or seditious language, thereby giving confidence to the loyal, over-awing the dis-affected, and, if possible, preventing such outbreak taking place."

On the 1st November the following letter was sent from the magistrates of Montego Bay :—

"Sir,   "Knockalva, Nov. 1, 1865.

"It having come to the knowledge of the under-signed that the negroes inhabiting the districts at the back of Kew Park, viz., Mountain Spring and Lamb's River, have been holding nightly meetings for some time past, and, moreover, have been seen in the early morning as if undergoing a drill; that conversations of a most rebellious and seditious nature have been very recently overheard, and reported to us, the magistrates in this interior, we deem it necessary, to prevent an outbreak, that a number of troops be despatched as early as possible in aid of the civil power.

"Ample accommodation can be given to the troops at Kew Park and elsewhere in this district, and it may be remarked that the population of the disaffected quarters numbers some thousands.

"Fifty stand of arms, wi·ᵗʰ were applied for yesterday, will be received this afte·_·n from Savanna la Mar, and will be used for the purpose of arming sundry Germans in Seaford Town, or other loyal subjects in this interior.

"I have, &c.,

(Signed)   "W. R. COOKE, J.P.
             "J. EDWARDS, J.P.
             "DE B. SPENCER HEAVEN, J.P."

That the first rising was not a mere local riot is conclusively proved from the fact that the wave of re-

bellion extended from Morant Bay 20 miles to the
north-west (between Arntully and Monklands) in two
and a half days, and from Morant Bay 40 miles to the
east and north-east, as far as Long Bay, in three and a
half days.   At Monklands, 17 miles (north-west) from
Morant Bay, Mr. Patterson, justice of the peace, was
obliged to fly for his life, and his place was plundered on
the 16th of October. At Mulatto River, 35 miles (north-
east) from Morant Bay, Mr. Hinchelwood, justice of
the peace, was obliged to fly for his life, and his house
was burned down on the 13th October.   Not only was
the rebellion universal throughout St. Thomas-in-the-
East (a parish which alone contained 215 square miles),
but it would have extended in a few more hours to
St. David's and Port Royal, where there were plenty of
sympathisers, but for the extraordinary energy shown
by the troops in heading it.

The number of troops in the whole island was only
1,000; of these about 500 were engaged in suppressing the rebellion and occupying the parishes of St.
Thomas-in-the-East, Portland, St. David's, and part of
Port Royal, upwards of 500 square miles in extent, *with
a population of fully* 40,000!   The other 500 troops
were employed in garrisoning and protecting Newcastle, Up-park Camp, and Kingston.   Even when
the additional troops arrived from Barbadoes and
Nassau, there were altogether only some 1,700 to
garrison and protect a country 140 miles long and 50

broad, containing an area of between 6,000 and 7,000 square miles, much of which consisted of mountain fastnesses or dense jungles, with few facilities for inter-communication.

Bearing all these circumstances in view, and considering the frightful and irretrievable ruin which must inevitably have overtaken the colony if the rebellion had been allowed to gain head or to extend itself, Mr. Eyre considered that he was fully justified in continuing martial law and trials by military tribunals, until the rebellion itself was so crushed out as to deter any attempt at a similar outbreak elsewhere.

The success which attended Governor Eyre's measures is in itself a justification of them; and to those who now, after the smoke of the battle has passed away, denounce the severity practised, it may be said, that in such a case instant and just punishment became eventual mercy, the deserved deaths of the few saving the lives of the many. What would have been said or thought of him, had he lost the colony, or occasioned the massacre of thousands, through any delay or hesitancy on his part to accept the responsibility which the emergency necessarily imposed upon him?

Nothing can be more ridiculous and absurd than to allege that there was no organization and combination on the part of the negroes. No persons in their senses can carefully go through the Parliamentary Blue Books without coming to the conclusion that the object of the rebellion was to exterminate the white population. However wild and visionary such a scheme may appear to Englishmen, it must be borne in mind that the success which attended the efforts of the Haytians against the French, and more recently of the St. Domingans against the Spaniards, afforded examples and encouragement which, from the vicinity of those republics to Jamaica, were constantly before the peasantry of that island; and those examples lost none of their force from the presence of many Haytians at Kingston living in wealth and idleness; and from the manner in which such examples were expatiated upon by designing demagogues and agitators, who, like G. W. Gordon, did not hesitate to tell the peasantry of the country "to do as the Haytians had done."

That some acts of wrong and injustice should be committed, and that in some cases the innocent may have suffered with the guilty, are incidents inseparable from the military occupation of a country in open rebellion; they could neither be foreseen nor prevented; they can only be lamented. Nor are such occurrences fairly chargeable against the authorities directing the general movements and policy, but necessarily unable to know the nature of or control all the subordinate details through such an extensive tract of country.

That the steps taken by Governor Eyre were, under God's good providence, the means of averting from

Jamaica the terrors of a general rebellion, and that they saved the lives and properties of her Majesty's subjects confided to his care, was the unanimous opinion of the whole of the intelligent and reflecting portion of the community of Jamaica ; and this opinion was fully, plainly, and deliberately expressed by the two branches of the Legislature in their legislative capacities, as well as by the ministers of the Church of England, of the Roman Catholic Church, and of the dissenting denominations ; by the custodes, magistrates, and vestrymen of parishes ; by planters, professional men, and artisans ; and by the ladies and women of the colony as a body, in the numerous and eloquent addresses expressing gratitude and thanks with which Governor Eyre was honoured.

No stronger proof could possibly be given of the full conviction of the colonists of the reality of their danger and the importance of taking steps against the recurrence of any similar risk than the fact that the Legislature of the colony voluntarily resigned into Governor Eyre's hands the functions and privileges which they had enjoyed under a system of representative institutions for upwards of two hundred years, in order to create a strong Government, and thereby better provide for securing the safety and welfare of the colony, in future.

In a previous chapter it has been noted that Mr. Eyre came into violent collision with several members of the

Legislative Assembly soon after his arrival in the island, some of the members being most bitterly hostile to him, and at last petitioning for his recall, and refusing to transact business with him. This very Assembly, and these very same gentlemen passed the highest eulogiums upon him after the suppression of the rebellion.

Governor Eyre never lost sight of the importance of effecting a change in the machinery which worked so unsatisfactorily, or rather did not work at all. Through his own influence and exertions he induced the Legislature to give up their own existence and to place all in the hands of the Crown. If he did nothing else during his four years' tenure of office, he did what no previous Governor managed to do, and conferred the greatest blessing upon the colony. He secured a power which will enable future Governors to do good and prevent evil, neither of which were possible under the old *régime*. The importance attached to this change by the Home Government may be seen in their final despatch to Mr. Eyre, dismissing him from the service —its value cannot be over-estimated.

Mr. Eyre may justly feel proud of the change he effected in the constitution. When the present troubles are almost forgotten, the blessings resulting from it will remain to future generations. Those only who have had practical experience of the working of the old West Indian Constitution can appreciate what has been effected by doing away with it in Jamaica. And yet Mr. Eyre has gained no advantage—reaped no credit from it. Other Governors will be praised and honoured for what his act has enabled them to accomplish.

On the 8th November Governor Eyre opened the legislative session, and the following important extracts are made from his speech, and from the addresses of the Legislative Council and House of Assembly to him :—

Extract from Mr. Eyre's Speech.

" It is my duty to point out to you that, satisfactory as it is to know that the rebellion in the Eastern districts has been crushed out, the entire colony has long been, still is, on the brink of a volcano which may at any moment burst into fury.

" There is scarcely a district or a parish in the island where disloyalty, sedition, and murderous intentions are not widely disseminated, and, in many instances, openly expressed. The misapprehensions and misrepresentations of pseudo-philanthropists in England and in this country, the inflammatory harangues or seditious writings of political demagogues, of evil-minded men of higher position and of better education, and of worthless persons without either character or property to lose ; the personal, scurrilous, vindictive, and disloyal writings of a licentious and unscrupulous Press, and misdirected efforts and misguided counsel of certain ministers of religion, sadly so miscalled, if the Saviour's example and teaching is to be the standard, have led to their natural, their necessary, their inevitable result (amongst an ignorant, excitable, and uncivilized population)—rebellion, arson, murder.

"These are hard and harsh words, gentlemen, but they are true ; and this is no time to indulge in selected sentences or polished phraseology.

"A mighty danger threatens the land, and, in order to concert measures to avert it, and prevent, so far as human wisdom can, any future recurrence of a similar state of things, we must examine boldly, deeply, and unflinchingly into the causes which have led to this danger.   I know of no general grievance under which the negroes of this colony labour.   Individual cases of hardship or injustice must arise in every community ; but, as a whole, the peasantry of Jamaica have nothing to complain of.   They are less taxed, can live more easily and cheaply, and are less under an obligation to work for subsistence, than any peasantry in the world. The same laws as to the imposition of taxes, the administration of justice, and the enjoyment of political rights, apply to them and to the white and coloured inhabitants alike.   They ought to be better off, more comfortable, and more independent than the labourers of any other country.   If it is not so it is due to their own indolence, improvidence, and vice, acted upon by the absence of good example and of civilizing influences in many districts, and by the evil teaching and evil agencies to which I have already referred, in all.

"It is a remarkable fact, too, that many of the principal rebels in the late outbreak have been persons well off, and well to do in the world, possessing lands, cottages, furniture, horses, mules, or other property, and with an education above the average of the peasantry.

"It is necessary to bring these facts before you in order to convince you how widely spread and how deeply rooted the spirit of disaffection is ; how daring and determined the intention has been, and still is, to make Jamaica a second Hayti, and how imperative it is upon you, gentlemen, to take such measures as, under God's blessing, may avert such a calamity. Those measures may be summed up in a few words : Create a strong Government, and then, under a firm hand to guide and direct, much may be accomplished.

"In order to obtain a strong Government there is but one course open to you, that of abolishing the existing form of Constitution, compensating the officers whose offices are abolished, and establishing one better adapted to the present state and requirements of the colony—one in which union, co-operation, consistency, and promptness of action may, as far as practicable, be secured. I invite you, then, gentlemen, to make a great and generous sacrifice for the sake of your country, and in immolating on the altar of patriotism the two branches of the Legislature, of which you yourselves are the constituent parts, to hand down to posterity a noble example of self-denial and heroism."

Extract from Address of Legislative Council.

" While joining your Excellency in acknowledging the zealous and able services of his Excellency the General Commanding, the senior naval officer, and of the military and naval forces, as well as of the Volunteers, we desire also to record our grateful thanks to your Excellency for the energy, firmness, and wisdom with which you have carried the island through this momentous crisis.

" We are well aware that the slightest hesitation on your part would have been fraught with the most imminent danger to the lives of the loyal inhabitants throughout the island; and we are well assured that all our loyal fellow-colonists unite in the expression of gratitude which it is now our privilege to convey to you.

" We entirely concur in the painful statement your Excellency has made, that there is scarcely a district throughout the island where disloyalty, sedition, and murderous intentions are not widely disseminated and openly expressed. We agree with your Excellency as to the causes which have created the dangers that now threaten the country, and will heartily co-operate with you in endeavouring to remedy this grievous state of affairs."

Extract from Address of House of Assembly.

" We assure your Excellency that the advice and co-operation which you seek of the Legislature in a crisis consummated by rebellion, and which threatens, by a most diabolical conspiracy, the lives of the white and coloured inhabitants of the colony, will not, on the part of this assembly, be withheld.

" We most readily acknowledge that, while the thanks of the island are due to his Excellency Major-General O'Connor, for the readiness and promptitude with which he met the occurrences of the outbreak, and no less to all the other civil, naval, and military authorities engaged in its suppression, as well as to the Maroons, for their fidelity and loyalty, the gratitude of the island is chiefly due to the unexampled skill, energy, and self-devotion which characterised all your Excellency's measures.

" We desire to express our entire concurrence in your Excellency's statement, that to the misapprehensions and misrepresentations of pseudo-philanthropists in England and in this country, to the inflammatory harangues and seditious meetings of political dema- gogues, to the personal, scurrilous, vindictive, and dis- loyal writings of a licentious and unscrupulous press, and to the misdirected efforts and misguided counsel of certain miscalled ministers of religion, is to be attributed the present disorganisation of the colony, resulting in rebellion, arson, and murder.

"We cordially agree with your Excellency, that this great wickedness cannot be attributed to any just grievances under which it can be said that the peasantry suffer. On the contrary, we entirely coincide with your Excellency in the opinion that they have advantages which the peasantry of no other country enjoy, and that it is owing to the causes to which your Excellency alludes that they have failed to reap the benefit of their position.

"Deeply impressed with the full conviction that nothing but the existence of a strong Government can prevent this island from lapsing into the condition of a second Hayti, we shall cheerfully take into consideration any measures recommended by your Excellency.

"We feel ourselves bound, in this emergency, to aid, so far as the resources of the country will admit, the Government in all steps which may be necessary for ensuring the security of the colony, and the protection of life and property."

It will thus be seen that those who, prior to the rebellion, were Governor Eyre's most bitter enemies, who had refused to transact business with him, who had actually petitioned for his recall, were, at its close, constrained to acknowledge that he saved the island of Jamaica, and the lives of all the loyal inhabitants throughout the colony.

CHAPTER XI.

UPON the news reaching England of the energetic and determined manner in which Governor Eyre had suppressed the rebellion and saved the island of Jamaica, the Government, the press, and the people of England almost universally declared that his services were deserving of the highest recognition.

Mr. Cardwell, as Colonial Minister, in a despatch, dated the 17th of November, thus wrote to Mr. Eyre: —"I wish you to inform the inhabitants of Jamaica how deeply her Majesty's Government deplore the losses which the colony in general has sustained, and how sincerely they sympathize with those who have to lament family bereavements incurred under circumstances so distressing. I have next to convey to you my high approval of the spirit, energy, and judgment with which you have acted in your measures for repressing and preventing the spread of the insurrection. I have also to express my gratification at the clear and succinct manner in which, under all the great difficulties of your position, you have been enabled to communicate to her Majesty's Government the narrative of the transactions. It was the first duty of your Government to take, as you did, effectual measures for the suppression of this horrible, rebellion, and I congratulate you on the rapid success by which those measures appear to have been attended."

But, in the meanwhile, the Anti-Slavery Society were busy at work. Meetings were held at Exeter Hall and elsewhere, and placards posted about the streets of London of the most disgraceful character. These placards represented that inconceivable atrocities had been committed upon the blacks by the soldiers and sailors engaged in suppressing the insurrection. One placard in particular spoke of "nine miles of dead bodies" strewing the road! Governor Eyre was held up to public execration, and the style adopted by his traducers may be gathered from the following specimen, culled at haphazard from the mass of violent invective hurled at him : —

"As for those who incited the privates and seamen to commit the abominations laid to their charge, we must ferret them out. They must be brought to trial. If guilty, their names shall be handed down to everlasting infamy ; they shall be branded as the first murderer, Cain ; they shall hang as high as Haman ; or, better still, be caged side by side with the wild beasts in the Zoological Gardens, so that men may spit at them when they pass by. When dead, their carcases shall be thrown to the dogs, their ashes scattered to the four winds of heaven ; and as for their souls, so blackened must they be, that hell itself will scarce care to receive them."   Such is philanthropy!

A deputation, in the course of a few weeks, waited upon Mr. Cardwell, and insisted upon a Commission of inquiry being sent out to Jamaica; and so great was the pressure brought to bear on Earl Russell's Government (which at that particular moment could not afford to quarrel with the violent and extreme political party who professed to espouse the cause of the negro), that the Premier finally acceded to their demands.

And here it may be as well to refer back to the course pursued by Earl Russell in 1851 in a similar emergency, when it was proposed that a Royal Commission should be sent out to Ceylon to inquire into the means employed by Lord Torrington to suppress an insurrection in that island in 1848. The cases are so exactly parallel that the speech of the noble lord might have been delivered almost verbatim in defence of Mr. Eyre. Earl Russell then said :—

" But, sir, what is the blame to be imputed to Lord Torrington with respect to this insurrection? Be it observed that the news of that insurrection came suddenly upon the Governor. He immediately sent for Colonel Fraser, an officer who had been engaged in the previous insurrection, to whose discretion and whose experience he might well trust for an able and a sound opinion upon that matter. He acted according to that opinion. He immediately saw the General commanding the forces. He took means by which troops should be at once sent to the points at which the insurrection had broken out. He took other means by which the rebels might be promptly met, and the rebellion promptly suppressed, and, in order to do that more effectually, with the concurrence of General Smelt and the Queen's Advocate, and the advice of Colonel Fraser, he proclaimed martial law in that district of the colony which was disturbed. The effect was immediate and most salutary; because, as the right hon. gentleman (Mr. Gladstone) says, in two days, though I cannot agree with him as to that term, but in a few days the armed resistance had ceased.

* * * * * *

So far, Lord Torrington was not to blame for the step which he had taken. But the right hon. gentleman says he continued martial law. The right hon. gentleman omits one remarkable circumstance, which was that he acted in concert and with the advice of his Executive Council in this respect. He had the opinion of one gentleman of that Council, Mr. Anstruther, strongly opposed to his own; but he had the opinion of four others in his favour; and, with his own opinion, there was, therefore, a preponderance of five to one in that Executive Council in favour of continuing martial law. The Major-General commanding the district, above all, was strenuous in advising that the operation of martial law should be continued. * * * *

Now, sir, I submit to the House that it is a totally different thing to act in the manner which those resolutions describe—at his sole will and sole caprice—and to take the deliberate advice of his Executive Council, of those who were best acquainted with the colony, and with their advice to continue martial law for a short time. The whole time during which this martial law was continued was ten weeks. But I must admit that it is a most serious resolution to come to, the establishment of martial law in any district, or in any part of a colony. I must admit that those acts which have been gone into in great detail by the hon. and learned gentleman the member for Abingdon (Sir Frederick Thesiger), whether accurately or not I will not at this moment stop to inquire, such as irregularities in taking evidence, want of proper defence and cross-examination, and many of those circumstances which are inherent and inseparable from martial law, which the Governor then took upon himself.* But at the same time the Governor had to consider—and this was the question for Lord Torrington; this was the question for the Government at home; and this is the question for the House to-night, in its more general feature—that if on the one hand martial law cannot be continued without the risk of punishments which may reach not the most guilty, but those who have appeared in arms, and are guilty according to the law of high treason and rebel-

* *Sic* in original.

lion—if such may be the consequence, on the other hand, the consequence of refusing to continue martial law, the consequence of refusing even to put it in force may be this—that rebellion may gain a head ; that insurrection, which at first is weak and may be easily crushed, may become formidable ; that the whole order of the colony may be destroyed ; that the allegiance which is due to the Crown may be withheld ; that property to an indefinite extent may be spoiled and ruined ; but, above all, that humanity, for the sake of which · martial law was withheld, that humanity itself may be lost sight of, and many more lives may be lost in the struggle that may ensue than would have been lost if martial law had for a few weeks been continued.

" In the last despatch which Earl Grey wrote, he stated that her Majesty's Government still believed that Lord Torrington was guided by opinions which he had conscientiously formed—supported as he was by those who ought to advise him in the colony—that in proclaiming martial law, and in punishing those who suffered, he was acting, as he believed, in the only way that could maintain the tranquillity of the country, and provide for the welfare of her Majesty's subjects. That, sir, is our belief.   It is our belief that when you send a Governor to a distant part of the globe—when you find that he is zealously performing his duty—when you find that he is endeavouring by all the means in his power to preserve the colony in allegiance to her

Majesty, and at the same time is consulting the peace, the welfare, the prosperity of such colony—we think that confidence ought to be held out to that Governor, that confidence ought to be placed in him, and that we ought not, as a Government, to attempt to throw any censure upon questions upon which we believe, if there could be any difference of opinion, he is more likely to judge right from the circumstances before him, and the assistance of his advisers, than we should be able who form our judgments of them at a distance. I believe we came to a right conclusion on that subject, and I believe that, looking at colonial government in general, this House ought to come to an entirely opposite conclusion to that of the hon. member for Inverness-shire. I believe that if at the first beginning of an insurrection a Governor were to say to himself, 'I must take care how I crush the rebellion; I must be careful how I punish the offenders; I may be brought before a Committee of the House of Commons; I may be censured by the Government under which I serve; I may undergo the pains and penalties of a resolution of the House of Commons, and therefore I must be careful not to extend the verge and boundary of strict law'—I believe if you teach such a lesson to your Governors, while you will diminish their energy—while you will diminish the security of her Majesty's subjects in the colony, you will do nothing for humanity. On the contrary, whenever an insurrection springs up, you will have a long and bloody contest—you will have the lives of her Majesty's troops sacrificed on the one hand, and you will have the lives and property of innocent colonists destroyed or endangered on the other; and, for my part, I must say I think it better that one guilty man should suffer, than ten innocent men should suffer death.   I, therefore, come to an entirely opposite conclusion from that of the hon. gentleman (Mr. Baillie).

*   *   *   *   *   *

"I trust that none will join in this vote who have not considered the colonial question fully, and that none will vote in favour of the motion who do not feel bound to pronounce a vote of censure upon the late Governor of Ceylon, upon the Secretary of State for the Colonies, and upon the Government.   If that be the case, I shall cheerfully leave the decision to the House.   I believe, whatever that decision may be, that the rules and maxims that we have laid down must be the rules and maxims by which any Government will be guided which seeks to preserve this empire; and that if *any Government was to take the dastardly part of sacrificing a Governor because there was a clamour raised against him, got up with great perseverance and industry—I believe that the Government, while it would sacrifice the colonies, would meet with the reprobation, the deserved reprobation, of the people of England.*"

Earl Russell having acceded to a Royal Commission being sent out to inquire into Governor Eyre's conduct, the gentlemen who had formed the deputation to Mr. Cardwell, without a moment's loss of time, turned themselves into an Association, under the title of the "Jamaica Committee," for the purpose of holding a court of inquiry themselves, both in London and in Jamaica. Attorneys, barristers, clerks, and a host of other persons, were appointed by them ; and when the members of the Royal Commission, Sir Henry Storks, Mr. Russell Gurney, and Mr. Maule sailed from England, the Commission despatched by the Jamaica Committee, took ship in the same vessel, with express and significant instructions in writing from the attorneys to the barristers sent out by the Jamaica Committee that " there were, besides the inquiry before the Commission, two other kinds of proceedings which might hereafter become expedient," viz., indictments against the parties implicated, and actions to be brought for damages. It need scarcely be wondered at that, with such instructions, both indictments and civil actions have followed.

After a protracted inquiry, the Royal Commission terminated its proceedings with the following results :—

Conclusions arrived at by the Royal Commission.

Upon the subjects proposed for our inquiry we have come to the following conclusions :—

I.

That the disturbances in St. Thomas-in-the-East had their immediate origin in a planned resistance to lawful authority.

II.

That the causes leading to the determination to offer that resistance were manifold :—

    (1.) That a principal object of the disturbers of order was the obtaining of land free from the payment of rent.

    (2.) That an additional incentive to the violation of the law arose from the want of confidence generally felt by the labouring class in the tribunals before which most of the disputes affecting their interests were carried for adjudication.

    (3.) That some, moreover, were animated by feelings of hostility towards political and personal opponents, while not a few contemplated the attainment of their ends by the death or expulsion of the white inhabitants of the island.

III.

That though the original design for the overthrow of constituted authority was confined to a small portion of the parish of St. Thomas-in-the-East, yet that the disorder in fact spread with singular rapidity over an extensive tract of country, and that such was the state of excitement prevailing in other parts of the island that, had more than a momentary success been obtained by the insurgents, their ultimate overthrow would have been attended with a still more fearful loss of life and property.

IV.

That praise is due to Governor Eyre for the skill, promptitude, and vigour which he manifested during the early stages of the insurrection; to the exercise of which qualities its speedy termination is in a great degree to be attributed.

V.

That the military and naval operations appear to us to have been prompt and judicious.

VI.

That by the continuance of martial law in its full force to the extreme limit of its statutory operation the people were deprived for a longer than the necessary period of the great constitutional privileges by which the security of life and property is provided for.

Lastly.

That the punishments inflicted were excessive.

> (1.) That the punishment of death was unnecessarily frequent.
>
> (2.) That the floggings were reckless, and at Bath positively barbarous.
>
> (3.) That the burning of 1,000 houses was wanton and cruel.

With regard to the opinion of the Royal Commissioners on the subject of martial law being kept in force " to the extreme limit of its statutory operation," it should be remembered that the Commissioners were sitting in judgment upon the actions of a general when the smoke had cleared off the battle-field,* and that martial law was kept in force only with the express advice of the Council of War, to whose opinions Governor Eyre was bound to defer.†

---

* See Professor Tyndall's able reply to Jamaica Committee, in Appendix.   Marked B.

† Mr. Eyre thus gave his reasons for the continuation of martial law in his examination before the Royal Commission :—

" I now give the reasons which induced me to think that martial law should be continued.   They are very short :—

" 1st. In order to deal summarily with the cases excepted from the operation of the amnesty, many of the parties being as guilty as

Whether the punishment of death was unnecessarily frequent, and the floggings reckless, we refer to a pamphlet published by the Jamaica Committee itself, wherein it is stated that "*the rioters were Africans as uncivilized as they were in their native wilds.*" However much, therefore, it may be regretted that excesses took place (as they always unhappily must where a country is in a state of insurrection and military law an absolute necessity), the blame rests with those who

---

those tried by courts-martial previous to the amnesty, and there being no valid reason why they should not be dealt with in the same manner.

" 2ndly. To preserve peace and good order in the districts where the rebellion had existed, and to afford time to reorganize the civil institutions. The custos, the magistrates, the clergy, and other principal inhabitants, had been killed, wounded, or driven away. The inspector of police had been killed, and the force become disorganized and demoralized. The court-house itself was burnt to the ground. It was impossible to re-establish civil institutions and relations at such a juncture, or without a sufficient time being allowed for reconstruction, and for the return of magistrates, clergy, and other inhabitants who had been compelled to fly during the rebellion. I think that is one very important reason why it was impossible to have suspended martial law."

And in answer to your next question, 46,635,—" What, in your opinion, would have been the evils that would have arisen from taking that particular course on the 30th of October ?" he proceeds,—

" 3rdly. It was important that for some short time longer, at least, the Government should continue martial law, to operate as an example and a warning *in terrorem* over the disaffected of other districts without the necessity of imposing it in those districts.

" 4thly. The indication which the continuance of martial law in the county of Surrey for some days after the amnesty gave of the determination of the Government to deal promptly and decisively with persons guilty of rebellion, or the concomitant crimes of murder and arson, was the most efficacious step it could take to overawe the evil-disposed in other parts of the colony, and thereby prevent any rising amongst the negro population of the districts where disaffection and seditious tendencies were known to exist. Those were the four principal reasons which operated with the Government at the time."

have been the cause of such insurrection, and not upon the men who have been compelled to adopt stern remedies.

The burning of 1000 houses, to English ears, appears startling, but the pamphlet published by the Jamaica Committee, from which we have just quoted, throws some light as to the character of these houses. It styles them " miserable little huts," in which the negroes " live like pigs in a sty."   And, moreover, no hut was destroyed except where plunder was found.

The Report of the Royal Commission having been sent home; on the 18th June, 1866, Mr. Cardwell, Secretary of State for the Colonies, addressed a letter to Sir Henry Storks, in which he expressed the approval of the Home Government for the cheerful assistance rendered to the Commission by Governor Eyre, in the prosecution of its inquiries.   Mr. Cardwell continued, and we think it advisable here to quote his own words:—" Though the original design for the overthrow of constituted authority was confined to a small portion of the parish of St. Thomas-in-the-East, yet there can now be no doubt that the disturbances there had their origin in a planned resistance to that authority. It is further evident, *looking to the singular rapidity with which disorder spread over an extensive tract of country, and to the state of excitement prevailing in other parts of the island, that the ultimate defeat of the insurgents would have been attended with a still more fearful loss of life and property had they been permitted to obtain a more than momentary success.* Under these circumstances Governor Eyre fully deserves all the commendation which you have bestowed upon the skill, promptitude, and vigour, which he manifested during the early stages of the insurrection, to the exercise of which qualities on his part you justly attribute in a great degree its speedy termination."

If this means anything at all, it means that but for Mr. Eyre's " promptitude and vigour " the whole island of Jamaica would have risen in insurrection, and that had the insurgents been allowed " more than a momentary success." more hangings, shootings, and floggings, must of necessity have taken place; therefore, that Governor Eyre's prompt severity was really the most merciful course in the long run that could possibly have been adopted. But let us go further. Mr. Cardwell continues :—

" As regards the proclamation of martial law under the Island Act of 1844, her Majesty's Government agree with you that the Council of War had *good reason for the advice which they gave,* and the Governor was *well justified in acting upon that advice.* Her Majesty's Government agree in your conclusion that the military and naval operations were prompt and judicious, and, *considering the large share personally taken by Governor Eyre in the direction of those operations, they attribute to him a large share also of the credit which is due for their success.* The addresses of the Legislative Council of the House of Assembly, of the various parishes of the island, and of others, testify the sense generally entertained by the white and *coloured* inhabitants of their obligation to Governor Eyre, for the promptitude and vigour of those measures."

This, be it remembered, was not written by Mr. Cardwell before the whole facts of the case were before him, which may possibly be urged by Mr. Eyre's detractors, when referring to the Secretary of State's despatch quoted in the beginning of this chapter; it was written after the Royal Commission had given its verdict, and after careful consideration on the part of her Majesty's Government.

This despatch is of vital importance at the present moment, and no excuse is necessary for quoting further from it, and at some length. With regard to the continuance of martial law to the extreme limit of its statutory operation, and to the excessive nature of the punishments inflicted, Mr. Cardwell writes :—" The greatest consideration is due to a Governor placed in the circumstances in which Governor Eyre was placed. The suddenness of the insurrection; the uncertainty of its possible extent; its avowed character as a contest of colour; the atrocities committed at its first outbreak; the great disparity in numbers between the white and black populations; the real dangers and the vague alarms by which he was on every side surrounded; *the inadequacy of the force at his command to secure superiority in every district;* the exaggerated statements which reached him continually from distant parts of the island ; the vicinity of Hayti, and the fact that a civil war was at the time going on in that country ;—all these circumstances tended to impress his mind with a conviction that the worst consequences were to be apprehended from the slightest appearance of indecision. Nor must it be forgotten that he resisted the proposal urgently made to him by the Custos and the magistrates to proclaim Kingston ; that he refused to accede to the suggestion of Colonel Whitfield to proclaim the parishes of Trelawney, St. James, Hanover, and Westmoreland, or to that of Major-General O'Connor, who thought that from the first the whole island ought to have been placed under martial law ; and that in respect both to the assistance offered by the Governor of Cuba, and to the summoning of British troops from Halifax, Nova Scotia, he showed himself *superior to feelings of alarm expressed and entertained by those around him.*"

Has the " greatest consideration," which Mr. Cardwell says " is due to a Governor placed in the circumstances in which Governor Eyre was placed," been shown to that gentleman ?

Mr. Cardwell concludes this most important despatch with the following paragraph :—

" Finally, I have to express on the part of her Majesty's Government their sense of the promptitude and judgment with which Governor Eyre submitted to the late Legislature the views which he entertained, and in which they so readily concurred, as to the expediency of effecting a decided change in the mode of Government of the colony. Those views have been confirmed by the sanction of the Crown, and by an Act of the Imperial Parliament, and the new form of Government is about to be established under the Governor who shall succeed you (Sir H. Storks) when you are relieved of your temporary duties. It remains, therefore, to decide whether the inauguration of the new Government shall be accomplished by Mr. Eyre, or whether her Majesty shall be advised to intrust that arduous task to some other person who may approach it free from all the difficulties inseparable from a participation in the questions raised by the recent troubles.

*   *   *   *   *   *

" They (the Home Government) do not feel, therefore, that they should discharge their duty by advising the Crown to replace Mr. Eyre in his former Government ; and they cannot doubt that, by placing the new form of Government in new hands, they are taking the course best calculated to allay animosities, to conciliate general confidence, and to establish on firm and solid grounds the future welfare of Jamaica."

The plain English of the last few lines of the above paragraph is that Mr. Eyre, after a lifetime devoted to the service of his country, in every climate and every quarter of the globe, and within a few months of his retiring pension, has been turned adrift without a sixpence !

When Mr. Eyre left Jamaica, he had been in the public service five-and-twenty years, and twenty years of that long period as the representative of his Sovereign, as Lieutenant-Governor or Governor. During this period he had under his government the various colonies of New Zealand, Saint Vincent, Antigua, the Virgin Isles, Nevis, Montserrat, Saint Christopher's, Dominica, Turk's and Caicos Island, British Honduras, and Jamaica. Wherever he went he made warm friends, and gained always the good-will and the affectionate esteem of the colonists.

When it became known that Mr. Eyre had been removed from the Governorship of Jamaica, there was a feeling of indescribable sorrow throughout the entire island.

On the 24th July, 1866, at a quarter to three o'clock, Governor Eyre started from the residence of Capt. Cooper, R.N., and drove to the Royal Mail Steam Company's wharf, the place of embarkation. Throughout the way the windows of the houses were filled and the roads crowded with spectators, who pressed forward to say, "God bless Governor Eyre!" As he drew nearer the wharf, the streets were almost impassable, so densely were they thronged with people of all classes, but principally with negroes, who cheered him warmly, shouting, "God bless your Excellency!" Numberless were the expressions of affection and good-will bestowed on him by the lower classes, such as, "God bless Governor Eyre!" "A good and prosperous voyage to you, sir!" "God bless Mrs. Eyre and your children!" On reaching the place of embarkation the crowd was still more intense, the enthusiasm still greater. The respectable and influential people of all classes had collected here to receive him ; and, on his getting out of his carriage, people thronged around to catch a last look, and to say good-bye. Every gentleman who could be present was there, and every lady also. The utmost order prevailed. The military band played "God save the Queen" as Governor Eyre passed on to the ship, amidst the earnest blessings of the high and low, rich and poor of the land, who had met to pay him this last act of respect. On reaching the steamer, Governor Eyre found the vessel also crowded with gentlemen and ladies, who had come from far and near to bid him and Mrs. Eyre farewell. Here the bishop and clergy presented him with a farewell address, after which Governor Eyre moved to the stern of the ship, to afford the crowds who flocked on board the opportunity of shaking hands with him. This continued till the steamer got under weigh, and as she moved off, renewed cheers and renewed blessings were showered upon him and upon his family.*

* For further newspaper reports on the subject, see Appendix F, which contains the addresses and Mr. Eyre's farewell speeches, in which he vindicates his own official course of action.

And Mr. Eyre is now, in England, subjected to a criminal prosecution. A committee has raised a fund, to indict him for murder; but his reputation will rest upon the foundation of honourable service and zealous devotion to the cause of his country. Calm before real danger; amongst savages; in the desolate wilderness; amidst insurrection, rebellion, and anarchy; he is not likely to quail before those who are now banded together to persecute him. He may say (as was said by another great man, placed in the same position as himself) that the inventions of malice and the credulity of ignorance are equally unable to affect his mind or influence his conduct in any situation or circumstance of life. The libels which have outraged truth, and endeavoured to corrupt the sources of public justice, have neither succeeded in alarming his apprehensions nor irritating his disposition. The good will of his countrymen is to him an object of virtuous ambition, and to such reputation as is based on the conscientious discharge of his duty he confidently but calmly aspires.

APPENDIX.

A.

EVIDENCE IN THE CASE OF MR. GORDON.

(Extracted from the Report of the Royal Commissioners.)

THE affairs of the parish of St. Thomas-in-the-East were the subject of great interest among many of the parishioners who were friends of Mr. Gordon. Many looked to him for advice, which they relied on and followed.

Among these was Paul Bogle, who cultivated a few acres of land at Stony Gut, a village in the hills about six miles inland from Morant Bay.

A chapel belonging to him of small dimensions stood on his land, and was opened about Christmas, 1864. He was a member of the "Native Baptists," a sect so called as being independent of and distinguished from the London Baptist Mission. Mr. Gordon was *an intimate friend and correspondent* of Bogle.*

Mr. Gordon had himself become a Baptist, and had a Tabernacle of his own on the Parade at Kingston. To Paul Bogle he addressed a short note when about to become such member, as follows:

"11th December, 1861.

"Mr. PAUL BOGLE,—I am to be *baptized* on *Christmas* Day, this day two weeks. Remember me on that day.

"G. W. GORDON."

---

* Although G. W. Gordon declared most solemnly at his trial, and elsewhere, that Paul Bogle was a stranger to him.

S

On the 26th February, 1864, Mr. Gordon wrote from Kingston to Paul Bogle at Stony Gut, as follows (*inter alia*):

"DEAR BOGLE,—Things are bad in Jamaica, and will require a great deal of purging."

When Paul Bogle's house was searched in October, a list of ten names was found there in the handwriting of Mr. Gordon. Mr. Gordon's own name was at the head of this list, and the nine other names were those of persons connected with Bogle's party. *A much larger list of names*, most of which were original signatures or marks, was afterwards taken from the *private writing-table of Mr. Gordon* at Cherry Garden. This last list was headed by the name of Paul Bogle, and contained 148 other names, many of which belonged to persons *who were implicated in the outbreak at Morant Bay.*

Mr. Henry James Lawrence was Mr. Gordon's manager and resident agent on his estate called "Rhine," near Bath, in St. Thomas-in-the-East.

He thus writes to Lawrence:

"They (Ketelholdt and Herschell) are a very wicked *band*, and the Lord will yet reward *them all* . . . . I note what you say of   . He is a sort of fiend who, altho' chastised, has remained hardened. We can afford to spare him, and perhaps England will better agree with him. *Mark, the reign of others will also soon be cut short.*"

Again, on 6th March, 1865, he writes to Mr. Lawrence:

"I note what you say re Oxford and Walker and Ketelholdt,—the parish will be well rid of Walker, but the evil will be doubled (?) in Baron, and I quite agree with your *sentiments. We must wait and see what the end will be of all these evil doers!* . . . . Thanks also for arranging with Kirkland. I shall treat him as he merits. What an unreliable SETT (*sic*) they all are. I am DISGUSTED with *them* and must try to keep aloof and above them. The Ex. Com. Gov. and

Bishop! what a set, can *any reliance be placed on these?* and can matters go on with such men *at the helm?*"

Again he writes to his manager, 27th April, 1865:

"The case of Gordon *v.* Ketelholdt was a great triumph to Baron and all the Cookes, for in spite of everything which was clearly in my favour, they got a jury of five to give a verdict for defendant. What a fresh victory is this for them all! How well it looks, and how diminished is my head! *but wait, it is not yet all over!* . . . . . The Attorney-General disgraced himself by low conduct. Sneddes proved a traitor, and M'Kenzie a MOST *worthless lying fellow.* Having nothing to do with the man, he is a *great villain (sic).*"

And again, on the 29th April, 1865:

"I have no doubt there are dual actions and strong under-currents against me, but wait and see the end of it, *be not cast down*, the Lord is at hand . . . . There is a sort of present exultation in the Baron, Herschell, Cooke, &c., all *their* points *being carried.* . . . . I note the great and glorious gathering at Rhine House; *this is very beautiful.*

"Messrs. Warmington and Henry Seymour Kennedy are new J. P.'s for St. Thomas-y'-East, and some few more expecting. All very *beautiful.* Great concerns for great men! *Keep you quiet and see the end of it all.*"

On the 4th of May he wrote, "I know the inveterate dislike of Herschell and all his *confreres. They will soon all find their level, and go like chaff against the wind.*"

Mr. Gordon was staying at Hordley in the Plaintain Garden district of the parish in June, 1865, and in conversation there with Mr. Harrison, he was spoken to about the state of the feeling among the people, and told that he could not control it. In reply, " Oh!" said Mr. Gordon, "if I wanted a rebellion I could have had one long ago. I have been asked several times to head a rebellion, but there is no fear of that, I will try first a demonstration of it, but I must upset that fellow Herschell, and kick him out of the vestry, and the Baron also, or bad will come of it."

On the 13th of July he wrote to Lawrence at the Rhine. " Herschell has got another £40 for pews at Bath Church, through the aid of his friend Price.   What will these (?) men, surely some calamity *will come* on them."

About the same time, conversing with Mr. Arthur Beckwith at Kingston, about a meeting held on the subject of labourers and wages, Mr. Gordon was told it was calculated to excite a spirit of disaffection amongst the people; to which Mr. Gordon answered, " Ah! well, we must have it some way or the other; this is the great movement; and if we do not secure it in this way, *in six months there will be a revolution in the country, and as I have always stood by the people, I will stand by them then.*"

On the 11th August a printed address to the people of St. Thomas-in-the-East, headed "State of the Island," was posted up on a cotton-tree in the main road at Morant Bay, opposite William Chisholm's house.   The original draft of this address, in the writing of Mr. Gordon, was given by him to a compositor at Kingston shortly before to be set up in type, with directions to forward copies to one Rodney, at St. Anne's Bay, others to James Sullivan at Bath, and further copies to Paul Bogle and to William Chisholm at Morant Bay.

These copies were sent.   In this address is found the following passage:

" People of St. Thomas-in-the-East! You have been ground down too long already; shake off your sloth, and speak like honourable and free men at your meeting.   Let not a crafty, Jesuitical priesthood deceive you.   Prepare for your duty. Remember the destitution in the midst of your families, and your forlorn condition.   The Government have taxed you to defend your own rights against the enormities of an unscrupulous and oppressive foreigner, Mr. Custos Ketelholdt.   You feel this. It is *no wonder you do.* You have been dared in this provoking act, and it is sufficient to extinguish your long patience. This is not time when such deeds should be perpetrated, but as they have been, it is your duty to speak out and to act too. We advise you to be up and doing, and to maintain your cause. You must be united in your efforts."

An open-air meeting on Saturday, August 12th, held in the market-place in front of the Court House, at Morant Bay, under a gynnep-tree, was presided over by Mr. Gordon, at which Paul Bogle and Moses Bogle were present. Resolutions on the conduct of the Government, and on the depressed state of the labouring classes, and the price of labour, and low rate of wages, were passed ; and in reference to the circular, called the " Queen's advice to the people," Mr. Gordon said that " The Queen's message to the working classes of Jamaica is not true ; I say it is not true ; it is a lie ; it does not come from the Queen ; the Queen does not know anything about it."

At the time of this meeting Mr. Gordon was staying at his cottage on the Rhine Estate, sixteen miles from Morant Bay.

In familiar conversation with Mrs. Major, the wife of Dr. Major, his tenant of part of that estate, he was told by her that in his speeches which she had recently been reading, he was certainly guilty of high treason, and she would accuse him of it. He replied, " Oh no, they have printed it wrong ; I never made use of such expressions, and you can't do it. *I have just gone as far as I can go, but no further.*"

In this conversation he spoke of the Governor as "a wicked man," and said " that it would be a blessing to the country if some one would shoot him ;" and that Mr. Herschell and the Baron were " bad and wicked men, and it would be a blessing if these three men were removed."

On the night of the 15th August, a meeting was held at a house belonging to Mr. Gordon, at Morant Bay, opposite the Wesleyan Chapel, at which James M'Laren acted as Secretary, with about thirty persons present ; from this meeting five persons were turned away as spies, who had not previously attended the meeting on the 12th of August.

Mr. G. W. Gordon attended and spoke at a meeting held at the " Alley " in Vere, on the 4th of September.   He said : " They report to the Queen that you are thieves.   .   .   .   . The notice that is said to be the Queen's advice is all trash ; it is no advice of the Queen at all.   .   .   .   .   I was told by some of you that your overseers said that if any of you attended this meeting they would tear down your houses. Tell them that I, George William Gordon, say they dare not do it. *It is tyranny.   You must do what Hayti does.   You have a bad name now, but you will have a worse one then.*"

The following is a passage in a letter addressed to Dr. Bruce, by Mr. Sydney Levien, the editor of a local newspaper, in reference to this Vere meeting :—" I could scarcely command vital thought enough yesterday to do justice to your meeting, and, against the wish of William, I wrote the feeble editorial that appeared to second the noble exertions of the Vere people. *All I desire is to shield you and them from the charge of anarchy and tumult, which in a short time must follow these fearful demonstrations.*   How I succeeded you must judge for yourself."

About three weeks before the events at Morant Bay, and shortly after his speech at Vere, Mr. Gordon was at the Bank of Jamaica at Kingston, conversing with Mr. James Ford, the Secretary, on the subject of that speech ; and Mr. Ford then said to him, " Supposing, Mr. Gordon, the people were to be such fools as to rise in rebellion, do you think that even in the event of their being successful in their cutting all our throats, which is perfectly possible, in the first rising, if they took us by surprise, that England either could not, or would not, avenge us amply, so that every one of them would be killed and done away with ?" Mr. Gordon said, " Ah, Mr. Ford, you are quite mistaken there ; all the powers of the Great Napoleon could not put down the rising in Hayti, and that was successful, for the troops died of disease before they could meet the people in the mountains." Mr. Ford then said, " But in India, a very short time ago, an organised, armed, and formidable rebellion of millions arose against the Government, and we know how they were successful at first, but it was very quietly, steadily, and determinedly put down, and England's power has been kept, and so it would be here." Mr. Gordon then replied, " Mr. Ford, India is not at all a case in point, for India is a flat country, and the English troops would overrun it and conquer it ; but this country is a mountainous country, and before the British troops could reach the people in the mountains they would die of disease here."

He then went away, observing, " Of course, this is mere abstract talking."

Mr. Lawrence, writing from the Rhine on the 8th of September to Mr. Gordon on private business, makes the following remark on local affairs : " I see by the papers that Mount Pleasant and Hall Head have been offered for sale by the Hon. W. P. Georges. . . . . I suppose this green bay-tree (Hon. W. P. Georges) will continue to spread *while the day of retribution draws nigh for his numerous transgressions,* and the ex-member of Assembly (Mr. D.) humbled."

On the 14th of September, he wrote to Mr. Lawrence at the Rhine Estate, " I fear we cannot mend public matters in St. Thomas-ye-East, so we had better look to our individual circumstances more clearly. I believe the Governor and his nest of Custodes are capable of anything, *but the Lord will soon scatter them as the chaff before the wind."* . . . . " There is just now great exultation, and a second verdict against me, and Jackson removed to satisfy the Baron ! *'Anguis in herba.'* I fancy you know that this means the character you refer to, and I have apprehensions that your opinions may be correct.

Let it all *go on! Just wait and see the result."* . . . Again, on the 18th of September, he wrote to Lawrence,—" The enemies now exult, and justice is silenced for a time, but it will raise its head. . . . . The Lord will soon pluck his hand out of his bosom, *and so confound the whole band of oppressors.* I believe this is to be about one of their last *flickers.* Let us wait and see."

On the 28th of September he wrote to Mr. Lawrence: " The·man, Mr. Eyre, is an arch liar, and he supports all his emissaries. . . . The *wicked shall be destroyed.* This is decreed. God is our refuge and strength, a very pleasant (*sic*) help in trouble."

The news of the events of Wednesday evening, the 11th of October, did not reach Kingston till the 12th October at noon.

On the 11th of October, Mr. G. W. Gordon was residing at his property, " Cherry Garden," in St. Andrews, a short distance from Kingston.* He was engaged in trade, and had business offices in that town, where he went on that day, returning home in the evening. On his return, he is said *by his wife* to have informed her of the outbreak at Morant Bay.†

---

* It is abundantly proved that Mr. Gordon's *residence* was at " Cherry Garden," in St. Andrews, a *district under martial law,* and when he was captured in Kingston (not under martial law) he was in point of fact a dissenter or absentee from his own home, and it was to " Cherry Garden " (in martial law district) that a detachment of police was sent to try and capture him. It is a singular fact that G. W. Gordon's will was made on the day after the massacres, and he therein described himself as of St. Andrews (martial law district).

† The fact brought out by the Royal Commissioners from Mrs. G. W. Gordon, that she learned from her husband *on the Wednesday* that the disturbances had taken place at Morant Bay, is a most important one. They had not in reality then occurred, or at least as they were only occurring that evening, it was impossible that any information subsequent to the occurrences could have reached Mr. Gordon in Kingston, 30 or 35 miles from the scene. The truth is that two messengers had been despatched by Paul Bogle and the other conspirators with a letter for Mr. Eyre. One of the two men went on to Spanish Town, and delivered the letter about the middle of the day; the other man remained in Kingston at Mr. Gordon's place of business, and there can be no doubt that from him Mr. Gordon learnt what was about to take place (not what had taken place) and so was enabled to tell his wife, as she gave evidence before the Commission.

As the outbreak took place at a distance of more than thirty miles, late on the afternoon of the 11th, and was not known in Kingston till the middle of the following day, it was suggested to Mrs. Gordon that probably it was on Thursday, the 12th, that Mr. Gordon first spoke to her on the subject. Upon this she replied, that "*Wednesday evening he brought the news*," and that "Mr. Gordon came up on the 12th, and said the outbreak at Morant Bay was true that we heard of on the Wednesday." He added, "that the feeling seemed to be so strong to put (*sic*) a pistol to him, and get rid of him, as they did the President of America."

When the news of the events of October 11th reached Kingston, on the following day, they were not fully believed by many persons there in the first instance.

On this day, about two o'clock, Mr. Lee, a friend of Mr. Gordon, mentioned to him the news of what had happened at Morant Bay, and Mr. Gordon seemed much distressed.

Mr. Lee said, "George, I fear your agitation at Morant Bay has been the cause of all this." Mr. Gordon said, "I never gave them bad advice. I only told them the Lord would send them a day of deliverance." And, when speaking of Baron Ketelholdt being killed, Mr. Gordon added, "*I told him not to go*, but he was such an obstinate man."

Dr. Major, Mr. Gordon's tenant at Rhine, about sixteen miles from Morant Bay, was at seven o'clock on the morning of October 11th, leaving the Rhine in order to attend the meeting of the vestry at Morant Bay. He met Mr. Lawrence, Gordon's overseer, as he came out of the gate, who tried to dissuade him from going, by saying, "I should strongly advise you not to go." Dr. Major went, however, and about two o'clock Mrs. Major sent to Lawrence for intelligence, at which hour he called on her at the Rhine, saying that "he heard nothing further than that there was a great disturbance, but that she need be under no apprehension about the Doctor, he would be quite safe, *but the Baron and Mr. Herschell he feared were doomed*." This conversation was, in point of time, *before* the fight had begun at Morant Bay, where, according to all evidence, the Baron and Mr. Herschell were not killed till after five o'clock.

About three o'clock the same afternoon, Mrs. Major again made inquiry by note sent by her servant to Lawrence, and he then sent word by the servant to her, " that the Doctor would be quite safe, *but Mr. Herschell and the Baron he had no hope of.*"   About the same time he also wrote to her the following note :

" DEAR MADAM,—Things seem in a fearful way ; the Doctor did not seem to know of the rebellion at Morant Bay till I told him, but I beg you will not be troubled.   I have no doubt the feeling will be quieted.   The Volunteer force moved on the scene of action this morning at one o'clock.   I will let you know if anything more transpires."

This note was received before four o'clock on the 11th of October, and at that time the events had not yet ended in the deaths of the Custos and Mr. Herschell, nor could the news of what had happened at Morant Bay have reached the Rhine at a distance of sixteen miles.

On the 12th of October, the next day, Lawrence wrote to Mrs. Major as follows :

" DEAR MADAM,—I am sorry I have no reliable news for you.   I have heard a good deal, but think much of what I hear is false.   There is a report about the Doctor, but the same is not true.   *The negroes know full well who fit for retribution.*"

On Friday morning, the 13th October, he went over to Spanish Town before ten o'clock in the morning.   The case of Gordon *v.* Ketelholdt had been fixed for argument in Court there that day.   He called at the office of his attorney there, and asked how the matter stood, and was told that the suit was at an end, in consequence of the death of the Baron, if

that fact was true. He then made inquiries as to the costs
of the suit, whereupon his attorney declined under the serious
existing circumstances to enter into such details. A person
then present remarked to him that there was plenty of time
for him to go to St. Thomas-in-the-East, and to exercise his
influence on the side of order; to which Gordon replied, "If
I go to St. Thomas-in-the-East, the moment martial law is
proclaimed I shall be the first man hung."

*　　*　　*　　*　　*　　*　　*

APPENDIX.

B.

PROFESSOR TYNDALL'S REPLY TO THE JAMAICA COMMITTEE.

Gentlemen,—You have done me the honour of sending me certain papers " relating to the atrocities of the authorities in Jamaica," during the suppression of the late "alleged rebellion."

I am far from being insensible to the opinion which your courtesy in sending me these papers implies : namely, that I am incapable of defending any line of conduct to which the term " atrocious " could with fairness be applied.

Amid the many distracting lights which fall upon this question, the notions which I have been able to form regarding Jamaica, and the interpretation which I have been able to put upon occurrences you so earnestly denounce, are these:

That through the absence of necessary guidance and governance, the negroes of the colony had fallen into a very chaotic and bad condition, presenting a deplorable contrast with their brethren in other colonies, who, favoured with less leisure, have become far better men. The Jamaica negroes are, I am informed, as a general rule, lazy and profligate, while many of the authorities I have consulted, and who have lived among these people, add a third and weightier adjective, which I refrain from writing down.

It is not, I believe, contended, even by their friends, that the Jamaica negroes are not lazy : it is only urged in extenuation that white men under the same circumstances would be lazy too.

Be he black or white, the man who illustrates this doctrine, and who lives as the negroes of Jamaica are reported to live, soon ceases to be a civilised being.

But he may be harmless and docile notwithstanding. Though absolutely useless, he may not be dangerous. Is this the character of the West Indian negro, or is it not?

History, written without reference to the Jamaica insurrection—written long years before the committal of the deeds you denounce—gives the following answer to this question :

" This vast conspiracy (that of the negroes in St. Domingo), productive in the end of calamities in the island, unparalleled even in the long catalogue of European atrocity, had for its object the total extirpation of the whites, and the establishment of an independent black government over the whole colony. So inviolable was the secresy, so general the dissimulation of the slaves, that the awful catastrophe was in no way apprehended by the European proprietors, and a conspiracy which embraced nearly the whole negro population of the island, was revealed only by the obscure hints of a few faithful domestics, who, without betraying their comrades, warned their masters of the approach of an unknown and terrible danger. The explosion was sudden and dreadful, beyond anything ever before seen among mankind. At once the beautiful plains in the north of the island were covered with fires, the labours of a century were devoured in a night, while the negroes, like unchained tigers, precipitated themselves on their masters, seized their arms, massacred them without pity, and threw them into the flames. . . . The cruelties exercised on the unhappy captives on both sides in this disastrous contest exceeded anything recorded in history. The negroes marched with spiked infants on their spears instead of colours, they sawed asunder the male prisoners, and violated the females on the dead bodies of their husbands."—Alison's *History of Europe*, vol. vi. p. 104.

It was people of this race and temper who, called together by the sound of horns and shells, assembled in hundreds round the Court House of Morant Bay on the 11th of October, 1865. It was such people who then and there fell upon our countrymen, and, after driving them by fire from the Court House, slew, hacked, and mutilated them; and who, after having done this, proceeded to spread the flame of insurrection elsewhere.

At the time here referred to, discontent, and disaffection prevailed throughout the whole island of Jamaica. This I gather from your own documents. The colony then resembled the dried grass of a prairie, ready to be set on fire from beginning to end by a spark of successful insurrection.

But lest what I gather from your documents should be tinctured by any bias of mine, I offer to your notice the first of a series of letters bearing upon this subject, which comes to my hand.

On the 20th of July, 1865, Mr. Hudson, of Jamaica, writes thus to Mr. Salmon, of the same island :

" Spring Vale, July 20, 1865.

" DEAR SIR,—I think it incumbent on me to inform you of certain reports of a serious nature which are in circulation in my neighbourhood.

"For the past few weeks there have been rumours of a rebellion among the peasantry, but I did not attach any importance to them, but conceived they originated from want of understanding the causes of the recent meetings held in this and the adjacent parishes until lately. I have been led by sufficient information to believe they are more than passing reports, and which require some notice.

" It appears that there is an organised plot among the people in this vicinity for a rebellion about the early part of August ensuing. My reasons for believing there is truth in the matter are these :

"A house girl of mine has stated several times to my family's

hearing that the black people have agreed upon rising in arms
at the above period for the purpose of murdering the upper
classes, and destroying and afterwards seizing their properties. She does not deny that she obtained this information
from her friends. For the present she will not say anything
more on the subject, but only states, 'We must wait and see.'
Other persons have likewise given us intelligence of a similar
nature. Dr. M'Catty mentioned something to me of a like
import which tends greatly to strengthen them. He stated
he had already acquainted you with the purport of his information.

"I do not think it would be wise to treat these rumours
merely as ' idle tales.' My district is hot to join with other
parts of the island in a move of the kind, if made.

"My delicate state of health prevents my calling to see you,
but I shall be glad to give you whatever further information
in my power, and to receive any directions from you on the
subject.

"It would not be prudent to allow these strong reports to
continue, without preparing, as far as we are able, against an
attempt of disturbance, should it turn out to be correct.

"I have, &c.,
(Signed) "John Hudson.

"The Hon. John Salmon, Custos."

" A house girl of mine" :—You, gentlemen, are far better
acquainted than I am with what an illustrious member of
your body calls " the law of inseparable association," and no
doubt you will recognise an illustration of this law in the
promptitude with which the warnings preceding the troubles
in St. Domingo suggest themselves on reading this letter.

On the 11th of October, as above stated, the much dreaded
action began. The Governor of the island had then thrown
upon him the responsibility of preserving the property, lives,
and honour of 14,000 British men and women, who were
scattered in isolated and unprotected positions among a
negro population of 350,000.

And it is to be remarked, that the leaders of these people were well aware of the advantages of their position. That they were not held back from revolt and rapine by the fear of subsequent retribution. In the neighbouring island of Hayti they had the example of a people which had successfully defied the power of France. In reply to an intimation of the swift vengeance of England in case of insurrection, Mr. G. W. Gordon was able to point out that "all the power of the Great Napoleon could not put down the rising in Hayti, and that was successful, for the troops died of disease before they could meet the people in the mountains." And when the power displayed by England in crushing the Indian mutiny was urged upon his attention, Mr. Gordon was able to respond, "India is not at all a case in point, for India is a flat country, and the English troops would overrun and conquer it; but this is a mountainous country, and before the British troops could reach the mountains they would die of disease here."

Taking all these things into account, I endeavoured to clearly realise the position of the Governor who had this problem suddenly thrust upon his attention by the butchery at Morant Bay. How, with the force at his disposal, to preserve the lives of 7000 British men, and the honour of 7000 British women, from the murder and the lust of black savages capable of the deeds which history shows to be theirs in St. Domingo; and a re-enactment of which had, to all appearance, begun under the said Governor's eyes.

I will not dwell upon the measures taken then and there by the Governor to solve this problem. For his deeds in the first instance have won for him the praise of his censors, and have challenged, without hostile response, the judgment of yourselves. But you denounce him for extending martial law beyond the necessary period, and for inflicting the punishment due to rebellion "for days and weeks after all resistance had ceased."

I am not prepared to question the truth of these allegations; I am not prepared to deny that the period of punishment was too long, or that its character was too severe. Now that the smoke of battle has cleared away, you perhaps see more truly the character of the field. But I would invite you to transport yourselves to that field while the smoke still hung upon it ; to remember that a former rebellion in Jamaica which everybody supposed to be quelled in May broke out "with redoubled fury in June ;" to think of Governor Eyre with the blood of his slaughtered countrymen before his eyes ; with the memories of St. Domingo in his mind; with the consciousness that the whole island round him was near its point of combustion, and with no possible means of estimating *how* near. In what way, gentlemen, some of your number would have acted under these circumstances, God only knows. In all probability they would have acted kindly and calamitously, for philanthropists can unconsciously become shedders of blood. How others of your number would have acted I believe I *do* know. They might have acted with more tact, and thus given less offence, but their measure of mercy to the murderers would not, I am persuaded, have exceeded that of Governor Eyre.

It appears to me that you practically forget the circumstances which I am here endeavouring to bring before your minds. There seems a tendency on your part to tone down the crimes of the negro and to bring his punishments into relief. You speak, for example, of the massacre at Morant Bay as "a local riot." But, looking at the historic antecedents, what right had Governor Eyre to come to this conclusion? Had he come to it and acted on it, he might have earned for himself the execration of the English people, if not of mankind. To his knowledge the whole island was disaffected, and history had informed him what a disaffected negro population can do. He knew how they could plot in secret, and spring like tigers on their victims the moment their plans were matured. Only think of his position, knowing that such things had occurred, and with a horrible practical intimation before him that they were about to occur again. The height and span of a bridge, gentlemen, must be regulated with reference to the larger floods, and the action of Governor Eyre had to be determined, not by the hypothesis of a local riot, but by the contemplation of the calamities which were certain to overwhelm the whole island if the insurrection were permitted to expand. No narrower assumption than this could, under the circumstances, be entertained. Had the local riot hypothesis been demonstrable *at the time*—could it have been proved that the insurrection was confined to a single parish, and that the culprits at large would not spread the fire of rebellion throughout the colony, I would join you in condemning Governor Eyre. But no such thing was demonstrable. Had he had a force at his command sufficient to cope with insurrection, even though the whole island were engaged in it, I would let him answer for himself. But he had no such force. The power opposed to him, if permitted to organise itself, was sufficient to swallow him and those for whose lives he was accountable. He was, therefore, obliged to augment his relative strength, by damping everywhere the spirit of rebellion, and this could only be done by making the name, power, and determination of England terrible throughout the island. That errors should be committed, that cruelties should be perpetrated, that wrong should be done, is, I fear, under such circumstances, unavoidable; but the error, the cruelty, and the wrong, so far as they were committed, were, for the most part, beyond the control of Governor Eyre.

You have directed my attention to the case of Mr. Gordon, and I have looked into it again. I pass without comment the evidence of Lieut. Edenborough, the extreme gravity of which cannot be overlooked, because, through the miscarriage of a letter, his evidence, though in the blue-book, was not taken before the Commissioners. From the speeches of Mr. Gordon in the House of Assembly; from his relationship to Mr. Paul Bogle, one of the principal murderers of Morant Bay; from his letters to Mr. Lawrence, his manager; from his conversations with Messrs. Harrison, Beckwith, Ford, and others; from his published address to the negroes, and from his other addresses, the conclusion seems indubitable, that he was the taproot from which the insurrection drew its main sustenance, and that Governor Eyre was justified in concluding that no man concerned in the murder of our countrymen was more guilty than he. When, therefore, the sentence on Gordon, after having been approved by his officers, was submitted to him, he did not stay judgment, but ratified the decision that others had pronounced. Whether, in the details of this proceeding, he committed or did not commit a legal blunder, I am not able to say. If he did, he has surely paid dearly for it by the ruin of his career. I notice throughout his entire conduct the clear conviction on his part that he was doing his duty, the undoubting trust in the justice of his countrymen which caused him to neglect the personal safeguards which a more adroit person would have employed. To associate the term "murder" with his name is, in my opinion, without justification. There is no propriety in the term unless it is backed by assumptions which no man has a right to make. And if in the prosecution, which, to the detriment of this country, is now invoked against Governor Eyre, the execution of Gordon, from a lawyer's point of view, be deemed indefensible, I trust the common sense of Englishmen will perceive that it was caused by those whose own bloody atrocities had, for the time, stifled mercy and abrogated law.

Such, gentlemen, are the notions and interpretations which your courtesy in writing to me induces me to lay before you. And such being my notions, when asked to join the Eyre Defence Committee, I felt that cowardice, or a dislike to the worry involved in the act, was the only reason which opposed my doing so. Concluding from what I had observed in society, that Governor Eyre was more likely to suffer from timidity than from conviction—that the dread of you, gentlemen, and of those whom you represent, was very widely spread—I overcame my strong reluctance to mingle in any matter of the kind. I pledge you my word of honour, gentlemen, that during this inquiry I have had laid before me the testimony of men of approved valour, coolness of judgment, and capacity, who have occupied positions of the most critical danger, who have extricated themselves and others from such positions in a manner which has secured for them the unanimous applause of the people of this country, and who, from data gathered on the spot, conclude that in the month of October, 1865, Governor Eyre saved the whole white population of Jamaica from massacre. I have the solemn assurance of such men, that England has few sons as noble, few men so equal to a great emergency, few who have done the state such service as Governor Eyre. And I now call upon you, with the most solemn emphasis that man can address to man, not to permit personal pride, the love of victory, or the desire to substantiate that to which you have committed yourselves, because you are so committed, to influence your further action in this matter. I call upon you in the name of all that is wise and dignified in human nature—in the name of all that is just and manly in the English character—not to permit the folly of Governor Eyre's admirers, if such folly should, in your estimation exist, to colour your judgment in this grave question. And whether you will hear, or whether you will forbear, I call upon the men of England who share the views here set forth, to throw themselves without delay between you and Governor Eyre, and to prevent you from adding to the harm which he has already experienced at your hands.

I have the honour to remain, Gentlemen,
with profound esteem for many of you,
and with brotherly affection for some,
Your obedient servant,

JOHN TYNDALL.

Athenæum Club,
November 7, 1866.

APPENDIX.

C.

REPORT OF A MEETING OF THE EYRE DEFENCE COMMITTEE HELD AT WILLIS'S ROOMS.

A MEETING of the general committee of the Eyre Defence Fund was held at Willis's Rooms, on Monday, the 18th inst., the Right Hon. the Earl of Shrewsbury and Talbot in the chair.

The HON. SECRETARY read the notice convening the meeting, and letters of apology for non-attendance from Lord Boston and Sir James Clark, who both regretted that they were unable to be present.

The EARL OF SHREWSBURY—My Lords and Gentlemen,—This meeting is convened for the purpose of giving efficient action to the working of the executive committee of this fund. You are aware that steps of a serious nature have been taken by the prosecution ; the time has therefore arrived for us to be prepared to act vigorously. We have for our object the protection of a persecuted man, and a man who I conscientiously believe has done his duty faithfully to his Queen and his country. You, gentlemen, I am sure, will feel that our best course is to be calm and quiet, but resolute and determined. Some proceedings have already taken place, and I believe I can do no better than to ask the solicitor, who is a most able, and at the same time zealous adviser, to inform you of what has occurred, and to state the reasons which have induced the executive committee to request Mr. Eyre to remain in the county in which he is now residing, and not by any action of his own to recognise in the smallest degree the validity of the proceedings now being instituted against him.

Mr. Rose, the solicitor, stated the proceedings that had taken place, and read the correspondence between himself, Mr. Eyre, and others.

The Hon. Secretary informed the meeting that having forwarded to Mr. Eyre two addresses transmitted to him, Mr. Eyre had replied as follows :

"I beg to acknowledge your communication informing me that addresses to me, expressing their good opinion of and confidence in my public character and conduct, and their sympathy with me under the circumstances of my present position, have been forwarded to you by a large number of the influential residents of Sheffield and the neighbourhood, and by the members of the Bradford Working Men's Conservative Association. Whilst I am deeply grateful for the good feeling which has prompted these demonstrations in my favour, I am sure I shall not be misunderstood if I add that, as a judicial inquiry into my conduct (unmerited as I believe it to be) is now approaching, it would be more in accordance with my own feelings and wishes if the presentation of any addresses containing a manifestation of public feeling or opinion could be suspended until that inquiry has terminated."

Professor Tyndall—My Lords and Gentlemen,—I am asked to propose a resolution regarding the application of the Defence Fund : and if you will allow me, I will preface the resolution by a few remarks, with a view of clearing up misconceptions possible and actual. The controversy about the conduct of Mr. Eyre seems to be regarded by some as a struggle between political partisans. I have, for example, heard myself called a Tory for refusing to join in denouncing the conduct of Mr. Eyre. Now, I did not come here to take up your time in listening to a profession of political principles, but, lest my position should be mistaken, I must avow that I have about as much right to membership in the Tory party as

I have to a seat in Convocation, with Archdeacon Denison as my guide, philosopher, and friend. In fact, my leanings are quite the other way. When asked, for example, prior to the late general election, whether I had a vote for Westminster, my reply was "No! but if I had a hundred votes I would give them all to John Stuart Mill." In fact, a glance over their names will show that Liberals as well as Conservatives throng. our subscription lists, proving that the motives which actuate us are altogether above those of party. Gentlemen, Mr. John Stuart Mill has more than once recommended the outspoken manly utterance of conviction. I hope he will bear it with good temper when he finds such utterance to be in opposition to himself. He doubtless sees in himself the assertor of constitutional principles. I see in him the prosecutor of a man who has done the State incalculable service. I see him endeavouring to fix the brand of murder upon one who, whatever his legal errors may have been, and whatever may have been the excesses committed by his subordinates, saved the colony which he ruled from excesses a million times more terrible —who by swift action, and the prompt quenching of a conflagration already ignited amid the most combustible materials, saved the island of Jamaica from scenes of bloodshed and dishonour, which, had they been permitted to occur, would have called down both upon him and upon those who had trusted an English colony to his unworthy hands the curses of the English nation. This manner of viewing the subject is the result of all that I have been able to learn regarding the character of the Jamaica negro. It is based on the historic atrocities committed on white men and women by the negroes of a neighbouring island; it is based on a knowledge of the state of Jamaica for months prior to the insurrection, during which time the colony was ripe for revolt; it is based on the bloody and cruel character of the outbreak at Morant Bay, which was the first bud and blossom of the disaffection. Finally, it is based on the almost unanimous testimony of the white population. But it may be urged that antipathies of race so affect the testimony of the Jamaica planter as to render it unworthy of acceptance. Well, I have not trusted to it alone. I hold in my hand a private letter from a British officer whose coolness of head and soundness of judgment are well known and appreciated ; a man above all panic, and whose name, wherever it is uttered in these islands, is received with respect. That officer is Sir Leopold M'Clintock, and these are the terms in which he expresses himself regarding Mr. Eyre and the Jamaica insurrection. "I write this to tell you that the Eyres go home by this packet. I met them yesterday. They both seem greatly harassed and cut up by all the vexation they have gone through. Eyre is a noble fellow—a man whom England may well be proud of. He acted vigorously in a great emergency, and saved the white population of this island from massacre. He is no lawyer, but he behaved with cool judgment and with a clear conscience. . . . . . . He stands higher in my estimation at this moment, notwithstanding 'the cloud,' than he did previous to the late events, which have proved him to possess great qualities." This is a specimen of the testimony which has influenced my judgment. As a political philosopher, Sir Leopold M'Clintock will not bear comparison with Mr. Mill ; but as regards capacity to form a practical judgment of the character of the Jamaica insurrection, and of Mr. Eyre's conduct therein, Mr. Mill, I hold, will not bear comparison with Sir Leopold M'Clintock. I hope Mr. Mill will not be offended with me if I compare him to a theoretic navigator, who, well versed in books and well instructed by lectures, holds, and will fearlessly apply, the general truth that the variation of the compass in our locality is 23 degrees west. It is so in Kew Observatory ; it is so on Salisbury Plain ; and it may be so in Mr. Mill's library. But it is not so on board ship. Here we may have the disturbance of local forces—of attractions and repulsions which our navigator's previous education does not in the least qualify him to deal with, and which render altogether nugatory, if not in the last degree perilous, the application of his general knowledge. Accept the pilotage which Mr. Mill so courageously undertakes, and there are cases in which he will wreck you with greater certainty than if you had abandoned your craft without chart or compass to the blind currents of the sea. It is constantly urged by the supporters of the Jamaica committee that the execution of Gordon is a frightful precedent, without a word to indicate the extent of ground covered by this phrase. Now I would beg to say that if the precedent be restricted to Jamaica, and to men of Gordon's stamp, who provoke insurrection there about four times in a century, it is not frightful, and if it be extended to England the extension is unwarrantable. Who dreams of making Jamaica a precedent for England? Certainly not the defenders of Mr. Eyre. We do not hold an Englishman and a Jamaica negro to be convertible terms, nor do we think the cause of human liberty will be promoted by any attempt to make them so. Five and twenty years before worth and unworth ran into unnatural coalition in the Jamaica committee—at a time when a million and a half of paupers existed in England and Wales alone — when the famished crowds of Lancashire met the military in the streets and were quieted by musket bullets; at that time Thomas Carlyle, in the interest of British workers, thus apostrophised the estimable members of the Anti-Slavery Convention: "Oh, Anti-Slavery Convention! loud-sounding, long-eared Exeter Hall; but in thee, too, is an instinct towards justice, and I will complain of nothing. Only black Quashee over the seas being once sufficiently attended to, wilt thou not perhaps open thy dull, sodden eyes to the 'sixty thousand valets in London itself, who are yearly dismissed to the streets to be what they can when the season ends?' Or to the hunger-stricken, pallid, yellow-coloured free labourers in Lancashire, Yorkshire, Buckinghamshire, and all other shires? These yellow-coloured for the present absorb all my sympathies. If I had twenty millions, with model farms, and Niger expeditions, it is to these that I would give it! Quashee has already victuals and clothing; Quashee is not dying of such despair as the yellow-coloured pale man's. Why, in one of those Lancashire weavers, dying of hunger, there is more thought and heart, a greater arithmetical amount of misery and desperation, than in whole gangs of Quashees." Is this view of matters consistent with a moment's tolerance of the proposition that the treatment of negroes in insurrection should be made a precedent for the treatment of Englishmen? It is very easy to be eloquent upon the question of colour; easy to talk of the administration of British law without regard to colour, as if it were at bottom a question of colour at all. Let me explain myself by a scientific illustration. There are two kinds of rock crystal, which nine persons out of every ten here present would pronounce identical in appearance; but a close observer notices certain minute facets in the one that are absent in the other. Now, that small external difference is infallibly associated with an entire inversion of the optical powers of the crystal. And so it is with colour. I do not object to black. I rather like it; but I accept black as indicative of other associated qualities of infinitely greater importance than colour. Nor have I lightly come to this conclusion. I have already quoted for you the views of Sir Leopold M'Clintock with regard to Mr. Eyre; let me now give you the opinion regarding the negro of Dr. Joseph Dalton Hooker — a man in whom righteousness, mercy, and truth are blended with the highest intellectual excellence, and with knowledge garnered from all corners of the earth. Neither he nor I, let me say, ever had the slightest sympathy with negro slavery. Both of us equally abhor cruelty; both of us are ready to join in denouncing it, but neither of us is willing to commit himself to that "falsehood of extremes" which is the vice of the position of the Jamaica committee. This, then, is the opinion which extensive reading, much questioning of travellers, and some personal contact have forced upon Dr. Hooker: "That the negro in Jamaica," he writes to me, "and even in the free towns of Western

Africa, is pestilential, I have no hesitation in declaring; nor that he is a most dangerous savage at the best." But my friend Hooker, if he had a word to say in favour of the Fiend himself, would be careful not to repress it, and he takes care to explain that though the negro is cruel, he is not so in the sense of the North American Indian, cruel for cruelty's sake. Still he regards the negro as essentially cruel, "inasmuch as when his blood is up, very cruel acts are his first acts, and these in great number." In a second note to me he thus repeats the conviction expressed in his first: "I consider him a savage, and a most dangerous savage too. I believe the power and position given to him in the free towns of Western Africa, to have had a pestilential influence; and the liberty given to him in Jamaica to have proved equally detrimental to the prosperity of that island." With testimony of which this is but a sample before me, I decline accepting the negro as the equal of the Englishman, nor will I commit myself to the position that a negro insurrection and an English insurrection ought to be treated in the same way. I approve of the conduct of those British officers in India who shot their wives before blowing themselves to pieces, rather than allow what they loved and honoured to fall into the hands of the Sepoys. I should not approve of the shooting of wives through the fear of prospective insult in the case of an English insurrection. Either this is mere sentimentalism or it is not. If any man thinks it so, let us have his name for the information of the women of England. If it is not—if the falling into the hands of a Jamaica negro be a different thing from falling into the hands of an Englishman, then the conclusion is mathematically evident that we are justified in going further to prevent the one calamity than to prevent the other. The women of England ought to have a voice in this matter, and to them I confidently appeal. They remem- the story of the Sabine girls who were treacherously carried away by the Roman youth, and who, afterwards, when their fathers had collected to avenge the insult, threw themselves between the combatants, offering themselves to the spears of both. I ask the women of England; I ask the wives and daughters of our antagonists, whether it is likely the conduct of the Sabine maidens would have been the same had Jamaica negroes played the part of the Roman youth? If the effort to repress crime is to bear any proportion to the agony which its committal would inflict, then I say the repression of a Jamaica insurrection ought to be more stern than the repression of an English insurrection. There is something in the soul of man to lift him to the level of death, and to enable him to look it in the face. But there is nothing in the soul of woman to lift her to the level of that which I dare not do more than glance at here, but which any woman desirous of information will find described in the history of the negro insurrection in Saint Domingo. For my own part, while intensely sympathising with animal suffering of all kinds—while capable of feeling for the moth which singes its innocent wings in the flame of a candle, cowardice alone would prevent me from braving a score of criminal prosecutions sooner than allow my countrywomen to run the risk of those unutterable horrors which threatened them in the autumn of 1865 in the island of Jamaica. Thus, gentlemen, however I may deplore, or even denounce, some of the occurrences associated with the quelling of the Jamaica insurrection, I cannot allow the contemplation of details to hide the cardinal fact that Jamaica is still a British colony, that the men of England within its boundaries have been saved from massacre, and the women of England from a fate which is left unexpressed by the term dishonour. Errors have been committed, but the really deadly error—the error of weakness, which in its effects is equivalent to that of wickedness, has been avoided. And now let me turn in conclusion to the resolution confided to me. Mr. Eyre is assailed by two classes of men. The one class, though, as I believe, mistaken, high-minded, and honourable; the other, if we may trust their own language, absolutely thirsting for the blood of Mr. Eyre. It is against this portion of the Jamaica committee that I ask you to defend him now. For men of this type, if they fail in their grand effort—the criminal prosecution—will seek to ruin Mr. Eyre in other ways. Their nobler colleagues, with whom, by the most extraordinary chance, they have come into momentary osculation, are above all this. I should not be surprised if they discountenanced all this; but I ask you not to leave Mr. Eyre trusting wholly to their interposition. I ask you to defend him from every assault, civil and criminal, made upon him in consequence of his conduct in Jamaica, and I therefore beg to submit to you the following resolution—"That the steps taken by the executive committee, for the defence of Mr. Eyre from proceedings, civil and criminal, are approved and adopted by the general committee."

General SIR WILLIAM GOMM—My Lords and Gentlemen,— I beg to second the resolution which has been moved by the learned professor; and while doing so, I would beg briefly to explain why I never seconded a resolution in my life with greater satisfaction to myself. I know Jamaica. I know it intimately—most intimately. I know the various orders of its strange community, and the exceptional character of the relations these bear to each other; and thence I was fully prepared to receive the distinct admissions, after mature deliberation, both of the Royal Commissioners and of her Majesty's late Government, that it was owing to the skill, the energy, and the promptitude of Governor Eyre that the whole colony was saved from a calamity incalculable. It is my firm belief that the means adopted by Governor Eyre were pressed upon him by difficulties and dangers rarely paralleled. It is further, gentlemen, my deliberate opinion that he saved the island of Jamaica to the British Crown. I am, therefore, much pleased at this opportunity of expressing my opinion, and of seconding the resolution proposed by the learned and eminent professor on my left. I may add one word in conclusion. I have no personal acquaintance with Mr. Eyre, and no communication has ever passed between myself and that distinguished, and, at the same time, most shamefully calumniated and persecuted public servant.

The resolution proposed by Professor Tyndall and seconded by Sir W. Gomm, was carried unanimously.

Sir Roderick Murchison—My Lords and Gentlemen,—As a vice-president of the Eyre Defence and Aid Fund, and therefore necessarily one of the executive committee, I beg to assure you that the vote you have just passed has been as gratifying to me as I am sure it must have been to all my associates. Being an old friend of Mr. Eyre, and having long admired his conduct as a great traveller, a philanthropist, a protector of the aborigines of Australia, and also as having through life maintained a high and spotless character, I participated in the general feeling of thankfulness to him when I learnt that the appalling outbreak and massacre in Morant Bay was so speedily followed by the announcement of the prompt and vigorous conduct of the man who thus saved the important colony of Jamaica from ruin. How then was I astounded when the same man who had been thus extolled was, through the declaration of certain public orators, held up to public opprobrium as a murderer! This was not to be borne by one who knew the true character of Mr. Eyre, and I at once wrote to the *Times* newspaper in my own name, beseeching my countrymen not to prejudge the question through any such appeals, and expressing my conviction that my friend would fully justify his conduct. Well, gentlemen, I do not hesitate to say, that after the elaborate judicial inquiry which has taken place in Jamaica I remain as satisfied as ever that my honoured friend Eyre acted on the first impulse, as every loyal governor ought to act when, at a great moral responsibility, he saved the lives of the colonists committed to his care. After the telling address of my eloquent friend Professor Tyndall, and the sanction given to it by so distinguished a general as Sir William Gomm, one of the true heroes of the wars of Wellington, and who formerly commanded the forces in Jamaica, it would be unpardonable and most out of place on my part if I were to weaken by any further observations the effect of their addresses. But, abstaining myself, I think I cannot better strengthen the good cause in which we are all embarked than by reading to you part of a letter I have received from that excellent and respected man Sir James Clark, who, earnestly sympathising with us, has been alone prevented from appearing here this day by the state of his health. From this letter I will read the following:—"My first acquaintance with Mr. Eyre was his bringing to me two little native Australian boys, whom he had brought with him to this country with the object of giving them some education, and then returning them to their own country. This thoughtful attention and kindness to these little black fellows produced on me a very favourable impression of Mr. Eyre's benevolent disposition, and all our intercourse since that time—some twenty years ago—has been to satisfy me that the impression then made was a correct one—that Mr. Eyre was a kind-hearted man, who had the good of his fellow-creatures at heart. I can now add that nothing which has transpired of Mr. Eyre's conduct during the suppression of the unfortunate Jamaica insurrection has diminished the high opinion I had formed of his character. Mr. Eyre's position was one of the most anxious and responsible in which a man could be placed: the preservation of an important colony and the lives of many thousands of his countrymen and their families hung upon his conduct. He preserved both by his judgment and decision. Had he failed by lack of either, those who are now accusing him of cruelty, and even murder, would have been equally ready to stigmatise him as unfit for his position. I can only add that my own conviction, founded on my knowledge of Mr. Eyre's character, is, that in his whole conduct during the Jamaica insurrection he was guided by the purest motives, his sole object being to save the colony." The chivalrous desire of Mr. Eyre to appear at Bow-street and sink or swim with his subordinates was only checked by the unanimous resolution of the executive committee, that he be urged to remain at his house in Shropshire, and not forward the design of his prosecutors. That, however, was our act, and we cannot allow Mr. Eyre to be unjustly accused, as he has been by a weekly newspaper (doubtless through ignorance of the facts), of having declined to face the responsibility which his subordinates have faced more bravely. Colonel Nelson and Lieutenant Brand are defended by her Majesty's Government; but, as upon us lies the burden of defending Mr. Eyre, so he was bound to be guided by the advice given us by the eminent counsel to whom we referred the points, and on which we acted. Gentlemen, there is still a pleasing duty left for me to perform, and I call upon you to return your best thanks to the Earl of Shrewsbury for his conduct in the chair. In espousing the defence of ex-Governor Eyre, he has evinced a feeling which is shared by many a brother admiral, and I rejoice to say by many a loyal subject of our gracious Queen. I move, therefore, that the hearty thanks of this meeting be given to Admiral the Earl of Shrewsbury.

LORD DE BLAQUIERE seconded the vote of thanks to the chairman.

After a few words from the EARL OF SHREWSBURY and TALBOT, the meeting separated.

APPENDIX.

———

D.

The following letters have, with many others of a similar nature, during the past six months, been addressed to the honorary secretary of the Eyre Defence and Aid Fund:

No. I.

FROM THOMAS CARLYLE, ESQ.

" Ripple Court, Ringwould, Dover,
" 23rd August, 1866.

" SIR,—The clamour raised against Governor Eyre appears to me to be disgraceful to the good sense of England ; and if it rested on any depth of conviction, and were not rather (as I always flatter myself it is) a thing of rumour and hearsay, of repetition and reverberation, mostly from the teeth outward, I should consider it of evil omen to the country, and to its highest interests, in these times. For my own share, all the light that has yet reached me on Mr. Eyre and his history in the world goes steadily to establish the conclusion that he is a just, humane, and valiant man, faithful to his trusts everywhere, and with no ordinary faculty of executing them ; that his late services in Jamaica were of great, perhaps of incalculable value, as certainly they were of perilous and appalling difficulty,—something like the case of ' fire,' suddenly reported, ' in the ship's powder-room ' in mid ocean, where the moments mean the ages, and life and death hang on your use or your misuse of the moments ; and, in short, that penalty and clamour are not the thing this Governor merits from any of us, but honour and thanks, and wise *imitation* (I will further say), should similar emergencies

U

rise, on the great scale or on the small, in whatever *we* are governing!

"The English nation never loved anarchy, nor was wont to spend its sympathy on miserable mad seditions, especially of this inhuman and half-brutish type; but always loved order, and the prompt suppression of seditions; and reserved its tears for something worthier than promoters of such delirious and fatal enterprises, who had got their wages for their sad industry. Has the English nation changed, then, altogether? I flatter myself *it* has not—not yet quite; but only that certain loose superficial portions of it have become a great deal louder, and not any wiser, than they formerly used to be.

"At any rate, though much averse, at any time, and at this time in particular, to figure on committees, or run into public noises without call, I do at once, and feel that as a British citizen I should and must, make you welcome to my name for your committee, and to whatever good it can do you. With the hope only that many other British men, of far more significance in such a matter, will at once or gradually do the like; and that, in fine, by wise effort and persistence, a blind and disgraceful act of public injustice may be prevented; and an egregious folly as well,—not to say—for none can say or compute—what a vital detriment throughout the British Empire in such an example set to all the colonies and governors the British Empire has!

"Further service, I fear, I am not in a state to promise; but the whole weight of my conviction and good wishes is with you; and if other service possible to me do present itself, I shall not want for willingness in case of need. Enclosed is my mite of contribution to your fund.

"I have the honour to be, yours truly,

"T. CARLYLE.

"To Hamilton Hume, Esq.,
  "Hon. Sec. Eyre Defence Fund."

No. II.

FROM THE BISHOP OF JAMAICA.

"Personally I have an earnest sympathy with Mr. Eyre. I warmly admire his character and history as far as they are known to me, and I firmly believe that the speedy suppression of the murderous insurrections in Jamaica is attributable, under God's providence, to the promptitude, courage, and judgment with which he acted under circumstances of peculiar difficulty and danger. From all that I have heard of Mr. Eyre's career, I believe that his humanity and kindness of heart, his love of justice and mercy, and his eminently Christian principles, qualified him in a very high degree for the discharge of his arduous and painful duties at a most critical period of the history of the colony whose government he had to administer.

*　　　*　　　*　　　*　　　*　　　*　　　*

"I am fully sensible of the honour conferred on me by your request; and while I trust that no exigence for the further defence of Mr. Eyre's conduct will arise to render any application of the fund raised by the Committee necessary to that particular purpose, I shall rejoice to find that some compensation shall have been provided by the successful exertions of the Committee for the loss unhappily entailed on Mr. Eyre by his disconnection from the public service in which he had been so long and so honourably employed."

No. III.

FROM ALFRED TENNYSON, ESQ.

" I sent my small subscription as a tribute to the nobleness of the man, and as a protest against the spirit in which a servant of the State, who has saved to us one of the islands of the Empire, and many English lives, seems to be hunted down. . . . . In the meantime, the outbreak of our Indian mutiny remains as a warning to all but madmen against want of vigour and swift decisiveness."

APPENDIX.

E.

Extracts from the Jamaica Newspapers.

WE forget for the moment whether it is Bridges or Bryan Edwards who, in their histories of Jamaica, remind us of an ancient Roman custom of constraining Pro-consuls and Governors to remain for forty days after the expiration of their term of office at the seat of Government, and suggests that if such were the case in the West Indies, the true light in which the conduct of certain Governors is regarded would be manifested. This test has been applied to Governor Eyre, and the ovation of Tuesday afternoon is the practical result.

We have good reasons for knowing that Mr. Eyre is a God-fearing English gentleman. That he is, to use the language of the poet Tennyson, one " who reverences his conscience as a king;" but next to the approval of his own conscience, he must have been immeasurably delighted by the testimony which was borne on Tuesday to the estimation in which he is held by vast masses of the community. We were quite unprepared for what we then witnessed. Other Governors have left our shores rejoicing in the approval of their Sovereign, so far, at least, as that can be expressed by the individual who presides at the Colonial Office; but no Governor has, in our memory, departed from us in whose favour the voice of the loyal and intelligent portion of our population has been so loudly declared.

Be it remembered, also, that the multitude who congregated on the wharf, or found standing-room on board the stately vessel, were not merely the white inhabitants, or the property classes, but men of all colours and conditions, and the loud cheers which were wafted across the water as the ship passed away, came from the representatives of all sections of our community. We do not deny that there are hundreds in our midst who would have rejoiced in seeing Mr. Eyre sent from us under widely different circumstances ; but still the vast gathering of Tuesday was most emphatically an expression of the feeling which actuates the lovers of law and order in our midst. We happened, on leaving the wharf, to overhear a fragment of a conversation between two black women :— " We want a Governor like Mr. Eyre," said one, " to protect the decent black people, and the buckra, from the lazy worthless negroes." The distinction which this woman made between " decent black people" and " worthless negroes" may not be obvious to all. Some, perhaps, may regard it as ridiculous ; others, as a distinction without a difference ; nevertheless, it embodies an idea which is gaining ground among the intelligent negroes of the colony, that the old cry of colour is a delusion and a snare, and that the wide gulf which lies between vast masses of the people arises from character and not from colour. We know that many of the " decent black people " estimate Mr. Eyre as did the woman whom we undesignedly overheard.

Reverting again to the parting ovation, we would call attention to the fact, that it was given not "forty days " after the virtual expiration of Mr. Eyre's government, but six months after his suspension by the Colonial Minister, and when the Report of the Royal Commissioners and the dispatch which accompanied it had been received, and therefore when no feeling of sycophancy, and no motive of self-interest could possibly influence a single individual who was present. Mr. Eyre was no longer the Governor of the colony ; he was simply an English gentleman, about, as he tells us, to " retire into private life, dismissed from the public service after nearly a lifetime spent in it ;" and it is on behalf of this ill-used and dismissed gentleman the great heart of the community has spoken.

No language has been too violent for certain writers and

speakers in the mother country to indulge in, when referring to those amongst us who have ventured to lift up their voices on behalf of the late Governor. We can hurl back their calumnies; we can treat their misrepresentations with disdain, and at least urge that we are not guilty of neglecting a fallen hero, or afraid to reiterate the convictions of our conscience, despite the rancour of the Jamaica Committee and the censure of a Colonial Minister.

We do not know that any Colonial Governor has borne the test which Mr. Eyre has done. For six months he has remained since his suspension in our midst, and when the moment of departure arrives, men and women of all classes press to say farewell, and bid him God speed; men who had been associated with him in Government, and who had often differed with him in political views; Ministers of all denominations, some of whom had been censured by the bodies with which they are connected because they had fearlessly borne their testimony to the service he had rendered; multitudes of men in less prominent walks of life; hard-handed and honest-hearted mechanics, and women too, whose numbers would have been greatly increased had they thought it would have been possible to be present on such an occasion.

It detracts nothing from the value we attach, and which we think Mr. Eyre will attach, to this farewell, if we add our personal conviction that his conduct will yet be seen in its true character, and that the British nation, often for a time, but seldom long, beguiled, will retract their baseless censures and hail with joy the act of the Minister, whoever he may be, who shall bestow upon him some signal mark of approval. But should this atonement to outraged justice be withheld, should Mr. Eyre be suffered to remain in retirement, POSTERITY WILL DO HIM JUSTICE. "There is," says the immortal Milton, "a resurrection of names as well as of bodies." Future Macaulays shall yet arise to continue the history of the British Empire. And the historian of the future, when he writes the page which shall portray the late rebellion and the events which followed it, will soar above the mists of ignorance and prejudice by which multitudes are now blinded, and tell how the noble-hearted man, who saved a splendid colony from anarchy and ruin, was dismissed from his position in obedience to the dictates of an irresponsible clique. He will tell also that the Government of the day, though professing, under other circumstances, to listen to the voice of representative intelligence, turned a deaf ear to the opinions of those whose homes, lives, and property had been preserved by the energy and promptitude of this ill-requited public officer, and that thus the unanimous vote of those who alone could be the right judges of the dangers by which they had been surrounded, and the measures by which they could be averted, was all but disregarded. To the honour of these men it will be added that they failed not in the expression of their gratitude, or suffered former differences of opinion to restrain the becoming utterance of those sentiments towards the ill-used Governor, who, in a terrible crisis, proved himself, as few could have done, to be the right man in the right place.

WE have to record a most *touching and thrilling incident* connected with the recent departure of Governor Eyre from Jamaica. It is well known that the venerable and deservedly beloved "Vicar Apostolic" of the Roman Catholic Church in Jamaica, "Father Dupeyron," has of late been most seriously indisposed, and quite unable to pay those formal official visits which, we doubt not, he earnestly longed to make. He, a few days since, expressed a wish to meet Governor Eyre in public, previous to his departure from Jamaica, *and before the assembled people* to shake hands with his Excellency, and express to him his (Father Dupeyron's) sympathy with the Governor under the heavy trials to which he had been subjected, since his successful efforts in the suppression of the late rebellion. The worthy Vicar, *at the risk of his life*, had himself driven on Tuesday to the Royal Mail Company Steamer's Wharf, where, after some time spent in waiting, he met his Excellency Governor Eyre, and they bade farewell in language which we do not now care to repeat. Suffice, that it was, on the one side, expressions of esteem, confidence, and sympathy, and on the other gratitude for the feelings entertained and expressed by the head of the Roman Catholics of Jamaica.

We have not space here to dwell on this subject, but shall return to it, and strive to do justice to our fellow-citizens, who have, in a *catholic* spirit, expressed their confidence in and sympathy with Governor Eyre.

THE Kingston farewell to our late Governor, Mr. Eyre, and the echo of it from all parts of the country, show that the heart of the island is true to the man who saved it from imminent ruin and lasting disgrace. Whatever may for a time be said by those in England who do not understand the state of society here, or who, under the influence of old and deeply-seated prejudices, will not consider all the facts of the rebellion and its suppression, and so form a just judgment in regard to both, the judgment of the intelligence and respectability of this country cannot now be upset. The most cautious minds—those which habitually desire to have their opinions tested by discussion, and the repeated and varied application to them of facts—must now feel satisfied that the views which have all along prevailed here on the subject of the inquiry entrusted to the Royal Commissioners have been shown to be just. The whole subject has not only been sifted here in the island press, and in every private circle, but it has now been fully handled by the English press, by the Commissioners, by the Ministers of the Crown, by Mr. Eyre; and the result is a clear knowledge of the points of agreement and disagreement; and we repeat that after all this discussion the opinions which prevail, and have for months prevailed here, are shown to have been well-founded. The judgment, the heart, and the conscience of the island in reference to Mr. Eyre are unmistakably sound. So are they in regard to the negroes and the late G. W. Gordon. Kingston never did itself more honour than when it gave Mr. Eyre the enthusiastic and sympathising farewell of last week. It fairly represented the sentiment of the whole island, and it will have much influence in England along with Mr. Eyre's reply to the Kingston Address in leading and forming the current of public opinion in that country.

Articles still appear in some of the English provincial papers, which show how little the writers of them have yet properly considered the facts reported by the Royal Commissioners; but enough has already been written by them to show that the current of opinion has been flowing into new channels, and will, the more the subject is kept before the English public, come to accord with the opinions which prevail here. The Jamaica Committee may do much injustice by their proceedings and by the writings and speeches of some of its members, but ultimately, and at no distant period, the effect will, we cannot doubt, be what they do not wish or anticipate. The case for the much-abused and maligned Mr. Eyre is so strong, that the more it is discussed the better for him. We have no doubt that Mr. Eyre sees this; that he knows he has a good cause, and fears no amount of injury. Let the Jamaica Committee then persevere; they will injure none but themselves in the end. Their wrong-doing will recoil upon themselves. One of the unavoidable consequences of the Report of the Commissioners must be a more correct knowledge than now prevails in England of the moral condition of the great bulk of the labouring population. Their crass ignorance, the ease with which they can be duped by designing rogues and demagogues, and their dangerous excitability, cannot fail to be seen through the aid of the Report. The conduct of Mr. Eyre and the island authorities will then be seen in its true light—that is, when it is known with whom they were dealing when they found it absolutely necessary to adopt severe measures in suppressing insurrection.

THE history of his Excellency Edward John Eyre, so far as it relates to his government in this colony, requires but a few lines from us to bring that chapter to a close. Notwithstanding the praise he received for "the skill, promptitude, and vigour which he manifested during the early stages of the insurrection," by Sir H. Storks and the Royal Commissioners, he was recalled by Mr. Cardwell, the late Colonial Minister, and left Jamaica on Tuesday, the 24th July, beloved and respected by a large majority of the inhabitants, who, from an ever-abiding sense of gratitude for the services he rendered to the country in 1865, looked upon his departure with unmeasurable sorrow and disappointment.

The narrative of his embarkation on board the Solent will be no doubt communicated by Sir Henry Storks to the Earl of Carnarvon, who has succeeded Mr. Cardwell in the Colonial Office under the Ministry of the Earl of Derby.

The Royal Mail Company's Steamer Solent it was known would sail on Tuesday, the 24th ult., at four o'clock, and it was pretty generally understood that Mr. Eyre was to leave his residence at three o'clock for the wharf. From about one o'clock in the afternoon, the line of road between Park Lodge, the residence of his honour the Custos, and Paradise Pen, the temporary residence of Mr. Eyre, by way of East Queen and Duke Streets began to exhibit signs of unusual bustle, and the pathways became crowded by citizens of all classes. Every window where a view could be obtained was filled with anxious observers, while the balconies of private houses and public offices on the way were filled by ladies and gentlemen from the fashionable circles of Jamaica society. On the Mail Company's wharf, and the windows and balconies immediately overlooking it, we observed :*

On the wharf, a company of the 3rd West India Regiment, under Major Anton, with the national and regimental colours, were in attendance as a guard of honour, and were accompanied by the magnificent band of that regiment.

* Here follows an enormous list of names.

The wharf-landing was carpeted, and the British ensign floated on the company's staff, at the French and other consular offices of the city, on the foremast of the Solent, and upon all the shipping of Kingston Harbour.

At a few minutes before three o'clock, the sound of distant cheering announced the approach of Mr. Eyre. The cheering increased as the party made progress down Duke Street, and continued, with the waving of hats and handkerchiefs, until they reached the entrance to the Mail Company's gate, when one tremendous shout of right welcome greeting arose from a crowd of black persons of both sexes who had thronged the entrance to the wharf, and in rolled triumphantly the carriage with that great, good man, Mr. Eyre, his amiable wife, and happy children, bowing gracefully to renewed and oft-repeated manifestations of welcome and hearty greeting.

As the cheer broke forth outside the gate, it was instantly taken up by the company inside the wharf.

His Excellency, with Mrs. Eyre and children, having alighted, were accompanied to the steamer, and were received by the band and the company of the 3rd West India Regiment, the national and regimental colours, the company presenting arms, and the band playing "God Save the Queen." The immense throng stood uncovered throughout the long line formed to receive his Excellency, who gracefully bowed as he passed along with Mrs. Eyre and family. Three cheers again met his Excellency as he ascended the stage, both sides of which were canvassed and carpeted, forming an enclosure; and on his Excellency leaving the gangway, three times three, thrice repeated, assailed his Excellency, who appeared on deck uncovered, and bowed in acknowledgment.

His Excellency embarked amidst great manifestations of popular feeling, and this feeling was somewhat heightened by the touching strains of a national melody from the band of the 3rd West India Regiment:

> " Should auld acquaintance be forgot,
> And days o' auld lang syne ?"

Captain Cooper, the indefatigable superintendent of the Mail Company, whose arrangements for the occasion were most satisfactory, seeing so many persons anxious to take a farewell of his Excellency, communicated the popular wish to Mr. Eyre, and, having procured an assent to the request—that the public might be permitted to pass along the deck of the Solent and wish Mr. Eyre adieu—with admirable judgment and presence of mind succeeded in making such arrangements as permitted of a ready ingress to and egress from the ship for so many hundreds of persons, awaiting and anxious to show that in their opinion Mr. Eyre had suffered no degradation in his recall from the Government.

The large company were then invited on board, which was generally responded to ; and each gentleman and lady shook hands heartily with his Excellency, almost all accompanying the act with a few appropriate observations, to all of which his Excellency gave a gracious reply.

It having been announced to his Excellency that the Lord Bishop and clergy of Jamaica desired to approach his Excellency with an address, his Excellency was pleased to receive the same, and his Lordship the Bishop, attended by the clergy of the Established Church, and other clergymen present, read in an audible and emphatic voice the following :

"JAMAICA.

" SIR,—We, the undersigned clergymen of the neighbourhood of Kingston, desire respectfully to convey to your Excellency, on the eve of your departure from this colony, the imperfect expression of our feelings on this painful termination of the period of your government. In conjunction with a large number of our brethren in other parts of the island, who would, we doubt not, most cordially join with us on the present occasion, if time allowed us to invite their concurrence, we not long ago tendered to you the heartfelt expression of our gratitude, our esteem, and our confidence. (Applause.)

" We desire to reiterate these sentiments now.   No former Government has ever rendered to Jamaica greater services than your Excellency has done.   You have not only secured the island from most imminent peril of a general insurrection by your courage, promptitude, judgment, and administrative skill, but, by the exercise of the same high qualities, prepared the way for such a reconstruction of the form of our constitution as—while we are not forgetful of our debt of gratitude to the House of Assembly for its liberal support of our anciently Established Church—the present emergency seemed to demand—a reconstruction to which, if any human means can avail to effect it, the future prosperity of the colony will primarily be due.   (Renewed applause.)

" For ourselves we would gratefully acknowledge the uniform kindness and courtesy which the clergy have ever experienced at your Excellency's hands, and the lively and discriminating interests which you have ever manifested in the welfare of the Church.   (Applause.)

" But even for those eminent services we would not thus warmly thank you, did we not know your Excellency to have been actuated by the purest motives, to be a devout worshipper of Him whose ministers we are, and to be influenced by feelings of true humanity towards the people to whom we minister.   (Deafening applause.)

" But knowing these things, we assure your Excellency of our heartfelt sympathy, and our earnest hope that you may, ere long, be called by our gracious Sovereign to another sphere of honourable and important public service.   (Uproarious applause.)

" It is our sincere desire and prayer, that wherever your lot be cast, the Divine blessing may attend you and all the members of your family, and we would beg you to accept and to convey to Mrs. Eyre, who has merited for herself the esteem and regard of so many amongst us, our respectful and most cordial farewell."   (Applause.)

His Excellency in a firm tone, his eyes betokening the

emotions of his heart, yet without a tear, replied, and was received with cheering at the end of each sentence, which, although not customary among British subjects, could not be restrained on this occasion. The personal farewell to his Excellency was again resumed—and Mrs. Eyre very condescendingly joined in the manifestations of acknowledgment in which his Excellency had engaged.

At four o'clock the bell rang, and again hearty shaking of hands with his Excellency took place, the band of the 3rd West India Regiment striking up with very singular appropriateness a national melody from the songs of old Scotland:

> " There's nae luck about the house,
> There's nae luck ava' ;
> There's little pleasure in the house,
> When our gude man's awa'."

At this moment a gentleman remarked to a friend, " Well, if this is degradation, I should like to be degraded every day in the same way."

Thos. Hendrick, Esq., proposed three cheers for Mr. Eyre, which was immediately responded to, and re-echoed from the living mass that crowded the shore, and the wharves that are adjacent. Three more for Mrs. Eyre were taken up with equal enthusiasm, and three for Queen Victoria were lustily given and oft repeated by the loyal inhabitants of the colony there assembled.

J. S. Williams, Esq., Advocate-General, as an old creole, then in a few words expressive of the obligation which the inhabitants of Jamaica owed Mr. Eyre for having saved their homes from desolation, proposed three cheers again for his Excellency, which was enthusiastically responded to.

When the stage had been finally removed, a concourse of persons who had remained on the wharf, with uncovered heads, rang the air with vociferous cheering, which was taken up along the shore by a crowd of people who had waited quietly and patiently for the moving of the ship. The guard of honour then presented arms, and the band gave the "general salute," which was immediately followed by the strains of "Auld Lang Syne." It is impossible to describe the enthusiasm, and at the same time the order and decent appearance, of those who thronged the shoreside during all these scenes. His Excellency bowed with hat in hand till the good ship Solent had fairly turned to sea.

The British ensign at the Royal Mail Company's Wharf was dipped three times on the arrival of his Excellency; the flags at the French and other Consulates were hoisted; and the shipping in harbour dipped three times as the noble vessel passed each of them with the ill-used but faithful and true servant of the British Crown, and the heroic and valiant rescuer of the well-disposed and peaceable and loyal inhabitants of poor Jamaica.

On the arrival of the Solent at Port Royal, a salute of seventeen guns from the Fort was fired in honour of his Excellency. The vessels of war dipped their ensigns, and the band on board H.M.S. Doris struck up "The National Anthem," which was immediately followed by the well-known air :

> " 'Mid pleasures and palaces though we may roam,
> Be it ever so lowly, there's no place like home."

Commodore Sir Leopold M'Clintock, LL.D., &c., and a number of gentlemen, were in waiting in the steamer's track, and, as soon as she stopped, all went on board to pay their respects to Mr. Eyre. A large number of other boats crowded around the steamer from shore, filled with passengers, all equally desirous, as had been the Kingstonians, of expressing their grateful sentiments to Mr. Eyre for his prompt action in having so vigorously suppressed the late rebellion.

No Governor has ever left these shores with such demonstrations of public gratitude and esteem as Mr. Eyre did on Tuesday, the 24th of July.

The public here, like the colonists of Australia, have been busily engaged in getting up a memorial to the Queen, praying that Mr. Eyre may be permitted " to accept the grateful

tribute intended for him" in a handsome testimonial, "in'
lasting record of our appreciation of his services." This testimonial has been most handsomely subscribed to, and embraces
the names of almost every class and creed in the colony. It
has been asserted by those opposed to the administration of
Mr. Eyre, and numbering but a mere unit of the community,
that large sums have not been subscribed, although announced ;
but although such assertions and insinuations are made, the
source from which they emanate is quite sufficient to remove
any anxiety regarding our representations. The memorial is
now in course of signature, and subscriptions are coming in
every day from the country districts to the committee, to be
added to the general fund. On the lists are to be found the
names of several BLACK PERSONS, who are no less grateful than
the European inhabitants of Jamaica for the delivery afforded
them in October last by Mr. Eyre.

APPENDIX.

—

F.

FAREWELL ADDRESSES TO GOVERNOR EYRE, AND HIS VINDICATION.

Yesterday morning a number of gentlemen assembled at the Royal Mail Company's wharf, at Kingston, to form themselves into a committee, representing over 1200 subscribers to a farewell address to his Excellency Governor Eyre, on the eve of his departure from this colony.

The deputation consisted of the Hon. L. Q. Bowerbank, Custos ; Hon. J. H. M'Dowell, Captain Cooper, R.N., J. S. Williams, A. L. Malabre, R. Nunes, G. Henderson, J. S. Brown, A. De Cordova, and W. Lee, Esqrs. At the hour appointed they drove off to Paradise Penn, the residence of his Excellency, where they were received at the door by Colonel Hunt, A.D.C., and conducted in.

The Hon. Dr. Bowerbank then read the address to his Excellency as follows :—

"We, the undersigned inhabitants of Kingston, and others, cannot refrain from offering to your Excellency and Mrs. Eyre, our most sincere sympathy with you on your departure from the colony.

"We rejoice that after a searching inquiry, the Royal Commissioners have reported to her Majesty that praise is due to your Excellency for your skill, promptitude, and vigour, in the recent insurrection ; and that to the exercise of such qualities by you, its speedy termination is to be attributed ; and we heartily congratulate your Excellency that there has been evinced, both in this country and abroad, a general approbation of your conduct, in having saved a colony to the Queen, and homes and lives to the Queen's subjects in this her island of Jamaica.

"It is our firm conviction that a more intimate acquaint-

x

ance on the part of the Imperial Government with the local affairs of the colony and its condition, as well as with the true nature of events which had endangered, and might continue to threaten the peace and welfare of the country, would have shielded from censure a faithful servant of the Crown.

" We nevertheless feel assured that when political passions shall have given place to reason and to justice, the vast majority of your fellow-subjects, and others interested in the maintenance of public safety and order, will consider that an officer who (unaided by any instructions from superior authority, in times of extreme and sudden difficulty and very grave national peril) has, on the whole, done his duty nobly and well, ought not, for any minor error, or excess of his subordinates, to be otherwise than most favourably dealt with.

" We earnestly trust that a time will soon arrive when the momentous services which your Excellency has recently rendered to Jamaica may meet with that distinguished reward which her Most Gracious Majesty the Queen so well knows how to confer on those whom she cannot doubt to be meritorious officers.

" That every blessing may be heaped upon your Excellency, Mrs. Eyre, and your children, is, we believe, the fervent hope of all the loyal and grateful people of Jamaica."

To which his Excellency read his reply in the following words:

"TO THE HON. L. Q. BOWERBANK, J. S. BROWN, J. M'DOWELL, W. S. COOPER, W. TITLEY, J. S. WILLIAMS, R. NUNES, E. EBBEKE, F. LYONS, A. MALABRE, A. DE CORDOVA, ESQS. &C.

"Mr. Custos, Rev. Gentlemen, and Gentlemen,—I thank you most sincerely for your very gratifying address of sympathy with me on the occasion of my departure from Jamaica.

"It is only natural, that after serving my Queen and country zealously, and, I hope, not uselessly, for twenty-five years (since September, 1841), and, after having had the honour of representing my Sovereign in both hemispheres as Lieutenant-Governor or Governor for nearly twenty years (since 1846), I should feel some pain and regret that my career should now be abruptly terminated by removal from the public service under the disapproval and censure of the Colonial Minister.

" But this pain and regret are greatly lessened by the reflection, that however able or impartial the parties may be by whom my conduct has been inquired into and adjudicated upon, it is impossible that persons imperfectly acquainted with the negro character, with the country, and with the circumstances that surrounded me at the time, can judge adequately or justly, after the event, of the necessity or propriety of the action I found it imperative to take under a great emergency.

" The points on which I am condemned are three :—1st For permitting the trial and execution of G. W. Gordon.

" 2nd. For continuing martial law and the trials by courts martial after the proclamation of the amnesty on the 30th of October.

" 3rd. For not being aware of the excesses committed under martial law, and for not issuing instructions which would have prevented those excesses.

" With regard to the first, I can only repeat my conviction that however defective it may have been in a strictly legal point of view, Mr. Gordon was the proximate occasion of the insurrection, and of the cruel massacre of particular individuals whom he regarded as his personal enemies, and that, therefore, he suffered justly.

" No impartial person can, I think, read the report of the Royal Commissioners without coming to the same conclusion.

" The court before which he was tried was not a court of law, but it was a perfect legal court.

" To have issued a special commission to try him was wholly impracticable at the time ; whilst to have kept him as a prisoner for future trial would have had a very bad effect, and might have been dangerous in the extreme, in the excited and precarious state the country was then in.

" I believe that it was only through the firmness and decision of the Government in dealing with this case summarily that seditious teachings and the spread of the rebellion were checked.

"Indeed, in my opinion, the prompt trial and execution of G. W. Gordon had more effect in preventing further risings in other parishes than any of the steps taken by the Government.

"Mr. Gordon was regarded by the negroes generally throughout the island as an obeah-man is by his immediate neighbours, as all-powerful and beyond the reach of ordinary jurisdiction.

"His trial and execution removed this delusion, and showed that the authority of the Queen was supreme. Nor was he the only person of better position and education engaged in stirring up and exciting the negro mind.

"It was absolutely necessary that a stop should be put to this action, and it could only be done by the immediate trial of the chief agitator, and that trial could only take place by court-martial under the then existing circumstances.

"With regard to the continuance of martial law and trials by courts-martial after the 30th October, it must be remembered that during the whole period for which martial law was in force, and for some time afterwards, the accounts daily received from the various parishes in the island led the Government to believe the whole country to be still in a state of great excitement and peril, and that further risings amongst the negroes might take place at any moment or in any direction; and although additional troops had arrived, the total number in the colony was still very insufficient to cope with anything like a general insurrection, or even to occupy and protect many districts at a time, had active military operations become necessary.

"It was essential to overawe the disaffected, known to be numerous in most parishes of the island.

"For this, continuance of martial law became requisite, and it was only by the continuance of the trials and punishment of those guilty of rebellion that the existence of martial law would be believed in.

" But there were also no gaols or prisons in which any large number of prisoners could be kept for future trial ; and even had it been practicable, delay in dealing with prisoners charged with the more serious offences committed during the insurrection would have had a most injurious effect in other parts of the colony, ripe as they were for rebellion.

" With regard to the trials which thus took place before courts-martial, after the most searching scrutiny which practised lawyers could institute—a scrutiny to which, I believe, proceedings under martial law were scarcely ever before subjected, and from which, I venture to think, that few would have come out with less of censure—the Commissioners report :—' In the great majority of the cases the evidence seems to have been unobjectionable in character, and quite sufficient to justify the finding of the court. It is right also to state, the accounts given by the more trustworthy witnesses as to the manner and deportment of the courts were decidedly favourable.'

" That the Government earnestly desired to show as much leniency as considerations affecting the safety of other parts of the island permitted is evidenced by the early date at which an amnesty was proclaimed, under which large numbers of persons were absolved from the penalties of all lesser crimes, though the more serious ones were still, for a limited time (prescribed by act), to be dealt with by courts martial.

" I may here state that as soon as it was known that martial law was to terminate at the end of the statutory period of thirty days, I was waited upon by members of the legislature and custodes to urge upon me an extension of it, and I am quite certain that had I attempted to curtail the limited period which by law it had to run, consternation and apprehension would have been universal.

" Even after martial law had expired, and notwithstanding the very numerous trials which had taken place under it, a large number of prisoners charged with the graver offences committed during the rebellion still had to be dealt with, of whom very many were found guilty on trial before a special commission, and were sentenced by a civil court in some cases to death, in others to a long term of imprisonment.

"In reference to my not having been aware of the excesses committed during martial law, I would only ask, how was it possible that I, necessarily detained at the seat of government in watching over the interests, and providing for the safety of the island generally, as well as in attending to the laborious duties of a most important legislative session, could make myself acquainted with occurrences which even Brigadier-General Nelson, the able officer commanding in the districts where they were taking place, heard nothing of?

"Those who know anything of the nature of the country in Jamaica, and the few facilities which exist for intercommunication, will readily understand that at any time, but especially during the rainy season, which was at its height during the suppression of the rebellion, it is physically impossible to learn or to control all that is going on throughout a tract of country so extensive as that occupied by our troops during martial law.

"But the truth is, that excesses must always take place under martial law, and especially when black troops, who are often wholly beyond the control of their officers, are employed. No one can regret these excesses more than I do. It is, however, upon those whose acts made martial law necessary, or upon the people who, by not coming forward to uphold the Queen's authority, and protect life and property, encouraged such acts, that these excesses are chargeable, not upon the authorities, who are compelled to resort to that stern remedy to put down, or prevent, the extension of rebellion.

"Did no excesses occur in repressing the Indian mutiny? or were the authorities there made responsible for not knowing of or not preventing them?

"In that case it was not thought necessary, as it was here, to appoint a commission of inquiry to rake up and parade before the world every allegation of injury which an ignorant and excitable population, in many respects little removed from savages, whose habit is untruthfulness, and vindictive at having been foiled in their recent rebellion, could be induced to bring forward, whether well or ill founded, against those who had the onerous and thankless task of putting down that rebellion.

" With regard to the non-issuing by me of instructions for the guidance of the military, I have only to point out that her Majesty's instructions to Governors lay down the rule that it is the duty of the Governor to give all necessary orders for the march and distribution of troops, but expressly enjoin him to leave all details connected with the carrying out those orders to the military authorities.

" When martial law is proclaimed in a district, the case is even still stronger, for then all civil jurisdiction is absolutely superseded, and the entire and sole management of the district so circumstanced becomes vested in the General in command.

" I have thought it right to make these observations, not to repudiate any responsibility properly attaching to me, or to excuse any shortcoming or errors in my own conduct, but as feeling it due to myself, to you, and to the British public to state some few of the considerations which influenced me in reference to the particulars in which my conduct has been most strongly condemned.

" And I the more gladly make these statements to you, gentlemen, because from your having been in the colony at the time, and from your long and practical acquaintance with the country, the people, and the circumstances which existed during the period referred to, you are in a better position than any other persons can be to judge of the value of them, and to know how far I did my duty to the colony and to my Sovereign in the hour of difficulty and danger.

" Even the Royal Commissioners, labouring as they did under all the disadvantages of unacquaintance with the

character of the country, the people, and the circumstances
of the moment, and making their enquiries after the event
from a people naturally untruthful, and stimulated by the
impression seduously instilled into them by designing persons,
that the Queen was on their side, and desired to obtain
evidence against and punish the authorities engaged in suppressing the rebellion — even the Royal Commissioners,
labouring under all these disadvantages, have been compelled
to admit that 'though the original design for the overthrow
of constituted authority was confined to a small portion of
St. Thomas in the East, yet that the disorder in fact spread
with singular rapidity over an extensive tract of country ;
and that such was the state of excitement prevailing in the
island, that had more than a momentary success been obtained
by the insurgents their ultimate overthrow would have been
attended with a still more fearful loss of life and property.'
And they have very justly remarked, that 'sometimes the
success of the measures adopted for the prevention of an evil
deprived the authors of those measures of the evidence they
would otherwise have had of their necessity.'

"Had I hesitated, there would have been evidence enough
of this necessity ; but what would have been said of me for
not having prevented the 'still more fearful loss of life and
property ?'

"The Royal Commissioners and her Majesty's Government
have been pleased to give me credit for 'skill, promptitude,
and vigour' on the occurrence of a great emergency, and to
state that 'to my exercise of these qualities the speedy
termination of the insurrection is due.' I am told that I
'showed myself superior to the feelings of alarm expressed
and entertained by those around me ;' and her Majesty's
Government further 'expresses their sense of the promptitude
and judgment with which I submitted to the Legislature the
views which I entertained, and in which they so readily concurred, as to the expediency of effecting a decided change in
the mode of government of the colony'—views which have

since been confirmed by the sanction of the Crown and an act of the Imperial Government. Why should they not equally give me credit for having exercised a sound judgment in the lesser matter of continuing martial law for a limited time after the proclamation of the amnesty, although they, acting as my judges after the event, without the necessary local experience, and when the very success of my measures had deprived me of the evidence of their necessity, are unable to appreciate so clearly the force of the considerations which influenced me in this matter, as they do in the circumstances which surrounded the commencement of the rebellion or the change effected in the constitution?

"With regard to the case of Mr. Gordon, the Royal Commissioners, labouring under the disadvantages already adverted to, and looking at the proceedings as lawyers naturally would do, that is, in connection with the strict rules and practice of courts of law (though I have already shown the court before which Mr. Gordon was tried was not a court of law, though a perfectly legal court) whilst expressing their opinion that they 'cannot see in the evidence which has been adduced any sufficient proof (that is, I presume, according to the strict rules and practice of court of law) either of his complicity in the outbreak of Morant Bay, or of his having been a party to a general conspiracy against the Government,' yet distinctly record, 'We have formed the opinion that the true explanation of Mr. Gordon's conduct was to be found in the account he has given of himself—"I have just gone as far as I can go, but no farther. If I wanted a rebellion I could have had one long ago. I have been asked several times to head a rebellion, but there is no fear of that: I will try first a demonstration of it; but I must first upset that fellow Herschell, and kick him out of the vestry, and the baron also, or bad will come of it!"'

"Mr. Herschell was not kicked out of the vestry, nor the baron upset; and they were two of the first victims of the insurrection.

"Again, the Commissioners distinctly record their opinion, 'Mr. Gordon might know well the distinction between a rebellion and a demonstration of it; he might be able to trust himself to go as far as he could with safety and no further; but that would not be so easy to his ignorant and fanatical followers. They would find it difficult to restrain themselves from rebellion when making a demonstration of it.

"'If a man like Paul Bogle was in the habit of hearing such expressions as those contained in Gordon's letters, as that the reign of the oppressors would be short, and that the Lord was about to destroy them, it would not take much to convince him that he might be the appointed instrument in the Lord's hand for effecting that end; and it is clear that this was Bogle's belief, as we find that after the part he had taken in the massacre at Morant Bay, he, in his chapel at Stony Gut, returned thanks to God that he had gone to do that work, and that God had prospered him in his work.

"'It is clear, too, that the conduct of Gordon had been such as to convince both friends and enemies of his being a party to the rising.

"'We learn from Mr. Gordon himself that in Kingston, where he carried on his business, this was the general belief as soon as the news of the outbreak was received.

"'But it was fully believed also by those engaged in the outbreak. Bogle did not hesitate to speak of himself as acting in concert with him.

"'When Dr. Major was dragged out of his hiding-place on the night of the 11th October, he saved himself by explaining that Mr. Gordon would not wish to have him injured; and when Mr. Jackson made a similar appeal for his own life to the murderers of Mr. Hire, it appears to have been equally successful.

"' The effect which was likely to follow the meetings which took place during the spring and summer of 1865, in some of which Mr. Gordon took a part, was foreseen by one of his most ardent supporters, who, writing to a common friend on the subject of an article he had inserted in a newspaper respecting the Vere meeting, used these words :—" All I desire is to shield you and them from the charge of anarchy and tumult, which in a short time, must follow these powerful demonstrations." '

"Again the Commissioners report :—' It appears exceedingly probable that Mr. Gordon, by his words and writings, produced a material effect on the minds of Bogle and his followers, and did much to produce that state of excitement and discontent in different parts of the island which rendered the spread of the insurrection exceedingly probable.'

"The British public may judge from these extracts from the report of the Royal Commissioners how far Gordon was morally guilty of causing the rebellion, and therefore justly punished, whatever may be the doubts entertained as to the proof of his complicity having been sufficient, in a strictly legal point of view, to satisfy a court of law ; but they can never know the full weight and pressure of the circumstances which made it necessary, in order to save the colony from the general massacre and pillage which further risings would have occasioned, to act promptly and decisively upon proof only of his moral guilt (and this, be it remembered, is all that is required before a court-martial under martial law).

" I am not a lawyer, but I understand there are legal gentlemen of high ability who dissent entirely from the opinion expressed by the Royal Commissioners, that there was not sufficient proof (that is, such as would be received in a court of law) of Gordon's complicity in the outbreak at Morant Bay, and who consider that the evidence adduced before the court-martial, taken in connection with concurrent circumstances, would have been both legally admissible in a civil court, and sufficient to satisfy a civil jury of his guilt.

" Be this as it may, I had myself no doubt whatever as to Gordon's having occasioned the rebellion, or of the danger to the colony if his case was not promptly and summarily dealt with. Under such circumstances, it was impossible to hesitate as to the course which I considered my duty to the Crown and to the colony made it imperative on me to take.

"And now, gentlemen, I come to the hardest part of my task, that of saying farewell to those who have been kind to me ; who supported me in the difficulties and dangers through which the colony has so recently passed, and who now sympathise with me under the obloquy and misrepresentations to which I am subjected.

"I have lived amongst you for nearly four years and a half, during which you well know I have had more than the usual share of hard work and political strife.

"You will, I am sure, do me the justice to believe that in these, as in all other matters, I have been actuated by the single desire to do what I conscientiously believed to be my duty.

"I have necessarily sometimes had to say or to do hard things, but you will, I know, at least acquit me of mixing up any personal feeling with my public action.

"And in taking leave of you I would only add that, as I bear no ill-will to any individual, I trust that none is borne towards myself, but that when I am gone from amongst you all will unite in believing that I wished well to the colony and to yourselves, and that I did my best to serve you.

"I now retire into private life, dismissed from the public service, after nearly a lifetime spent in it ; but I have at least the consolation of feeling that there has been nothing in my conduct to merit it, nothing to occasion self-reproach, nothing to regret.

"On the contrary, I carry with me in my retirement the proud consciousness that at all times, and under all circumstances, I have endeavoured to the best of my ability to do my duty as a servant of the Crown, faithfully, fearlessly, and irrespective of personal considerations.

"With such convictions, deeply as my removal from the public service must necessarily affect my future and the interests of those most dear to me, I can submit to the forfeiture of position, to the sacrifice of twenty-five years' career in the public service, or to any personal indignity entailed, counting my individual losses as utterly insignificant when so largely counterbalanced by the undeniable fact that the very acts which have led to my dismissal have saved a noble colony from anarchy and ruin.

"Your generous and valued testimony to the integrity of my conduct in this my last and most important goveru-ment will ever be most highly cherished by me, and will be handed down to my children, and their children, as an encouragement and a stimulus to them to do their duty also, under whatever circumstances of trial they may at any time be placed.

"Again, gentlemen, I thank you, in Mrs. Eyre's name and in my own, for your warm-hearted sympathy and for your good wishes towards ourselves and our children.

"We shall always remember most gratefully your great kindness and good feeling.

"Our best wishes and our fervent prayers for your indivi-dual and collective interests and welfare will still be with you, and we earnestly trust that the change recently made in the government of the country (and which I shall ever regard as a proud monument of my administration amongst you) will, when time has permitted its development, and matured that reorganisation which is essential, lead to a renewed confidence in Jamaica at home, and to progress and prosperity within the colony itself, that must eventually largely promote its material interests, and add to the comfort and happiness of all within it.

" E. EYRE.

"Kingston, July 23, 1866."

We may state here that the address has 1230 signatures, 613 of which are those of persons residing in this city, and the rest are of individuals from other parts.

The following address was also presented to Mr. Eyre, on

behalf of the bishop and clergy of Kingston and the neighbourhood:

"TO HIS EXCELLENCY EDWARD JOHN EYRE, ESQ., LATE GOVERNOR
OF JAMAICA, ON HIS DEPARTURE FROM THE ISLAND.

"SIR,—We, the undersigned clergy of the neighbourhood
of Kingston, desire respectfully to convey to your Excellency,
on the eve of your departure from this colony, the imperfect
expression of our feelings on this painful termination of the
period of your government. In conjunction with a large
number of our brethren in other parts of the island, who
would, we doubt not, most cordially join with us on the present occasion if time allowed us to invite their concurrence,
we not long ago tendered to you the heartfelt expression of
our gratitude, our esteem, and our confidence. We desire to
reiterate those sentiments now.

"No former Governor has ever rendered to us greater
services than your Excellency has done. You have not only
rescued the island from most imminent peril of general
insurrection, by your courage, promptitude, judgment, and
administrative skill, but by the exercise of the same high
qualities prepared the way for such a reconstruction of the
form of our constitution as, while we are not forgetful of our
debt of gratitude to the House of Assembly for its liberal
support of our anciently established Church, the present
emergency seemed to demand—a reconstruction to which, if
any human means can avail to effect it, the future prosperity
of this colony will primarily be due.

"For ourselves we would gratefully acknowledge the uniform
kindness and courtesy which the clergy have ever experienced
at your Excellency's hands, and the lively and discriminating
interest which you have ever manifested and exercised for the
welfare of the Church.

"But even for these eminent services we could not thus
warmly thank you did we not know your Excellency to have
been actuated by the purest motives, to be a devout worshipper of Him whose ministers we are; and to be influenced
by feelings of true humanity towards the people to whom we
minister.

"But, knowing these things, we assure your Excellency of
our sincere sympathy with you, and our earnest hope that you
may ere long be called by our gracious Sovereign to another
sphere of honourable and important public service.

"It is our sincere desire and prayer that wherever your lot may be cast, the divine blessing may rest on you and on all the members of your family ; and we would beg you to accept, and to convey also to Mrs. Eyre, who has conciliated to herself the esteem and regard of so many amongst us, our respectful and most cordial farewell.

"We have the honour to be, Sir, your Excellency's most obedient servants,

"REGINALD KINGSTON, Bishop of Kingston.
THOMAS STEWART, D.D., Archdeacon of Surrey.
WILLIAM MAYHEW, Rector of St. Andrew," &c.

To the foregoing address Mr. Eyre returned a reply in these terms :

"TO THE RIGHT REV. THE LORD BISHOP OF KINGSTON, THE VENERABLE ARCHDEACON STEWART, THE REV. T. MAYHEW, &c.

"My Lord Bishop and Rev. Gentlemen,—I thank you very gratefully for your generous and warm-hearted address of regard and sympathy on my removal from the government of Jamaica.

"I assure you that it is both gratifying to me and greatly consolatory to know that after a long residence amongst you, and after having had to guide the colony through scenes of great difficulty and trial, I retain the confidence and esteem of the clergy of the country, whose good opinion (living as they have done on the spot, and knowing intimately all the circumstances connected with the late rebellion) is in itself the strongest testimony I can offer that I have not merited the imputations which have been alleged against me by persons not in the colony at the time, and imperfectly acquainted with the true nature of the events, of having acted either with injustice or with undue severity in repressing an insurrection which imperilled the lives and property of the inhabitants and jeopardised the safety of the colony.

"I heartily concur with you in regarding the change recently effected in the form of government of the island as likely to confer great and lasting benefits upon the community, and I shall ever feel proud that it was accomplished during my administration of the government, and in a great degree through my own personal exertions.

"It is most gratifying to me to think that when I am gone from amongst you there will still remain this permanent proof of my anxiety to benefit the colony, and that my efforts were not unsuccessful.

"For the good feeling and friendly intercourse which have ever characterised my connection with the clergy of Jamaica, I am most deeply indebted to you.

"It has been a great pleasure to me to co-operate cordially with you in all matters affecting the interests of the Church, and I pray that God's blessing may rest upon your continued labours to promote His honour, and advance the temporal and spiritual welfare of the people entrusted to your charge.

"Mrs. Eyre unites with me in sincere and affectionate thanks for your good wishes towards ourselves and children.

"E. EYRE.

"Kingston, July 24."

LONDON: PRINTED BY W. CLOWES AND SONS, STAMFORD STREET AND CHARING CROSS

London : 8, New Burlington Street,
March, 1867.

A LIST OF WORKS

PUBLISHED BY RICHARD BENTLEY,

Publisher in Ordinary to Her Majesty.

ADAM AND THE ADAMITE; or, The Harmony of Scrip-
ture and Ethnology. By Dr. M^cCAUSLAND, Author of 'Sermons in Stones.' Crown 8vo.
7s. 6d.

"Dr. McCausland is an eminent geologist and an orthodox Christian, and in this work he
endeavours to harmonise the statements of Science and of Revelation. He heartily accepts
the recent discoveries of a pre-Adamite mankind, as proved by the flint instruments of
France and England, the metallic weapons of Denmark, and the submerged dwellings in
the Swiss lakes. He accepts the theory of three distinct races of mankind – the Mongol, the
Negro, and the Caucasian, as having each made their appearance at a separate date and on a
different portion of our globe. He puts the latest conclusions of science on these points in
an intelligible and popular way, and argues that these conclusions are far more in accordance with the statements of the book of Genesis than the opinion of the unity of mankind,
and their common descent from Adam about six thousand years ago. The book is interesting, attractive, and useful."—*Notes and Queries.*

AFTER THE STORM; or, Brother Jonathan and his Neigh-
bours in 1865-6. By J. E. HILARY SKINNER. 2 vols.

"An amusing and genial record of travel at an interesting time over interesting countries,
presented to us in a spirited and lively narrative, at times humorous and at times pathetic,
the results of much acute observation."—*Guardian.*

AFRICAN HUNTING FROM NATAL TO THE ZAM-
BESI, LAKE NGAMI, KALAHARI, FROM 1852 TO 1860. By WILLIAM CHARLES
BALDWIN, F.G.S. In a handsome Volume, 8vo., with Fifty beautiful Illustrations
by WOLFF and ZWECKER, with a Map, and Portrait of the Author. Second Edition.
Price 10s. 6d.

"Mr. Baldwin's is one of the most extraordinary records we have ever met with; and
a more exciting, interesting, or genuine book has seldom fallen into the hands of the
public."—*Daily News.*

ANECDOTES OF ANIMALS. With Eight Spirited Illus-
trations by WOLFF. Gilt edges. 5s.

"Specially adapted to be put into the hands of young readers."—*John Bull.*

ANDERSEN'S (HANS CHRISTIAN) ICE MAIDEN.
Translated from the Danish by Mrs. BUSHBY. Small royal, with 39 beautiful Illustrations by ZWECKER. 7s. 6d.

"A perfectly new and fanciful Swiss story."—*Examiner.*
"With exquisite illustrations."—*Dublin Evening Mail.*

——————————————————— IN SPAIN. Translated
from the Danish by Mrs. BUSHBY. Post 8vo. 10s. 6d.

"A very interesting travel-book, by a writer always graceful and attractive.
Andersen is the most picturesque of modern Danish writers."—*Examiner.*

B

ANDROMACHE OF EURIPIDES; with Suggestions and

Questions at the foot of each page; together with Copious Grammatical and Critical Notes: also with a Brief Introductory Account of the Greek Drama, Dialects, and Principal Tragic Metres. By the Rev. C. HAWKINS, D.C.L., Ch. Ch., Oxon, and one of the Upper Masters of Christ's Hospital, London. Used at Eton. 4s. 6d.

ARCHBISHOPS OF CANTERBURY, FROM ST. AU-

GUSTINE TO DR. HOWLEY, LIVES OF. By the Rev. WALTER FARQUHAR HOOK, D.D., F.R.S., Dean of Chichester.

Vol. I. 15s. Vol. II. 15s. Vols. III. and IV. 30s.

"The work of a man of unusually strong and practical sense. Had Dr. Hook spent his whole life in a cloister, his work would doubtless have gained something in perfect accuracy and scholar-like finish; but, on the other hand, it would probably have lost much more of that shrewd and living knowledge of men and things which is displayed through-out the volume. For Dr. Hook's sterling practical good sense we were fully prepared, but another great merit of the book took the form of an agreeable surprise. There is a most remarkable power of entering into the feelings and position of men of remote ages and of various schools of theology. Dr. Hook is throughout fair, and more than fair. He really understands his characters, and does not praise or condemn from any cut and dried nineteenth-century standard. In a work chiefly biographical this is the first, and one of the rarest of all merits. And we know no strictly ecclesiastical writer—one, we mean, who writes with a theological as well as a historical purpose—who can lay claim to this pre-eminent merit in a higher degree than Dr. Hook. His thorough fairness of dealing is shown on almost every controverted point which he approaches."—*Saturday Review, January* 26, 1861.

AUSTEN'S (MISS JANE) NOVELS. A complete Library

Edition. In 5 vols. crown 8vo., with Ten Illustrations. 21s.

Vol. 1. SENSE AND SENSIBILITY.	Vol. 4. NORTHANGER ABBEY and
2. EMMA.	PERSUASION.
3. MANSFIELD PARK.	5. PRIDE AND PREJUDICE.

"Miss Austen has a talent for describing the involvements and feelings, and characters of ordinary life, which is to me the most wonderful I ever met with. Her exquisite touch, which renders commonplace things and characters interesting from the truth of the description and the sentiment, is denied to me."—*Sir Walter Scott.*

"'Pride and Prejudice,' by Jane Austen, is the perfect type of a novel of common life; the story so concisely and dramatically told, the language so simple, the shades and half-shades of human character so clearly presented, and the operation of various motives so delicately traced—attest this gifted woman to have been the perfect mistress of her art."—*(Extract from page* 446 *of Thomas Arnold's Manual of English Literature.*

AUTOBIOGRAPHY (THE) OF THE EARL OF DUN-

DONALD (LORD COCHRANE). Library Edition. 2 vols. 8vo., with Portrait. 21s.

—————————————— Popular Edition, with a Portrait and

Four Charts. Small 8vo. 5s.

"Is full of brilliant adventures, described with a dash that well befits the deeds."—*Times.*

BENTLEY'S FAVOURITE NOVELS. With Illustrations

to each volume. Crown 8vo. 6s. each, or by Post 6s. 6d.

ANTHONY TROLLOPE'S THREE CLERKS.
UNCLE SILAS. By J. SHERIDAN LE FANU.
THE SHADOW OF ASHLYDYAT. By the Author of 'East Lynne.'
TOO STRANGE NOT TO BE TRUE. By Lady GEORGIANA FULLERTON.
LADYBIRD. By the same Authoress.
QUITS! By the Author of 'Initials.'
EAST LYNNE. By Mrs. HENRY WOOD.
THE CHANNINGS. By the Author of 'East Lynne.'
MRS. HALLIBURTON'S TROUBLES. By same Author.
NED LOCKSLEY, THE ETONIAN.
INITIALS. By the Author of 'Quits!' 'At Odds,' &c.
LAST OF THE CAVALIERS. A Romance.
GUY DEVERELL. By the Author of 'Uncle Silas.'
THE HOUSE BY THE CHURCHYARD. By the Author of 'Uncle Silas.'

BENTLEY'S (GEORGE) ENQUIRY INTO THE AUTHOR-
SHIP OF THE SINAITIC INSCRIPTIONS. 8vo. 1s.

BENTLEY BALLADS (THE). A Selection from 'BENT-
LEY'S MISCELLANY,' including Ballads and Legends by DR. MAGINN, FATHER
PROUT, SAMUEL LOVER, ALBERT SMITH, THE IRISH WHISKEY DRINKER,
LONGFELLOW, &c. In small 8vo. 5s.

BENTLEY (TALES FROM). Being a Selection of the best
Stories that have appeared in 'BENTLEY'S MISCELLANY.' 6 vols., 1s. each ; or
sold separately. Or 2 vols. cloth. 6s.

BOUTELL'S (Rev. C.) HERALDRY: HISTORICAL AND
POPULAR. By the Rev. CHARLES BOUTELL, M.A. Third Edition, 850 Illustrations.
Demy 8vo. 21s.

"We have now to direct the attention of our readers to a third edition, entirely revised,
and greatly enlarged. Thus, the chapters entitled 'Marshalling' and 'Cadency' now appear
enlarged and rearranged, and 'Cadency and Differencing.' A chapter has been devoted
exclusively to 'Royal Cadency.' The chapter on the 'Royal Heraldry of England' has
been in part rewritten, and that on 'Foreign Heraldry' has been considerably extended.
Lists of plates and illustrations, and a very copious index, give completeness to a work
which is clearly destined to supplant the excellent introduction, which the best heralds
have hitherto regarded as the most complete—we mean Porny's well-known 'Elements'—
and to become for the future the recognised text-book for students of this interesting branch
of historical learning."—*Notes and Queries.*

"Mr. Boutell's arrangement of his book is a very good one, and cannot fail to be useful
to all readers. They may learn the meaning of any heraldic term, and a great deal of its
history, in the readiest manner ; and any one may leave the book with a tolerably complete
comprehension of the science."—*Athenæum.*

BRITISH NAVY (HISTORY OF THE) FROM THE
COMMENCEMENT OF THE REVOLUTIONARY WAR TO THE BATTLE OF
NAVARINO. By W. JAMES. In 6 vols. small 8vo. 36s.

"A work of which it is not too high praise to assert, that it approaches as nearly to
perfection in its own line as any historical work ever did."—*Edinburgh Review.*

BROWNE'S (Professor) HISTORY OF ROMAN CLASSI-
CAL LITERATURE. By R. W. BROWNE, M.A., Ph.D., Prebendary of St. Paul's, and
Professor of Classical Literature in King's College, London. 8vo. 12s.

"Professor Browne is not only a classical scholar, but one of the most graceful of English
modern writers. In clearness, purity, and elegance of style, his compositions are unsur-
passed; and his sketches of the lives and works of the great authors of antiquity are
models of refined taste and sound criticism. This is a work which, for utility of design and
excellence of execution, may challenge comparison with any which the present century has
produced ; nor can we hesitate to regard it as a very valuable instrument for the instruction
of the national mind, and the elevation of the national taste."—*Morning Post.*

BUCKLAND'S (FRANK) CURIOSITIES OF NATURAL
HISTORY. 1st Series. Rats, Snakes, Serpents, Fishes, Frogs, Monkeys, &c. Small
8vo. 6s.

———————————— (Second Series). Fossils, Bears,
Wolves, Cats, Eagles, Hedgehogs, the Rigs, Eels, Herrings, Whales, Pigs, &c., &c.
Small 8vo. 6s.

———————————— (Third Series). Wild Ducks,
Salmon, Lions, Tigers, Foxes, Porpoises, Fleas, Wonderful People, &c. 2 vols. 12s.
See also 'Curiosities of Natural History.'

BREAKFAST BOOK (THE). A Cookery Book for the
Morning Meal. By the Author of 'Everybody's Pudding Book.' 2s. 6d.

BURY'S (VISCOUNT) EXODUS OF THE WESTERN
NATIONS. 2 vols. 8vo. pp. 1,000. 32s.
"Lord Bury's work well deserves attention."—*Edinburgh Review.*

CASHMERE AND THIBET, DIARY OF A PEDES-
TRIAN IN. By Captain KNIGHT, 48th Regiment. 8vo., with 45 fine Woodcuts and Lithographs. 21s.

CAWNPORE—CAPTAIN THOMSON'S STORY OF. By
Captain MOWBRAY THOMPSON. Post 8vo. 10s. 6d. Illustrations.

CHANNINGS (THE). By Mrs. HENRY WOOD. Uniform
with 'East Lynne.' Forming one of the Favourite Novels. With Two Illustrations. Crown 8vo. 6s.

CHATTERTON'S (LADY) SELECTIONS FROM THE
WRITINGS OF PLATO. Fcap. 8vo. 4s.
" An elegant volume of selections."—*Quarterly Review.*

CLIFFORD'S (EDMUND) LIFE OF THE GREATEST
OF THE PLANTAGENETS; an Historical Sketch. 8vo. 12s.

CLUB LIFE OF LONDON. With Anecdotes of the Clubs,
Coffee-Houses, and Taverns during the 17th, 18th, and 19th Centuries. By JOHN TIMBS, F.S.A. In 2 vols. crown 8vo. With Portraits.

COLLINS' (W. WILKIE) RAMBLES BEYOND RAIL-
WAYS; or Notes taken afoot in Cornwall; to which is added a Visit to the Scilly Islands. Crown 8vo. 6s.
" A very pleasant book, in which the most is made of a happily-chosen subject. The author takes us through all the rocky wonders and beauties of the Cornish coast, from St. German's to the Land's End."—*Times.*

CONSTANTINOPLE DURING THE CRIMEAN WAR.
By Lady HORNBY. Royal 8vo., with Chromo-Lithographs. 21s.
" We can only recommend every one to read this very thoughtful and lively volume."—*Saturday Review.*

COOK'S GUIDE (THE). By CHARLES ELMÉ FRAN-
CATELLI, Author of the ' Modern Cook.' In small 8vo. With Forty Illustrations. 5s.
" Exceedingly plain."—*Times.*
" Intended mainly for the middle class."—*Observer.*

COOKERY (STANDARD WORKS ON).
1. FRANCATELLI'S MODERN COOK. 8vo. 1,400 Recipes. 12s.
2. ———— COOK'S GUIDE. 1,010 Recipes. 5s.
3. WHAT TO DO WITH THE COLD MUTTON. 2s. 6d.
4. THE BREAKFAST BOOK. 2s. 6d.
5. EVERYBODY'S PUDDING BOOK. 2s. 6d.
6. THE LADIES' DESSERT BOOK.
7. THE TREASURY OF FRENCH COOKERY. By Mrs. Toogood. 5s.
8. GOOD COOKERY. By the Right Hon. LADY LLANOVER. 10s. 6d.

" The destiny of nations depends upon their diet."—*Brillat Savarin.*
" There's no want of meat, sir;
Portly and curious viands are prepared
To please all kinds of appetites."—*Massinger.*

CREASY (SIR EDWARD)—THE FIFTEEN DECISIVE
BATTLES OF THE WORLD—FROM MARATHON TO WATERLOO. Sixteenth Edition. 8vo. 10s. 6d.
" It was a happy idea of Professor Creasy to select for military description those few battles which, in the words of Hallam, ' A contrary event would have essentially varied the drama of the world in all its subsequent scenes.' The decisive features of the battles are well and clearly brought out; the reader's mind is attracted to the world-wide importance of the event he is considering, while their succession carries him over the whole stream of European history."—*Spectator.*

CREASY (SIR EDWARD), HISTORY OF THE RISE
AND PROGRESS OF THE ENGLISH CONSTITUTION. A Popular Account of the
primary Principles, the formation and development of the English Constitution, avoiding
all party politics. Eighth Edition. Post 8vo. 7s. 6d.

" The study of English History would be incomplete without the perusal of a work on
the English Constitution. Sir Edward Creasy's work, which is clear, full, and impartial,
will give the student all needful information on this important subject."—*Reader.*

CUMMING'S (REV. DR. JOHN)—THE GREAT TRIBU-
LATION COMING ON THE EARTH. Crown 8vo. 5s., or by post 5s. 6d. Thirteenth
Thousand.

" There is no doubt that the barometer of Europe singularly corresponds with Dr.
Cumming's deductions from prophecy."—*Times.*

———————— THE GREAT PREPARATION; OR, RE-
DEMPTION DRAWETH NIGH. Crown 8vo. 5s., or by post 5s. 6d. Sixth Thousand.

———————— THE GREAT CONSUMMATION; OR,
THE WORLD AS IT WILL BE. Crown 8vo. 5s., or by post 5s. 6d. Third Thousand.

———————— READINGS ON THE PROPHET ISAIAH.
Fcp. 8vo. 5s.

CURIOSITIES OF CLOCKS AND WATCHES. By E. J.
WOOD. Post 8vo. Two Illustrations, 400 pp. 10s. 6d.

" A mass of anecdotes about horology."—*Pall Mall Gazette.*

CURIOSITIES OF NATURAL HISTORY. By FRANK
BUCKLAND, ESQ. In Two Series. Small 8vo. 12s.

1st Series, Containing Rats, Serpents, Fishes, Monkeys, &c. 6s.
2nd Series, Containing Wild Cats, Eagles, Worms, Dogs, &c. 6s.
3rd Series, Containing Lions, Tigers, Foxes, Porpoises, &c. 2 vols. 12s.

" These most fascinating works on Natural History."—*Morning Post.*

DANES (THE). SKETCHED BY THEMSELVES IN
a Series of their best Stories by their most popular Writers. Translated by Mrs.
BUSHBY. 3 vols. post 8vo.

DAVIS'S (DR.) CARTHAGE AND HER REMAINS;
being an Account of the Excavations and Researches on the Site of the Phœnician
Metropolis in Africa. Conducted under the auspices of Her Majesty's Government by
Dr. N. DAVIS, F.R.G.S., &c. 8vo. Thirty Plates. 10s. 6d.

DELANY'S (Mrs. MARY GRANVILLE)—THE AUTO-
BIOGRAPHY AND CORRESPONDENCE OF MARY GRANVILLE (Mrs. DELANY),
with Interesting Reminiscences of King George III. and Queen Charlotte. Presenting a
Picture of the Fashionable Society during nearly the whole period of the Eighteenth Century.
Edited by the Right Hon. Lady LLANOVER. First Series. 13 Portraits. 3 vols. 8vo. 15s.

———————— (2nd Series). Nine Portraits and
Copious Index to the whole work. 3 vols. 8vo. 36s. Or the whole work complete in
6 vols. for £2 10s.

DOBELL'S (SYDNEY) THE ROMAN: A DRAMATIC
POEM. Post 8vo. 5s.

DORAN'S (DR.) WORKS. A Complete Set of Dr. DORAN'S
Works. In 10 vols. post 8vo. handsomely bound in half-calf. 4l. 4s.

———————— LIVES OF THE QUEENS OF ENG-
LAND OF THE HOUSE OF HANOVER. In 2 vols. post 8vo. 21s.

———————— TABLE TRAITS AND SOMETHING ON
THEM. Crown 8vo. 7s. 6d.

DUNDONALD'S (EARL) AUTOBIOGRAPHY OF A
SEAMAN. Library Edition, with Portrait. 2 vols. 8vo. 21s.

———————————————— Popular Edition. Small 8vo. 5s.

EAST LYNNE. By Mrs. HENRY WOOD, Author of 'The
Channings,' 'Mrs. Halliburton's Troubles,' &c. With Two Illustrations. Crown 8vo. 6s.

EDEN (Hon. Miss), UP THE COUNTRY. A Diary in India
during the Governor-Generalship of Lord Auckland. New Edition, crown 8vo. 6s.

> "A brighter book of travel we have not seen for many a day. In ease and grace of style
> Miss Eden reminds us of Lady Duff Gordon, in wit and satire and suggestion of Lady
> Morgan. We regard this bright and merry Indian book as one of happy inspiration."—
> *Athenæum.*

ELLET'S (Mrs.) WOMEN ARTISTS OF ALL AGES
AND COUNTRIES. Post 8vo. Handsomely bound. 5s.

ELLIS (Mrs.)—THE MOTHERS OF GREAT MEN.
Handsomely bound for a Present Book. Crown 8vo. 6s.

———————————— CHAPTERS ON WIVES. Crown 8vo. 5s.

ELLIOTT'S (Mrs. DALRYMPLE) NARRATIVE OF HER
ADVENTURES AND IMPRISONMENT DURING THE FRENCH REVOLUTION,
WITH SKETCHES OF MANY CELEBRITIES WITH WHOM THIS BEAUTIFUL
WOMAN WAS ACQUAINTED. With Three beautiful Portraits from Miniatures of
Cosway, &c. 8vo. 6s.

EYRE'S (Miss) WALKS IN THE SOUTH OF FRANCE.
Second Edition. 8vo. 12s.

> "A very clever book, by a very clever woman, full of vivid descriptions of the scenery
> of the Pyrenees, the manners of the Béarnais, with plenty of legendary and folk lore, and
> some very charming specimens of minstrelsy."—*Illustrated News.*

———————————— OVER THE PYRENEES INTO SPAIN.
Crown 8vo. 12s.

ENGLISH CONSTITUTION, (HISTORY OF THE RISE
AND PROGRESS OF THE.) By Sir EDWARD CREASY. Author of 'The Fifteen
Decisive Battles of the World.' Sixth Edition. Post 8vo. 7s. 6d.

ENGLISH GOVERNESS (THE) IN EGYPT; or, Harem
Life in the East. By EMMELINE LOTT, formerly Governess to Ibrahim Pacha. 2 vols.
post 8vo. Portrait. 21s.

ENGLISH MERCHANTS: Memoirs in Illustration of the
Progress of Commerce. By H. R. FOX BOURNE, Author of a 'Memoir of Sir Philip
Sidney.' 2 vols. With numerous Illustrations. 24s.

EVERYBODY'S PUDDING-BOOK; OR, TARTS, PUD-
DINGS, &c., IN THE PROPER SEASON FOR ALL THE YEAR ROUND. Fcap. 8vo.
Third Thousand. 2s. 6d.

FAIRE GOSPELLER, PASSAGES IN THE LIFE OF
THE (Mistress Anne Askew). By the Author of 'Mary Powell.' Crown 8vo. Antique
binding. 10s. 6d.

FISHER'S (LIEUT.-COL.) PERSONAL NARRATIVE OF
THREE YEARS' SERVICE IN CHINA. By LIEUT.-COL. FISHER. 8vo. With
many Illustrations. 16s.

FITZGERALD'S (PERCY) CHARLES LAMB: his Friends, his Haunts, and his Books. Crown 8vo. Imperial 16mo. 7s. 6d.

FLETCHER'S (LIEUT.-COL.) HISTORY OF THE AMERICAN WAR. 8vo. In 3 vols. 18s. each.

> "The conception and execution of this history are most creditable. It is eminently impartial; and Colonel Fletcher has shown that he can gain reputation in the field of literature as well as in the camp of Mars."—*Times.*

FORSTER'S (REV. CHAS.) SINAI PHOTOGRAPHED; or, Inscriptions in the Rocks of the Wilderness by the Israelites who came out of Egypt. With Photographs, Glythographs, and Lithographs. Folio. 4l. 4s.

———— **ISRAEL IN THE WILDERNESS.** A Popular Account of the Inscriptions on the Rocks round Mount Sinai. Crown 8vo. 6s.

> "This is a work which will be read with much interest by all who hang fondly over every detail of Holy Scripture, and delight to identify every spot, and verify every circumstance connected with the exodus of the Israelites."—*Notes and Queries.*

———— **LIFE OF DR. JOHN JEBB, BISHOP OF LIMERICK.** Post 8vo. 6s.

———— **SERMONS ON THE LIFE OF ST. PAUL.** 8vo. 7s. 6d.

———— **THE ONE PRIMEVAL LANGUAGE.** Traced experimentally through Ancient Inscriptions in Alphabetic Character of Lost Powers from the Four Continents. In Three Parts, 8vo. with Chart, 42s.

Or sold separately as under:—

PART I. THE VOICE OF ISRAEL FROM THE ROCKS OF SINAI. 21s.

PART II. THE MONUMENTS OF EGYPT AND THEIR VESTIGES OF PATRIARCHAL TRADITIONS. 21s.

PART III. THE MONUMENTS OF ASSYRIA, BABYLONIA, AND PERSIA: with a New Key for the Recovery of the Lost Ten Tribes. 10s. 6d.

FRANCATELLI'S (C. E.)—THE MODERN COOK. By CHARLES ELMÉ FRANCATELLI, Pupil of the celebrated Carême. In 8vo. Seventeenth Edition. 1500 Recipes. With Sixty Illustrations. 12s.

> "The *magnum opus* on which the author rests his reputation."—*Times.*

———— **THE COOK'S GUIDE.** By the Author of the 'Modern Cook.' In small 8vo. 1000 Recipes. With Forty Illustrations. 5s.

> "The whole book has the merit of being exceedingly plain, and is an admirable manual for every household."—*Times.*

FRANCE A CENTURY AGO. By Admiral Sir GEORGE COLLIER. Being a Diary of a Visit to France and the Austrian Netherlands. Edited by his Granddaughter, Mrs. GERTRUDE TENNANT. 8vo. Portrait. 10s. 6d.

FULLERTON'S (LADY GEORGIANA), THE NOVELS OF. 2 vols. Crown 8vo. 6s. each.

    1. LADYBIRD.
    2. TOO STRANGE NOT TO BE TRUE.

> "I lately read one of the most fascinating and delightful works I ever had the good fortune to meet with, in which genius, goodness, and beauty meet together in the happiest combination, showing the additional charm of an historical basis—'Too Strange not to be True,' by Lady G. Fullerton."—*Einonnach, in Notes and Queries.*

FULLERTON'S (LADY GEORGIANA) LIFE OF THE

MARCHIONESS GIULIA FALETTI OF BAROLO. By SILVIO PELLICO, Author of 'Le Mie Prigione.' Translated by Lady GEORGIANA FULLERTON. In 1 vol. small 8vo. 6s.

GALLENGA'S (ANTONIO) NARRATIVE OF THE IN-

VASION OF DENMARK. By A. GALLENGA, Correspondent of the 'Times' at the Danish Head-Quarters. 2 vols. post 8vo. 10s. 6d.

GLADSTONE'S (THE RIGHT HON. W. E.) ADDRESS

TO THE UNIVERSITY OF EDINBURGH. 8vo. 1s.

GRAHAM'S (COL.) HISTORY OF THE ART OF WAR.

By COLONEL GRAHAM. Being a history of War from the earliest times. Post 8vo. 5s.

GREENHOW'S (Mrs.) NARRATIVE OF HER IMPRI-

SONMENT IN WASHINGTON. Post 8vo. With Portrait. 5s.

"The story of her captivity is very interesting."—*John Bull.*

GUBBINS' (MARTIN) HISTORY OF THE MUTINIES

IN OUDH; and an Account of the Siege of the Lucknow Presidency. By M. R. GUBBINS, Financial Commissioner for Oudh. In 8vo. with Illustrations and Map. 10s. 6d.

GUILLEMIN'S 'THE HEAVENS.' *See* Heavens.

GUIZOT'S (M.) FRANCE UNDER LOUIS PHILIPPE

from 1841 to 1847. 8vo. 14s. Forming Vol. VII. of his 'Memoirs.'

—————— MEMOIRS OF A MINISTER OF

STATE from 1840 to 1841. 8vo. 14s. Forming Vol. VI. of his 'Memoirs.'

—————— EMBASSY TO THE COURT OF ST.

JAMES. Crown 8vo. 6s. Forming Vol. V. of his 'Memoirs.'

—————— PERSONAL MEMOIRS, FROM THE

TIME OF THE FIRST NAPOLEON TO THE YEAR 1840. 4 vols. 8vo. 31s. 6d. Each volume can be had separately, price 14s.

—————— LIFE OF OLIVER CROMWELL. Crown

8vo. With a fine Portrait of Oliver Cromwell. 6s.

"M. Guizot has unravelled Cromwell's character with singular skill. No one, in our opinion, has drawn his portrait with equal truth. M. Guizot's acquaintance with our annals, language, customs, and politics is altogether extraordinary."—*Quarterly Review.*

"M. Guizot has given us an admirable narrative, far more candid than any from an English pen."—*Times.*

GUY DEVERELL. A Story. By J. SHERIDAN LE

FANU, Author of 'Uncle Silas.' Crown 8vo. 6s.

HALLIBURTON'S (Mrs.) TROUBLES. By Mrs. HENRY

WOOD, Author of 'East Lynne,' &c. Forming one of the 'Favourite Novels.' Two Illustrations. 6s.

HALL'S (MRS.) BIOGRAPHICAL MEMOIRS OF DR.

MARSHALL HALL, M.D., F.R.S., &c. By his Widow. 8vo. with Portrait. 14s.

HAREM LIFE IN EGYPT AND CONSTANTINOPLE.

By EMMELINE LOTT, formerly Governess to His Highness Ibrahim Pacha, son of the Viceroy of Egypt. 2 Vols. Post 8vo. 21s.

HAYES' (ISAAC) ARCTIC BOAT VOYAGE IN THE

AUTUMN OF 1854. By ISAAC T. HAYES. Edited, with an Introduction and Notes, by Dr. NORTON SHAW. Crown 8vo. 5s.

HEAVENS (THE): an Illustrated Handbook of Popular
Astronomy. By AMÉDÉE GUILLEMIN, Edited by J. NORMAN LOCKYER, F.R.A.S.
Imperial 8vo., with 225 Illustrations, Coloured Lithographs and Woodcuts. 21s.

"If anything can make the study of astronomy easy and engaging to ordinary minds, it will assuredly be a work of the attractive style and handsome—we may almost say sumptuous—aspect of M. Guillemin's treatise on 'The Heavens.' It deserves to be spoken of with all praise, as one towards which author, editor, illustrator, and publisher have equally done their best. Of the translation itself we cannot speak too highly. It has all the force and freshness of original writing."—*Saturday Review.*

"The publication of this splendidly illustrated handbook of popular astronomy is quite an era in the art of popularizing that most exciting of sciences. No book has ever been published calculated in an equal degree to realize the different astronomical spectacles of the heavens to the mind of an ordinary reader. Of all the marvels of astronomy M. Amédée Guillemin and his gorgeous illustrations give us a far more vivid conception than any work on the subject known to us."—*Spectator.*

HERBERT'S (LADY) IMPRESSIONS OF SPAIN. Royal
8vo., with 15 full-paged Illustrations. 21s.

———————— THREE PHASES OF CHRISTIAN ·LOVE:
being the Lives of St. Monica and Others. 8vo. 12s.

"This is an exquisite book, and men and women of all sects and shades of religious faith will thank Lady Herbert for her labour of love. It is a pure offering at the shrine of humanity, to show the world how divine a thing human nature may become when it is interpenetrated by the gift of charity, transforming and restoring it to the image of Him in whose likeness it was at first created. It is a charming gift-book."—*Athenæum.*

HISTORY OF THE BRITISH NAVY, FROM THE
EARLIEST PERIOD TO THE PRESENT TIME. By CHARLES DUKE YONGE.
In 3 vols. 8vo. 54s. *See* Yonge.

HOOK'S (DEAN) LIVES OF THE ARCHBISHOPS OF
CANTERBURY, ST. AUGUSTINE TO DR. HOWLEY. Vol. I., 15s. Vol II., 15s.
Vols. III. and IV., 30s.

"Written with remarkable knowledge and power. The author has done his work diligently and conscientiously. Throughout, we see a man who has known much of men and of life: the pure Anglican divine, who at every step has been accustomed to make good his cause against Romanism on the one hand, and against Puritanism on the other. We must express our high sense of the value of this work. We heartily like the general spirit, and are sure that the author has bestowed upon his work a loving labour, with an earnest desire to find out the truth. To the general reader it will convey much information in a very pleasant form; to the student it will give the means of filling up the outlines of Church history with life and colour."—*Quarterly Review, July,* 1862.

"If the grandeur of a drama may be conjectured from the quality of the opening symphony, we should be inclined to anticipate from the introductory volume that English literature is about to receive an imperishable contribution, and that the Church will in after-times, rank among the fairest and the ablest of her historians the author of this work."—*Athenæum.*

"The work of a powerful mind, and of a noble and generous temper. There is in it a freedom from any narrowness of spirit."—*Guardian.*

HORNBY'S (LADY) CONSTANTINOPLE DURING THE
CRIMEAN WAR. Royal 8vo. With Chromo-Lithographs. 21s.

HOUSE BY THE CHURCHYARD. By J. SHERIDAN
LE FANU. Crown 8vo. Illustrations. 6s.

ICELANDIC LEGENDS. By ARNASON. Translated by
GEORGE POWELL and E. MAGNUSSON. 8vo. With 28 Illustrations. 10s. 6d.

"This beautiful volume cannot fail to take its place in every good library, and be equally welcome to the young. The style is beautifully pure."—*Spectator.*

ICE MAIDEN (THE). Translated from the Danish, by Mrs.
BUSHBY. Small royal. With 39 very beautiful Illustrations by ZWECKER. 7s. 6d.

"A perfectly new and fanciful Swiss story."—*Examiner.*
"With exquisite illustrations."—*Dublin Evening Mail.*

INGOLDSBY LEGENDS (THE); OR, MIRTH AND

MARVELS. The Illustrated Edition. With 60 beautiful Illustrations by CRUIKSHANK, LEECH, and TENNIEL; and a magnificent emblematic cover, designed by LEIGHTON. Printed on Toned Paper. Eighth Thousand. 1 vol. Crown 4to. cloth. 21s.; or morocco 42s.; or bound by Rivière 52s. 6d.

"A series of humorous legends, illustrated by three such men as Cruikshank, Leech, and Tenniel—what can be more tempting?"—*Times.*

"Abundant in humour, observation, fancy; in extensive knowledge of books and men; in palpable hits of character, exquisite, grave irony, and the most whimsical indulgence in point and epigram. We doubt if even Butler beats the Author of these legends in the easy drollery of verse. We cannot open a page that is not sparkling with its wit and humour, that is not ringing with its strokes of pleasantry and satire."—*Examiner.*

"The time for discussing the merits and artistic peculiarities of Thomas Ingoldsby has long since past. His name is duly inscribed on the long roll of English humorists; and his quaint fancies, characteristic refashionments of old legends, and unrivalled facility for narrating the grotesque stories of the old hagiographers, or parodying the plots of modern dramatists in verse, as flowing as the rhymes are startling, has made that name a household word. In re-issuing this collection with some additions to the admirable and popular illustrations by Cruikshank, Leech, and Tenniel, Mr. Bentley has done excellent service to those who love a good story well told; and in every Tappington Hall in England the illustrated edition of the 'Ingoldsby Legends' ought to find a place."—*Notes and Queries.*

———————————————————— The Library Edition, in 2 Vols.
8vo. With the original Illustrations by GEORGE CRUIKSHANK, and JOHN LEECH. 21s.

———————————————————— The Carmine Edition, in crown
8vo. With six Illustrations by Cruikshank and Leech, with gilt edges and bevelled boards. 10s. 6d.

———————————————————— The Popular Edition. Crown 8vo.
Seventy-fifth Thousand. 5s., or in calf or morocco 12s. 6d.

INITIALS (THE). By THE BARONESS TAUTPHOEUS.

Uniform with 'East Lynne,' &c. Crown 8vo. With 2 Illustrations. 6s.

IRVING'S (WASHINGTON) LIFE AND LETTERS. By

his Nephew, PIERRE IRVING. In 4 vols. Post 8vo. Price 21s.; or each Volume separately, price 6s.

JAMESON'S (Mrs.) ESSAYS IN ART AND LITERA-

TURE. Crown 8vo. 2s. 6d.; or handsomely bound, 4s.

JERUSALEM, THE GOLDEN, AND THE WAY TO IT.

By the Rev. HERMAN DOUGLAS, M.A. With an Introduction by the Author of 'Mary Powell.' In small 8vo. with Illustrations. 6s.

KAVANAGH'S (JULIA) MADELINE. A Tale of Auvergne.

Fcp. 8vo. gilt edges. 4s.

"One of those rare books which at once touch the feelings by a simple and forcible truthfulness to nature. It is destined to permanent popularity, and the name of the writer will be marked with those of Madame Cottin and St. Pierre."—*Atlas.*

KNIGHT'S (Captain) DIARY OF A PEDESTRIAN IN

CASHMERE AND THIBET. 8vo. With 45 fine Woodcuts and Lithographs. 21s.

"The book is an excellent and welcome addition to our records of daring travel."—*Saturday Review.*

LACORDAIRE (Abbé) MEMOIR OF THE. By the Count

de MONTALEMBERT, one of the Forty of the French Academy. In 8vo. 12s.

"The life of a man of exalted character and talents, whose story is told in the eloquent language of Count de Montalembert."—*John Bull.*

LADY'S WALKS IN THE SOUTH OF FRANCE. (See

EYRE.)

LADY'S DESSERT BOOK (THE). By the Author of

'Everybody's Pudding-Book.' Fcp. 8vo. 2s. 6d.

LAKE'S (General ATWELL) DEFENCE OF KARS: A
Military Work. With numerous fine Plans and Plates. 8vo. 10s. 6d

LAMARTINE'S (ALPHONSE DE) MEMOIRS OF RE-
MARKABLE CHARACTERS: Nelson, Bossuet, Milton, Oliver Cromwell, &c. Post 8vo.
5s.

LAMB (CHARLES): his Friends, his Haunts, and his Books.
By PERCY FITZGERALD, Author of 'The Life of Laurence Sterne.' Imperial 16mo.
7s. 6d.

LAST OF THE CAVALIERS (THE). Uniform with 'East
Lynne,' &c. Crown 8vo. With 2 Illustrations. 6s.

LEE'S (Dr.) LAST DAYS OF ALEXANDER OF RUS-
SIA AND FIRST DAYS OF NICHOLAS. A Diary kept during a stay in Russia in
1825-26. Small 8vo. 3s. 6d.

LE FANU'S POPULAR STORIES. In crown 8vo. 6s.
each. With 2 Illustrations.
    1. UNCLE SILAS.
    2. GUY DEVERELL.
    3. THE HOUSE BY THE CHURCHYARD.

LEGENDS OF A STATE PRISON. By PATRICK SCOTT.
Fcap. 8vo. 6s.

LETTERS FROM HELL. From the Danish. In 2 vols.
Post 8vo. 21s.
"There is a fearful but natural intensity of incident, and a strong vehement satire,
mingled with a sweet pathos and tenderness, ringing through the pages like a dirge from
'sweet bells jangled.'"—*The Eclectic Review.*

LLANOVER'S (Lady) GOOD COOKERY FROM THE
RECIPES OF THE HERMIT OF ST. GOVER. 8vo. With Illustrations. 10s. 6d.

MAGINN'S (Dr.) ESSAYS ON SOME OF SHAK-
SPEARE'S CHARACTERS. Falstaff, Jacques, Romeo, Bottom the Weaver, Lady
Macbeth, Iago, Hamlet, &c. Crown 8vo. 6s.

MARSDEN'S (Rev. J. B.) DICTIONARY OF CHRISTIAN
CHURCHES AND SECTS FROM THE EARLIEST AGES OF CHRISTIANITY.
By the Rev. J. B. MARSDEN. 8vo. 12s.
"The best book on the subject current in our literature."—*Athenæum.*
"Characterized by great candour. It is a production of great utility."—*Daily News.*
"Mr. Marsden's information is well digested, his judgment sound and impartial, his
manner of statement not only clear, but with a sustained vividness. The work has somewhat the appearance of an Encyclopædia, but it is only in appearance. The exposition has
the freshness of an original work. The philosophic impartiality of the author should not
be passed over. He has, of course, opinions, but he indulges in no violence or harshness of
censure. The arrangement is well adapted for the important point of conveying complete
and full information."—*Spectator.*

M^cCAUSLAND'S (Dr. Q. L.) SERMONS IN STONES;
OR, SCRIPTURE CONFIRMED BY GEOLOGY. Tenth Edition. Fcap. With 19
Illustrations. 4s.
"The object of the author in this work is to show that the Mosaic narrative of the
Creation is reconcilable with the established facts of geology; and that geology not only
establishes the truth of the first page of the Bible, but that it furnishes the most direct and
sensible evidence of the fact of Divine Inspiration, and thereby authenticates the whole
canon of Scripture. The word of God is thus authenticated by His works."
"The object of this work is to reconcile the discoveries in geology with the Mosaic
account of the Creation. The case is clearly made, and the argument cleverly managed."
—*Spectator.*

—————————————— **LAST DAYS OF JERUSALEM AND**
ROME. 8vo. 10s. 6d.
"The book of a reverent student of Scripture."—*Guardian.*

M^cCAUSLAND'S (Dr. Q. L.) ADAM AND THE ADAMITE.

Crown 8vo. 7s. 6d. Plates.

"Dr. McCausland is an eminent geologist and orthodox Christian, and in this work he endeavours to harmonise the statements of science and revelation. He heartily accepts the recent discoveries of a pre-Adamite mankind, the theory of three distinct races of mankind—the Mongol, the Negro, and the Caucasian—and puts the latest conclusions of science on these points in an intelligible and popular way. The book is attractive and useful."—*Notes and Queries.*

MIGNET'S LIFE OF MARY QUEEN OF SCOTS. Two

Portraits. Crown 8vo. 6s.

"The standard authority on the subject."—*Daily News.*

"A good service done to historical accuracy. This work will continue to occupy its place in our libraries."—*Morning Post.*

MITFORD'S (MARY RUSSELL) RECOLLECTIONS OF

A LITERARY LIFE, with Selections from favourite Poets and Prose Writers. By MARY RUSSELL MITFORD. Crown 8vo. With Portrait. 6s.

MODERN COOK (THE). *See* FRANCATELLI.

MOMMSEN (Dr. THEODORE)—THE HISTORY OF

ROME FROM THE EARLIEST TIME TO THE PERIOD OF ITS DECLINE. By Dr. THEODORE MOMMSEN. Translated with the Author's sanction, and additions, by the Rev. W. P. DICKSON. With an Introduction by Dr. SCHMITZ. Crown 8vo. Vols. 1 and 2, 21s. Vol. 3, 10s. 6d. Vol. 4, in two Parts, 16s.

"A work of the very highest merit: its learning is exact and profound; its narrative full of genius and skill; its descriptions of men are admirably vivid. We wish to place on record our opinion that Dr. Mommsen's is by far the best history of the Decline and Fall of the Roman Commonwealth."—*Times.*

"Since the days of Niebuhr, no work on Roman history has appeared that combines so much to attract, instruct, and charm the reader. Its style—a rare quality in a German author—is vigorous, spirited, and animated. Professor Mommsen's work can stand a comparison with the noblest productions of modern history."—*Dr. Schmitz*

"This is the best history of the Roman Republic, taking the work on the whole—the author's complete mastery of his subject, the variety of his gifts and acquirements, his graphic power in the delineation of natural and individual character, and the vivid interest which he inspires in every portion of his book. He is without an equal in his own sphere. The work may be read in the translation (executed with the sanction of the author) not only with instruction, but with great pleasure."—*Edinburgh Review.*

"A book of deepest interest, and which ought to be translated."—*Dean Trench.*

"Beyond all doubt to be ranked among those really great historical works which do so much honour to our own day. We can have little hesitation in pronouncing this work to be the best complete Roman History in existence. In short, we have now, for the first time, the complete history of the Roman Republic, really written in a way worthy of the greatness of the subject. M. Mommsen is a real historian; his powers of research and judgment are of a very high order; he is skilful in the grasp of his whole subject, and vigorous and independent in his way of dealing with particular questions. And an English critic may be allowed to add, that his book is far easier and more pleasant to read than many of the productions of his fellow-countrymen."—*National Review.*

"An original work, from the pen of a master. The style is nervous and lively, and its vigour fully sustained. This English translation fills up a gap in our literature. It will give the schoolboy and the older student of antiquity a history of Rome up to the mark of present German scholarship, and at the same time serve as a sample of historical inquiry for all ages and all lands."—*Westminster Review.*

"Dr. Mommsen is the latest scholar who has acquired European distinction by writing on Roman history. But he is much more than a scholar. He is a man of genius, of great original force, and daring to the extreme in his use of it; a philosopher in his power of reproducing men; witty, with a dash of poetic fancy; and humorous, after a dry, sarcastic fashion, which, combined with his erudition, recalls Scott's Oldbucks and Bradwardines. His elaborate portrait of Cæsar is, we venture to say, one of the best pieces of biographical delineation that this century has produced. Dr. Mommsen's style of character-drawing is his own. He neither reveals a face by lightning flashes, like Mr. Carlyle, nor sets it in a framework of epigrammatic oil-lamps, like M. de Lamartine; nor dashes it off by bold crayon strokes, like Lord Macaulay. But his keen and rather naturally satirical genius softens in the presence of what he admires. He analyses skilfully, describes with fine pencil lines, and colours with a touch that is not too warm, and yet quite warm enough to give the hues of life."—*Pall Mall Gazette.*

MONTALEMBERT'S (Count De) LIFE OF THE ABBÉ
LACORDAIRE. In 8vo. 12s.
"The picture is fascinating."—*Blackwood's Magazine.*

MOODY'S (SOPHY) WHAT IS YOUR NAME? Being a
Popular and Succinct Account of the Meaning and Derivation of Christian Names. Post
8vo. 6s.
"The information is of an entertaining character, and the work is a most comprehensive compendium of information."—*London Review.*

NATURALIST IN VANCOUVER ISLAND AND BRITISH
COLUMBIA. By JOHN KEAST LORD, Naturalist to the Boundary Commission.
2 vols, crown 8vo. Many Illustrations 24s.

NED LOCKSLEY, THE ETONIAN. Uniform with 'East
Lynne.' Crown 8vo. Two Illustrations. 6s.
"The new comer whom we now hail writes with force, with heart, and, what we want
most in a novel—with freshness."—*Times.*

NOTES ON NOSES. By EDEN WARWICK. Fcap. 8vo.
2s. 6d.
"Worthy of Laurence Sterne."—*Morning Post.*

OVER THE PYRENEES INTO SPAIN. By MARY
EYRE, Author of 'A Lady's Walks in the South of France.' Crown 8vo. 12s.

PLANTAGENETS (LIFE OF THE GREATEST OF THE).
An Historical Sketch. By EDMUND CLIFFORD. 8vo. 12s.

PLATO (SELECTIONS FROM THE WRITINGS OF). By
Lady CHATTERTON. Fcap. 8vo. 4s.

POWELL AND MAGNUSSON'S LEGENDS OF ICE-
LAND. By ARNASON. Translated by GEORGE POWELL and E. MAGNUSSON. 8vo.
With 28 beautiful Illustrations. 10s. 6d.

PRENDERGAST (THOMAS), THE MASTERY OF LAN-
GUAGE; OR, THE ART OF SPEAKING FOREIGN LANGUAGES IDIOMATI-
CALLY. 8vo. 8s. 6d.

QUITS! By the Author of 'The Initials.' Uniform with
'East Lynne.' With 2 Illustrations. Crown 8vo. 6s.
"A most interesting novel."—*Times.*
"Witty, sententious, graphic, full of brilliant pictures of life and manners, it is positively
one of the best of modern stories, and may be read with delightful interest from cover to
cover."—*Morning Post.*

REDEMPTION DRAWETH NIGH; OR, THE GREAT
PREPARATION. By the Rev. Dr. JOHN CUMMING. Sixth Edition. Crown 8vo. 5s.

ROMAN CLASSICAL LITERATURE (HISTORY OF).
See BROWNE.

RUSSELL'S (EARL) LIFE OF CHARLES JAMES FOX.
In 3 vols. Crown 8vo. Vols. 1 and 2, 21s. Vol. 3, 12s.
"Must be ranked with the companion biography of Pitt, by Lord Stanhope, in the front
rank of our political classics."—*Pall Mall Gazette.*

SAM SLICK'S SEASON TICKET. Fcap. 2s.

SCOTT'S (LADY) TYPES AND ANTITYPES OF THE
OLD AND NEW TESTAMENT. Post 8vo. 5s.

SHAKSPEARE'S CHARACTERS (ESSAYS ON SOME OF).
By Dr. MAGINN. Crown 8vo. 6s.

SMITH'S (Dr.) RAMBLES THROUGH THE STREETS
OF LONDON: with Anecdotes of their more ancient Residents. Crown 8vo. 6s.

STEBBING'S (Dr.) LIVES OF THE PRINCIPAL

ITALIAN POETS. Crown 8vo. 7s. 6d.

TALES FROM BENTLEY'S MISCELLANY: Being a

Selection of the Best and most entertaining Stories that have appeared in 'BENTLEY'S MISCELLANY,' by its most Eminent Writers. 6 Vols. 1s. each; or 4 vols. 1s. 6d. each, sold separately.

THE THREE CLERKS. By ANTHONY TROLLOPE.

Crown 8vo. 6s. With 2 Illustrations.

"Mr. Trollope amply bears out in this work the reputation he acquired by 'Barchester Towers.' We regard the tenderness and self-sacrifice of Linda one of the most graceful and touching pictures of feminine heroism in the whole range of modern novels."—*John Bull*.

"Here are scenes from family life, more true, more pathetic, and more skilfully sustained than any that can be found, except in the writings of family novelists."—*Saturday Review*.

THIERS' (M.) HISTORY OF THE GREAT FRENCH

REVOLUTION, FROM 1789 to 1801. By M. THIERS. In 5 vols. small 8vo. With Forty-one Fine Engravings and Portraits of the most eminent Personages engaged in the Revolution. 30s.

ATTACK ON THE BASTILLE	PORTRAIT OF CAMILLE DESMOULINS
PORTRAIT OF THE DUKE OF ORLEANS	CONDEMNATION OF MARIE ANTOINETTE
PORTRAIT OF MIRABEAU	PORTRAIT OF BAILLY (MAYOR OF PARIS)
PORTRAIT OF LAFAYETTE	TRIAL OF DANTON, CAMILLE DESMOULINS, &c.
ORGIES OF THE GARDES DU CORPS	PORTRAIT OF DANTON
PORTRAIT OF MARIE ANTOINETTE	PORTRAIT OF MADAME ELIZABETH
RETURN OF THE ROYAL FAMILY FROM VA-RENNES	CARRIER AT NANTES
PORTRAIT OF MARAT	PORTRAIT OF ROBESPIERRE
THE MOB AT THE TUILERIES	LAST VICTIMS OF THE REIGN OF TERROR
ATTACK ON THE TUILERIES	PORTRAIT OF CHARETTE
MURDER OF THE PRINCESS DE LAMBELLE	DEATH OF THE DEPUTY FERAUD
PORTRAIT OF THE PRINCESS DE LAMBELLE	DEATH OF ROMME, GOUJON, DUQUESNOI, &c.
PORTRAIT OF MADAME ROLAND	PORTRAIT OF LOUIS XVII.
LOUIS XVI. AT THE CONVENTION	THE 13TH VENDEMIARE (Oct. 5, 1795)
LAST INTERVIEW OF LOUIS XVI. WITH HIS FAMILY	SUMMONING TO EXECUTION
PORTRAIT OF LOUIS XVI.	PORTRAIT OF PICHEGRU
PORTRAIT OF DUMOURIEZ	PORTRAIT OF MOREAU
TRIUMPH OF MARAT	PORTRAIT OF HOCHE
PORTRAIT OF LAROCHEJACQUELEIN	PORTRAIT OF NAPOLEON BONAPARTE
ASSASSINATION OF MARAT	THE 18TH BRUMAIRE (10th November, 1709)
	PORTRAIT OF CHARLOTTE CORDAY.

"The palm of excellence, after whole libraries have been written on the French Revolution, has been assigned to the dissimilar histories of Thiers and Mignet."—*William H. Prescott*.

"I am reading 'Thiers's French Revolution,' which I find it difficult to lay down."—*Rev. Sydney Smith*.

TIMBS' (JOHN) ANECDOTICAL WORKS.

1. CLUB LIFE OF LONDON. 2 Vols. Portraits. 21s.
2. THE ROMANTIC LIFE OF LONDON. 3 Vols. 31s. 6d.
3. A CENTURY OF ANECDOTE FROM 1750. 2 Vols. 21s.
4. LIVES OF WITS AND HUMORISTS. 2 Vols. 12s.
5. LIVES OF PAINTERS. 1 Vol. 6s. Portraits.
6. LIVES OF BURKE AND EARL OF CHATHAM. 1 Vol. 6s. Portraits.
7. ECCENTRIC CHARACTERS. 2 vols. 21s.

"Mr. Timbs' notion of condensing the salient points, events, and incidents in the lives of distinguished men, and presenting them by way of anecdote in chronological order, is a very happy one."—*Notes and Queries*.

—————————— CLUB LIFE OF LONDON. With Anecdotes of the Clubs, Coffee-houses, and Taverns during the 17th, 18th, and 19th Centuries 2 Vols. 21s.

TIMBS (JOHN), THE ROMANCE OF LONDON. 3 vols. post 8vo.

———————— CENTURY OF ANECDOTE FROM 1750 TO 1850. 2 vols. post 8vo. Portraits. 21s.

    " The best collection of anecdotes which modern times have produced."—*Athenæum.*

TOO STRANGE NOT TO BE TRUE. A Novel. By LADY GEORGIANA FULLERTON, Author of ' Ladybird.' Two Illustrations. Crown 8vo. 6s.

TRIBULATION (THE GREAT) COMING ON THE EARTH. By the REV. DR. JOHN CUMMING. Thirteenth Edition. Crown 8vo. 5s.

TROLLOPE'S (ANTHONY) THE THREE CLERKS. Crown 8vo. Two Plates. 6s.

    " A really brilliant tale, full of life and character."—*Times.*

UNCLE SILAS. By J. SHERIDAN LE FANU. Crown 8vo. Two Illustrations. 6s.

    " We conclude by cordially recommending this remarkable novel to all who have leisure to read it, satisfied that for many a day afterwards the characters there portrayed will haunt the minds of those who have become acquainted with them. Shakespeare's famous line, ' Macbeth hath murdered sleep,' might be altered for the occasion; for certainly Uncle Silas has ' murdered sleep' in many a past night, and is likely to murder it in many a night to come, by that strange mixture of fantasies like truth and truths like fantasy which make us feel as we rise from the perusal as if we had been under a wizard's spell." —*Times.*

UP THE COUNTRY. *See* EDEN.

WEBB'S (MRS.) MARTYRS OF CARTHAGE. By MRS. WEBB, Author of ' Naomi,' &c. Handsomely bound. 5s.

WHALLEY (REV. DR. S.)—LIFE, JOURNALS, AND CORRESPONDENCE OF THE REV. Dr. THOMAS SEDGWICK WHALLEY, LL.D. Including an Interesting Correspondence with Mrs. Siddons, Madame Piozzi, Miss Seward, Mrs. Hannah More. &c., &c. Edited by the Rev. HILL D. WICKHAM, Rector of Horsington, Somersetshire. 2 vols. With 4 Fine Portraits. 30s.

    " Filled with lively and forcible sketches; with scenes so delightfully comic, as almost to recall the more farcical bits of Molière."—*Saturday Review.*

WHATELY (RICHARD), MEMOIR OF, late ARCH- BISHOP OF DUBLIN. With a glance at his Contemporaries and Times. By W. J. FITZPATRICK, Esq., Author of ' Lady Morgan, her Career, Literary and Personal;' ' The Life, Times, and Contemporaries of Lord Cloncurry,' &c. 2 vols. post 8vo. 21s.

————————, SELECTIONS FROM THE WRITINGS OF (late Archbishop of Dublin). Fcp. 8vo. 5s.

    " Contains the pith, the cream, the choice bits of Archbishop Whately's writings. His style is as clear as Cobbett's or Paley's."—*Athenæum.*

WHAT TO DO WITH THE COLD MUTTON. Fcap. 8vo. 2s. 6d.

WOOD (Mrs. HENRY.) The most Popular Stories of this favourite Writer. In 4 volumes, price 6s. each. With 2 Illustrations to each book. Each work can be had separately.

    1. EAST LYNNE.
    2. THE CHANNINGS.
    3. MRS. HALLIBURTON'S TROUBLES.
    4. THE SHADOW OF ASHLYDYAT.

YONGE'S (C. D.) HISTORY OF THE BRITISH NAVY,

FROM THE EARLIEST PERIOD DOWN TO THE PRESENT TIME. By CHARLES DUKE YONGE. In 2 vols. 8vo. with Maps, 45s.; or 3 vols., 54s.

"Mr. Yonge here tells us some of the most delightful episodes in English History. There are no brighter pages in the history of human strife than those detailing the sea-fights of sixty and seventy years ago."—*Reader*.

"For the industry, research, and ability, which characterize these volumes, they merit high commendation. The great naval battles are described with extraordinary power and distinctness."—*Daily News*.

YONGE'S ENGLISH-LATIN DICTIONARY.   Post 8vo.

9s. 6d. In use at Eton, Harrow, Winchester, and Rugby.

———— LATIN-ENGLISH DICTIONARY.   Post 8vo.

7s. 6d. Or the two together, strongly bound in roan, 15s.

"A very capital book, either for the somewhat advanced pupil, the student who aims at acquiring an idiomatic Latin style, or the adult with a knowledge of the language, who wishes to examine the difference between the structure and expressions of the English and Latin tongues by a short and ready mode. It is the best—we were going to say the only really useful—Anglo-Latin Dictionary we ever met with."—*Spectator*.

———— NEW VIRGIL.   With the Notes of HAWTREY,

KEY, and MUNRO. Post 8vo. 7s. 6d. In use at Eton, Harrow, Winchester, and Rugby.

AGGREGATE SALE, 57,000.

BENTLEY'S FAVOURITE NOVELS.

In crown 8vo., each volume with 2 Illustrations.

UNCLE SILAS. By J. SHERIDAN LE FANU.

TOO STRANGE NOT TO BE TRUE. By LADY GEOR-GIANA FULLERTON. 6s.

EAST LYNNE. By Mrs. WOOD. 6s.

QUITS. By the Author of 'The Initials' and 'At Odds.' 6s.

THE CHANNINGS. By the Author of 'East Lynne.' 6s.

NED LOCKSLEY, THE ETONIAN. 6s.

THE INITIALS. By the Author of 'At Odds' and 'Quits.' 6s.

THE LAST OF THE CAVALIERS. 6s.

MRS. HALLIBURTON'S TROUBLES. By the Author of 'East Lynne.' 6s.

THE SHADOW OF ASHLYDYAT. By the Author of 'East Lynne.'

LADYBIRD. By LADY GEORGIANA FULLERTON.

ANTHONY TROLLOPE'S THREE CLERKS.

GUY DEVERELL. By the Author of 'Uncle Silas.'

THE HOUSE BY THE CHURCHYARD. By the Author of 'Uncle Silas.'

LONDON : PRINTED BY W. CLOWES AND SONS, STAMFORD STREET AND CHARING CROSS.